TARA DUNCAN

AND THE

FORBIDDEN BOOK

TARA DUNCAN

AND THE

FORBIDDEN BOOK

 HRH Princess Sophie Audouin-Mamikonian

TRANSLATION BY **William Rodarmor**

Sky Pony Press
New York

Sky Pony Press books may be purchased in bulk at special discounts for sales promotion, corporate gifts, fund-raising, or educational purposes. Special editions can also be created to specifications. For details, contact the Special Sales Department, Sky Pony Press, 307 West 36th Street, 11th Floor, New York, NY 10018 or info@skyhorsepublishing.com.

Sky Pony® is a registered trademark of Skyhorse Publishing, Inc.®, a Delaware corporation.

Visit our website at www.skyponypress.com.

10 9 8 7 6 5 4 3 2 1

Library of Congress Cataloging-in-Publication Data is available on file.

ISBN: 978-1-61608-969-6

Printed in the United States of America

CONTENTS

TARA DUNCAN
AND THE
FORBIDDEN BOOK

CHAPTER 1

MURDER, THEY SAID

The glittering mask was black with fury. The dark figures huddled around its wearer were careful not to move.

"So, that fool dares to defy me!" roared their leader. "Very well! I can't kill her openly. My fellow Bloodgraves would never forgive me. But if it happened by accident . . ."

The master began to laugh, and his mask slowly turned blue with satisfaction.

"Yes, an accident. . . . An accident that would both destroy my adversary and trap my enemy—a happy coincidence! Once the girl's in my power, I'll have access to all the demonic power objects, and nothing will be able to ever stop me. Here's what we are going to do . . ."

Hearing the complicated plan the master had devised, one of the dark figures trembled. *No, that can't happen! The girl mustn't be captured alive.*

There was no longer any choice.

Tara Duncan had to die!

The shadow moved stealthily along the wall, silently cursing the silver moonlight shining in through the windows. It skillfully avoided sofas, chairs, and tables while making for its goal: an office door behind which angry voices could be heard.

The figure took out a transparent object, carefully set it against the wall, and smiled as the voices in the office became clearly audible. What they were saying was very interesting.

First came a male voice—that of the dragon wizard Chemnashao-virodaintrachivu, Master Chem for short. He sounded defensive and ill at ease. The second voice was also male and sounded cultured, but seemingly unable to easily pronounce certain words. It belonged to Manitou, a wizard currently in the body of a Labrador retriever. The third, very angry voice was that of the wizard Isabella Duncan. The fourth belonged to Selena Duncan, Isabella's daughter.

"Of course I am!" Isabella snapped, apparently in answer to a question. "For crying out loud, Chem, you didn't even tell me Tara had been kidnapped! If you weren't already a big batrachian, I'd turn you into a toad this instant!"

"Saurian!" protested the dragon. "I'm a saurian, Isabella. Please don't insult me. Anyway, what more could you have done than I did? Besides chewing your fingernails to the bone, that is."

"You have no excuse, Chem," she thundered, "and you know it!"

"But everything turned out fine in the end, didn't it? We found Tara, we freed the kidnapped apprentice spellbinders, and we defeated Magister."

"No thanks to you," growled Manitou. "Tara, Fabrice, Robin, Sparrow, Fafnir, and I escaped from the Gray Fortress without your help. And we're the ones who fixed Magister's hash, not you!"

Master Chem, who was feeling cornered, tried to change the subject.

"Speaking of hash, we've been getting complaints about you, Manitou," he said. "A half-dozen female spellbinders in Lancovit would like to skin you alive."

The black Lab groaned. "All right, what did I do now?"

"You probably can't remember it, but about ten years ago you sold them an eternal youth potion," said Chem. "Which wasn't exactly eternal, since it aged them fifty years overnight. We got the latest cases a few days ago, but I've been trying to treat one of the women for a year now. The problem is that your potion's side effects are unpredictable. I've been able to cure the others and restore their looks, but this one woman's case seems hopeless."

"*Woof*?" barked Manitou. "Darn, I mean, 'What?' If I did sell that stuff, I don't remember doing it, so I can't help you! As you know, I only regained my human consciousness a month ago, and my memory is a disaster. I don't have lapses, I have black holes. My mind is just shot."

"Well, it's a good thing you're here on Earth and not many people know you've been turned into a dog," said Chem with a chuckle. "Otherwise your hide wouldn't be worth a plugged nickel."

"Are they really that angry?"

"What do you expect? Their husbands and boyfriends went to bed with twenty-year-old girls, and in the morning woke up next to grandmothers! Imagine the shock! You shouldn't have written 'Forever Young' in your ads."

Isabella interrupted them. "Let's not get sidetracked by the problems my father has such a talent for causing whenever he performs magic," she said irritably, unwilling to let the dragon off the hook so easily. "I'd like to get back to our initial topic, namely Magister, the Bloodgrave who nearly opened the rift between Earth and Limbo, which would have allowed the demons to invade the planet. That's more important than some poorly concocted potion. It was very lucky that Tara was smart and powerful enough to destroy the Throne of Silur."

"That's right, so let's not beat ourselves up about what could've happened and what we should or shouldn't have done," said the old dragon, who was getting tired of being yelled at. "You got your daughter Selena back, whom you thought was dead, and your granddaughter Tara is thriving. So, let's please discuss our other problems instead, namely: Who is hiding behind Magister's mask? Who is this Hunter he mentioned to Tara? And who tried to kill her in the vortex? It couldn't have been Magister himself, since Tara is the key that gives him access to the demonic objects. We have a lot of questions and can't even begin to answer them. I hate that."

"Hmm . . . What do you make of the Rigibonus?" asked Manitou, who was thinking hard.

"The what?"

"That strange ray that one of Magister's henchmen used at the manor house. Remember when Magister first tried to kidnap Tara? He sent one of his Bloodgraves, who tried to kill Isabella while he was at it. The ray starts as a Rigidifus, to petrify the victim, and then becomes a Carbonus to burn them. That's why I call the spell a 'Rigibonus.' It would have cooked Isabella's goose, except that Tara grabbed the burning ray—we don't know quite how—and fired it back at the Bloodgrave. It seriously wounded him. And since it's a double spell, only Tara can heal it. In the meantime, the guy's face must look like charcoal-broiled steak."

"Yuck!" said Selena. "Spare us the gory details, Manitou. But that means that he'll recover automatically if Tara dies, right?"

"Exactly," said the dog. "So, do we know the guilty party?"

4

"I don't think so," rumbled the dragon after a few moments' thought. "I imagine the pain must be so intense that he's probably not good for much. The only thing he can do right now is blow bubbles."

"Bubbles?"

"That's right. He probably puts his head into icy water to dull the pain and must make a lot of bubbles when he screams," Chem explained, sounding amused. "So I'm afraid we have to look elsewhere."

Chem's black humor was greeted with silence.

"Tara picked up some hairs from Magister's hairbrush," said Manitou. "Did that yield anything?"

"When we captured the Gray Fortress, we got the brush and some of dear Magister's clothes—even his underpants. We turned the lot over to the hunter-elf crime laboratory, but it was all so steeped in demonic magic that we didn't learn much. We weren't able to identify the rat or locate him."

"Magister always wears that mask," Selena said softly. "In the ten years he held me prisoner I never learned who he was."

"And I didn't hear about any of this until later," said Isabella, "so I have no idea either, unfortunately. But right now I have a much more important question: How are we going to deal with the fact that Tara is the heir of the Omois Empire? I have a few thoughts on that, but . . ."

The listening shadow remained glued to the wall, careful not to make any noise. It was so concentrated that it didn't see the enormous puma silently creeping up behind it. Ears flat against its skull, the cat approached stealthily, eyes focused on its prey. Suddenly the figure moved, and the cat froze, hugging the ground. Its lips drew back, revealing gleaming fangs.

Alerted by some mysterious sixth sense, the shadow turned around, but it was too late. The great cat pounced, and the two crashed to the floor together.

Chem, Selena, Manitou, and Isabella were startled to hear a fierce roar followed by a scream and the tinkle of breaking glass.

"Ahhhhh!"

Selena yanked the office door open and gasped. A young boy with black hair lay on the ground among shards of glass, pinned down by a huge golden puma affectionately licking his face.

"Are you completely out of your mind?" the boy furiously yelled at the cat, as he dodged its rough tongue. "You're totally nuts! You can't go around jumping people like that!"

"Caliban?" asked Manitou. "What in the world are you doing here?"

"Let him up, Sembor!" Selena ordered her feline familiar.

The cat reluctantly backed off, freeing its victim. Selena helped Cal to his feet.

"I was just passing by—" the young spellbinder began.

"At two o'clock in the morning?" snapped Isabella.

"Is it really that late?" He sounded surprised, his gray eyes wide with innocence. "Oh boy, I really better get to bed! If you don't mind, I'll just—"

He was about to run off when Chem grabbed him by the collar.

"Just a second, young man! I'd like to know what you were doing up in the middle of the night."

Glancing at the glass on the floor, Chem recited: "By Repairus, take these shattered bits and assemble them so each one fits."

The fragments immediately flew together to form a drinking glass that floated obediently in front of the dragon wizard.

"As I was saying, in the middle of the night, with a glass. An empty glass."

Cal considered concocting a plausible lie, but the look of fury on Isabella's face stopped him.

"As you know, we thieves live for information," he said. "So, when I realized that you were having a secret meeting, I took a glass from the kitchen and set it against the wall so I could hear you."

Selena looked baffled. "A glass?"

"Yeah, it's an old thief trick. The sound vibrations hit the wall and are transmitted by the glass. You can hear almost as well as if you were in the room yourself."

"Just so you know, young man, we weren't talking secrets. In fact, Lady Duncan had me on the carpet again for not telling her that her granddaughter had been kidnapped," said the old dragon with a forced chuckle. "But we've moved beyond that stage of our discussions, haven't we, Isabella?"

She glared at him. "Don't think for a moment that I've forgiven you, you old snake. We'll be talking about this again, believe me!"

"Saurian!" moaned Chem. "I'm a reptile, all right, but I belong to the class of higher saurians. I don't call you an old she-ape whenever I get angry with you, do I? So please, let's stop beating each other over the head with our family trees each time we have an argument!"

Isabella's eyes narrowed at the insult. Ignoring her daughter's quiet chuckle, she coldly retorted: "You're right Chem, you're a saur-ian. Just talking with you makes my head sore."

That was a declaration of war, and Cal decided to make himself scarce before he became collateral damage. Selena gave the relieved boy an embarrassed smile as he slipped out of the living room. As a nighttime expedition, this one still needed work, he had to admit. Cal entered the bedroom he was sharing with Robin and Fabrice. His two friends were awake and anxiously waiting for him, as was his familiar, Blondin the fox.

"Hey, weren't you supposed to be discreet?" said Fabrice sarcastically. "'I can't take you with me,' you said, 'you'd make too much noise!'

Well, when it comes to noise, I thought the house was collapsing. A real my first is a feline, my second is a donkey, and my third a rhythmic system composed of two or more lines repeated as a unit."

"A real *what*?" asked Robin the half-elf, who had trouble with the young Earthling's odd habit of dropping riddles into his conversation.

"A cat + ass + strophe = catastrophe," Fabrice helpfully explained.

"That stupid puma!" snapped Cal. "Sembor was crouching in a corner of the room, and I didn't see him. Until he jumped me, that is."

"Bummer!" said Robin sympathetically. "So much for your licensed thief training! Weren't you able to learn anything at all?"

"Not a thing. They were talking things over with Master Chem. Well, more like they were chewing him out. Isabella is still mad that he didn't tell her about the time Tara was kidnapped. In other words, same old, same old."

"So much the better," said Robin, his crystalline eyes bright. "That means we'll be able to enjoy our vacation in peace. Personally, I like being on Earth. It's a nice change from OtherWorld."

Delighted to get their apprentices back safe and sound, the high wizards of Lancovit had given the young heroes three weeks' vacation. The five friends had now been on Earth for a week. But Tara had already missed the start of school, unfortunately, and was due to start classes in just two days.

Upon their arrival from OtherWorld, Fabrice had invited them to stay at his father's castle, but the two boys wanted to stay nearby at Isabella's manor house with Tara and Sparrow. So that Fabrice wouldn't feel left out, Isabella invited him over as well. Add Selena and Master Chem, and the old pink stone house was full to bursting. Using magic, that wasn't a major problem. But if the manor house had turned into a huge castle overnight, the nonspells would certainly have noticed. So

Isabella simply made each individual room bigger, to accommodate everyone comfortably.

Just then, a discreet knock on the door sent the three boys diving under their covers. False alarm. It wasn't Selena—or worse, Isabella—just Sparrow and Tara. Standing at the door, the girls looked in at their three friends affectionately. There was Fabrice, blond and athletic; Cal, small and graceful, with the face of an angel; and Robin with his glittering eyes, who was much taller than the other boys. The two girls were accompanied by their familiars, Tara's pegasus Gallant and Sparrow's panther Sheeba. Framed in the doorway, they were quite a sight.

The pretty picture wavered a bit when they burst out laughing at an apocalyptic description of Cal's failed expedition.

"Okay, you girls, that's enough," grumbled the little thief. "Quit laughing like whaloons. I'm dead tired, so get out of here! Beat it!"

Tara was grateful for Cal's effort to help her and gave him a kiss, which made him blush. The display of affection was slightly undermined by the girls' amused comments once they were back in their room next door.

The next morning, the five young spellbinders decided to explore the country around the manor.

"The easiest way would be by bike," suggested Tara.

"What's that?" asked Cal, Sparrow, and Robin in unison, none of whom had ever seen a bicycle before.

"One of these," said Tara with a sly grin, and she climbed on her bicycle. "You just get on, like this. To make it go, you press the pedals. You'll see, it's easy."

After crashing headfirst twice into the manor lawn, Cal decided that Tara and Fabrice had had enough fun laughing at his expense. Discreetly, the young spellbinder recited: "By Stabilus, steady this thing so it cruises, and spare me all the bumps and bruises."

Magic on Earth was much less powerful than on OtherWorld, but Cal's stabilizing spell worked, and his bike began rolling perfectly straight.

"Cheater!" yelled Sparrow as she bailed out at speed to avoid crashing into a large chestnut tree.

"Yeah, well, there'll be two of us cheaters, 'cause I'm fed up with these bikes," muttered Robin. "By Stabilus, steady this mechanical steed, so o'er hill and dale I'll lightly speed."

Tara smiled, thinking that Robin's spells were usually more elegant than Cal's.

Suddenly, Sparrow screamed. Her bike was out of control again and was heading toward a big rosebush full of long, sharp thorns.

Instinctively, the slim girl shape-shifted.

The curse that had affected her ancestor, changing him into a beast five hundred years earlier, acted instantly. Instead of the young Princess Gloria Daavil, known as Sparrow, riding the bike, it was a monstrous ten-foot-tall beast, a terrifying mix of bear, bull, and wolf, and equipped with enough fangs and claws to scare a psychopath.

Her transformation was fatal for the bicycle, alas, as it was for the rosebush and her clothes.

"Hoo, boy! I'm so sorry," said the hairy beast apologetically. "I think I busted your vike."

"It's *bike*," Tara corrected her automatically, while biting the inside of her cheeks so as not to laugh. "It's no big deal. But Sparrow . . ."

"Yeah?" said the beast, pulling rose branches out of her fur.

"People around here aren't exactly used to critters like you. Would you mind changing back, please?"

"Oh, sorry! I'll go inside and get some other clothes. I'm pretty sure I ripped my jeans. Hmm—my shirt, too. Won't take me a minute!"

With a quick magic pass, Robin made the crumpled bicycle good as new.

Finally, they were all ready. The familiars were tired from their recent adventures, so they elected to stay behind at the manor house.

The Earth summer was acting like a real summer for once: clear and warm. The gang toured the area, admired some old castle ruins, and had a picnic. (At first, the three OtherWorld spellbinders were perplexed by the PowerBars Tara brought along as a snack. When they wanted power, they didn't unwrap it; they conjured it.)

Heading home, they were about to turn onto the main road leading to the manor when Tara, who was in the lead, suddenly slammed on the brakes. Twenty men dressed in black were standing in front of her house!

Without thinking, she laid her bike down in the grass and ran to hide in a small grove of trees. Greatly surprised, Cal, Sparrow, Robin, and Fabrice followed her.

"What's going on?" asked Fabrice worriedly.

"There's a bunch of suspicious guys near the manor house. They look like they're trying to surround it."

"Oh no!" he moaned. "Not again!"

"If they're enemies and they're here to attack Grandma, they're going to get a big surprise," said Tara, who was craning her neck to see through the bushes. "She and Chem and Mom will make hash out of them. Chopped nice and fine."

"Spare us!" protested Sparrow, who had an overly vivid imagination.

"Actually, they don't look as if they're planning to attack," announced Robin after taking a quick peek. "They're just standing around, as if they're waiting for something."

"Something or someone," said Sparrow, nodding at Tara. "Until I'm told otherwise, I'm assuming you're Magister's target."

Fabrice's eyes widened.

"So you think they're from OtherWorld? More Bloodgraves here to kidnap Tara?"

"No idea," answered Sparrow. "Bloodgraves are usually masked, and those guys aren't. That said, it could also be a trap. Let's stay hidden for the time being—especially you, Tara."

Just then, Chem, Selena, Isabella, and Manitou all emerged from the manor. The young spellbinders tensed, ready to join the fight.

But nothing happened. The leader of the men in black said something, and then made a gesture. A kind of hologram instantly appeared in mid-air: a tiny figure who gravely recited a speech.

In case its hearers were deaf, its words also appeared in fiery letters above its head. A bit pale, but letters of fire just the same. Master Chem nodded, listening carefully.

From where the five friends were huddled, it was hard to make out his expression, but Tara sensed that the old wizard was very troubled.

"Listen, we can't stay behind these trees all evening," said Sparrow, who had become much less timid since conquering her childhood stutter. "I suggest Cal, Fabrice, and I go see what's happening. Tara stays here with Robin to protect her. If everything is okay, I'll signal you to come. If it's dangerous, we'll barricade ourselves in the house, and it'll be up to you to somehow contact OtherWorld's High Council of Wizards and have them send reinforcements."

"But I don't want to stay here!" protested Tara, who was now sick with worry.

"You don't have any choice," Sparrow countered. "If you come with us and those guys attack and try to grab you, we'll have to defend ourselves. We'll be risking our lives to protect you."

"As arguments go, that's completely bogus," growled Tara.

"Maybe," Sparrow admitted, "but it can't be beat. See you later."

Before Tara could try to change their minds, Sparrow, Fabrice, and Cal hopped back on their bikes and raced toward the manor house.

Tara was very anxious and watched her friends while savagely chewing on her white forelock. Robin, who had taken human shape to disguise his half-elf traits, was feeling just as worried.

The three kids rode through the line of black-clad men without causing a reaction. Their leader was asking Master Chem a question and he responded by pointing at Cal.

Two of the men immediately grabbed the young thief, lifting him off his bike.

Frozen, Tara understood. The men in black had seized her friend! They were taking a hostage to force her to give herself up.

Well, she wouldn't disappoint them.

To Robin's surprise, she jumped on her bicycle and started pedaling furiously toward the manor house.

Since she'd started using magic, however reluctantly, Tara understood that she had to visualize what she wanted. So she now imagined herself striking her adversaries like a thunderbolt, blasting them away from Cal and the manor house.

Unfortunately, she had forgotten a small detail: that the living stone, the repository of OtherWorld's magic, was in her pocket. The stone was an intelligent entity that Tara had freed from imprisonment on the Island of Black Roses, and it lent Tara its powerful magic. When their two powers combined, Tara became a disaster waiting to happen.

The stone had only a vague idea of how much damage it could do. It hadn't yet absorbed the fact that humans were fragile.

"Power?" sang the stone in Tara's mind. "You want power to destroy the evil people who are causing harm? Power I give you? Here, take it."

Tara had no time to react. Her bicycle suddenly took off, soaring overhead like a hawk. Then it dove toward the men in black while she desperately clung to the handlebars.

Hearing a loud "Aaahhhh!" they looked up. For some reason, the scream sounded more like girlish panic than warlike fury.

They didn't have time to think. Tara and the stone's combined magic sent the attackers flying in all directions, and they had a painful landing twenty yards away. Isabella liked both roses and blackberries, and a thicket of blackberry bushes surrounded the property. The men in black yelped as they landed in the thorns.

Tara's bike slammed to a stop an inch above the ground, and only then did she stop screaming in terror. She jumped off, glowered at the stone in her pocket, and lifted her hands, which immediately started glowing with blue light. She was ready to rescue her friends.

"Cal! Fabrice! Sparrow!" she yelled. "Run for it! I'll cover you."

But Cal didn't budge, just gaped at her in astonishment.

"Tara!" roared Master Chem. "Stop that right now! These are imperial guards!"

Before Tara could obey, a new arrival added to the confusion by joining the fray: It was her familiar, Gallant, flying to the rescue. The lacerated leader of the black-clad men was limping toward them when he found himself facing the enraged pegasus's claws.

At that, the guard captain lost his legendary cool. Pointing at Gallant, who had just ripped off a chunk of his trousers, he screamed: "By Pocus, I'm stopping this fight by force, and paralyze the winged horse."

Unable to avoid the paralyzing ray shooting from the man's hands, Gallant crashed to the grass with a loud thud.

Turning to Tara, he continued: "By the authority of the Empress of Omois, I order you to surrender immediately!"

Tara's reaction was purely instinctive, unfortunately. This man had just paralyzed her beloved pegasus, and she hadn't been fast enough to stop him. Now the imperial Omois guard captain flew through the air and landed with a loud splash, which told everyone that he had just met the manor house's beautiful swimming pool.

He emerged spluttering and enraged. He'd lost his black cape during his short flight, and Tara could see that his uniform was indeed the purple and gold Omois livery. Also, his dissimulation spell had dissipated, revealing the guards' characteristic four arms, which were very useful for carrying their array of both sharp and blunt weapons.

Surprised, Tara dialed back her magic power, despite protests from the living stone, who always enjoyed a little fight.

"But . . . but . . . didn't they come here to kidnap me?"

"Not at all," said the old wizard, frowning. "They came to get Caliban."

"Cal?" asked Tara, completely at a loss. "Whatever for?"

"They came to arrest him," Master Chem confirmed somberly. "He's wanted for murder."

CHAPTER 2

THE ARREST

"This is serious, Tara!" said Sparrow, pale with fear. "They arrested Angelica, too. And Master Chem has been summoned to the palace to explain the circumstances surrounding the boy Brandis's death in the vortex. You and I have been 'invited' to come as well."

This news hit Tara like a punch in the stomach. Even though it had been a tragic accident, Cal and Angelica had been partly responsible for the young spellbinder's death.

"I'm going with you," said Master Chem. "Tara, we have to get ready—"

"That's out of the question!" interrupted Isabella sharply. "Tara can't go to Omois."

The guard captain frowned.

"And why can't Miss Duncan visit our beautiful capital?" he asked very politely, his four hands inching closer to his gleaming swords.

"Because she can't!" answered Isabella. "That's all there is to it."

The guard scowled and his hands moved a little lower.

Master Chem intervened. "There have been several attempts on Tara's life," he said diplomatically. "She can't risk going to OtherWorld. It's too dangerous."

From the expression on the captain's face, he seemed to feel that it was Tara who was dangerous to other people, not the other way around. Anyway, it didn't really matter. His mission was to bring Cal back and not the two girls, whose presence had simply been requested.

"I would never do anything to endanger the young lady's safety," the captain said, bowing. "I will inform the empress." Then, looking coldly at Isabella, he added, "However, I will come back if Her Imperial Majesty decides that Miss Duncan's presence is required after all."

"I'll go," said Sparrow to the guard. "I'll represent you, Tara."

"Is that okay with you, Cal?" asked Tara, trying bravely not to cry.

Still dumbfounded by what was happening to him, the little thief frowned, then forced a thin smile. "Let's just say I've been in more pleasant situations. But don't worry; this will all be cleared up real fast. The Truth Tellers will read my mind and see what really happened. I didn't kill that boy. It was whoever tried to kill you by expanding the vortex."

Tara gave Sparrow a look of anguish, then nodded and kissed Cal on both cheeks, to his acute embarrassment.

Robin and Fabrice merely gave him manly thumps on the back.

Without a word, the guard signaled to his men to take charge of Cal and Blondin, then released Gallant from the paralysis spell. The bleary-eyed pegasus stumbled over to Tara to be petted. Looking very preoccupied, Master Chem headed toward Count Besois-Giron's castle, which held the Transfer Portal to OtherWorld. The imperial guards followed with Sparrow and Cal.

"Wait a minute!" shouted Isabella. She was rubbing her painful wrists and suddenly looked as pale as her silvery hair. "You can't go walking around this planet looking like that. Dry your uniforms and put your cape back on, Captain. And don't frog-march that boy along as if he were a dangerous criminal. The nonspells might get suspicious."

The captain scowled at her. His velvet purple-and-gold uniform was soaking wet and looked ready for the garbage. Sighing, he summoned a hot blast of wind to quickly dry it.

Bad idea! Everyone knows that if you heat velvet too fast, it shrinks. In moments, the captain was gaping at his bare calves and two pairs of forearms sticking out of a mini-uniform.

Repressing a nervous giggle, Selena solemnly held his black cape out to him. The captain wrapped himself in it along with whatever dignity he had left, then strode in annoyance toward the castle, followed by his men.

Selena took Tara in her arms, but the girl tensed. She still wasn't used to physical contact. But then she relaxed. Her mother didn't want to strangle her, she realized, just to give her a hug.

"Are you all right, darling?"

Tara was also not used to having anyone worry about her, and she relaxed a little more, touched by her mother's kindness.

"No, I'm not all right!" she blurted. "I'm scared to death for Cal. And I'm furious at him at the same time. I don't know how he does it, but he's always getting himself into impossible situations."

"I'm worried for your friend too," said Selena. "Murder is a very serious charge. And I thank Demiderus that you weren't charged as well."

Isabella rolled her eyes—she didn't want Selena worrying Tara—and went into the manor, still rubbing her wrists. Before she was out of sight, both Selena and Tara glimpsed the two shiny red glyphs pulsing

19

on her forearms. Tara frowned. She knew that if she became a wizard, the blood oath Isabella had sworn to her father would kill her grandmother. Tara forgot that when she flew to Cal's rescue, but using her power so close to her grandmother visibly caused the woman pain. Tara absolutely had to be more careful.

Selena sighed and reluctantly released her daughter. As she turned to go inside, she said, "I think I'm about to get yet another lecture on how to raise children, and what they should and shouldn't be told. I'll see you later."

Tara smiled slightly. Her mother and grandmother had spent the last week making up for their ten years apart. Isabella was surprised to discover that her sweet, gentle daughter had developed a strong character during her decade of imprisonment.

"So, what do we do now?" asked Fabrice.

Tara watched Cal and Sparrow disappear around the bend of the road and made up her mind. She took a deep breath, and said, "Let's follow my grandmother."

Without waiting for the others, Tara ran inside. They followed, surprised to see her sneaking from place to place to reach the living room without being spotted.

"Er, why are we hiding?" asked Fabrice, who felt silly crawling across the carpet.

"I want to find out what my grandma's plotting," whispered Tara. "And with her, the only way to do that is to listen at keyholes."

"That didn't work out too well for Cal last night," he answered, nervously glancing around for Sembor, Selena's familiar.

"Shhh!" Tara hissed. "Listen!"

When they put their ears against the door, the two women's voices were clearly audible. It was easy to imagine slender Selena sitting in a comfortable armchair, carefully watching her mother.

"I can't say that I ever much liked your late husband Danviou," Isabella was saying, "but look at the wonderful surprise he left us!"

So, they had gotten past the child-rearing chapter and were now reliving the "good old days."

"What wonderful surprise?" asked Selena, clearly perplexed.

"That he was the emperor! The Emperor of Omois! Actually, I always suspected something odd was up with your husband. I saw how nervous he got whenever we met new people. I thought he must be some minor Omois nobleman who had run away from his family. I didn't realize he was actually running away from an *empire*! And to think that I didn't want him for you because I wanted you to marry someone more important. That little sneak!"

What Selena said next knocked Tara for a loop: "No kidding! But did you really hate him so much that you had to lock me up in that tower to keep him from seeing me?"

Isabella cleared her throat before answering. "Well, maybe I did go a little overboard."

"*Overboard*? You had trolls guarding the tower! And then you sent those half-dozen 'highly presentable' princes and spellbinders to woo me—and then fried or flattened them when they failed. You should really quit reading those old Earth romance novels, Mom. They just aren't for you!"

"All right, all right. I admit the trolls were a bit much. But I only wanted what was best for you, darling. And how could I trust some stranger who suddenly dropped into our lives and wanted to marry you?"

Tara was flabbergasted. Her grandmother had opposed her parents' marriage? So that was why Isabella had always avoided talking about them! Lots of things were suddenly becoming clear to her.

But Selena wasn't interested in bringing up the past. Changing the subject, she came back to the present: "Does Tara realize that by refusing the empress's invitation she could be making her friend Cal's situation worse?"

"I couldn't care less about that boy's fate," said Isabella. "There's no way my granddaughter's going to Omois. It's too dangerous. Just think, Magister could capture her again!"

"I'm not minimizing the danger," Selena said calmly. "But Tara is very loyal to Cal, and she'll never abandon a friend. Anyway, what would you do to stop her? Lock her up in a dungeon, like me?"

"I hadn't thought of that," Isabella answered slowly. "But it's not a bad idea!"

On hearing this, Tara jumped away from the door and signaled her friends to do the same. Her heart was pounding.

"Man, your grandmother is pretty radical, isn't she?" said Robin, expressing what they were all thinking. "So, what do we do now?"

"Seems pretty obvious, doesn't it?" whispered Tara. "We're going to Omois. Cal needs us!"

"I could've bet you were going to say that," Fabrice said with a groan. "And I suppose it's up to me to get us there."

"I'm really sorry," said Tara, who didn't like putting her friend in such a predicament, "but your father is the guardian of the Transfer Portal to OtherWorld. And I think we better get out of here right away, before Grandma turns me into another Sleeping Beauty."

"What about you, Robin?" Fabrice asked, without much hope. "You wanna go too?"

"Will there be fighting?" asked the half-elf, his eyes bright.

"All right, I get it." Fabrice signed with resignation. "What a fourth letter of the alphabet + an old cloth!"

"D-rag?" guessed Tara.

"You said it!"

The preparations were soon complete. Carefully avoiding Tachil and Mangus, the two spellbinders who worked for Isabella, the kids grabbed their robes and a change of clothes for OtherWorld.

Those spellbinder robes were much more than simply things to wear. Thanks to the magic spells woven into the fabric, they were warm in winter, cool in summer, stain-resistant, and fireproof. They also had the most-extraordinary pockets. You could stick absolutely whatever you wanted into them, provided it wasn't alive, because it wouldn't be able to breathe. But aside from that, the pockets could handle anything from a needle to a bathtub, because the objects were made weightless and stored in another dimension. (Sparrow once tried to explain how this worked, but Tara's eyes glazed over when she got to quantum mechanics, atomic disincorporation, and parallel universes, so she gave up.) Also, you could magically change the robes' colors and decorate them, which OtherWorld fashionistas found very handy.

Tara carefully packed her gold immuta-credits as well as her magic map. This was the extraordinary map she had originally bought for Isabella, but kept for herself when it turned out to be incredibly useful. *Too bad*, thought Tara. *I'll get Grandma something else on OtherWorld.*

For his part, Robin put the green twig of the living tree in one of his pockets. A gift from the grateful tree, it had the power to make any plant sprout and grow in seconds. Fabrice took a half-dozen cartoons and comic books. He explained to his surprised friends that he had trouble falling asleep without reading, but found OtherWorld books too exciting for his taste.

The young spellbinders then slipped away to the stables to get Gallant, who was waiting for them. Robin changed the pegasus into a large dog, which made the handsome white stallion speechless with indignation.

It only took them a few minutes to walk over to Besois-Giron Castle. Busy with his rosebushes, Igor the gardener only gave them a distracted wave. When they pushed the large entry door open, it creaked, startling them.

"Wait for me here," whispered Fabrice when they were inside. "I'll go get the Transfer Room keys from the office."

"I thought your father always carried them in his pocket," murmured Tara.

"He does, but there's an extra copy, just in case. It'll only take me a minute."

Just to be on the safe side, Tara and Robin hid behind the suits of armor lining the castle's black-and-white tiled entryway. Tara felt torn between a deep concern about Cal and regret at leaving her mother, with whom she had so recently been reunited. She didn't like magic, which kept intruding in her life willy-nilly. She had no faith in Other-World justice and hated the idea of having to go back there. But to help Cal, she was prepared to confront all the demons of Limbo.

Standing beside Tara and looking at her out of the corner of his eye, Robin felt awkward and agitated. He admired her long blond hair, with that distinctive white forelock, and her unusual deep blue eyes. She was so beautiful; it sometimes made him catch his breath.

"What if this is all a trap?" he whispered. "Magister knows it's hard to get to you on Earth. Suppose he's concocted this whole business as a way of luring you to OtherWorld?"

"I thought of that," Tara somberly replied, absentmindedly grabbing her white strand and chewing on it. "But what choice do we have? Trap or no trap, we can't leave Cal all alone."

"You're probably right. But let's keep our eyes peeled."

While they were talking, Fabrice was upstairs on the third floor, sweating bullets. His plan had hit a snag.

The spare keys were in his father's office all right. The problem was, so was his father.

Standing behind the half-open door, Fabrice took a deep breath and recited: "By Somnolus, please catch some z's, so you won't hear me take the keys."

Because magic is so much weaker on Earth, Fabrice's father didn't get sleepy right away. The boy waited, annoyed at the idea that he might have to ask his friends for help. But then his father's eyelids began to droop. He rubbed his eyes, let his head slump, and started snoring.

So far so good. Now Fabrice had to get the keys. How he wished Cal were with him. The little thief would have searched the room three times while Fabrice was mustering all his courage to take a single step.

Tiptoeing as quietly as possible, he headed toward the desk. To his dismay, the drawer squeaked loudly enough to wake the dead.

Forget it, he thought. *I'll leave the drawer open and just hold my breath and cross my fingers.*

Teeth clenched, Fabrice picked up the keys, silently cursing when they clinked. In two steps he was at the door, when he suddenly heard a loud voice behind him.

"Don't set the beam down over there! Put it here!"

Fabrice whipped around, his heart in his mouth. His father's eyes were still closed and he was waving his arms. He was dreaming.

When a swarm of black butterflies started dancing in front of his eyes, Fabrice realized he was about to pass out. He took a deep breath and heaved a sigh of relief. Then he quietly closed the door and raced downstairs to his friends.

"Okay, I got them. Let's go!" he said.

"You're white as a sheet," remarked Robin tactlessly. "Is everything okay?"

"Oh yeah. Everything's totally peachy spectacular!" he replied weakly. "I just cast a spell on my own father and nearly had a heart attack. Let's hope he never finds out, otherwise I'm going to be grounded for the next fifty years!"

It only took them a few minutes to climb the tower. The large Transfer Portal Room was empty, guarded only by the brightly colored tapestries that represented OtherWorld's five races: human spellbinders, giants, elves, Lilliputian fairies, and unicorns.

The kids and their familiars went to stand in the center of the room. Fabrice took the transfer scepter from an alcove and set it on the tapestry with the matching pattern, then joined his friends. The scepter hummed, and a bright white glow lit them up. Rays of blue, yellow, red, and green light shot from the other tapestries, creating a miniature rainbow. Fabrice was about to shout out their destination when he suddenly choked, leaving the words unsaid.

The door to the room had just opened!

The transfer stopped immediately and the light faded. Rigid with fear, the spellbinders watched as a black dog padded into the room.

"Great-grandpa?" cried Tara in astonishment. "What are you doing here?"

"Tara, how many times do I have to tell you not to call me Great-grandpa," said the Labrador, sounding miffed. "It makes me feel a hundred years old. Call me Grandpa or Manitou."

"How about Popsicle?" asked Tara, who couldn't resist. "Popsicle would be nice, wouldn't it? And you didn't answer my question."

"Popsicle is totally unacceptable," he said firmly. "Pops is about as far as you can go. As to why I'm here, I knew you were up to something stupid, so I followed you. And I'm coming too. At least you'll have a cautious adult along, which might save you from spending the rest of your days on bread and water when Isabella and Selena realize what you're up to. Besides, I want to be far away when your grandmother notices you're gone. I've got sensitive ears."

"Grandpa, I *adore* you!" said Tara.

Manitou gave her a wolfish smile and went to join the others in the center of the room. Fabrice launched the transfer again. When the four beams of light hit them, he shouted: "Omois, Tingapore Imperial Palace!"

Their image wavered, and in the next instant, they vanished.

When they appeared in Omois, they were greeted by a thicket of razor-sharp spears. The imperial guards hadn't been warned of this unexpected arrival and, following their habit of skewering first and asking questions later, very nearly brought the travelers' lives to an early end.

Fortunately, Head Palace Housekeeper Kali was there. She shouted, and the guards' spears froze.

"Unannounced arrivals are not authorized," she snapped, waving her six arms. "You're lucky that I was in the Transfer Room, otherwise . . ."

She didn't specify what that "otherwise" was, but Fabrice shivered.

Tara stepped forward, calmly ignoring the guards' baleful stares.

"I am Tara'tylanhnem Duncan," she announced graciously. "The empress requested our presence to help shed light on the death of one of her subjects in an uncontrolled vortex. We were supposed to come with High Wizard Chemnashaovirodaintrachivu, but were delayed."

Tara looked as cool as a cucumber, but inside she was shaking like a leaf. She desperately hoped the Kali would swallow her story.

To her great relief, Kali smiled, then bowed deferentially.

"I will immediately send word of your belated arrival to the empress and emperor. Damien, one of our apprentice spellbinders, will accompany you to your suite."

The boy with shiny black hair who had been so hostile to them during their previous visit to Omois bowed in turn. Since learning that their friend Sparrow was able to turn into a monstrous beast ten feet tall—and was royalty to boot—Damien had become the most courteous and attentive of guides.

The Omois Imperial Palace hadn't changed; it was as extravagantly dazzling as ever. People with sensitive eyes were well advised to wear sunglasses, so as not to be blinded. Jewel-studded gold statues stood everywhere, bathed in beams of light; valuable carpets were scattered underfoot; yellow and green marble streaked with opalescent mother of pearl made the walls look like flowing rivers. Elegant pieces of furniture wandered around, rushing over to anyone who felt like sitting or lying down.

Suddenly, Tara cried out. An aged spellbinder had let himself fall to the floor in front of them. An armchair popped out of nowhere and materialized under his bony posterior just in time to cushion his fall. The man pulled out an ornate pen, and a one-legged table hopped over lickety-split to stand before him. A sheet of parchment appeared and he started dictating. Hearing his words, the pen displayed a pair of little arms, stretched, yawned deeply, and began to write.

Okay, got it, thought Tara. *When somebody falls, don't react. It's completely normal.*

All the same, she found herself catching her breath when courtiers would suddenly sit down in midair and have an armchair sprint over on its little wooden legs to catch them.

But it was when they reached the interior palace gardens that they fully appreciated the empress's unusual taste in decor. They were about to cross a vast park—more a jungle than a park, actually—when Fabrice suddenly screamed, making them jump. A monstrous foot had crashed down in front of him, followed by a pair of sharp-toothed jaws that seemed to have him in mind. He backed away in terror to escape the monster that was trying to swallow him, but Damien merely smiled.

"Don't be afraid," he reassured them. "The drago-tyrannosauruses can't harm you. When we entered the jungle, we automatically activated force-field bubbles. The animals can see us, but they can't get to us."

Fabrice looked up at the enormous saurian drooling onto the protective bubble and trying in vain to pierce it.

"I hate this!" he screamed. "Whenever there's some huge, hungry thing around, why does it always go after me? I want out of here before the whole security system breaks down."

"There's no risk of that," answered Damien.

"Yeah, right!" snapped Fabrice. "It's like they said in *Jurassic Park*: that there is nothing to be scared about, just a power malfunction. Get me out of here!"

Damien obeyed, but his perplexed look suggested he had serious doubts about Fabrice's mental stability.

The group then entered a kind of gigantic aquarium where fish in water bubbles floated among the furniture and plants. Tara felt the empress had gone a bit far when she found herself nose to nose with what looked very much like a whale—except that it must have gotten a bad sunburn, because it was bright red.

The next hall made them feel they had stepped into a refrigerator. In a glacial landscape, large furry balls were browsing on the frozen white grass. A snowstorm was raging, and they advanced with difficulty. In the crevasses, animals that looked like lobsters waved their claws, waiting for one of the fur balls to fall in. Piles of bones at the bottom showed that this must happen often enough.

The empress had apparently decided to recreate all of OtherWorld's environments inside her palace, complete with their fauna and flora.

Purple ifrits were busy everywhere. These minor demons from Limbo couldn't harm OtherWorld peoples, which is why they were allowed to remain on the planet. In Omois they cleaned and guarded the Imperial Palace, directed Tingapore's insane traffic, and served as messengers. Within a few centuries they had become essential to the empire's life and workings. Tara, who had awful memories of her passage through Limbo, kept well away from them.

When the group reached their suite of rooms, Damien formally introduced them to the door. It opened an eye, a mouth appeared and greeted them very politely, and an arm turned the handle. They went in and, when Damien left, heaved a collective sigh of relief.

Seeing them, Sparrow and Sheeba jumped to their feet. "Tara! What are you doing here? I thought your grandmother forbade you from coming to OtherWorld."

"We couldn't abandon Cal," said Tara, stroking Sheeba. "And let's say we didn't exactly ask her permission. It seemed more important to come to try to help. How is he doing?"

"I don't know. We were separated as soon as we got here. I'm waiting to be called to testify."

Robin looked around the room disapprovingly.

"Good grief!" he said, waving an arm at the suite's sumptuous decor. "A quarter of all this would be enough to sustain an entire village in Selenda. It's almost indecent!"

The half-elf had a point. The luxurious room was immaculately white, with everything in it shading from silver to the purest opalescent: beautiful albino snaptooth furs from Gandis, silver arachne silk curtains, woven kalorna fiber carpets, and crystal OtherWorld statues. The only touch of color was a magnificent bouquet of red flowers with waving petals that gave off a sweet scent.

The suite had four bedrooms around a large central living room. In an alcove, perches and bedding awaited the familiars. Gallant let Tara know that he wanted his wings, and he flapped them with pleasure when she transformed him back into a pegasus. Then he settled next to her and laid his light head on her knees so she could scratch him between the ears.

Manitou jumped onto a sofa that was so soft he almost sank out of sight.

"All we can do now is to follow Sparrow's example, and wait," he said. But do you think we could order something to eat in the meantime? It's been ages since I've had fried kalornas, kraken tentacles, or manuril shoots. Not to mention brrraaa chops, roast leg of mooouuu with fines herbs, slurp juice, yellow string beans from the Meus plains, and—"

"I don't know if we have the time," Robin interrupted, not unkindly. "The empress is sure to have us called in soon. We let it be known that we're here to stand by Cal, so—"

"Stand! That's the word for it," said Fabrice with a sigh. "I can't *stand* always having to get Cal out of the tight spots he gets into. Professional, for short, plus second letter of the alphabet, plus Lunar Excursion Module, for short = pro + b + LEM = problem. That's Cal, all over."

Tara was about to reply when a big mouth and an eye took shape on the door. "A visitor requests permission to meet you," said the mouth. "Should I let him in?"

"Who's the visitor?" asked Robin cautiously.

The eye blinked, and they got the impression that the door was feeling uncomfortable.

"I'm guessing it's a gnome, but I've never seen one before. Would you like me to ask the other doors what race he belongs to? They're sure to know."

"No, that's all right," said Sparrow. "Let him in."

The door didn't stir. Oops! Sparrow had forgotten the magic word.

"Er, please!"

The mouth smiled, and the door shortly opened to reveal a very odd individual. Tara looked down . . . and down . . . and down, to find a tiny blue figure wearing a mud-colored doublet and pants and a matching bonnet from which protruded a big tuft of orange hair.

"It's a Smurf!" said Fabrice, laughing.

"Miss Tara'tylanhnem?" the creature asked in a tiny, high-pitched voice. "I am Glul Buglul, a gnome, and Sir Caliban Dal Salan's compensator. I was not originally assigned to this trial, but the empress specifically insisted that I work with Sir Dal Salan. Though you are free to request another compensator if I do not suit you."

"Compensator?" wondered Tara, who was fascinated by the odd character.

"He'll be assisting Cal at the hearing," explained Sparrow. "The Truth Tellers will read Cal's mind to find out what happened, and the compensator will interpret what they transmit to him."

"Why?" Fabrice asked, surprised. "Can't the Truth Tellers speak?"

"They're telepaths," Sparrow said with a shiver. "They can read our minds, but they never developed vocal cords. So the compensators receive the Tellers' brain waves and speak for them. They're the only ones who can do that, in fact."

Tara frowned. "But if the compensators are the only ones who can communicate with them, how can you be sure they're telling the truth?"

"The Tellers may be mute, but they are not deaf!" said the gnome with great dignity. "If one of us shaded the truth, they would hear it immediately."

"Sorry. I didn't mean to insult you," said Tara, who had been thinking out loud. "It's just that everything is so different on your world. And I'm very worried about my friend."

"If he is innocent of the crime the empire has charged him with, he is in no danger," explained the gnome. "However, to better understand the situation, I will need your testimony. Do I have your permission to take your depositions?"

This made Fabrice uncomfortable. He had seen plenty of movies on Earth where the friendly cop asks witnesses if he can interview them, and the next thing they know, the witnesses are behind bars. He opened his mouth to refuse, but Tara beat him to the punch.

"Of course you can," she said. "We all saw what happened, and we'll tell you everything."

The gnome pulled out a small box with two large ears that seemed to be listening very carefully. One after another, the friends described the boy's tragic death, or at least as much of it as they could. Master Chem hadn't lifted the Informatus spell he'd cast on them, so they weren't able to talk about Angelica's plot against Tara.

When they were finished, Buglul bowed.

"The case seems simple to me," he said. "If the Truth Tellers confirm your story, the worst the defendant faces will be a reprimand for distracting the apprentices. The real guilty party is whoever transformed the vortex and thereby caused the boy's death. You did say that the counter-spell seemed to come from the area where the high wizards were standing. Is that correct?"

"Yes," said Robin. "It was very clear. Some sort of dark power countering all our efforts. That power is what killed the boy!"

"Thank you," said the gnome, bowing again as he folded the two ears and put the box in his pocket. "You will be summoned in a few minutes for the start of the trial."

Fabrice was impressed. No doubt about it—telepathy was pretty darn practical. "My first retransmits image and sound," he muttered to himself. "My second is a kind of road, my third is the biblical you, and my whole is a very useful faculty."

"I'm guessing *tele* and *path*," said Tara, "but I'm stumped on the third."

"Thee," said Fabrice. "Tele + path + thee = telepathy." He paused, then asked, "So, what do we do while we're waiting?"

"Nothing, I'm afraid," said Tara. "The imperial guards are pretty well armed, so we can't really stroll around without permission."

But as it turned out, they didn't have long to wait. A purple ifrit came and led them through the lush interior gardens to the Double Throne Room, where the empress and the emperor were waiting.

The impressive hall was so big one practically had to pack a lunch just to get across it. On the wall were colorful frescoes of unicorns leaping, imps picking flowers chided by fairy dragonflies, and giants munching on hills. In short, a lot was going on.

There was gold everywhere, of course. The gold animal sculptures were so beautiful—they almost seemed alive. A gorgeous crystal and gold pegasus—Tara's gift to the two sovereigns on her previous visit— stood center stage, a sign of their gratitude toward the young spell-binder.

A number of crystalists were observing everyone carefully. These were OtherWorld's journalists, easy to recognize because of the little-winged cameras, called scoops, that always hovered around them. Tara was surprised to note that many of the female spellbinders had copied the empress's distinctive white forelock in their hair. So much the better, she thought. The Empress of Omois didn't know that Tara was actually her niece, and it hadn't occurred to Tara to hide her telltale white forelock.

Few courtiers seemed interested in the trial, but the high wizards of Omois and Lancovit were out in force, floating around the twin thrones under the direction of Lady Auxia, a brown-haired high wizard who was the empress's cousin and the palace administrator. To Tara's great surprise, Master Chem had brought a whole contingent from Lancovit: Master Dragosh, the vampyr; Lady Boudiou; the elf Master Den'maril; Lady Sirella, a mermaid floating gracefully in her water bubble; the cahmboum Master Patin; Master Sardoin; and Master Chanfrein. The only Lancovit wizards missing were Lady Kalibris, whose administrative duties probably kept her back at the Living Castle, and the medical shaman, Master Night Bird.

Tara shuddered to see the vampyr, whose fangs always looked ready to bite her. And she gulped when Master Chem spotted her. The old dragon looked angry enough to turn them into toads.

But when Tara turned her attention to Empress Lisbeth'tylanhnem, she was so dazzled by the young woman's beauty that she forgot the vampyr and the dragon. The first time Tara saw the empress, her incredible mass of hair had been red. This time, it was its natural color and flowed like a golden river down to the matching sandals on her tiny feet, its magnificence highlighted by a single white forelock. Enveloped in this silky stream and wearing a cream-colored robe studded by jewels in the pattern of the imperial emblem, Empress Lisbeth'tylanhnem literally glowed. Her milky skin was highlighted by a touch of pink on her cheeks and red on her scarlet lips. Beneath the heavy gold crown sparkled a pair of large, deep blue eyes. Taken as a whole, the picture was almost too perfect, and Tara wondered if the empress used magic to enhance her natural beauty.

Seated next to her on a matching throne, under the hundred-eyed purple peacock, Emperor Sandor was wearing a plain steel half breastplate inlaid with gold. His blond hair was woven in a braid that lay across one broad shoulder. He looked bored to death, but sat up when he saw the four friends and the dog, his interest piqued.

The granite-faced majordomo asked for their names and titles, and announced them: "Her Royal Highness Princess Gloria Daavil, called Sparrow. High Wizard Manitou Duncan. Apprentice Spellbinder Tara'tylanhnem Duncan, called Tara. Apprentice Spellbinder Robin M'angil. Apprentice Spellbinder Fabrice Besois-Giron. The princess, the high wizard, and the spellbinders are here in response to your Imperial Majesties' summons in the matter of the defendant, Caliban Dal Salan."

The empress's eyes widened when she heard Tara's full name. At their first meeting, she had been surprised by the name, which was normally reserved for the imperial family. But she had forgotten about it when the vortex raged out of control and nearly destroyed her palace. The emperor, however, was now alert and paying Tara his full attention.

Master Chem and the empress opened their mouths to speak, but Sandor beat them to it.

"Tell me, child, how do you happen to have such a distinctive name?" he asked in a well-modulated purr. "Are you aware that it is normally forbidden to have the same last name as the empress?"

In coming to Omois, Tara knew that she might face the problem of being the legitimate heir to the empire—well, the secret heir, anyway. And from the look on Master Chem's face, he clearly didn't want her revealing this little detail in the middle of Cal's trial.

Let's see if a diversion will get me out of this fix, she thought.

"Oh, really? I'm terribly sorry," she said, ducking the issue. "We came here to support our friend Cal, who has been unjustly accused of the boy's death. Since we all witnessed the event and I closed the vortex (*may as well remind him that she was the one who saved the palace from destruction*), it seemed essential that we give our testimony."

"I see," murmured the emperor in a vaguely malevolent tone. "Have you come to claim the imperial favor that my half-sister granted you, so you can save the guilty party?"

This time Master Chem spoke up.

"What do you mean, guilty party?" he exploded. "The boy's death was an accident, as you know perfectly well. We only came to prove Caliban's good faith. I suspect there's a malicious plot behind all this, and I plan to uncover it, believe me!"

Chem was so furious that he began to hiccup, to the point where a worried Lady Boudiou started pounding him on the back. Despite her efforts, the old wizard's face turned an interesting eggplant color.

Empress Lisbeth was about to turn her attention back to Tara when the little crowd suddenly screamed in terror. Under their horrified eyes Master Chem had begun to swell. He grew larger and larger, and sharp claws grew from his fingertips, a white mane replaced his hair, his skin became covered with blue and silver scales, a spiny crest shredded his robe, and huge fangs burst from his throat. Within seconds, a magnificent and imposing dragon stood where the old wizard had been. With an excited *zoom* the buzzing scoops rushed to transmit the images to their crystalists.

"*Hic!*" The huge blue dragon hiccupped and belched a blast of fire that just missed the highly inflammable wooden ceiling.

As diversions go, Tara thought to herself, *this one takes the prize!*

The emperor was slack-jawed for a moment until he remembered that he was the empire's military chief, after all, and bravely drew his sword. Next to him, the guard captain brandished his own swords, but looked no more confident. From the corner of his eye he noticed the scoops filming him, so he tightened his grip on his weapons, trying to look martial.

"Stop that!" the empress raged at the guards who were trying to pull her to safety. "Unhand me!"

In a fury, she went to stand in front of the dragon, hands planted on her hips.

"Master Chemnashaovirodaintrachivu!"

"Yes, Your Imperial Majesty, *hic!*" he rumbled.

"This is an insult to our court! You will immediately shape-shift back, or I will have you thrown in prison for outrage to our person."

The dragon bowed graciously, bringing his terrifying muzzle down level with the angry young woman's face.

"Very well, Your Imperial Majesty. I hear, *hic!*, and I obey."

"Good," she said, wrinkling her nose. "And stop that huffing and puffing! You reek of sulfur, and it stinks!"

The dragon began to shrink and its fangs disappeared, as did its scales. Soon the old wizard was again standing in front of them, wearing a robe that he barely had time to conjure, so as not to wind up naked in front of the empress. She glared at him for a moment, then turned back to Tara.

"Very well. So, what were we saying before we were so rudely inter-rupted?"

"That you were going to give us permission to help our friend Caliban?" suggested Tara, displaying her sweetest smile.

The emperor opened his mouth, and Tara sensed that he might be about to ship them right home, but the empress spoke first.

"Of course you can assist your friend, child. That's why we requested your presence. We will summon the Truth Tellers immediately, and then we can get back to this name business."

Maybe the emperor could be fooled, but the empress was too clever not to have noticed that Tara had carefully avoided answering her.

The four friends respectfully bowed to the sovereigns and were awkwardly imitated by Manitou, Sheeba, and even Gallant, whose body wasn't really designed for bowing. Then they stepped aside, leaving room for Cal and the telepaths.

The Truth Tellers appeared a few moments later and Fabrice whistled with surprise. They didn't have any mouths! Their bright, intelligent eyes lit on people and things with interest and patience. Wrapped in long white tunics, they moved slowly, gliding gracefully over the ground. Their heads were covered with big black helmets that ended in a point at the back.

Glul Buglul, the gnome, followed them, accompanied by Cal, Blondin, and Angelica. Tara was startled to see the tall brunette, having completely forgotten that she had also been charged. As she passed, Angelica shot Tara a look of hatred.

Well, there never was much friendship between them to begin with.

A fat, balding man and a skinny woman whose hair was much too black to be natural accompanied Angelica, whispering advice and suggestions. Given their haughty and scornful looks, they were probably her parents. Cal was accompanied by a slim, nervous-looking man and a pretty woman with gray eyes, who carefully observed everything around her. Tara knew that Cal's mother was a licensed thief, a kind of super spy in the Lancovit government. From the way she was studying the hall, Tara felt she had already spotted all the emergency exits, estimated the number of guards, and had chosen several ways to eliminate any possible opponents.

Angelica's parents went to stand next to Master Dragosh and Cal's parents near Master Sardoin.

Facing them on a floating silver disc stood a man with a woman who was weeping into a handkerchief: the unfortunate parents of the boy who'd been sucked into the vortex.

Under the scoops' watchful lenses, everyone stood, sat, lay down, floated, or hovered, and the trial began.

Master Buglul recited the facts. How during the apprentices' competition two candidates had opened a Transfer Portal. How a loud scream had broken the young spellbinders' concentration, causing them to lose control of their magic. How for some reason the vortex grew to enormous size and swallowed a familiar—Angelica's flying lizard Kimi—and Brandis T'al Miga Ab Chantu, one of the boys who had materialized the portal. Finally, how a charge of murder had been brought by the boy's parents. As soon as the gnome was finished, he gestured to the Tellers. Leaving Angelica aside for the time being, they formed a circle around Cal, who was very pale and seemed to be having trouble breathing. A heavy silence fell on the hall, intermittently broken by Master Chem's persistent hiccups.

Manitou stirred restlessly. As the Truth Tellers began their work, the dog felt a sort of mental tendril brushing his brain. It was completely abnormal, and he knew he should be concerned, since the Tellers were probing only Cal, but a heavy lethargy clouded his mind. The tendril continued to probe and press, its pressure now extending to his entire body—including his bladder.

The uncomfortable feeling roused him and promptly ended the mental investigation. The Lab shook his silky black head and looked around the hall.

Raising a leg and peeing on one of the thrones in the middle of the trial probably isn't a great idea, Manitou thought. *Better to find some place more appropriate.* He discreetly backed toward a door and went out.

Once in the hallway, he raced to the part of the interior park reserved for this kind of urgent business and gave a silent sigh as he relieved himself on a big tree. He'd felt the pressure lift the moment he left the hall, which also seemed odd. If he'd had eyebrows, he would've frowned.

The Lab had just finished when he heard approaching footsteps. His dog nose recognized the person's scent.

"Fabrice! What are you doing here?"

"I saw you go out, and I was concerned," said the boy. "Are you all right?"

"Yes and no. I think a Truth Teller decided to take a little trip around inside my head, and it wasn't especially pleasant. What happened while I was away?"

Fabrice didn't know enough about OtherWorld to grasp the implications of what Manitou had just revealed.

"Nothing much," he said with a sigh. "They're just standing around Cal wide-eyed, shaking their heads, that's all."

"Hmm, that's very strange. Normally it would've all be over in a few minutes. Let's go back inside. I have to speak with Chem."

Coming around a grove of trees, they were startled to see two spellbinders in conversation near an exit door. That in itself was nothing unusual, but where their faces should have been there was just a shiny space. And they were wearing gray!

"Oh my god!" whispered Fabrice. "Bloodgraves!" He shrank back into the trees, well aware that he was no match for Magister's evil minions.

From where Fabrice and Manitou were standing, they could overhear what the two spellbinders were saying.

"The master's plan worked perfectly!" said the first with a chortle. "That stupid Chem raced here to protect Caliban Dal Salan, leaving the *Forbidden Book* unguarded. Magister will have no problem seizing it!"

"With the demonic spells it contains, the dragons will never be able to resist us. They'll soon bow before our power!"

"Oh no!" groaned Manitou. "Bloodgraves in Omois! That takes the cake! So, was it Magister who managed to get Cal charged in order to draw us here? Now I *really* have to talk to Chem!"

The moment the Bloodgraves left, Manitou rushed to the Double Throne Room, with Fabrice hot on his heels. They found the hall in total pandemonium. People were yelling and shouting and making a terrific din.

"That's enough!" thundered Xandiar, the captain of the guards. "Let the gnome speak!"

A tense silence fell, and everyone could see Buglul swallow hard.

"As I was telling Their Imperial Majesties and this honorable assembly," he announced solemnly, "we are facing an unprecedented situation. Our Truth Tellers are unable to read this young spellbinder's thoughts!"

"Why does everyone look so worried?" whispered Fabrice in surprise.

"Because if the Tellers have lost their power," answered Manitou gravely, "it could mean the end of OtherWorld!"

CHAPTER 3

THE TRUTH TELLERS

The empress's clear voice cut through the stunned silence. "This is ridiculous! Just because we're having a problem with this spellbinder doesn't mean there's a problem with everyone. Xandiar!"

"Yes, Your Imperial Majesty?" said the guard captain, bowing.

"Go stand in the middle of the Truth Tellers. We're going to have a test."

"Me, Your Majesty?" he stammered.

Empress Lisbeth'tylanhnem sighed and rubbed her head. "You're the only Xandiar around here, as far as I know. So yes, I mean you!"

"Very well, Your Imperial Majesty."

With martial stride, the captain went to stand among the Truth Tellers and rested his hands on the pommels of his four scimitars. Everything about his attitude warned the Tellers to be very careful with what they were going to say.

Glul Buglul gulped, the Tellers' eyes widened, and almost immediately, the gnome began to speak.

"Attention, everyone! The Tellers declare that the captain of the guards' first thought is a constant concern for Their Majesties' safety. His second thought is a yen for a cold pitcher of beer from Mount Tador. His third thought focuses on the attractive Lady Bom—"

"Stop!" shouted the guard captain, who had turned beet red. "That's a pretty conclusive test. The Tellers haven't lost any of their powers."

The entire hall sighed with relief. The reason there are so few crimes on OtherWorld is largely due to the telepaths' invaluable work. If they had lost their priceless faculties, it would open the way to chaos.

"That's perfect," said the empress. "Now, let's try with the girl. Tellers!"

Angelica obediently took her place in the circle, but the result was the same as with Cal. Her mind was impenetrable, and the telepaths had to admit they were powerless.

"I don't understand why the Truth Tellers can't access these children's thoughts," said the emperor. "Unless someone has managed to create a protective spell to mask their guilt. Which would call for enormous power. And only the dragons—"

"As I said before—*hic*," interrupted Master Chem, who wasn't about to let himself be accused, "we accepted your summons because Caliban and Angelica are innocent—*hic*. We assumed the Tellers would confirm this for us *hic*. Now that this seems to be impossible, there seems to be only one thing left to do."

"I agree," said the empress soberly. "We will have to summon the manes of Brandis T'al Miga Ab Chantu. That will require a great deal of preparation, and I suggest we get some rest beforehand. The hearing will resume tomorrow."

"What are 'manes'?" whispered Tara to her friends.

"They're the boy's psychic remains," said Sparrow. "His spirit, if you like. They can be summoned just once and only asked a single question."

"A ghost!" sighed Fabrice. "Here I think I know everything about this world and *bam!*, something like this hits me. So, Cal and Angelica are going to be judged by a ghost? What if he says they're guilty?"

"They'll be condemned to death," said Sparrow gravely.

"To *death*?" asked Tara, appalled. "You're joking, right?"

"Afraid not. Whether children or adults, spellbinders on Other-World are responsible for their actions as soon as they come into their powers. The death penalty may have been abolished in Lancovit, but it's still in force here in Omois."

"Stay calm, Tara," said Robin. "Getting worried won't do you any good. It clouds your mind, and it's very bad before a fight. Odds are, everything will go well and Cal will be acquitted."

Tara smiled feebly. The half-elf was thinking like a warrior. She straightened and took a deep breath. *He's right*, she thought. *We may as well wait and see what happens.* If things turned out badly, then she would have a perfect right to panic.

The little crowd streamed out of the Throne Room buzzing with questions and conjectures, with feet, tentacles, pseudopods, and hooves sliding and clicking on the purple marble floor. The crystalists whispered furiously into their crystal balls and cubes, spreading the news. All in all, the session had been fascinating.

To Tara's great surprise, Cal strolled over and joined them, while Blondin skipped merrily around. The imperial guards seemed completely unconcerned about what the two were doing.

"I'll be darned!" exclaimed Sparrow, who was equally surprised. "Aren't you in prison?"

"In prison? Why? I haven't done anything," said Cal with a smile.

"But they arrested you!"

"No, they 'kindly invited' me to the palace to 'help clear up a few points.' Unless or until I'm convicted, I'm considered to be innocent." Then he added, sounding oppressed, "But I swear, I'd rather be in jail. Because Angelica is also charged, they stuck us in the same room together, believe it or not."

"No!" exclaimed Sparrow. "That's not so great."

"It's a total drag, you mean. I spend as much time as I can wandering around this blasted palace and only go back there to sleep. And you know what the worst is?"

"What?"

"She snores!"

Their burst of laughter attracted the attention of Master Chem, who was talking with Fabrice and Manitou. He turned to them and said, "Come over here. I'm just about—*hic!*—to hear something that Manitou and Fabrice found out."

When the dog related the conversation between the two Bloodgraves, Chem lost his hiccups completely.

"By my pile of gold!" he roared. "Not again!"

The group cautiously backed away, but this time the dragon wizard controlled himself. Not a single fang or scale appeared.

"You didn't really expect Magister to give up, did you?" said Tara calmly. "We know he's crazy about getting power. And as long as he hasn't found a way to defeat and replace you, he'll continue searching for the demonic objects. Using *The Forbidden Book* is a good way to get to Limbo, isn't it?"

"He doesn't need the book to travel to the demon kingdom," answered Chem soberly. "He can go there whenever he likes. But he needs certain spells that are forbidden even to demons to increase his power, and he can't be allowed to acquire them!"

"He must have cast a spell or something on the boy's parents to make them accuse Cal and to get you to come here," observed Manitou. "To stop him, the simplest thing would be to go get the book and keep it with you."

"I can't," said Chem.

"What do you mean, you can't?"

"You have no idea how much power that book has. It's not just an object, it's a creation of the demons of Limbo, and it has a life of its own. When I study it, I touch it as little as possible. If I carried it around, it could overcome and corrupt me within a few hours. I have too much power to risk that!"

"But you're not in Lancovit now to keep anyone from stealing it!" said Manitou, sounding very concerned. "What are we going to do?"

"I'll ask Safir Dragosh to go back immediately and watch over the book. Our vampyr friend is a powerful wizard. He'll know how to protect it."

"Is that all?"

Master Chem shrugged. "The hunter-elves have long known that I have valuable and dangerous objects in my keeping that must not be stolen. They watch the whole castle very carefully. Besides, nobody knows where the book is hidden or how to get to it. So I'm not really worried."

"Oh, really?" asked the surprised dog. "Well, if you don't mind I'm going to worry a little. Just in case."

Sparrow took a deep breath. The old dragon had forgotten one small detail. Because of the group's earlier trip to Limbo, the secret hiding place wasn't so secret anymore. She was about to speak up, but hesitated, deciding to say nothing.

"Well, I think it's totally cool!" said Cal with a grin.

"What? You think it's cool?" asked Fabrice.

"Well, yeah. For once, Magister doesn't need Tara to get hold of the book. So no one's going to try to enchant me, petrify me, cook me, or drown me to get it. Life could actually get kind of boring!"

There was only one proper response to Cal's statement. Tara stuck her tongue out at him.

After dinner, the friends gathered in their suite. Soothsuckers had been served with dessert, and after savoring an amazing cherry/apricot/cinnamon/pepper one, Tara reached the message at the heart of the lollipop: "You can see the trap, but it's not where you think"—which didn't tell her anything all that helpful.

Cal's room was near the suite, but since he had to share it with Angelica, he was trying to stay away. The friends were deep in conversation when the mouth on the door opened and spoke: "An ifrit wishes to speak with Miss Tara'tylanhnem Duncan. Should I let it in?"

"Sure," said Tara, a little surprised.

A red djinn floated into the living room. Ifrits don't have legs, and the lower part of their body ends in a kind of whirlwind. This one bowed politely and in a strident voice said, "My imperial mistress requests your presence in her gold boudoir. I have been sent to take you there."

When Tara's friends got to their feet, it added, "Alone."

"Don't you want us to go with you?" asked Robin, ignoring the ifrit's remark. "After all, there are Bloodgraves in the palace."

"Thanks, but you don't have to worry about me," said a smiling Tara, who appreciated the half-elf's courtesy but wanted to speak to the empress in private to plead Cal's case. "I'm not going far. See you soon!"

As she followed the ifrit down the palace hallways, Tara noticed that the light grew noticeably dimmer. The farther they went, the less busy the halls were, until they reached a dusty and vaguely gilded room that didn't correspond at all to her notion of an imperial boudoir.

The ifrit bowed again, said that someone would come for her soon, and left. Tara walked around the room. It was furnished with several large tapestries showing the exploits of Omoisian hunters, three chairs so delicate you'd be afraid they would collapse under you, a pair of purple velvet sofas, and a pretty table with an inlaid top and curved legs.

The three chairs practically fought each other for the privilege when Tara decided to sit down. As she looked at them with mistrust, she suddenly caught her breath. She could feel the weight of an icy gaze on her, a feeling she knew well. *A Bloodgrave was watching her!* She spun around just in time to see a burning ray shooting toward her, and she dove to the floor, barely avoiding being hit.

The table exploded and one of the tapestries caught fire. Tara stood and ran to hide behind a sofa. Her attacker was behind the door, and she could see two hands brandishing a ball of fire. Tara wished for a shield with all her might, and the living stone intervened without being asked. Their combined magic conjured a wall eight inches thick that abruptly hid her from view.

Not exactly what I asked for, but it'll do for now! Tara thought.

Once over the initial surprise, Tara's enemy gathered its power, which was unfortunately considerable.

A fireball shattered part of the wall. Tara huddled to avoid flying debris and conjured enough water to put out the resulting blaze. But a second fireball was already shooting toward her, and she again had to dive to the floor. She absolutely had to come up with something stronger before the whole wall was demolished! She was thinking fast.

Tara couldn't see the Bloodgrave, but she could see a pair of hands when it launched its magic. During a lull she peeked cautiously through a crack in the wall. The hands were busy with another fireball, making it bigger. *Perfect!*

Summoning her power, she fired an ice beam like the one she had used against the Throne of Silur.

Maybe Tara had seen too many cartoons, because she imagined that when she fired her ray, the hands and the fireball would freeze, trapped in a sheath of ice.

It didn't work that way at all.

When the ray hit the fireball, it merely fizzled out. The Bloodgrave cursed, but its hands were still free. Now furious, it cast a new spell, preparing to blast her. Tara trembled, aware that she couldn't resist another attack.

Suddenly she heard the sound of running feet, and the hands disappeared. Moments later, Lady Boudiou and Xandiar burst into the room, closely followed by a group of soldiers. When he saw the damage, the guard captain whipped out his four swords and posted men all around the room. Lady Boudiou rushed over to Tara, who could hardly believe she was still alive.

"My heavens!" cried the old lady wizard, astonished by the destruction in the room. "What happened here?"

"Someone tried to kill me," Tara answered, still shaking with fear. "You just saved my life. A few seconds more and *pfft!*, no more Tara!"

"By Demiderus! Come here, darling!" The good woman wrapped Tara in a motherly embrace, and the girl burst into racking sobs.

When Xandiar interrogated her, however, he looked frankly suspicious. Ever since their first encounter, the guard captain seemed to take everything Tara did as a personal affront. And she had the painful feeling that he didn't believe her at all. Especially when the investigation revealed that the empress had never actually summoned her.

Naturally, it was impossible to find the ifrit that had delivered the message—or even find one who would confess to having done so, since they all looked exactly alike.

Robin and Fabrice were furious when they heard the news and decided that they would stick to Tara like her shadow from now on. Cal, who was just as shaken, requested and got permission to spend the night with his friends. Lady Auxia, the palace administrator, had guards posted at the door. To settle Tara's nerves, Auxia's shaman Master Bison Lightfoot made her drink a series of brews, each more revolting than the last.

Despite the soothing potions, Tara didn't have a very good night. Robin had seen too many OtherWorld movies about valiant knights, and wanted to sleep on the floor in front of Tara's bed, but she refused. For Tara's part, terrible nightmares left her feeling exhausted and shaky the next day. She couldn't understand what was happening. Magister would never try to kill her; he needed her too much. So, who wanted to get rid of her? And why? Like most people, Tara had dreamed of a life of high adventure. Now, she would pay good money for the most dull, stale, and insipid existence possible.

Soon after breakfast, Damien came to escort them to the hearing. Crossing back through the jungle on the way to the Throne Room, Fabrice was relieved to see that the pterodactyls soaring in the distance didn't see him as a mid-morning snack. A pair of soldiers escorted Cal into the huge purple-and-gold hall and the trial resumed.

The events of the previous day had clearly made the rounds of the palace, because the hearing was jammed. Crowded around the twin thrones were silver unicorns, gold chimeras, lemon-yellow imps, two-headed tatris, some twenty suspicious centaurs with war paint on their flanks, blue gnomes—in short, representatives of many of the planet's races. Human courtiers in unusual, colorful costumes wandered here and there or sat on benches and chairs.

Suddenly, Tara got a shock. A gorgeous blonde next to her had unexpectedly turned into a balding, skinny old woman, causing her companion to pull back in surprise. The old woman stamped her foot angrily on the floor, fiddled with something in her hair, and turned back into the gorgeous blonde. Her dismayed companion was about to upbraid her when his own magic spell failed. Instead of a handsome courtier, a reedy teenager appeared, looking with horror at his nonexistent biceps. The blonde gave a sarcastic cackle. The boy glared at her and stormed out of the hall.

Tara gathered that Omoisian spellbinder courtiers seldom showed themselves in their true form. The only glitch in the system was that maintaining a fictional appearance was too tiring to do for long. *Well, the day I want to stand 5 foot 10 with a 36-inch bust,* thought Tara, *I'll know how to make it happen!*

Just then, the majordomo gestured to the crowd and the assembly quieted. The empress and emperor took their seats on the thrones, surrounded by high wizards.

Empress Lisbeth had chosen silver to accentuate her beauty this time. Her hair, caught in a stunning chignon, framed her head like a metal helmet. Her silver robe was covered with luminous birds fluttering from branch to branch. A platinum and diamond crown circled her brow and temples, making her look even taller.

In keeping with the silver theme, Emperor Sandor was wearing light-steel armor decorated with silver runes. A slim metal band rested on his hair, which he wore hanging down his back. Made cautious by his previous experience, he had traded his short saber for a long sword and was scowling at Master Chem as if to dare him to shape-shift again. His entire attitude screamed, "If you so much as twitch an ear, dragon, I'll cut you to ribbons."

The fact that the dragon wasn't paying him the slightest attention seemed to annoy him even more.

The scoops hovered around the imperial couple, recording every detail.

When Tara was able to tear her attention away from the fascinating empress, she noticed that Master Dragosh was missing. The vampyr had probably returned to Lancovit to protect the famous *Forbidden Book*. So much the better.

Cal and Angelica went to sit in a large golden circle painted on the floor in front of the sovereigns. The dead boy's parents stood outside it. A heavy silence fell on the assembly.

The high wizards began their incantations. These clearly required considerable effort, because sweat began to run down their faces.

"By Convocatus, we summon you, Brandis T'al Miga Ab Chantu," they chanted. "By Convocatus, we bind you, and through that binding, you will answer us! By Convocatus, spirit, appear and materialize before us!"

A flickering glow started to dance in front of the wizards, then grew brighter and taller, taking the shape of a boy. His body was somewhat transparent, but perfectly visible. Tara was surprised to realize that she could see its colors. She'd thought that it would be white or colorless, like ghosts in the movies. In fact, aside from the fact that you could kind of see through him, you would've thought the boy was completely normal.

And he was completely naked.

Well, not quite. The middle of his body was sort of blurry. Clothes obviously didn't accompany the dead to the hereafter.

"Something . . . something called me," murmured the ghost.

"We did, darling boy," said his mother, her cheeks streaming with tears.

"Where . . . where am I? I can't remember. Why are you crying, Mom?"

For a moment the crowd thought the woman was going to collapse, but her husband squeezed her hand and she held on.

"You're dead, my love. You were killed by the uncontrolled vortex of a Transfer Portal. We've called you back so you can judge those who caused your death." She pointed at Cal and Angelica.

"I'm dead?" exclaimed the ghost, sounding very surprised. "Are you sure? It's strange, I don't feel dead."

"But you are, unfortunately" said his father, his jaws clenched. "You were killed, and we're trying to find out what happened. When you activated the Transfer Portal, a loud scream made you lose your concentration and the portal went out of control. You died because of two Lancovit spellbinders, and all we have left of you now is your ghost. Justice must be done. Are these two spellbinders the guilty parties?"

The ghost seemed at a loss.

"Yes . . . I remember now. The scream . . . fear . . . the dark power. There was a little girl . . . She tried to help me." (Tara sat bolt upright— *little girl* indeed!) "But the vortex was too powerful, and it sucked me in."

The boy's voice strengthened, and he went on: "And you say I'm dead because of those two?"

"That's right, son," answered the woman.

"Then there's no doubt about it," said the ghost, his tone harsher. "They're guilty!"

"No!" Tara's scream cut through the buzz of excited comments. Deftly dodging a guard who tried to stop her, she ran to stand in front of the ghost.

"They distracted you, that's true," she said. "But they didn't kill you! You spoke of a dark force, a force that nearly swept us both away. Try to remember! That force wasn't coming from these two spellbinders. It was coming from somewhere else."

The ghost frowned, but something seemed to be interfering with his concentration.

"Yes . . . a dark force . . . something that kept the vortex from closing. If it weren't for that force, I'd still be alive."

"That's enough!" shouted the boy's father. "Miss, I understand that you want to protect your friends, but my son is *dead*! He's dead because of those two, do you understand? So step aside, and let my son pronounce judgment on his killers."

Tara had opened her mouth to reply when the ghost spoke: "I feel . . . I feel a force pulling me away. I have to leave. These two spellbinders must be condemned for what they did to me. But death . . . death is too great a penalty. They should be imprisoned for the rest of their lives."

With those terrible words, the boy's shape wavered, began to fade, and disappeared.

Tara refused to accept defeat.

"I claim my imperial favor!" she cried.

The emperor shifted on his throne.

"Your favor doesn't apply here," he said harshly. "It applies only to you personally; you can't use it for your friends. In any case, you can't claim an imperial favor in a matter of life or death."

Tara felt herself weakening, but she shouted again: "This is crazy! Cal and Angelica aren't guilty! And you know it as well as I do."

Tara had made a mistake. The empress didn't like being crossed, and she knew how to deal with insolence.

"That's enough," she said coldly. "The sentence has been pronounced. Take the defendants to prison. I have spoken."

Under Tara's helpless eyes, Empress Lisbeth'tylanhnem stood up and walked out.

Sparrow, Robin, and Fabrice stared at the condemned pair. Angelica was weeping on her father's shoulder as he raged against the empress, calling for a war against the empire. For his part, Cal seemed in shock. But oddly enough, his mother didn't seem worried. She whispered something into her son's ear and after a moment, he looked up and smiled.

The imperial guards had to tear Angelica away from her parents, but Cal followed them without any fuss. As Blondin leaped like a living flame by his side, Cal even gave his friends a little wave.

Tara collapsed at that point, slumping to the floor in tears. Sparrow was instantly at her side and started sobbing as well. The two boys bravely tried not to cry, but couldn't.

"It's unfair," moaned Tara. "The adults in this world are crazy. This is awful! What are we gonna do?"

Robin discreetly wiped his tears, then gave Cal a searching look as he was being led away.

"You know, Cal looks awfully cheerful for a guy who's just been given a life sentence," he said thoughtfully. "I wouldn't mind asking him a few questions."

"We're allowed to visit him in his cell," said Sparrow, blowing her nose. "And—"

She was interrupted by Master Chem's arrival. The old wizard seemed both furious and baffled.

"I don't understand any part of this whole business!" he groused. "It's obvious that Magister somehow set Cal and Angelica up. But what's crazy is that we aren't able to clear them. The Truth Tellers suddenly become unable to probe them, and the empress and the emperor have them jailed. And I'd bet my pile of gold that they know perfectly well that Angelica and Cal are innocent!"

"I agree," said Tara who had recovered a little. "Someone, somewhere is playing us for complete idiots. And if we don't find out why, they'll be right."

The old wizard scowled, and she smiled a little.

"Grandpa, you said that a Teller probed you, right?"

"No, I said that *someone* probed me," answered Manitou. "I don't know if it was a Teller."

"Then we better talk to the gnome," said Tara, chewing on her white forelock. The habit always annoyed Gallant, and he swatted the hair away.

"To the gnome?" asked Fabrice. "Why?"

"He's worked with the Tellers for a long time. He should be able to tell us if one of them read Grandpa's mind and maybe even why."

They had no trouble finding him. The gnome was in one of the palace's outdoor gardens, with two Truth Tellers. They had opened their white tunics and Tara was astonished to see that their brown bodies looked like wood.

So, the Tellers were actually *plants*!

Instead of arms, they had a tangle of budding branches. Their feet—roots, actually—were sunk into the earth. And the things that Tara had taken for helmets were actually large black petals that had opened around their heads and were hungrily soaking up sunshine. Their entire beings gave off a feeling of silent ecstasy.

The gnome's eyes widened when he saw the little group striding toward him, and he set down the watering can he'd been using.

"Hello, Master Buglul," said the dragon wizard. "Could you spare us a few minutes of your time?"

The gnome bowed, looking somewhat apprehensive. "Er, of course, High Wizard. What can I do for you?"

"High Wizard Manitou Duncan says he was probed by a Teller in the hearing room. Can you confirm that for us?"

The gnome was shocked.

"That is impossible!" he said indignantly. "No Truth Teller would ever probe a conscious individual without their permission, or the permission of a court of law. It is strictly forbidden."

"I'm sure that's true," Chem said smoothly. "But we all do something that's forbidden every once in a while. So, could you kindly answer my question, please?"

The two Tellers stirred. Buglul squinted, then spoke.

"High Wizard, the Tellers declare that if one of them had wanted to probe you or Master Duncan, no one would have detected the intrusion. So, if someone tried to read or penetrate his brain, it was certainly not a Teller."

"Is that so?" asked Chem in surprise. "I see. So they can 'read' people without their knowledge. That's very, very interesting."

"But they never, *ever* do it," said the gnome firmly. "Remember, many countries ship their worst criminals to Santivior, the Truth Tellers' home planet, where the Tellers guard them in exchange for the goods they need. Why would they trade that special relationship for the pleasure of snooping? Whoever read your friend was not one of them. You will have to look elsewhere. "

In the face of the gnome's determination, Chem bowed. "Thank you, Master Buglul."

As they left the garden, the friends knew one thing for sure: They had been trapped, and they couldn't make a move until Cal was free.

Master Chem decided to request another audience with the empress.

"I'll keep you all posted," he said. "Manitou, stay with the children and keep them from doing anything too stupid, like destroying the palace or launching an interplanetary war—you know, the things they seem to specialize in. Okay?"

"I'm not their babysitter," growled the dog. "And if they feel like doing something, I'll probably do it too, believe me."

Tara gave her great-grandfather a big smile, and he winked. Chem rolled his eyes in resignation and stomped off, muttering.

"None of this is getting us very far," said Fabrice as they headed for the palace's lower depths. "If what Buglul said is true, it wasn't the Tellers who probed your grandfather. So, who was it, and why? What does Manitou know that someone would want to rummage around in his brain to find it?"

"It's like a puzzle," ruminated Tara. "Lots of little pieces that don't fit, until the moment when something suddenly starts to make sense. And I wonder . . ."

"What do you wonder?"

"Hm, what? Oh, nothing. Let's start by seeing what Cal has to tell us. We can't let him rot in jail for a crime he didn't commit."

"Er, just to be clear," hazarded Fabrice. "We're going to see Cal to talk things over, right?"

"Of course not," said Tara brightly. "We're going to help him escape!"

CHAPTER 4

IMPERIAL PRISONS

"What?" shouted Fabrice. "Are you kidding?"

"Not at all," said Tara. "Someone wants Cal in jail. I don't know if Magister is the one who came up with the scheme, but by freeing Cal we'll be screwing up the plan."

"You know, for once I agree with Fabrice," said Sparrow. "Springing someone from an Omois prison is impossible. Can't be done."

"Oh, yeah? Finding and breaking out of the Gray Fortress was impossible too, wasn't it?" said Tara. "Defeating Magister and destroying the Throne of Silur was just as impossible, but we did it. For that matter, magic is impossible, and this world is impossible." She shrugged. "I've learned not to let that word stop me. In fact, I'm seriously considering eliminating it from my vocabulary."

Robin smiled at her. "You've got a point, Tara. If helping Cal escape will mess Magister up, facing the empress and her chatrixes and arachnes is worth it."

"What did you say?" yelped Fabrice. "Chatrixes and arachnes? Not again!"

"I'm really sorry," said Robin, who didn't look sorry at all. "Didn't I mention that the prisons are guarded by chatrixes? As for arachnes, I'm not so sure. They may have been replaced since my father was stationed in Omois. I seem to remember they once ate a guard who'd forgotten the answer to the riddle of the day."

Fabrice shivered. "I *hate* spiders!"

He immediately looked up, scanning the ceiling for them, and he nearly missed the prison's main protectors. When Fabrice eventually glanced down, what he saw sent him leaping backward in panic. He had almost bumped into a chatrix, a huge hyena-like animal with black fur and a poisonous bite. The beast was licking its chops and seemed to be thinking something like, "Dinner is served!"

There may not have been any arachnes around, but there were lots of chatrixes, all straining at their leashes at the sight of so many people invading their sanctuary. They were drooling over such appetizing prey and were extremely disappointed when the guards muzzled them to let the visitors pass.

Cal was in prison, all right. But the problem with most prisons is that they can't hold spellbinders. So the walls of this one were specially built of spellblock from the Gandis Mountains, which blocks magic spells. In addition, an artifactum that neutralized all magic in its vicinity was mounted on a column above the hallway. Since were-light couldn't be used, the prison was lit by ordinary electric bulbs, powered by a small generator.

The artifactum was just a simple statuette, but its outstretched arms hummed with all the magic power it was absorbing. When Tara walked under it, she felt the living stone move in her pocket.

Power? sang the stone, its voice sounding a bit muffled. *I feel it going away. Why go away?*

Don't worry, Tara answered mentally, though she hadn't expected the statuette to be strong enough to neutralize the living stone's power. *We won't stay long. You'll feel better as soon as we're outside its area of influence.*

Sleep, I will. Good night.

Gallant, whom Tara had miniaturized, whinnied, and they heard Cal's voice.

"Tal, Zegranbraz!" said the little thief happily. "Sal tan mir?"

Great, they couldn't understand a word he was saying! (What Cal actually said was, "Hey there, guys! Wassup?")

"Trus!" swore Sparrow. At least Tara guessed she was swearing. "Valendir!" (Which translated to, "Rats! Let's move away from here!")

She gestured for them to move out of the statuette's energy field. Once they were far enough, she spoke again.

"The palace translation spell doesn't work because the statuette neutralizes all magic in the area around it. You guys will have to learn our various languages, otherwise we won't be able to communicate."

"But I thought everybody used the Interpretus!" exclaimed Fabrice. "What are we gonna do?"

"We're going to use a spell that will allow you to learn all the languages I know," said Sparrow. "Lancovian, of course, plus Omoisian, Dwarvish, Gnomish, Elvish, and a couple of Earth languages I picked up on my visits there."

"Eh, how many do you know?" asked Fabrice, impressed.

"About twenty, I think. Once the spell is lodged in your brain, it's permanent. We'll be able to talk even when the statuette is neutralizing magic, because it won't affect us. Gather round, and I'll cast the spell on you."

They obeyed, and Sparrow chanted: "By Rosettus, take every single word I know, and on my friends instantly bestow."

Tara felt as if thousands of bees were suddenly buzzing in her head. Words, sentences, and expressions shot through her like lightning bolts.

"Are you all right?" asked Sparrow in Lancovian. "It isn't too uncomfortable, is it?"

Manitou shook his head, and his pink tongue lolled out.

"Geesh," he moaned in fluent Elvish. "I feel like I've been run over by a train. Or gotten a hangover without having a drop to drink."

Robin stared about wide-eyed and addressed Sparrow in guttural Gnomish: "Wow! That spell of yours really works!"

After a few experiments in different languages, they all decided to use Lancovian, which Cal spoke fluently.

They headed back toward his cell. The little thief was standing on the threshold of a large comfortable room. Its door, which was made of clear OtherWorld quartz, let images and sound through, even without magic. Perched on a big cushion, Blondin winked at them.

Cal had observed their comings and goings with some perplexity. "Are you guys all right?"

Robin frowned and answered in perfect Lancovian: "Seems to me we're the ones who should be asking the questions, don't you think?"

"Well, I'm fine. What's going on?"

"We were treated to an accelerated language course," explained Tara. "In fact, it was so accelerated, I feel like I've got every OtherWorld language in my head. Anyway, here's the question: Why do you look so cheerful?"

Cal grinned. "Mom said a similar misunderstanding happened to her a couple of years ago," he explained obligingly, "and she gave me some tips that might help get me out of here."

"Ab-so-lute-ly not!" said an icy girl's voice. "My father will take care of whatever is necessary to solve this problem. And since my fate is unfortunately connected to yours, you're not doing anything."

Cal rolled his eyes.

An image of Angelica in the next cell appeared, and Tara grimaced. Not only did she have to devise a plan to get Cal out of jail, she would probably have to free Angelica as well.

The tall brunette looked at them scornfully.

"What are you losers doing hanging around here? Hatching another of your little schemes?"

Cal didn't like Angelica, and the feeling was completely mutual. "What do you know?" he said. "The animal in the cage next to mine can speak! I thought she could only scream."

"Can it!" snarled Angelica. "I'll scream if I feel like it. And that stupid ghost is going to pay for getting us locked up."

"Really? What you plan to do, kill him?"

"That's a point for Cal," remarked Robin.

"A hit, a very palpable hit!" said Sparrow, grinning.

"That's enough out of you, Angelica!" said Tara angrily. "It's your fault we're all here. You're responsible for that boy's death, and the death of your familiar. So spare us the comments and mind your own business."

Angelica glared at her. If looks could kill, Tara would've died on the spot. The tall girl turned on her heel and went to sit on her bed, muttering insults under her breath.

Tara turned to Cal and whispered, "Is it safe for us to talk? If it is, explain why you look so pleased with yourself."

"I don't think there are any microphones," said Cal in a low voice, "but let's be careful anyway. I have two reasons to feel happy. The first is that this is going to be part of my final exam next year!"

"Your what?"

"My licensed thief final examination. I have to pass a whole bunch of tests to get my license. So, when my mother saw I was being put in prison, she went to the school dean and suggested I be graded on my escape."

Fabrice was dumbfounded. "And that's all you could think of? You're in jail, in a place where you can't perform magic, because you've been trapped by Magister, who attracted us here so that he could get hold of the *Forbidden Book*, and all you can say is, 'Cool, I'll be graded on this'? Those guards must've bonked you on the head when they arrested you, because you've completely lost your marbles!"

"I think I must've missed an episode somewhere," said a perplexed Cal. "Magister did what?"

When they explained, the little thief looked thoughtful.

"That's incredible," he said. "And it's kind of a far-fetched plan if all he wants is to get the *Forbidden Book*. To do that he could just spy on Master Chem and steal the book when he's away from Lancovit. After all, he travels a lot. But we can clear that up when I get out of here. The second reason I'm happy is that my mom came to visit, and she knows how to prove I'm innocent!"

"Hey, that's fantastic!" exclaimed Fabrice. "So we're saved. Let's go see the empress right away! The gorgeous, magnificent eighteenth letter of the alphabet + what we do to pants = m + pants = empress."

"Er, there's just one catch," said Cal.

"I should have known it was too good to be true," said Fabrice with a sigh. "Go on."

"According to my mother, there's a very particular entity embodied in a statue called the Judge of Souls. The entity was created by the demons in order to tell truth from lies. Everybody tells lies in the demon kingdoms, so this is the only way the rulers can exercise any control over their subjects, since the Truth Tellers refuse to go to Demon Limbo. Once we're in front of the Judge, we can recall Brandis a second time, which is normally impossible, and convince him that someone other than me caused his death. We'll record the whole proceeding with a taludi and turn it over to the imperial court. It's practically impossible to fool a taludi, so that should be enough to get me declared innocent."

Tara's eyes widened. "You want us to go to *Limbo*? To talk with *demons*? Fabrice was right. The guards must've hit you on the head. And what the heck is a taludi?"

"It's a little animal that records everything it sees. It can even see through spells and illusions. You can't fool a taludi, which makes them valuable witnesses in lawsuits and criminal cases. The little problem I mentioned is that the Judge of Souls statue is in the Demon King's court."

"Hold on," said Manitou, feeling very uncomfortable. "Do you mean the same Demon King who gave Tara that metaphor infection? I thought he was furious at her. You think it's wise to defy him again?"

"Well, she did yank his chain a little," said Cal with a chuckle. "I think she called him 'a babbling blob who talks a good game, but doesn't actually have any power.' That may have annoyed him—really, those demons have no sense of humor. But I didn't say anything bad to him, and since this was Mom's only suggestion for solving my problem, I don't have any choice. I'll go alone."

"No, you won't!" said Tara and Sparrow at the same time.

"Besides, you need me," added Sparrow. "Because I'm the only person who knows how to reach the 'object' that can get us to Limbo. And if you don't let me come along, then you can forget about me helping you."

Sparrow had stressed the word "object," and Cal snapped his fingers excitedly when he understood what she meant.

"Of course! How dumb I am! *The Forbidden Book!* The book Master Chem used to take us to the Demon King's realm! And you know how to get it?"

"That's right. First Master Chem reprogrammed my accreditation card so I could pass through his wall-door. Then he told me to memorize these instructions."

The pretty brunette closed her eyes and carefully recited what the dragon wizard had said:

"On the upper left-hand bookcase you'll see a book called *Comparative Anatomy of OtherWorld Fauna*. Take it down and put it on my desk. Tap three times on page 3, and then ten times on page 20. Be careful not to make a mistake. My desk will shift aside, revealing a glass staircase. Go down it, skipping the fourth and seventh steps. At the bottom you'll see two fire snakes. Crawl between them on your hands and knees. Whatever you do, don't walk between them standing up; they'll burn your head off. This passageway will bring you to *The Forbidden Book*, which is on a pedestal. Walk around the pedestal and pick up the flat stone hidden behind it. Quickly replace the book with the stone;

you'll have less than a second. When you've done that, climb the stairs, this time skipping the second step from the bottom, then the fifth. In the office, pick up the anatomy book without touching its pages. Put it around *The Forbidden Book* to hide its cover, and bring this to me."

Sparrow opened her eyes. "There you have it! If nothing has changed we shouldn't have too much trouble getting the book."

Tara gave her an enthusiastic hug. "Sparrow, you're terrific! So, what do you say, Cal? Do you have enough to go on?"

"It's perfect!" he exclaimed with a big grin. "Couldn't be better! Master Chem won't notice a thing—at least I hope not."

"Great," said Robin, smiling. "With that out of the way, we can concentrate on planning the escape. But what about the prison's security system?"

"Just guards and chatrixes," said Cal. "Oh, and Drrr, of course, but she isn't here on guard duty. It's more like she's the one being guarded."

"Drrr? Who's that?"

"A young arachne."

Fabrice blanched. "An arachne, here?" he whispered fiercely. "I didn't see any webs."

"No, because she's allergic to her own silk. She can produce it, but not spin it; it burns her. It's extremely painful and she's undergoing therapy, so she asked to be locked in a cell so she doesn't accidentally hurt anyone."

"Well, if she's locked up, everything's fine," said Fabrice, relieved.

"That is, she's locked up during her therapy sessions," said Cal with a small, wicked smile. "She didn't have a session today, so I think she's out somewhere, stretching her legs."

Fabrice took a deep breath and tried to speak slowly and deliberately. "Cal?"

"Yes?" The little thief's tone was perfectly innocent.

"I don't know when, and I don't know how, but you're going to pay for this."

"Come on, boys," interrupted Sparrow. "You can play games some other time. So what do we do now, Cal?"

"The cell door is no problem. I have everything I need to get myself out. They searched my spellbinder robe, but they didn't find my little lock-picking tools, because I hid them under fake scars and scabs. All I have to do is peel them off. But the chatrixes and the guards—that's more complicated. We can't cast spells on them because of the anti-magic statuette. Wouldn't do any good, anyway."

"Why not?"

"Because the guards have been heavily dosed with anti-enchant-ment spells. No one can use magic to put them to sleep, knock them out, blind them, wipe out their memories, and so on."

"And chatrixes are naturally immune to magic," noted Robin soberly.

Cal was thinking hard. "During the attack on the Gray Fortress, your fellow elves used drugged darts to put the chatrixes out of commission. Would they work on the guards? Those guys may be immune to spells, but not to drugs."

The half-elf's crystalline eyes narrowed as he thought it over.

"I don't know; putting the guards to sleep, then the chatrixes . . . Seems like a pretty tall order. I have to think. Give me a little time, and I'll see what I can come up with."

"Anyway, that's just the first stage," said Sparrow. "Once you're out of jail you still have to make it to the Transfer Portal to travel back to Lancovit. And the portal is guarded."

Cal's face fell. "Darn! I forgot about that! You're right. We'll have to figure how to put everybody out of commission."

"Are you sure that's the right way to go?" asked Manitou diplomatically. "Why don't we just ask Chem what he thinks about this? After all, he already used *The Forbidden Book* to save Tara's life once. Maybe he'd be willing to use it again to save Cal and thwart Magister's plans."

Sparrow answered, "He'd never agree; it's too dangerous. Last time, Tara was dying when he agreed to read it to take us to Limbo. If we approach him this time, there's a chance he'll do everything he can to keep us from getting the book, which would ruin all our efforts. No, I agree with Cal. Let's get him out of jail, get the book, then go to Limbo. We can disguise ourselves as demons in order to approach the statue. We ought to be able to fool them."

"If you say so," growled Manitou, unconvinced. "But my nose says this stinks!"

"Really?" asked Cal, laughing. "Since you're a dog at the moment, isn't that normal?"

"Very funny, Cal. Very funny. Keep laughing and you'll see what dog teeth can do to the seat of your pants."

Over the next days, the four young spellbinders and Manitou crisscrossed the palace back and forth and top to bottom. They noted the changing of the guards and the schedule of their meals and rounds, both day and night. Because the palace was so huge, their familiars were especially useful. Gallant flew to every nook and cranny, and Sheeba used her stealth to fetch whatever they needed.

But the panther was very annoyed at Robin over the matter of the traduc turds. Robin and Sparrow had concocted a potion similar to the one the elves had used to knock out the Gray Fortress chatrixes, and they planned to use it on the guards and animals here. Unfortunately for Sheeba, traduc excrement was an essential ingredient in the potion, and she was the only one able to slip into the stables to get it. She complained that her fur would stink to high heaven for a week.

The other ingredients were easier to obtain: kalorna seeds, green mud from the Drakorn Islands, magic water from the Sea of Fogs, a few pinches of salt from the mountains of Hymlia, snow from the Tador peaks, and the narcotic purple flowers the elves used in the Gray Fortress assault. Within an OtherWorld week, everything was ready for the escape.

Empress Lisbeth'tylanhnem, meanwhile, had been extremely busy. For the third time in a month, a delegation of gnomes had come to ask her help in resolving a very serious but mysterious problem. Nobody knew exactly what was going on, but the hunter-elves had been mobilized and the word "scandal" was being whispered among the courtiers.

One night, when most of the palace was asleep, Tara felt like getting some fresh air, so she and Gallant went for a stroll in one of the parks. Robin discreetly kept an eye on her. Since the attack, he wasn't letting Tara out of his sight, which sometimes got on her nerves. He was now hanging back in the shadows, so as not to disturb her.

A couple of hunter-elves stood chatting by the light of Other-World's two moons, Tadix and Madix. Tara didn't want to bother them and was about to move away when she overheard them say the empress's name. She casually edged closer—*I'm just out for a stroll, pay no attention to me*—and listened.

"It sure wasn't an ordinary search," one of the elves was saying. "Either the gnomes were lying, or he isn't guilty of anything."

"Hard to say," said the second. "After all, we did search the whole castle without finding anything. Besides, why would he do something like that? It doesn't make sense."

"Hey, the empress tells us to investigate, so we investigate." He changed the subject. "What did you think about the aerial polo match? That referee really . . ."

Tara moved away, having heard all she wanted.

During the following days, she expected to be summoned by the empress over the matter of her name, but Lisbeth'tylanhnem clearly had other fish to fry.

For his part, unaware of what his young spellbinders were plotting, Master Chem had made several trips to Travia, the capital of Lancovit. King Bear and Queen Titania were furious that Cal had been put on trial, and they lodged a formal protest, demanding that the verdict be overturned.

The empress answered by diplomatic courier that since the defendant had been judged by the victim's manes, changing the sentence was out of the question.

Relations between the kingdom and the empire quickly went from warm to chilly.

The kingdom threatened to recall its ambassador.

The empire threatened to call *its* ambassador.

In short, the political world was at a boil.

Tara strongly suspected Cal's mother of using her 007-style superspy skills to rattle a lot of skeletons in a lot of closets to get her son released. From the looks on the ambassadors' haggard faces, the skeletons must have been highly embarrassed.

And speaking of relatives, Tara's grandmother had nearly destroyed half of planet Earth over the past week.

When Isabella realized that her granddaughter had left for Other-World, her fear and rage sparked a terrifying storm that devastated several countries and blew down thousands of trees. She wanted to rush to Omois and immediately haul Tara back to Earth, but Selena stopped her. In spite of Selena's own anxiety, she understood Tara's desire to rescue her friend.

All this news reached the group by way of Master Chem, when he handed Tara a taludi that had just come in. Consisting of a white bony dome with three large round eyes, the taludi is a strange little animal that sticks on your face like a suction cup and covers your ears. When it's in place, it faithfully reproduces the image, sound, and even smell of the last person who spoke to it.

Somewhat apprehensively, Tara put the taludi on and was amazed to see her mother in front of her, looking so real she felt she could practically reach out and touch her. She could also see a swath of damage behind her. Lightning had shattered trees, the manor's blackberry bushes were but charred memories, and a smell of smoke hung in the air.

"I'm afraid we won't be making blackberry jam anytime soon," said Serena, gesturing at her surroundings. "As you can see, your grandmother was a little upset about your leaving without permission. But Chem says that everything's fine, at least for the time being."

Selena cleared her throat, and tried to look serious. "The next time you decide to take off somewhere—if there is a next time—you'd do well to tell me about it. Beforehand. This planet is fragile, and it would bother me if your grandmother damaged it. Let's avoid catastrophes, please. Anyway, we're anxious for you to get back home. Or to what's left of it."

Selena smiled, showing her dimples.

That's funny, thought Tara as she looked at her mother. *I never noticed that her dimples are just like mine!*

"I know you're incredibly independent, darling," the image was saying, "but I'd really like a chance to act like a mother. I was deprived of it for so long and then, no sooner are we reunited but *zip!* and you're gone. We still have so many things to share. So be very careful, darling, and come back quickly! Oh, and one more thing: I'd like you to keep me up to date on what you're doing. So please send me a taludi or a message. Your grandmother and I are worried, even though we know you're able to take care of yourself. I love you."

When Tara removed the taludi, she felt a bit weepy. She would've loved to run to her mother's arms and point to the bad guys so her mom could protect her from them. The only problem was that when it came to magic, Tara was much more powerful than her mother. Of the two of them, Tara would be in a better position to beat up the bad guys. Well, whatever; nobody ever said the world was perfect.

Tara positioned the taludi and explained her situation to her mother, while carefully glossing over the details she wanted to keep secret. Then Sparrow fed the animal some silver nitrate. The taludi wolfed it down and went to a corner to digest its meal in peace. Later, they would give it to the Omois courier service to be delivered to Earth.

"Yikes!" said Sparrow suddenly, examining her list.

"What's wrong?" asked Fabrice.

"We're missing an ingredient. To maximize the strength of Robin's potion, I need three hairs from an elephant's trunk."

"You're joking, right? Where do you expect us to find an elephant?"

"Actually, I saw one yesterday," said Robin with a smile. "In the empress's private garden."

"Oh, really?" said Tara. "That's interesting. I didn't know that garden was open to the public."

"It isn't."

Tara looked at him for a moment, then grinned.

"Oh, I get it. The empress has an elephant in her garden—right! She has Tyrannosauruses in her gardens and whales in her salons. So, why not an elephant?"

"And it's no ordinary elephant, either," he said. "It's the great sacred blue Talabamouchi elephant. It was given to the empress's grandmother as a gift a few centuries ago, and it's the apple of the empress's eye, because it's apparently immortal, like Manitou. They ran a whole bunch of tests to understand why, but without success. I'll go pluck three of its hairs and be right back."

"Wait, Robin!" said Fabrice. "I'm coming with you. I've never seen a real elephant up close!"

"It sure must be different from television," said Tara. "Why don't we all go? I'd be curious to see this famous pachyderm."

Robin opened his mouth, then closed it again. He found it very hard to resist anything Tara wanted, even when it made no sense. The girl had too much sway over him.

"Go and have fun, kids," said Manitou. "I'll stay here with Gallant and keep an eye on the potion."

As they followed the hallways to the garden, Tara noticed that the empress had decided to plant trees throughout the palace that day. They had taken root directly in the green marble and extended their branches in vaulting domes of golden leaves. Firebirds flew along the hallways. Their flaming wings were treated with an anti-fire spell, but it was wise to avoid their nests, so as not to get burned. Captivated by the birds' beauty, Tara and her friends paused to admire them. At the young people's feet, trash boxes trotted around on their tiny legs, hungrily looking for any scrap of paper, while large, shining globes with wings cast enchanted light everywhere. There were also suits of armor—lots of them. Their empty arms held weapons whose hooks, blades, and teeth made Tara shiver.

The kids passed a pair of elegant unicorns who were seriously discussing philosophical subjects, their cloven hooves in comfortable felt slippers to avoid scratching the marble floor. Tara was dazzled, and she had to make an effort not to reach out and touch their silvery coats.

Anyway, creatures who said things like, "The empress's idiosyncrasies are reflected in the *sui generis* nature of her palace" probably weren't inclined to let themselves be stroked without spearing the interlopers—after giving them a lecture in philosophy.

Walking the hallways, it was sometimes hard to know if you were dealing with an animal or a deep thinker. A kind of red cat whose lower body was encased in a pink shell lay purring in the branches of a green tree, and the tree was stroking it. But when Tara got closer, she saw that the cat held the tree on a leash, and she couldn't tell which was the master and which the companion. Further on, transparent palace walls formed a room for a delegation from the moon Tadix, whose gravity is much weaker than OtherWorld's. The delegates were strange, fragile-looking creatures, pale and elongated, whose eight-fingered hands reached almost to the ground. Their heads were crowned with a kind of green algae that wavered in the low gravity created especially for them, and very light clothes hung limply around them. Tara got the feeling that the slightest breeze might snap them in two.

Eventually, the four friends reached the empress's private garden. The huge gates were closed, but there were no guards in sight. Spotting a tall tree growing in the hallway with branches that extended over the garden wall, Robin jumped up, quickly climbed it, and disappeared over the wall. A few seconds later the gates silently swung open, revealing an astonishing landscape.

As elsewhere in the palace, magic had transformed everything. From inside the garden, the walls were invisible, and the place looked like Mentalir, the unicorn country. Blue meadows were dotted with little white flowers, and the trees hung heavy with fruit. Beautiful little fairies—tiny winged creatures—flitted from flower to flower in competition with the bizzz, OtherWorld's red and yellow bees. Gorgeous purple butterflies fluttered in strange patterns, and a choir of birds chirped unearthly melodies. It was almost night in the rest of the palace, but oddly enough, a beautiful red sun shone here, its rays turning the white blossoms pink. The air was sweetly scented, and a single breath of it drove all cares away. Tara sighed with happiness. It was a true fairytale landscape.

Suddenly, Fabrice let out a groan. Mesmerized by the sight of the fairies, he had stepped into what looked like an enormous cow pie.

As if in response to his noise, a huge footfall shook the earth, and the creature that had produced it strode directly toward them.

Tara gaped. This wasn't an elephant, it was a *mammoth*! A gigantic, very hairy blue mammoth with massive tusks that curved high on either side of its large head.

When it spotted the four teens, the mammoth stopped and stared at them with tiny, red, evil-looking eyes, then trumpeted shrilly.

"Robin, are you sure you want to pluck hairs from this monster's trunk?" shouted Tara, hands over her ears.

"This is very strange!" he yelled back. "It was completely calm yesterday! I don't know what's going on, but I'd get out of the way, you guys."

The enormous pachyderm swept the ground with its trunk, tossing bits of grass and earth here and there. It shifted from foot to foot for a moment, then seemed to make up its mind. Trumpeting loudly, it charged straight at Fabrice and Sparrow.

Instinctively, Sparrow shape-shifted. In the pretty brunette's place stood a ten-foot-tall beast armed with razor-sharp fangs and claws. But in the face of such a charging mass, Sparrow didn't have many options. With superhuman speed she dodged the mammoth's charge, snatching Fabrice—who was paralyzed by the sight of onrushing death—out of the way.

The mammoth was surprised at not finding anything to trample and dug in with all four feet. Carried by its momentum, however, it slammed into the invisible garden wall with a *boom!* so loud it that rattled the entire palace. A little stunned, it turned around and shook its head, panting with rage and pain. Then it spotted Tara and Robin racing toward a tree for safety.

Sparrow shivered. The tree wasn't tall enough! The pachyderm would still be able to reach them with its trunk. At top speed, she recited: "By Pocus, I summon the forces at large to stop this mammoth's frightening charge!" The spell flashed toward the animal—and stopped in mid-air.

"It's protected by a counter-spell," she screamed. "Watch out! It's been enchanted to attack us!"

"Get higher," Robin yelled.

"I'm not a squirrel!" answered Tara, who was climbing as fast as she could. To her alarm, the branches were thinning out just as fifty tons of demented mammoth drew closer.

Fortunately, the mammoth decided not to reach up and grab them. Instead, it wrapped its trunk around the tree and started to shake it.

"D-d-do s-s-something!" Robin managed to say through teeth rattling under the assault.

Living stone, help! cried Tara mentally. *Let's tie this animal up before it kills us!*

Power you want? sang the strange stone. *Power you take.*

Without bothering to recite a spell, Tara visualized a blue net dropping over the mammoth and trapping it.

The spell didn't work at all. When the net touched the mammoth, it made a kind of cracking noise and vanished. Now Tara was *really* frightened. Sparrow had been right: this animal was well protected.

While the two young spellbinders were clinging to the branches with despair, the mammoth must have realized that it wasn't accomplishing anything. Setting its huge head against the tree, it now began to push, planning to knock it down.

"All right, that does it!" muttered Robin through gritted teeth. From his spellbinder robe he pulled out a little twig with a silvery bud on top. He held this at arm's length toward the grasses, bushes, and brambles under the mammoth, and chanted: "By the tree that is alive, I want those plants to grow and thrive."

At first, the animal was too busy pushing against the tree to notice that the surrounding vegetation was getting taller. But it must have started to tickle, because it flailed with its trunk to get rid of the prickly bushes jabbing its belly.

Tara put her hand on Robin's, joining her magic to his, and recited: "By the tree that is alive, I want those plants to grow and thrive."

Galvanized by Tara's powerful magic, the plants made a great leap upward, trapping the pachyderm in a living prison. It struggled to free itself, but the grasses and bushes tangled its feet and trunk. In minutes, the mammoth was helpless, able only to trumpet furiously.

Tara and Robin climbed down from their tree and cautiously backed away.

"Very effective!" he said with a grin. "You can hold my hand any time you like."

Tara blushed. Sparrow and Fabrice, who were still shaken, joined them.

"Yikes!" said Fabrice, "I was so scared! I thought that monster was gonna flatten you like a pancake!"

"Hey, look out!" Sparrow's cry made them turn around.

Alarmingly, the vegetation entangling the mammoth had started to smoke. They were about to run out of the way when the monster suddenly burst from the scorched bushes and grabbed the nearest person: Fabrice.

The boy screamed as the huge trunk crushed his ribs. But just as Sparrow was about to leap into the fray with fangs and claws, and just as Tara was activating her power, something very odd happened.

The mammoth suddenly jerked to a stop, paralyzed, apparently unable to move. Then it gently set Fabrice down, whose cheeks were now wet with tears. The huge animal started shifting awkwardly from foot to foot while its trunk delicately stroked the boy's head.

"He . . . he . . . he *chose* me!" stammered Fabrice. "He says his name is Barune. He feels terribly sorry. He doesn't know what came over him. He . . . *chose* me!"

Jaws slack, the friends stared at Fabrice as if he'd gone crazy.

Then Sparrow started. "By my ancestors, *it's a familiar!*" she exclaimed. "This . . . this monster has become a familiar. Look at his eyes. They've changed, they're golden!"

She was right. The small, angry eyes had turned gold—and they looked very concerned.

Robin was so astonished that his legs buckled, and he slumped to the ground.

"No! I can't believe I'm seeing this!" he moaned. "Don't tell me Fabrice was just chosen by the empress's favorite animal!"

"I hate to say so, but that's exactly what happened," soberly said Tara, who could feel a giggle rising in her. "From now on, Fabrice's familiar is an immortal fifty-ton blue mammoth. Do you think we'll have any trouble hiding this little . . . detail?"

That did it. The terror they'd been feeling turned into a wave of hysterical laughter that left them bent over, with tears streaming down their cheeks. And every time one of them managed to say the word "detail," it started up all over again.

Still feeling overwhelmed, Fabrice came out of his trance and frowned.

"What are you guys doing, rolling around on the grass?" he snapped.

"Oh, sorry," said Sparrow, laughing and wiping the tears from her fur. "It's just wonderful. I'm very happy for you."

Fabrice's face immediately cleared. "Yes, it's extraordinary. Barune is fantastic. Do you realize what happened? He chose me—*me!* I can't believe it."

"Neither can I," said Robin with a sigh, still holding his belly. "All right. Now we have to take care of this . . . problem." (He was careful not to say the word "detail." His stomach muscles hurt enough already.)

"What problem?" asked Fabrice. He was lovingly stroking Barune's coarse hair, as the mammoth quivered with joy.

"Number one," said Robin, counting on his fingers, "we didn't have permission to come in here, so we've broken an imperial rule. Steal a couple of elephant hairs, nobody notices. But steal an elephant, that's a little harder to hide. Number two: This animal attacked us without any reason. Usually all he cares about is rummaging in your pockets for snacks of red bananas or popping peanuts. So I'm feeling cautious about his reactions right now. Number three: The empress *adores* this elephant. Number four: Her scientists have been studying him for years to find out why he doesn't age, so he's considered a national treasure. Aside from all that, you're right; we don't have any problem."

The only thing Fabrice picked up from Robin's little speech was that the half-elf distrusted his new friend.

"You don't have a familiar, so you don't know what it's like!" he shouted vehemently. "My mind and his are one now. He tells me that a dark figure approached him shortly before we arrived, and he can't remember anything after that. He was bewitched! Tara wasn't able to immobilize him, and you know how powerful she is. And what about the bushes? How do you explain that he was able to burn them up just like that? I'm telling you, our main problem isn't Barune, it's finding out who tried to kill Tara again."

"Fabrice is right," said Tara thoughtfully. "Whoever wants to get rid of me tried it indirectly this time. And it nearly worked! If Barune hadn't become Fabrice's familiar, the spell wouldn't have been broken, and he would've killed us all!"

Looking a bit green, Fabrice lowered himself to the ground.

"Ow!" he said, feeling his ribs. "That's true. Barune nearly squeezed me to death. All right, so what we—"

The garden gates swung open just then, admitting a group of very alert guards followed by a half-dozen high wizards, including Chem, Boudiou, and Chanfrein—and the emperor and empress.

"What's going on here?" thundered Xandiar, the captain of the guards. "We thought someone was attacking the palace!"

Emperor Sandor carefully studied the mammoth and the four kids, then frowned.

"Can you clear something up for me, my dear?" he asked unctuously. "Did you give your precious guests permission to take their ease in our private garden?"

"Unless I've been the victim of a sudden attack of amnesia," the empress answered playfully, "I don't believe I gave anyone that permission."

Sparrow, Fabrice, and Robin were rigid with fear and embarrassment.

All right, thought Tara, *I guess it's up to me, as usual.*

"Our friend Fabrice has been *chosen,* Your Imperial Majesty," she said. "That's why we're in your garden."

Okay, that was stretching the truth a little. But Tara really couldn't say they were preparing a potion to help Cal escape from prison.

Now it was the empress's turn to frown.

"He was *chosen?* What a stupid excuse! I don't see any animal here except for Barune—"

Gaping, the empress suddenly interrupted herself. She had just noticed her blue mammoth's golden eyes.

"No! Not Barune!" she moaned. "Don't tell me Barune chose this boy as his master?"

"Yup," said Tara flatly. "Sorry."

What happened after that is a little unclear. The empress had hysterics, because she loved the animal dearly. Xandiar suggested killing Fabrice as the only way to get the familiar back. Fortunately, the two rulers didn't listen to their bloodthirsty guard captain, though Fabrice got a chill when he found the emperor studying him thoughtfully. Lady Boudiou enveloped Fabrice in a protective embrace, then wanted to do the same to Barune but couldn't, given that the mammoth was four times taller than her. Master Chem, who was very worried about diplomatic relations between Omois and Lancovit, suggested they try breaking the link between Barune and Fabrice. However, the last linked pair that had been tried on—an arachne and a female Salterens salt harvester—had died, and he was counting on the empress's love for Barune to force her to reject his suggestion.

After half an hour of wails, cries, and tears, they had to face facts: Fabrice and Barune were joined and would be to the end of their days—period. Looking at Xandiar, Chem caught him clearly thinking that Fabrice's days just might end sooner than expected, so he made the empress and emperor promise that no attempt would be made on the boy's life. The imperial order was given, and Xandiar had to comply.

"Very well," said Empress Lisbeth dryly to Fabrice. "Since the matter is settled I may as well let you leave with Barune. But how do you plan to get him out? As familiars go, he certainly isn't small. I doubt he can even fit through the doors. And I'm warning you, I don't want my palace damaged just so he can leave."

"Is that all?" asked Tara, speaking for Fabrice. "Let me take care of that. I had the same problem with Gallant."

She quickly recited: "By Miniaturus, shrink this mammoth blue, so it can stroll around with me and you."

Barune trumpeted in panic as he felt himself shrinking. In a few seconds he was the size of a large dog. Now much closer to the ground, he just stood there, rolling his eyes in fear.

Feeling heartsick, Lisbeth'tylanhnem pursed her lips, then bent down to stroke the tiny blue mammoth, who was desperately clinging to Fabrice's leg with his trunk.

She wiped away the imperial tear streaking her porcelain cheek and gave her orders: "Go back to your rooms. You've done enough damage for one day. In fact, I've been meaning to warn you that a dwarf delegation from the Hymlia Mountains is coming tomorrow and I will need your suite. So, I'm afraid I won't be able to extend my hospitality to you much longer."

All right, it wasn't very elegant. But she certainly hadn't anticipated that her favorite mammoth would become the familiar of a little earthling.

Actually, she had hoped it would become her own. Or that of her children.

The empress wiped away a final tear, majestically turned on her heel, and left the garden.

But Master Chem stayed behind. Hands on his hips, he stood tapping his foot and looking very angry.

"All right," he thundered as soon as the last guard left, "will you kindly tell me the truth? If a link had formed between Barune and

Fabrice, the mammoth would've destroyed half the palace to go be with him. So, what *really* happened here?"

Despite Tara's great affection for the old dragon, she never forgot that he was, above all, a politician. Their escape plan would fall apart if he forbade them from interfering. So she decided to shade the truth a little.

"We only wanted see the mammoth," she said. "They haven't existed on Earth for thousands of years. When we got here, it attacked us for no reason, trying to trample us. It managed to catch Fabrice and was about to tear him to shreds when the choosing happened."

She fell silent. *Master Chem doesn't look too convinced. Maybe if I distract him . . .*

"Oh, and one more very strange thing," Tara continued quickly. "Barune was protected by a counter-spell. We couldn't control him. It was as if he was programmed to kill us!"

The wizard looked at them searchingly. Robin tried to flash an expression of wide-eyed innocence, but only managed to look stupid. Sparrow was smiling with her every fang. Fabrice was unconsciously imitating his new familiar by shifting from foot to foot and looking vaguely embarrassed.

"Okay," he grumbled. "As I see it, this is the second time someone's tried to kill you. Whoever's after you sure doesn't give up easily. Plots, and plots within plots. I'm getting a very bad feeling about all of this."

Tara had a hunch she wasn't going to like what came next. And she wasn't disappointed.

"You're all going back to Lancovit, then Tara's going to Earth," the old wizard said firmly. "I'll take care of Cal and Angelica. Don't worry; I'll stay here as long as it takes to get your friend released. You have my word as a dragon."

"By my bow and arrows," groused Robin, "you may wind up spending a few decades here, High Wizard. The empress doesn't seem at all inclined to release them!"

"We'll see about that. In the meantime, you're leaving first thing tomorrow morning."

"But we—"

"No buts. This isn't a suggestion; it's an order!"

Back in their suite, Sparrow hurried to finish concocting the potion. They now only had a few hours to carry out their plan. Barune trumpeted indignantly when she asked Fabrice to pluck three hairs from his trunk, but overall the operation went pretty well.

Except the fact that the potion came close to blowing up the palace and quite a bit of Tingapore.

When she was preparing the mixture, Sparrow had forgotten one small detail: She was still in her monstrous beast shape—her *hairy* beast shape. She'd been calmly chatting with Manitou and letting the mixture settle when a couple of things happened.

First, the potion started to glow a strange green color. Then it began to overflow and give off purple fumes.

"Hey, there!" called Fabrice, who was fascinated by the stages in concocting the potion and was watching the process. "Look at the time before the storm + English currency = calm + pound = compound. Are those colors normal?"

"What colors?" asked Sparrow in surprise.

"The green and the purple. And that smoke, is that normal too?"

"*Arf! Arf! Grrrr. Bow-wow!*" barked Manitou, who had briefly forgotten that he could also talk.

Fortunately Robin understood animal language. In a flash, he leaped over the sofa, grabbed a crystal vase, and tossed away its flowers. Then he dumped the potion onto the snaptooth fur rug with one hand while pouring water onto it with the other. The green glow and the vapors disappeared—along with half of the furs and a large swath of expensive wooden flooring, revealing the concrete foundation underneath.

"Yikes!" shouted Sparrow, mopping her brow. "That was a near thing! But what changed the potion into some kind of Destroyall?"

"A kind of what?" asked Fabrice shakily, as he stared at the hole in the floor.

"It's an extremely dangerous explosive that can melt practically anything," she said. "If you aren't very careful when compounding Destroyall, it can wipe out an entire country when it explodes. And the fumes are as dangerous as the liquid itself. But if I remember correctly, the ingredients for Destroyall are completely different from what we've been using."

"Maybe it was your hairs," Manitou suggested, as he carefully examined the remains of the potion. "You must have shed a few of them while you were preparing the mixture, and it caused a chain reaction."

"Well, at least we now know two things," said Robin, amused.

"Oh yeah? What are they?"

"One, how to use Sparrow's fur to make an explosive that can destroy everything, and two, that you now have to pluck three more hairs from your mammoth's trunk."

Barune, who understood him and was getting fed up, hid behind the sofa, trumpeting softly in protest. His life had been pretty quiet and now he was suddenly getting bewitched, shrunk, and slowly plucked bald. All he wanted was to eat a red banana and take a little nap. Nobody was about to pluck his nose hairs again!

It took an entire stalk of red bananas, but Fabrice was finally able to persuade him, and Sparrow prepared a second batch of the potion carefully. Very carefully.

This time, everything went well. No green glow, no purple smoke.

"Perfect!" said Tara. "Now, let's see if the trick they use in the movies to put the bad guys to sleep will work on this planet."

Gallant and Sheeba were outfitted with harnesses that carried several bottles of the potion. Before opening the bottles, Sparrow took cloths soaked with an antidote and covered everyone's face, muzzle, or trunk, which was no simple task. That way, their little group wouldn't be put to sleep along with the guards. Then she opened the bottles. Green fumes rose from them and began to spread. Sparrow opened the door part way to let the familiars out. The friends then cocked an ear and grinned when they heard a double *boom!* The two guards who'd been watching their suite since the attack on Tara had just passed out.

"Bingo!" she whispered through her makeshift gas mask. "It's working! In movies, they usually put the gas in the ventilation ducts, but since there aren't any here, I had to improvise."

"What?" yelped Fabrice in a strangled voice. "Are you saying you weren't sure it was going to work?"

"Well, no. How could I?"

"By Demiderus, as your grandmother says, I hate it when you do that!"

Moving like shadows, they made their way to the prison.

The courtiers, ifrits, and guards they met along the way that night would never understand why they woke up next morning sprawled in the hallway with splitting headaches.

Once within sight of the entrance to the jail, they watched as the two familiars slipped off into the darkness. A moment later, a clatter of spears falling to the ground was heard, followed by loud snoring.

"Let's go," said Robin, who had stealthily crept ahead to scout. "The guards and the chatrixes are all asleep."

And in fact, it was bedtime at the jail. People and animals slumped this way and that, each snoring louder than the next. The prisoners were asleep as well. Sparrow carefully sealed the bottles, and they were soon able to remove their masks. Within minutes, they were in front of the quartz crystal door to Cal's cell. Blondin's sleeping nest was empty, but they could see Cal under the covers.

Sparrow knocked loudly.

"Cal! Cal! Wake up and open the door."

The shape didn't move.

"Darn it!" said Sparrow worriedly, "I hope he covered his mouth and nose the way I told him to yesterday. Otherwise we won't be able to wake him until tomorrow morning."

"He was supposed to pick the lock," fretted Fabrice. "Without him we're stuck!"

"Maybe I can help, young man," came an icy voice behind them. "Could this be what you need?"

They spun around.

The chatrixes might still be asleep, but the guards were wide awake. Standing in front of the horrified young spellbinders was Xandiar, dangling a small silver key from one of his four hands.

"Ha, ha, ha!" chortled Angelica, who wasn't sleeping either. "You think I didn't overhear your stupid plan? I warned the captain of the guards that you would try to help Cal escape, and he took steps to stop you. This way, I'll get favorable treatment and Cal won't be able to ruin my parent's efforts to get me out of here."

"Angelica, you're very lucky to be locked up, believe me!" growled Robin, a light of fury glowing in his eyes.

She backed away, as if she could physically feel the menacing glare. Then, realizing she was safe, she drew herself up and spoke: "I haven't forgotten the way you treated me, you miserable half-elf. Why should I pass up a chance to get revenge?"

She raised her voice. "What about you, Cal? Don't you have anything to say?" But Angelica was answered only by silence.

Suddenly suspicious, Xandiar turned the key in the lock and slid the cell door smoothly aside. In two steps, he was at the motionless figure and yanked the blankets away. Everyone gasped.

Angelica's revenge was going to be short.

Very, very short.

Cal's bed held only two carefully positioned pillows.

The cell was empty!

CHAPTER 5

OF GNOMES AND KIDNAPPINGS

Cal was stressing out. He'd learned that expression while on Earth and found it fit his present situation perfectly. He may have been strutting his stuff (another expression he liked) for his friends, but he wasn't at all sure he could actually pull off his crazy scheme. Knowing that failure meant being locked up for the rest of his days did nothing to improve his mood.

He'd been nervously arranging his bedclothes in preparation for the escape when Blondin suddenly started to growl. The fur on the fox's back was standing straight up, and he was staring at the rear wall of the cell. The feeling Cal was getting from his familiar was strange. Blondin was sensing some sort of *force* trying to break in. Cal was about to walk over when a couple of stones from the wall crashed into the room, raising a cloud of dust.

Coughing, he was astonished to see four blue gnomes emerge from the cloud and bow deeply to him. It can be tricky for humans to tell gnomes apart, but he thought one of them looked familiar.

"Master Glul Buglul?" he gasped, trying to wave away the dust.

"Good day, Apprentice Spellbinder Caliban Dal Salan," said the gnome politely.

"Eh, good day," said the flabbergasted thief. Even without an Interpretus, Cal understood Gnomish fairly well, though he spoke it with an awful Lancovian accent.

Cal's sense of humor quickly returned. "Tell me, Master Buglul, do you have any special reason for destroying the prison, or did you just see a light and decide to go in?"

"Not the prison, Apprentice Spellbinder Caliban Dal Salan, just the wall of your cell. We have a proposal for you."

"You do know that people also come in through the door, right? And for pity's sake, call me Cal. Otherwise this could be a very long conversation."

"We do not wish to be seen," Buglul explained with dignity. "We have come to beg for your pity."

In perfect synch, the gnomes all kneeled down in front of Cal. And that's when the situation really got weird.

"You're going to get your pants dirty," Cal said, feeling acutely embarrassed. "Get up and tell me what you want. No point in your risking rheumatism."

The gnome smiled faintly and stood up. "My knees are not what they used to be, I admit. We need you, because we are being killed."

Cal opened his mouth, then closed it. Hard to make a sarcastic crack after that kind of statement. He waited for the rest—and wasn't disappointed.

"Unlike other races, we gnomes are able to burrow through anything," Buglul explained. "Stone, wood, metal—except for lava, nothing stops us. We have dug tunnels everywhere on OtherWorld. But we are careful because as we dig, we feed on the nutrients in the earth and that depletes the soil."

"Is that so?" exclaimed Cal in surprise. "I thought you only ate birds. Which is why I decided I'd never go to Smallcountry. No birds means too many insects for my taste."

The gnome frowned slightly. "'Never' is a very definite word, I find. And we only eat birds for gustatory pleasure; what nourishes us is actually the earth. But we are exhausting it and our excrement isn't fertile, unfortunately."

"So what?" asked Cal, in whom patience wasn't a major virtue. "What does this have to do with me? You said someone was *killing* you."

"I am coming to that. Here is what our excrement actually is."

Buglul slipped on a glove and pulled a small pouch from his pocket. With obvious revulsion, he opened it and poured glittering red, white, blue, and green stones into his hand, and then into Cal's. The thief was absentmindedly looking at the gemstones when his eyes suddenly widened.

"By Demiderus, you excrete *jewels*?"

"That is correct. Very few people know this. That secrecy protects us from greedy dragons, humans, and dwarves."

"I'm a thief," said Cal slowly. "True, I'm a licensed thief, but a thief all the same. I don't think it's such a great idea to put things like this in my hands."

"I know the honor code of your profession," said Buglul comfortably. "I know that you only act under orders from your government.

But that does not concern us now. We trust you to keep our secret because we can offer you freedom in exchange for your help."

Now Cal really lent an ear. This was suddenly getting very interesting.

"A few months ago, a powerful wizard discovered our . . . peculiarity," said the gnome. "He could have been content to ask us to supply him with stones, which we would have gladly done, but that was not enough for him. As the price of his silence, this wizard forced us go all over OtherWorld stealing magic objects from other spellbinders. When two of us died in a trap, we rebelled and told him we would no longer obey him. Unfortunately, the objects we stole had given him great power—power that he concentrated in an artifactum. Thanks to the power of that artifactum, he was able to imprison our wives and children in a place we are not able to locate. We think he has created a secret Transfer Portal, and he is holding his prisoners on some other planet.

"In desperation, we appealed to the empress for help, without revealing too many details. At first, she did not believe us. We came back a second time, then a third that month. Eventually, the empress sent hunter-elves to search the spellbinder's castle, but they did not find anything. Without proof, it was impossible to charge the blackmailer. Moreover, his new power shields him from the Truth Tellers. They know that he is guilty, but they are unable to read his mind. When the blackmailer realized that we had informed on him, he became furious. In reprisal he had thirty of our wives executed. And sent us their bodies."

As he spoke those terrible words, the gnome's voice broke. Cal felt tears stinging his eyes and furtively dabbed them away.

"We are not thieves," said Buglul with a weak smile. "The hunter-elves may be good investigators, but they are apparently not thorough enough. We decided that only a thief could unmask another thief. We therefore decided to secretly study the files on students at the University of Licensed Thievery. We discovered that your professors consider you one of the best future thieves of your generation."

"Really?" exclaimed Cal, who found this prodigiously interesting. "They're certainly secretive about it! They're always saying that I'll never be as good as so-and-so, or that my grades—"

"That may be," interrupted the gnome, "but it is the reason we have entered your cell. We need you to find the place where this fiend has imprisoned our wives and children. We also would like to see his artifactum destroyed. Once he is cut off from his power, the Tellers will be able to 'read' him, and the empress will have him executed for what he has done."

Suddenly, Cal had an awful suspicion. "Speaking of the Tellers, was the fact that they couldn't 'read' me something you came up with? So you could get thrown in jail, and then use me?"

"Heavens no!" exclaimed the gnome, recoiling in shock. "The Tellers say that someone cast a Mentus Interruptus on you, a spell that scrambles thought patterns. But they are sensitive enough to know if an individual is guilty or not—and you are not. Their word is good enough for us, even though it does not satisfy the empress. And now, we no longer have very much time. Will you agree to help us? In exchange, we will free you, which will allow you to find whoever has clearly set you up."

"That's impossible," said Cal, remembering his other escape plan. "There's, er, something I have to take care of first. Once I do that, I'll come help you, I promise. But my first concern is to prove that I'm innocent. I'm sure you understand that."

"We understand," the gnome assured him, "but we are desperate. With every passing minute, that monster acquires more power. He only has two more objects to obtain: a cursed book and a wooden wand carved by First Circle demons. He gave us four days to steal the book for him. Otherwise, he will kill again and again until we obey. When he comes into possession of that evil book, his power will be multiplied tenfold. And once he acquires the wand, not even the dragons will be able to resist him!"

"*The Forbidden Book*!" cried Cal excitedly. "Don't tell me you're supposed to steal *The Forbidden Book*!"

"Shhh!" hissed the gnome, shooting a worried glance at the cell door. "That is indeed the name the spellbinder gave us, but please keep your voice down, or the guards will hear us. So, will you help us, yes or no?"

"Amazing, the number of people who want that blasted book!" said Cal with a grimace. "Unfortunately, my answer is no. There's no way I can go with you, at least not now. But my mother is a lot more skilled than I am, you know. Ask her to help, and she'll find your secret portal in minutes."

The gnome bent his head and sighed. "We appealed to the empress, and that did not work. Your mother will fare no better. There would inevitably be political considerations and the negotiations would take time, which we no longer have. I had hoped it would not come to this but . . ."

"But what?" Cal was suddenly suspicious.

The gnome raised his head and looked him in the eye. "I am very sorry, but you leave me no choice."

With unexpected speed, Buglul leaped up and pressed something against Cal's neck.

The little thief felt like screaming, but couldn't. After a quick stab of pain, he found himself completely paralyzed. Blondin barked loudly, feeling his companion's distress, but without understanding what was happening to him.

"That was a t'sil," Glul Buglul calmly explained. "A parasitical worm from the Salterens desert. It paralyzes its host and burrows into its flesh, usually near the neck. It then enters a major artery and immediately seeds its eggs throughout the victim's body. This takes a few minutes. That done, it dissolves. The paralysis disappears and the eggs remain in stasis until they hatch. It takes about a hundred hours for them to activate. They hatch out as burrowing worms that feed on their host, and the cycle repeats.

"There are two ways to deal with t'sil. The first is to swallow the antidote. It enters the bloodstream through the stomach and attacks and destroys the eggs. It must be taken at least two hours before they hatch. The second is to die. When the heart stops beating, the eggs are deprived of blood oxygen and die immediately."

Buglul paused.

"You should be recovering from the paralysis about now. That is a sign that the eggs are in your bloodstream."

In fact, Cal could feel the stiffness leaving his muscles. The instant he regained the use of his arms and legs, he grabbed Buglul and slammed him against the cell wall, squeezing the gnome's slender throat. The other gnomes tensed, ready to intervene, but Blondin blocked their way, teeth bared. Buglul gestured to them not to move.

"We're going to take care of this problem pronto," snarled Cal furiously, squeezing tighter. "Either you give me the antidote right now, or I'll crush your windpipe."

"We cannot . . ." croaked the gnome, who was turning purple. "We do not have the antidote here. You will have to come with us. Otherwise, you will die."

"I can find that antidote at any drugstore!" Cal hissed through clenched teeth.

"No . . . you cannot," said the gnome, gasping. "T'sil only occurs deep in the Salterens desert. There is a Transfer Portal at Sala, the capital of Salterens, but none in the remote desert, and it takes at least three days to reach the salt mines. Besides us, the Salterian mine owners are the only ones who have the antidote. They use t'sil to control the slaves they kidnap from other races. You would never have enough time to go into the desert, bargain with them, and take the antidote. Besides, you might become their slave. You have no choice but to follow us."

Cal was still enraged, but he understood that he had no choice. He released the gnome, who fell to his knees, rubbing his throat.

"So, show me this blasted spellbinder of yours! I'll find his blasted hidden portal, and you and your people can go fry your little blue butts in Limbo hell."

The gnome made a protective sign against Cal's curse, then handed him a sticky brown mass.

"What in the world is that thing?" he growled suspiciously.

"It is an oxygenator," Buglul explained. "We gnomes do not need to breathe when we are digging because our bodies absorb oxygen directly from the soil. But you and your fox would suffocate. The oxygenator can synthesize any gas or liquid. Give it some of your blood, and it will supply you oxygen and recycle your carbon dioxide."

"*Some of my blood?* What do you mean, some of my blood? Let's be clear on what you mean by 'some' for this vampire-thingy of yours. If we're talking a couple of quarts, forget it!"

"Just a few drops, no more than if you scraped your knee. Put the device on your face and breathe deeply."

Glaring at the gnome, Cal did so. He gingerly put the sticky creature to his face, and it quickly spread and covered it. He felt a small twinge behind his ears, proof that the beast was feeding. Cautiously, he took a breath and was relieved to find that it worked perfectly, though the air was slightly musty. The mask also covered his eyes to protect them, but he could see quite well through the brown membrane.

Blondin, on the other hand, wasn't in the least cooperative. When the gnomes tried to put a mask over his muzzle, he backed into a corner and snarled. The fox was almost as big as the gnomes, so they prudently handed the oxygenator to Cal. Ignoring Blondin's teeth snapping inches from his fingers, he slapped the sticky thing over his muzzle.

"You'll have to crawl for quite some distance," warned the gnome. "Our nearest main gallery is more than a mile away."

Cal shrugged, uninterested in Buglul's explanations. Blondin didn't mind, since he was already on all fours, and he even gave a sarcastic little yip at the look on his companion's face. Once beyond the statuette's influence, Cal cast a double Interpretus spell, so he could communicate with the gnomes even when they were out of range of the Imperial Palace's general spell.

The trip was long, arduous, and extremely painful. Within a few hundred yards, Cal could no longer feel his hands, and his knees were killing him. They felt scraped raw. Behind him, two gnomes were filling the tunnel in as they went along.

Cal was curious at first, and he watched the gnomes at work. But the process was so revolting he soon looked away.

Dwarves tunnel by laying their hands on rocks and making them soft and easy to dig. If a layer is too hard, they disassociate the molecules of their bodies and flow into the rock until they reach easier going. But gnomes dig very differently. They open gigantic mouths, easily two or three times their size, and swallow earth at incredible speed. Their saliva sticks the soil together so their tunnels don't collapse.

When they left Cal's cell, the gnomes first replaced the stones in the wall. (The saliva, he noticed, made excellent mortar.) Then their enormous mouths started vomiting up the tons of rock and earth, filling the tunnel. A few minutes of this, and it would be impossible to imagine that Cal had dug his way out, especially since the gnomes carefully cleaned the cell by licking up all the dust.

As he crawled along, Cal suddenly remembered a device he'd seen on Earth: a skate-something. Those things had wheels! And the tunnel floor was perfectly level. Under his breath he chanted: "By Creatus, I want that wheeled doohickey, so I can move ahead more quickly."

From then on, things went much more easily. Lying on his board, Cal had only to push along the tunnel with his hands to move, and the gnomes could pick up the pace. Buglul examined the device with interest and admired how smoothly it rolled, but not to the point of wanting to get on board with Cal.

But things got sticky when the tunnel began to slope downward. Buglul heard a shout behind him and barely had time to leap aside before Cal went tearing by. The boy had obviously forgotten a small detail: his device didn't have any brakes.

When the anxious gnomes finally caught up with him, he lay in a crumpled heap, shaking. Sure that he'd been badly injured, they gently rolled him over and were startled when they saw his face, which was still covered by the thin membrane mask.

Cal wasn't hurt; he was laughing his head off.

"Wow! That was terrific!" came his slightly muffled voice. "Are there any more slopes around here?"

Buglul raised his eyes to heaven—to the tunnel roof, anyway. "No, none," he said dryly. "And even if there were, we would appreciate your not using that contraption of yours. You might hurt yourself. And us too."

To their great relief, they reached the main gallery without further problems, and Cal made his rolling board vanish. He was amazed to see a series of immense galleries, the highest of which disappeared in the shadows. Their walls were decorated with images of flowers, trees, and animals, and decorated with ocher, lapis-lazuli, malachite, gold, and silver. Globes of luminous water lit everything up. Everywhere, gnomes were busily hurrying around. With a shudder, Cal realized they were riding giant ants, termites, spalenditals, and arachnes; some were even mounted on enormous geometer moths and dragonflies. All this menagerie was swarming, stridulating, gurgling, and whistling. Insects are so small that Cal had never realized they could be so noisy!

He didn't see any women or children anywhere, which confirmed what Glul Buglul had told him.

"You can take off the oxygenator," said the gnome. "The air is breathable here."

Cal peeled the mask from his face and stuffed it in his pocket, noting that it had turned a vaguely reddish color.

"We are far from the Imperial Palace," continued Buglul. "We have nothing to worry about."

"Okay, so what do we do now?" asked Cal, struggling with his intense urge to throttle the blue gnome.

"We will ask the Truth Tellers to locate your friends Duncan, M'angil, Daavil, Brandaud, and Besois-Giron, and we will bring them here."

"My friends? What do they have to do with anything? I don't need them to take care of your problem. In fact, the fewer of us there are, the easier it will be."

The gnome shook his head stubbornly. "Your university file says you were able to defeat Magister as a group, all together. For the sake of our wives' and children's lives, we must take every possible precaution. Your friends will be coming here. That is not open for discussion."

Cal opened his mouth to protest, then closed it again. After all, he had no idea what he would be facing, and Tara's extra-powerful magic could well come in handy. He smiled at the irony. Poor Tara! She hated magic, yet spent all her time being forced to use it!

"As soon as we are sure that the wizard is occupied elsewhere, we will lead you to his castle," continued the gnome. "There, you will have to locate the Transfer Portal he uses to go to wherever he has imprisoned our wives and children, and where he keeps his artifactum. Once you have liberated our people, and if possible shattered the artifactum that holds his power, you will be free. Wait for me here. You will be brought something to eat and drink."

Cal was hoping for a nice steak, so he was a little disappointed when the gnomes handed him a basket of raw fruits and vegetables.

"Hey! I'm not a cruditor!" he protested. "Don't you have anything else?"

The gnomes bowed without replying and left Cal in communion with his carrots. *Well, I wasn't that hungry anyway,* he thought. He put the basket aside and settled down to wait.

Soon enough the gnomes returned to lead him to a very pretty bedroom. Obviously unaccustomed to having guests of his size, they had pushed several beds together so he could sleep comfortably. In the bathroom, showerheads floated in midair, ready to wash him down. But as Cal tried to scrub off the dirt from the tunnel, he realized that the shower heads—clearly set for someone much shorter—stubbornly refused to move higher than his belly button. He tried lying down, but that only made things worse, as the showerheads now blasted his face. Blinded and choking, he decided maybe he would skip showers for a while.

As Cal was being energetically rubbed dry by the towels, he suddenly imagined he felt something suspicious moving under the skin of his left arm. It was probably purely in his mind, but he thought he felt a kind of *swarming* in his veins. Petrified, he checked himself all over, looking for the slightest abnormal twitch.

While Cal was examining himself from stem to stern—and periodically checking his accreditation card's countdown of the hours and minutes he had left to live—the gnomes brought him one of their suits of clothes. Though clearly borrowed from the tallest of them, the mud-colored outfit still left most of the young thief's arms and legs bare.

Cal grimaced, and recited: "By Transformus, turn this outfit blue, and kindly make it fit me, too." The doublet and pants immediately lengthened, turning a handsome navy blue. So far, so good. Now all Cal had to do was to rid himself of the deadly t'sil worms and get his friends, his freedom, and his honor back, and all would be for the best in the best of all possible OtherWorlds.

When the gnomes returned with a basket of roots and fruits at the next meal, however, Cal lost some of his good humor. He sighed. It was going to be a long wait.

CHAPTER 6

THE BLUE GNOMES

When she realized that Cal was gone, Tara's heart sank. *Only one wizard can make people disappear like that: Magister!* The anxiety she read in her friends' eyes confirmed that they were thinking the same thing.

Suddenly, something snatched at Tara's robe, and she found herself dangling in midair. The infuriated guard captain had grabbed each young spellbinder in one of his hands and was shaking them like rag dolls.

Gallant, Manitou, Barune, and Sheeba were about to rush to help, but the thicket of spears raised by the guards deterred them.

"Where is Caliban Dal Salan?" screamed Xandiar. "Where've you hidden him? Tell me, or I'll—"

"Stop it!" cried Tara. "We haven't done anything!"

"Haven't done anything? You tried to knock my guards out and the prisoner escaped!" Xandiar was spitting mad and shook them harder. "Tell me where the thief is, or I'll rip your head off!"

If there was one thing Sparrow hated, it was being picked up by the scruff of the neck like a puppy. *Magic doesn't work here. All right, fine. Let's see if the beast curse can do its number . . . Yessss!* She felt her muzzle lengthening and her claws sprouting. In seconds her huge paws had reached the ground. Now the guard captain found himself nose to muzzle with a highly irritated beast.

"Let my friends go!" rumbled Sparrow, seizing Xandiar by the throat and lifting *him* in the air. "We didn't have anything to do with Cal's escape."

The other guards reacted instantly: scimitars, knives, swords, and other weapons, flew from their scabbards with a menacing hiss.

"Nobody move!" croaked Xandiar, who was enjoying a close-up view of Sparrow's enormous fangs. "I have the situation . . . under control."

He released Fabrice, Tara, and Robin. Little Barune, who didn't realize that his companion had been dangling overhead, peered around frantically, looking for him. When Xandiar set Fabrice down, the mammoth happily wrapped his trunk around the boy's leg.

"You should tell Barune to let go of you from time to time," whispered Robin, his eyes on the guards. "You'd have a hard time running away with him hanging on like that."

"Put me down," Xandiar ordered Sparrow with a strangled voice. "I won't touch you again, at least not for now."

The moment Sparrow loosened her grip, the guard captain drew his scimitars like lightning and pointed them right at her heart.

"Don't *ever* threaten me again!" he hissed, jaws clenched with fury.

"And don't *you* threaten *me*," Sparrow answered coldly.

Tara, Fabrice, and Robin all held their breath. The air was so tense, you could cut it with a knife.

Suddenly, a strident trumpeting jolted them all, and Sparrow nearly got skewered. Barely mastering his surprise, Xandiar put up his swords. Barune, who was tired of waiting and wanted a red banana, had just created a noisy distraction.

Fabrice, who had practically hit the ceiling in surprise, stroked his small blue familiar, and the tension eased. The guards sheathed their razor-sharp implements, and Xandiar elected to be reasonable, if not polite.

Despite their protests, he had them all locked in cells, including Manitou, who vainly pointed out his high wizard status. An expert in subtle torture, Xandiar first let them go to sleep, then woke them up in the middle of the night. They were sleepy, tired, and anxious, but persisted in what he called their lies: they simply didn't know where Caliban Dal Salan was.

At that point, Xandiar no longer had a choice. He went and delivered his report to the empress.

To his astonishment, not to say anger, Empress Lisbeth'tylanhnem greeted this startling news quite casually.

The young woman received him in her amber boudoir. As he always did when he entered that incredible work of art, the guard captain felt large and clumsy. Except for the yellow marble floor, every square inch of the room was covered with carved amber. The artists had sculpted the butterflies, birds, fishes, and animals so lovingly that they seemed almost alive. Warm light from the walls made the empress's skin glow like that of a ripe, sun-kissed peach.

Xandiar was so overcome by the adoration he felt for the slender young woman that his throat tightened. Helmet under one of his arms, he knelt and waited respectfully.

Two ladies-in-waiting were brushing their sovereign's incredible hair, and she grimaced when the brushes snagged a tangle.

"By my ancestors," she grumbled, "I'm going to have it all cut off one of these days!"

"But Your Imperial Majesty, you can't do a thing like that!" cried one of the pair, a beautiful, doe-eyed brunette. "Half the women in the empire would die to have hair like yours."

"Exactly, and it's only because of their envious sighs that I keep this blasted mop," said the empress as she looked at herself in the mirror. "But one of these days my impatience will be stronger than my vanity and *snip! snip!* Short hair and freedom!"

Waving her ladies-in-waiting aside, the empress turned to the kneeling guard captain. "While waiting for that day to come, tell me to what I owe your urgent presence at my morning *toilette*, Xandiar."

The guard reddened. "The boy Caliban Dal Salan has mysteriously disappeared, Your Imperial Majesty."

He tensed, prepared for the storm of anger that was sure to break over him.

Nothing happened.

Xandiar looked up and met Lisbeth'tylanhnem's oddly thoughtful gaze.

"Fine, fine," she eventually said. "Is there anything else?"

He was dumbfounded. "The young spellbinder's friends were able to concoct a mysterious portion to put the guards to sleep and help him escape. I locked them up, and I'd like permission to use enhanced interrogation techniques to make them talk. We will be able to find the prisoner that way."

Surely his news was catastrophic enough to make the empress furious this time. Xandiar cautiously closed his eyes.

But Lisbeth retained her Olympian calm. "Certainly not! Lancovit would never stand for children being tortured to get confessions. Release them."

"*What*?" The guard captain was so upset, he leaped to his feet, forgetting who he was speaking with. "But they knocked out half the palace! And the boy has—"

"Disappeared. Yes, I understand," said the empress, who didn't like having her orders questioned.

With a sudden chuckle, she turned to her doe-eyed lady-in-waiting.

"Mariana, do you remember the time I thought I was in love with the Prince of Trond'or and cast a sleeping spell over the entire palace?"

"You were only twelve, Your Majesty," said the girl, smiling at the memory, "but very powerful for your age. You didn't consider the fact that the prince himself would also be asleep."

"Yes. Not very romantic, to open your heart to a young man who is snoring. And when I finally managed to wake Mother up, she was fit to be tied. It took the high wizards nearly a month awaken everybody."

Empress Lisbeth'tylanhnem turned her attention back to the astonished officer, who was once again kneeling at her feet.

"So you see, these young people haven't done anything very serious. Leave them in peace." Then she abruptly changed the subject. "I imagine you saw Barune. Is that boy, the Guardian's son, treating him well?"

Better than you treat me, Xandiar almost answered bitterly. But he adopted a neutral tone. "It would seem so, Your Imperial Majesty."

"Well, he'd better. If that young fool hurts so much as a hair on my mammoth's head, he'll pay for it. You may withdraw, captain, and go about your duties."

Xandiar hadn't risen to become captain of the imperial guard by being an idiot. The eldest son of a minor provincial nobleman, he knew that the Omois court was a swarming clutch of intrigues and plots—and that he may have just blundered into one of them.

So, it was with some indifference that he greeted the news awaiting him back at the prison.

The new prisoners had done the same thing as the old one, vanished into thin air.

Well, at least he knew one thing: The empress was sure to be happy to hear about this latest escape from her impregnable prison.

While the guard captain was gloomily contemplating his prison's few remaining occupied cells, Tara was crawling along on her elbows, feeling unpleasantly like an earthworm.

The four friends, their familiars, and Manitou had been trying to get some rest after Xandiar's exhausting attempts to extract a confession when the gnomes showed up. Warned by a mysterious sixth sense that something was trying to break into her cell, Tara smashed a chair, grabbed two of the legs, and got ready to fight for her life. One gnome only avoided being clobbered by a chair leg when he quickly hissed, "We are here on Caliban Dal Salan's behalf!" thus saving all their lives.

But when the gnomes explained the deal they had made with Cal, Tara got so angry, they all backed away from her. Even now, in the tunnel, they tried to keep as far from her as possible.

For their part, Fabrice and Barune hadn't been especially upset and were happy enough to follow the gnomes who had awakened them. Sparrow, still in beast shape, had nearly eaten two of them before she understood what was happening. And Robin initially looked with dismay at the two gnomes he'd knocked out before realizing that they weren't enemies. His feeling of guilt evaporated when he learned what the little blue creatures had done to Cal, and he contemptuously left the two wounded gnomes in their fellows' care. Awakened with a start, Manitou had promptly followed the gnomes and was threatening to bite them if they didn't lead him to Cal immediately.

The gnomes were terribly disappointed not to be able to take Angelica with them, but she wasn't in her cell—a fact Tara regretted not one bit.

The gnomes dug so quickly that their various escape routes soon merged. Before long, the friends found themselves in the main gallery, stiff and out of breath, but free.

Their reunion with Cal was tearful, but he laughed long and hard when he learned how they had been locked up and then freed by the gnomes.

"Lord, how I would have liked to have been a fly on the wall then," he said, "just to see the look on Xandiar's face! His escape-proof prison leaks like a sieve!"

Having wiped away their tears of laughter, they settled down to discuss the situation.

"First thing we've got to do, is to get rid of those horrible t'sil eggs," said Tara with a shudder.

"But we can't let that wizard get hold of *The Forbidden Book*," Manitou objected. "That could endanger the entire balance of Other-World. Cal still has two more days before the t'sil hatch. I suggest we first make a little trip to Lancovit to retrieve the book and put it some-place safe where the gnomes won't find it. Then we'll try to deliver their wives and children."

"If Magister really is behind all this, I can't confront him directly," said Tara. "He's much too powerful. We were very lucky last time. We'll have to try and locate his hidden portal and plan an escape route when we know that lunatic is busy somewhere else."

"Obviously, it would be disastrous if he captured you," said Manitou. "So, are we all agreed? Lancovit and the book first, and the prisoners and the antidote next. What do you think of that plan, Cal?"

"Well, I'd like to say no," the thief answered candidly, practically feeling his skin twitching, "but between the t'sil and the chance of a demon invasion, there really isn't much choice. So it's okay by me. The quicker we carry out the mission, the sooner I'll get the antidote."

"I'm ready too," said Robin. "Let's go fetch the book, then save Cal."

"In the meantime," Manitou continued, "our only problem is how to explain to our little blue friends why we have to make a stop at Lancovit before coming back to help them."

"Are gnomes skilled at magic?" asked Fabrice, turning his attention from Barune for a moment.

"Not particularly," answered Cal. "They use spells, but ones they've bought, not created. I haven't been able to adjust their shower, and their towels almost rubbed my skin off. Why do you ask?"

Fabrice explained: "If they're as ignorant as I am, they probably wouldn't know whether you needed magic tools to do your work, would they? And if the Truth Tellers can't read your mind, you can say anything at all. That you absolutely have to go to Lancovit to get your thief tools, say. And that without them you won't be able to find the hidden portal."

"Fabrice, that's brilliant!" said Cal admiringly. "I only wish you could bring yourself to pay a little more attention once and a while."

"The link with Barune is so strong, I can't always tell his feelings from mine," said Fabrice, chewing on his lip. "He's having trouble getting used to being miniaturized. So, I'm sorry if I seem a little distracted these days."

Cal rolled his eyes. "That's fine. If it makes you forget your awful riddles, you can be as distracted as you like."

"I understand," said Tara with a smile. "It was like that for me in the beginning too, being unable to be away from Gallant. You'll see—the link gradually gets less compelling with time."

What do you mean, less compelling? asked the pegasus mentally, who hated being away from Tara as much as ever. She soothed him, stroking the soft hairs between his ears. She realized that she hadn't paid Gallant much attention in the last few days. *All right, as soon as we're done with this new crisis, I'll spend a whole week petting and pampering you.*

When Glul Buglul was told that his guests wanted to go to Lancovit, he objected. He was sure they were planning some trick to save Cal without making use of the antidote.

The little thief answered icily that he wasn't in the habit of working without his tools. He was the professional, he said, and if the gnome wanted to do the job instead of him to just say so.

Tara almost took pity on poor Buglul until the latter demanded they leave a hostage behind. That made her angry enough to grind the gnome into hamburger, but Fabrice intervened.

"It's all right," he said. "It won't take all of us to get Cal's tools. I'm not good for much right now, so why don't I stay here as a hostage with Barune? A fruit and vegetable diet is perfect for him. We'll just wait for you."

Despite his offer, Tara knew that Fabrice regretted seeing them go. He had already missed out on their earlier adventures when Magister kidnapped him by mistake, and now it was happening again. That said, he did look so absorbed by the little mammoth that leaving him behind wasn't necessarily a bad idea. His being distracted in the middle of a raid could be a problem.

The gnomes' Transfer Portal wasn't far. Buglul offered them arachnes and spalenditals to ride there, but Tara preferred to restore

Gallant to his normal size. She, Cal, and Robin flew on the pegasus behind Buglul, who had requisitioned a dragonfly. Sparrow ran along beside them in her beast shape with Sheeba, Manitou, and Blondin.

Once at the portal, Buglul again tried to pump them for information. "How long will it take to retrieve your tools, Apprentice Spellbinder Caliban Dal Salan?"

"Between two and twenty-six hours, depending on how many people are around. I'm still a fugitive, after all. I have to keep a low profile."

The gnome nodded. "I understand. You still have enough time. The t'sil will not be active for another two and a half days."

Cal shuddered and said nothing.

"Where will we arrive?" asked Robin prudently. "It probably wouldn't be a great idea to materialize right in front of the Living Castle guards."

"No, of course not, and we thought of that," said the gnome. "You will arrive at our Travia embassy. From there you will have to get to the castle on your own. We will be waiting for you here—and so will your friend."

That is a threat that's hard to ignore, thought Tara. But they really did plan to come back, so she had no reason to be anxious. Well, almost none.

The gnome opened the door to the Transfer Room, and the moment they stepped in, the five tapestries representing unicorns, spellbinders, fairies, giants, and elves began to glow, forming a shining halo around them. The gnome put the scepter in place and quickly stepped out. Sparrow cried "Lancovit embassy!" the rainbow touched the little group, and they were instantly transported.

A place where they landed put them face-to-face with rows of sharp, chitinous legs. The embassy Transfer Portal guards were enormous

praying mantises, who watched impassively as the humans materialized. The mantises were an attractive light green and had huge, spiked
forelegs. One of them, displaying the Smallcountry emblem of a bird
and an arachne on its abdomen, waved them forward. Their throats
tight, the friends filed past ranks of mantises whose large, multifaceted
eyes gazed at them with interest. Sparrow held her breath until they
were out of the Transfer Room.

A gnome was waiting for them.

"Welcome to our Travia embassy," he said, bowing. "I am Bulul
Bulbul, Smallcountry ambassador extraordinary plenipotentiary.
Would you like us to escort you to the place where Apprentice Spell-
binder Caliban Dal Salan has his tools?"

"No thanks, Your Excellency, that won't be necessary," Cal said
politely. "We'll meet you back here in a little while."

"We are at your disposal at any time, day or night. Do not hesitate
to rouse us. We have been instructed to assist you in any way we can."

"Thanks, Excellency. We'll be sure to do that if it proves necessary."

Leaving the embassy, Tara was glad to see Travia's beautifully-
colored houses again. Workmen had decorated and painted every wall
in the city with bright, cheerful frescoes. Gleaming roofs stood out
against the sky, which Tara suddenly realized was *striped*. Astonish-
ingly, the celestial dome above them displayed green, purple, yellow,
and blue stripes.

Sparrow glanced up and sighed. "Aunt Titania has been launching
new public works again, I see! Pay no attention, Tara. The urge
comes over her every so often. She likes to change the color of the
sky from time to time, because she thinks blue or black is a little too
conventional."

Cal gave the sky a dubious glance. Then he took a deep breath and
relaxed. "Wow! It's nice to be home. I didn't realize how nervous I've

been. Let's go to my house. The guards took all my daggers and other weapons, and I feel naked without them."

Unlike her friends, Sparrow was feeling very tense. The first time she'd picked up *The Forbidden Book,* it seemed almost to writhe in her hands, as if it were alive. This had been so unsettling that she forgot to crawl on her way out, and one of the fire snakes scorched her hair, coming within an inch of killing her. She shivered at the memory. And to think she was now going to have to do that again!

The Travia streets were crowded. Lilliputian fairies flitted here and there, carrying messages, flowers, or pollen. A group of little children on tethers were practicing floating behind a female spellbinder in a blue dress. Tara smiled. It almost looked as if the woman was carrying a big bouquet of children. Trumpets blared whenever a pedestrian took off or landed. Like scoops, the trumpets had wings and carefully watched the busy crowds to warn of takeoffs and landings. The overall effect was deafening. Some spellbinders were riding pegasi, but Tara was surprised to also see one mounted on a large winged bull; people gave its sharp, gleaming horns a wide berth.

As in Tingapore, the city's merchants had hundreds of items for sale. The stands were heaped high with fruits and vegetables, some of which looked unhappy to be there. Delicious southern cantaloops grumbled in their cages. Freshly picked kalornas waved bewildered eye-petals. A kraken that clearly didn't want to wind up on a skewer was trying to climb out of its tank to strangle the krakenmonger. The P'abo imps in the next stall complained loudly about getting splashed. They sold colorful candies, including their famous Soothsucker lollipops. Animated by magic spells, the goodies marched up and down the trays, commanded by bottles of Tzinpaf.

Farther on, two elves were selling bows and arrows next to a dwarf's stall. Robin's weapons had also been confiscated at Omois, and like Cal, he felt naked without them, so he went over to buy a bow. The ones on display had taut bowstrings and were delicately carved from handsome brown wood. Spotting the black streaks in Robin's white hair, one of the elves muttered something and laughed sarcastically. Tara didn't hear what the elf said but the tone was insulting, and she saw Robin stiffen. His status as a half-elf apparently wasn't going unnoticed.

Racists, thought Tara. *Even though the universe's races are clearly all equal.* Her grandmother knew how to deal with such people, and Tara decided to copy her attitude. She took out her immuta-cred purse and walked over. Thanks to Sparrow's language spell, she understood the elves' musical inflections perfectly.

"Well, Robin, do these little shopkeepers have anything halfway decent?" she said contemptuously in perfect Elvish. "I don't see why you're bothering. Let's go spend our money with people who know real work!"

"Well said, miss!" roared the dwarf. "Come, see what I've got. My axes and swords are worth any of those spindly toy weapons."

The second elf, who was about to turn Robin away, glared at the dwarf. "We sell the best bows in OtherWorld," he said in honeyed accents.

"Oh, really?" snapped Tara. "Not that I can see."

Robin swallowed hard.

"Eh, take it easy," he whispered, aghast. "My countrymen can be pretty touchy, and I don't think I can handle two of them at once."

Tara refused to back off. She and the elf were too busy staring each other down. Her anger was so intense that the living stone sensed it, and her hands began to pulse with blue light. The elf must have felt the girl's power because he suddenly blinked and bowed.

"The weapons here may not suit you," he said smoothly. "But I think we have something that would be more appropriate for your rank, my lady."

At a sign, the other elf stepped behind a glittering curtain and emerged with a carved wooden case. He opened it reverently, revealing an extraordinary-looking bow. As white as whaloon milk, it was inlaid with iridescent wood from the Hymlia Mountains. Runes underlined in gold and silver gleamed on the bow's body, and its upper and lower limbs glittered like diamonds. The grip was royal brrraaa horn inlaid with emeralds.

The bow was magnificent—and from the way Robin, Cal, and Sparrow were staring at it, unique.

"This is the bow of Lillandril Steel-Heart, one of our most famous women warriors," the elf proudly announced, pleased with the impression he'd made. "It was created for her, and it has been searching for a new master ever since her death two thousand years ago. But I must warn you: If you touch the bow and are not the person for whom it is destined, you will be badly burned."

"I know the legend of Lillandril's bow, and I also know that it would never accept a half-elf," said Robin with a shrug, "So, don't play games with me. I'll buy a regular bow. That one over there would suit me just fine," he said, pointing.

Tara could feel Robin's sadness, and it pained her. And then she got an idea. *A magic thing, eh? Let's see if my stone can lend a hand.*

Living stone, she called mentally. *Can you feel the magic in the bow before me?*

Bow? The stone had no idea what a bow was, of course.

Sorry. Look at the picture in my mind. Through Tara's eyes, the living stone could see the bow in its case.

Hmpf, not powerful, the stone whispered, mentally gauging the shiny weapon. *Not like me! But I understand when it talks.*

Ask it if it is bored.

A bit surprised, the living stone complied.

Yes, bored, she said with a sigh. *Like me before beautiful Tara, pretty Tara, came search me under black roses.*

Perfect, thought Tara, smiling at the extravagant compliments. *Tell the bow that the next person to touch it will give it more adventures than it ever had with Lillandril. And that it must not burn him.*

After a few seconds, the stone replied. *Lillandril put spell. Little bow not able to lift spell all alone.*

Really? You mean it burns everyone? That it actually can't choose a new master?

No. Lillandril put spell just to protect bow. Only she can touch it. But pfft!—sudden death.

In an ambush?

Fish bone, the bow answered through the stone. *Lodge in throat. Drop dead. But just before big battle, so elves say she die fighting. Fish bone less glorious.*

Tara repressed a mental chuckle.

I see. Living stone, can you neutralize the spell?

Hmpf, answered the stone with a touch of contempt. *You give your magic to help?*

I give, confirmed Tara.

Then easy!

The living stone seized Tara's power and combined it with her own. An invisible tendril discreetly reached out and probed the bow, then withdrew.

Done! the voice in Tara's mind shouted with satisfaction.

"Robin?" said Tara aloud.

"Yes?"

"Pick up the bow."

"But—"

"Don't argue, just pick it up. Trust me."

With a mocking smile, the elf held the case out to him. Robin hesitantly reached in and touched the bow's grip. When nothing happened, he seized the bow and took it from the case.

The elf's eyes almost popped out of his head. "By Jeduril and Brandmaril, it didn't burn him! That's impossible!"

Robin's grin was so wide, it practically took up all his face.

"It's fantastic," he said in a tone of wonder, gently stroking the gleaming wood. "So powerful and yet so light!"

The two elves had lost all their arrogance and were now looking at Robin as if he had grown a second head. Then, with a visible effort, they pulled themselves together.

"With arrows, the bow costs a thousand gold immuta-credits," one announced.

Yikes! A thousand credits! Tara had all of forty-five in her purse. Disappointment was sweeping over her when Sparrow stepped forward.

"Hold on a second!" she shouted. "I know the legend of Lillandril's magic bow too. And I know that the legend says the bow can't be sold, only given to the person brave enough to seize it. Which is what my friend just did. So don't try to jerk us around, or I'll complain to the High Council of Elves."

The annoyed arms dealers bent their heads.

"Oh, all right," grumbled the first. "Go ahead and take it. And be sure to tell the High Council that we *gave* it to you."

"Perfect!" said Tara, snatching up the arrows and ornate quiver that went with the bow. "It's a pleasure doing business with you."

At his stall next door, the dwarf was hooting with laughter.

"Ha, ha, ha! Looks like our little elves outsmarted themselves! They went fishing for puffer sardines but caught a slasher shark instead! Well done, miss. That was a sight worth seeing. As a token of my appreciation, please accept this dagger as a gift. Its name is Needle. Take good care of it. It doesn't have any magic, but it won't bend and it won't break. See you again sometime, girl. May your hammer ring clear."

Before Tara could protest the dwarf's sudden generosity—or respond with the polite, "May your anvil resound"—he had already turned away to serve other customers.

The friends walked for several blocks before Robin began to emerge from his wonderment. He was so distracted that he kept treading on Sparrow's heels.

"He's just like Fabrice with Barune," she said sarcastically. "Hey, would you mind looking where you're going, please? You'll have all the time in the world to get to know your new toy."

"It's beautiful, isn't it?" said Robin for the thousandth time.

"Gorgeous," answered Sparrow, also for the thousandth time.

"Oh, Tara, look! That girl's wearing a copy of your glyph on her neck."

The young shopper's neckline was low enough to reveal a shiny ornament at her throat. But it was a poor copy of the gift that the colors had given Tara in Limbo when she freed them from the Demon King. When Tara didn't keep it discreetly covered, her throat displayed a wild, baroque jewel that combined ebony, diamond, emerald, sapphire, and ruby.

As they walked, Tara began to pay more attention to the crowd. The fashion in OtherWorld was no fashion at all, she noticed. Since anyone could create whatever outfit they wanted and magic allowed every extravagance, the resulting spectacle was fascinating. There were lots of feathers, furs, and leathers of every color, plus materials she couldn't identify, probably made from the silk or spit of some exotic animal. Tailors and dressmakers only worked for the nonspells, who could be distinguished from spellbinders by their relatively sober clothing.

Sparrow pointed out a fat woman who ambled along wrapped in a kind of living dress created by a swarm of tiny brilliant balls. Another woman showed off her beautiful body thanks to lengths of muslin tossed about by a breeze she generated herself. One bystander, completely covered in purple feathers, was chatting with another whose body was encased in a shiny black carapace.

Gradually, the crowd began to thin. Cal led them through a maze of streets to an attractive house hidden behind a thick hedge of bushes that clicked their thorns at them. The bushes parted when Cal put his hands on them, but he grimaced as the thorns pricked his skin.

Suddenly Sparrow screamed and instinctively shifted into beast shape. Before her stood a monster with seven heads, each one hissing with bared teeth. Tara summoned her power and Robin nocked an arrow to his bow. But Cal stepped ahead of them, walking straight toward the drooling maws.

The monster bent down as if to swallow him, but let itself fall to the ground at Cal's feet with an earth-shaking *boom!* and rolled over on its back, yelping happily.

"Yes, Toto, it's me! How's my big boy? I've missed you!" Cal continued in this affectionate vein as he scratched around the eyes of every head he could reach.

"Toto?" exclaimed Tara incredulously. "You call this thing *Toto*?"

"Well, yeah," said Cal, sounding a little embarrassed. "My parents gave it to me for my third birthday. At the time, Toto seemed like a nice name."

"It's a hydra!" cried Sparrow, who was trying to get her heartbeat down from the stratosphere. She shifted back into human shape and her robe groaned as it regained its normal dimensions. "I thought hydras weren't allowed in the city."

"Mom has a special dispensation because she often keeps valuables at home," he said. Then to the hydra: "Go ahead and smell them, Toto. You can let them in; they're friends."

When a head as big as Tara swung over to delicately sniff her, she almost choked. Rising from the monster's armored, olive-green body were seven black heads with seven pink, wet tongues, and Tara knew some Doberman pinschers who would envy their teeth.

"Next time, Cal, please warn me!" said Robin in a friendly way, as he released the tension on his bow. "Your Toto nearly took seven arrows in its throats."

"Er, I'm really sorry," said Cal, who of course had done it deliberately, having forgotten that his friend was once again armed and on edge.

At his command the hydra obediently stepped aside, whining softly when Cal walked into the house.

The interior smelled of fresh roses, which made sense, since an entire bank of them cascaded down one of the walls. It was carefully tended by a half-dozen buzzing little fairies. The floor was covered with a kind of soft fur that purred as it wrapped itself around their ankles. They passed into what would be a spacious living room, except that it was terribly cluttered with books, maps, parchments, and gleaming, ornately carved objects. Delighted to be of service, the sofa and chairs bounded over to meet them.

The friends had barely sat down when plates and silverware rushed in from the kitchen accompanied by dishes being filled at top speed. This included tea, hot chocolate, and Tzinpaf, candies, and cream puffs. There was a steak for Cal, who tore into it as if he hadn't eaten any meat for the past two days, which was actually the case. Sparrow ate three cream puffs, Robin six, and as for Manitou, Tara stopped counting after the twentieth. She noticed that her hot chocolate tasted slightly of honey and nuts, and learned that the particular flavor came from cacao beans imported from Earth. The furry carpet watched for any falling crumbs and ate them, quivering with delight.

Tara and Sparrow were extremely curious to see Cal's bedroom, but he stubbornly barred the way. He wasn't about to let them make fun of him because of his posters of Shakira, an Earth singer whose voice he loved—along with her hypnotically swinging hips.

Cal quickly gathered a half-dozen sharp-edged implements and stuffed them into the pockets of his robe. As Tara had learned, those pockets could accommodate practically anything, yet never became lumpy or heavy. His choices made, Cal left a taludi for his parents informing them of his escape. He then filled a purse with immuta-creds, took a couple of parchments, and went out with his friends. Toto looked heartbroken when they left for the castle, and they could hear the hydra whimpering pathetically for a long time.

"We'll go in the side way," Cal explained as they walked toward the Living Castle. "It's an entrance the castle itself showed me a few years ago."

"You mean you *talk* with that big pile of stones?" asked a surprised Manitou. "It's the first time in my life as a high wizard that I've heard of such a thing!"

"Well, we don't exactly talk. More like I ask the castle for things, and it either does them or doesn't react. It's never been willing to make the walls of the girls' dormitory transparent, for example. No help there at all."

"Cal!" exclaimed Tara and Sparrow together, and Robin jabbed the little thief in the ribs.

"What? What have I said now?"

The Living Castle was well guarded. When Magister acquired demonic magic, the sovereigns, presidents, and other OtherWorld rulers finally realized the danger they faced, and the profession of guard grew by leaps and bounds. You could always tell new recruits: they went strictly by the book. On the other hand, they tended to paranoia and watched the castle and its surroundings obsessively. Rounds had been increased, and the friends had to wait for the guards to pass so they could get to the part of the castle that Cal had in mind.

Whistling casually—*I'm just an innocent stroller, pay no attention to me*—he stopped in front of a section of a wall that looked no different from any other.

"Hmm, let me see," Cal muttered, his brow furrowed. "What did it tell me? Oh, yeah! 'Castle, fairest of them all, let your friends pass through the wall.'"

"'Fairest of them all'?" repeated Robin incredulously.

"Hey, the castle's a bit vain. What can I say?"

The wall underwent a kind of spasm and its stones vanished, creating an opening. Cal raised a fist and recited: "By Illuminus, drive the dark away and brightly show and light our way." An intense light immediately began to glow.

They were apparently in the depths of the castle; the dungeons, in fact. Sparrow shivered as they passed dark cells in which she could make out skeletons, still in chains. Lancovit's past had apparently been a little more savage than the history books reported.

They climbed many, many stairs.

Cal had taken the precaution of changing his appearance. He couldn't maintain the subterfuge for long, but for the moment his hair was somewhere between red and chestnut, his eyes black instead of gray, and he had coarsened his delicate features. Blondin had been changed into an Arctic fox and was all white except for the black tip of his tail.

Finally climbing one last flight of stairs, they emerged into one of the main hallways—and into a raging storm.

The Living Castle was clearly in a bad mood. A very bad mood, indeed. A terrifying hurricane flattened trees and illusory landscapes. Icy gusts lifted the courtiers' robes, to their offended shrieks, and ruffled Gallant's mane and Sheeba's and Blondin's fur. The pegasus decided not to fly, to avoid risking being blown into a wall.

"Son of a gun!" exclaimed Cal. "What is it up to?"

The moment it heard his voice, the Living Castle seemed to hesitate. A patch of blue sky appeared among the heavy darkness weighing on its domes. Then a ray of sun timidly broke through the clouds. Soon, the lovely Mentalir landscape with its silvery unicorns and blue meadows returned, to the courtiers' great relief.

"Really, the castle has been simply unbearable!" said a fat woman bundled in her spellbinder robe. "Two days of hurricane weather is beyond the pale. I don't understand why Their Majesties didn't intervene."

"I think one of our young spellbinders was imprisoned in Omois," said her companion. "The castle has been in a lousy mood ever since we heard the news. But things must've worked out, which would explain this nice sunshine."

Cal was slack-jawed with astonishment.

"Did you hear that?" he stammered. "I had no idea that castle cared for me so much. It's . . . it's very unexpected."

Robin slapped him on the back so hard he staggered. "*All* your friends are unexpected: gnomes, a magic castle, a half-elf. Your reputation's made. You're an eccentric, my dear Caliban."

Suddenly, Tara screamed and stumbled backward.

In front of her a dark cave had yawned open. From it a monstrous, furious slug with a jaw full of mandibles emerged.

Tara held her breath. *All right, the darned Living Castle has obviously gotten its weird sense of humor back.* She had forgotten how much it loved to frighten young spellbinders with its ghostly projections.

The slug was barreling toward her, but Tara refused to be intimidated and stood her ground. The castle wasn't about to trick her again!

So she was totally surprised when a mandible snagged her robe and violently yanked her toward the monster's mouth!

Out of nowhere, an arrow brushed the tip of her ear and lodged in one of the slug's six eyes. Howling in pain, the beast pulled in the shattered eye. It released Tara, who fell to all fours and scuttled backward at top speed, helped on her way when a large paw swatted her. Sparrow had instinctively shape-shifted and used her strength to push Tara out of danger. Gallant gave a fierce whinny, flew onto the giant worm's back, and started biting it. Sparrow did the same, deftly dodging the mandibles and raking the giant gastropod with her claws. Hissing with pain, the slug swung its head sideways, tossing the beast against the wall.

Unable to avoid the impact, Sparrow screamed as she slammed into the wall. Then she fell to the ground, unconscious.

CHAPTER 7

A CRYSTAL TRAP

Sparrow shifted back into human shape under the impact, but remained unconscious.

The slug extended its mandibles, eager to devour the person who had been hurting it, but had to give up in the face of an enraged Sheeba and a fresh volley of arrows.

With Robin shooting at superhuman speed, the slug began to look like a monstrous porcupine. Meanwhile, the panther and the pegasus continued fiercely biting its back and flanks.

The number of arrows left in Robin's quiver was gradually diminishing. When the arrows eventually ran out, the slug took the opportunity to move dangerously close. But the arrows suddenly yanked themselves out of its body, making the slug writhe and shriek in pain. Then they obediently flew back into the quiver. Once over his astonishment, Robin started shooting again.

After taking arrows in five of its eyes, the slug finally retreated into its cave, nearly knocking Gallant out against the cave roof in the process. The pegasus quickly took to the air and landed triumphantly next to Tara.

Keeping an eye on the mouth of the huge cave, and with his bow still drawn, Robin shouted to Tara, "Are you all right?"

"I'm fine," said Tara, "but Sparrow's hurt. She isn't moving."

Tara was anxiously leaning over the unconscious girl. A deeply worried Sheeba stood near her companion, softly whining.

Cal quickly kneeled next to Sparrow and put his hand on her neck and intoned: "By Healus, ease this body's pain and make our Sparrow well again."

At that, Sparrow's oddly bent arm straightened, and she began to move her head.

"Ow, ow, ow!" she moaned, glassy-eyed. "By my ancestors, what happened?"

"What happened is that you charged without thinking and got yourself knocked out!" said Manitou severely. "Against something that big and aggressive, you're better off using a bow and arrow, or maybe a machine gun and, ideally, a cannon. Avoid hand-to-hand fighting at all costs. Don't they teach you *anything* in your combat training sessions?"

"Well, not how to fight giant slugs," muttered Sparrow, who was painfully struggling to her feet with Sheeba's help. "It wasn't on this year's curriculum, anyway."

The slug's attack had been so fast and unexpected, it caught the astonished courtiers off guard. Now they all started screaming and calling for the guards. But then the din abated just as abruptly, and Tara's heart skipped a beat when she saw who had just appeared at the end of the hall: Master Dragosh, Lady Boudiou, Lady Kalibris, and the chimera, First Counselor Salatar.

All right, I guess our low profile bit is pretty well shot, thought Tara. She could only hope that the empress hadn't labelled all five of them fugitives.

"Get out of here, Cal!" whispered Sparrow, who was still gathering her wits. "They might recognize you in spite of your disguise."

Nodding, the little thief slipped into the crowd.

Dragosh's red eyes widened when he spotted Tara.

"So, it's Miss Duncan!" the vampyr hissed malevolently. "I should've known you would be behind this commotion. What have you been up to now?"

"She didn't do a thing!" Robin said angrily, while keeping a sharp eye on the cave. "She was attacked by carnivorous Salterian slug. Take a look."

He pointed to a trail of slime left by the wounded slug glistening in the grass. The Living Castle canceled the Mentalir landscape, and they could clearly make out the viscous streaks on the bare stone.

"By Demiderus!" cried Lady Boudiou, "That slug is an *animatrap!*"

Sparrow started. "Of course! I should have realized that!"

"What's an animatrap?" asked Tara.

"It's a personal anti-personnel trap," said Robin. "If somebody wants to get rid of you but doesn't know when you'll pass a given spot, they set an animatrap there. The moment you enter its field, you're detected and the trap springs."

Sparrow chimed in: "Animatraps were used a lot in the last spellbinder wars, but fell out of favor long ago. Mom made me study them because many royal family members fell into traps like that when successions were . . . disputed, let's say. This one wasn't set for me, so I didn't see it."

"I see. Politics on your world is just *so* interesting! So, how can you detect these traps?" asked Tara.

"If you see something that looks blurry, like heat waves, it's probably an animatrap. Be very careful, Tara! They're hard to spot, which is why they're so effective."

"Great," she muttered. "Now whenever I see a blur or the weather turns hot, I'll be terrified. I just love this planet!"

"But whoever is after you hasn't had much luck," Lady Boudiou cheerfully pointed out. "You're surrounded by faithful and vigilant friends. Come here, darling. I think you need some comforting."

She tried to take Tara in her arms, but the girl quickly broke free.

Tara wasn't terrorized; now she was furious. When she got her hands on whoever was after her, she would make them sorry they were ever born.

Just then, she noticed that Robin was looking at his bow doubtfully.

"Are you okay, Robin?"

"Yeah, except that I've had a little difference of opinion with my new bow. It popped into my hands before I called for it, and it shot the first arrow without my say-so. And it didn't bother mentioning that it could call back its arrows. I think the two if us are going to have a little chat."

Tara was about to speak when Dragosh returned to her.

"To what do we owe the dubious honor of your presence in Lancovit?" the vampyr asked in a tone so threatening that Tara instinctively activated her power.

Her hands glowed blue. The vampyr immediately stepped back and his hands started glowing red. The courtiers casually but quickly moved away from the two adversaries, carefully opening a space between them. Tara couldn't help thinking that magic duels looked a lot like old Western shootouts.

Lady Kalibris, the castle administrator, sized up the situation and quickly intervened.

"Welcome back to our—" began Dana, her first head.

"—Castle. How—" continued the second head, Clara.

"—are you, dear?" Dana finished.

Tara was so focused on the vampyr that she didn't respond imme-diately. But the administrator had cleverly planted herself between the two opponents, and Tara's politeness was the strongest. The glow faded from her hands, and she answered: "Very well, thanks. And how are you, ladies?"

"We are—"

"—upset. Yes, very upset—"

"—at what happened to Caliban. That scamp—"

"—didn't deserve—"

"—such a harsh punishment. Do you plan—"

"—to stay long? Your room—"

"—is always ready for you, of course."

"Thank you, ladies. I don't yet know how long I'll be here, but I'll let you know when I'm leaving."

"That's perfect," Dana concluded. "You are our guest of honor, like last time."

Bingo! With a single well-chosen sentence, the administrator had made Tara untouchable.

Powerless, Dragosh gave her a long, burning look, but Tara remained unruffled.

"I'll never be far behind you, Duncan," he hissed, so quietly that only Tara could hear him. "I haven't forgotten that you're the portal through which the demons can invade our universe. If I have the slightest doubt about you, I won't hesitate. Guest or not, I'll destroy you."

Just then something shiny whistled between them and slammed into the wood with a resounding *thwock!* that made the Living Castle shudder indignantly.

"Sorry!" shouted a well-known voice. "Guess my axe got away from me. May your hammer ring clear, Master Dragosh. Yours too, Tara!"

The vampyr, who was staring at a steel blade a quarter-inch from his head, made no reply, but Tara smiled broadly.

"Fafnir!" she shouted joyfully, then gave the polite dwarf response: "May your anvil resound!"

Tara ran to hug the imposing dwarf, who received her assault with dignity. Fafnir had changed. The beard that had marked her as an adolescent was gone. She no longer wore her red hair in beribboned braids, but gathered in a simple ponytail that fell almost to the ground. Her striking green eyes were underlined in black, and the bracelets on her arms looked about to snap under the tension of her impressive biceps. Her black jerkin sported so many knives and cutting imple-ments that if she ever fell into a river, she would probably sink like a stone. And Tara suspected that her tight leather pants, whose red matched her hair, probably held an equal number of bad surprises for any eventual attacker. A large, beautifully worked pendant rested on her chest, clear evidence of her blacksmithing skill.

Fafnir looked spectacular, as usual. And she looked sincerely happy to see Tara and her friends.

Master Dragosh gave Fafnir a long, venomous once-over, then looked at the axe, which was still vibrating. He wasn't fooled. No dwarf would ever let their favorite weapon get away from them.

The slug, taking advantage of the relative calm, cautiously stuck out its last surviving eye.

Big mistake.

Dragosh reacted instantly. From his outstretched hands, a long jet of flame completely incinerated the giant gastropod. The cave opening wavered, and the destroyed trap disappeared, leaving only a blank section of wall.

The vampyr's reaction stunned the onlookers.

"What have you done?" yelped both of Lady Kalibris's heads at once.

"It would seem obvious," Dragosh answered curtly. "I just neutralized the trap."

"And it didn't occur to you—"

"—that the hunter-elves could have studied it to find out—"

"—who set it?"

"What you've done was completely stu—"

"—inappropriate!"

For a moment, the vampyr looked surprised at what he'd done. Then he scowled, turned on his heel in a great billowing of his spellbinder robe, and left without a word.

Counselor Salatar turned to Tara. The chimera opened his great lion's mouth with its darting tongues of flame, and spoke: "Hmm, well. Our friend Safir is a little jumpy right now. Please forgive him. As Their Majesties have commanded, you are welcome, Miss Duncan. However, I see that the attacks against your person have not ceased. Therefore, I would ask you to move around the castle as little as possible, and especially to stay well away from Their Majesties. High Wizard Manitou, I would appreciate it if you would see that your great-granddaughter complies with that request."

The Labrador looked at him coldly, without responding. Caught up in the joy of seeing Fafnir again, Tara said only that she didn't plan to stay very long, and Salatar had to settle for that cryptic statement. Lady Kalibris, Lady Boudiou, and the chimera departed, leaving behind a crowd of buzzing courtiers, who were sure to spread the news of the event around Lancovit.

Tara sighed and turned to Fafnir. "Did you hear about Cal? He's got big problems."

"So do I," said the dwarf soberly.

"He's been arrested, and . . . What do you mean, so do you?"

"If he was arrested, then why's he there, standing behind you," asked the dwarf, without answering Tara's question.

Cal heard her and came over.

"So you recognized me in spite of my disguise?" he murmured, surprised.

"We dwarves have sharp eyes," said Fafnir, shrugging her burly shoulders. "Didn't take me two minutes to see through your get-up. You'll have to transform yourself more than that to fool me. You escaped, I suppose?"

"He'll explain all that in a minute," said Tara cautiously, nodding toward some hovering courtiers. "Let's go to my room. Sparrow ought to lie down."

The Living Castle, probably feeling sheepish at being her attacker's unwitting accomplice, didn't project any crevasses or other pitfalls under Tara's feet. Instead, it outdid itself in creating gorgeous Other-World landscapes when she reached her suite. Sparrow was feeling so nauseated that she lay down on the blue canopy bed without complaint. A worried Sheeba leaped up to join her and rested her muzzle on the girl's arm. Cal was relieved to cancel his transformation spell, reverting to his gray eyes and thatch of black hair.

They told Fafnir all about their recent adventures, but kept their word to the gnomes and omitted the secret about the excreted jewels.

Dwarves can't stand being locked up, so of course she completely approved of their jailbreak.

"Well, none of that stuff is too serious," she finally said, "but what's happening to me is a real catastrophe."

"Oh yeah?" asked Cal, taken aback by that startling statement. "I could be eaten alive by parasite worms, and you don't think that's serious? In that case, I'm curious to know what's happening to you."

"I'm getting angry."

The five friends looked each other, then burst out laughing. Fafnir frowned.

"Did I say something funny?"

Robin took a deep breath, mastered his urge to laugh, and explained: "Let's just say that you dwarves aren't especially known for your calm and moderation."

Cal translated: "He means you have lousy personalities."

"That's not true at all," said Fafnir stiffly. "And in any case that's not the issue. Last time I got angry I almost wiped out our entire camp. We were exploring a new ore vein. We'd just come back up to the surface. I was broiling a brrraaa steak, and suddenly *poof!* Everything went black. When I awoke I was tied up, Tanir, Brendir, and Glenir were wounded, and I'd knocked out Blenda and Chantar. And it gets worse."

"Worse?" exclaimed Sparrow. "What can be worse for a dwarf than to attack another dwarf? Doing something like that usually brings a death sentence, doesn't it?"

Tara turned to her.

"Tell me something, Sparrow," she said. "In your world do you settle all your problems by killing people?"

"Each group of people deals with this sort of thing in its own way. Dwarves aren't known for their patience or their compassion. If a dwarf is guilty of attempted murder, they're executed. Period."

"The High Council of Dwarves recognized that I had extenuating circumstances," explained Fafnir.

"Oh really?" said a surprised Sparrow. "What were they?"

"That I wasn't myself. According to my friends, my skin turned purple, almost black, and my voice changed. I ordered them to bow down and worship me, like a god. When they laughed, I tried to kill them. It was one against five, but I almost whipped them because my blasted magic came back! Blendir said he heaved his war hammer at me, but a magic shield appeared and blocked it. It took three of them to take me down!"

The friends stared at Fafnir in astonishment. Dwarves hate magic. Actually, "hate" doesn't begin to describe it. "Makes them puke" is more like it. The friends thought Fafnir had rid herself of her magic when she drank the rose petal brew on the Island of Black Roses.

Clearly, that wasn't the case.

Cal said what they were all thinking: "So, they banished you again?"

The dwarf bent her red head. "Yeah. And if I don't get rid of this cursed magic, I'll be exiled for good."

"As I see it, we have a number of problems on our hands," said Tara, summing up. "Cal has to free the gnomes so he can get rid of the t'sil worms and avoid a horrible death. He also has to prove that he's innocent of the murder he's charged with. Fafnir has to rid herself of her magic and the possession that turns her into a megalomaniacal red monster. I have to find who's trying to kill me, while avoiding being captured by Magister. Isn't that awesome? Just think: a few months ago my biggest concern was picking which modern language to study in school, and buying a new bathing suit!"

Manitou gave a wolfish smile. "I remember that when you were little you often said you were bored and wished your life would be more exciting. So, what are you complaining about? Your dreams have come true!"

"Grandpa?"

"Yes, dear?"

"Next time I make a wish, do me a favor and bite me!"

"I never bite members of my own family," said the dog quite seriously. "Only strangers."

"It was the black roses, wasn't it?" interrupted Fafnir. "There was something in their juice. And that something got into me."

"Wait a moment," said Tara, feeling in her pocket. "I'm going to ask the living stone if it can tell us a little more about the entity that imprisoned it on the island."

She pulled out the glittering stone and explained the situation.

Friend, you, show, ordered the stone.

Tara obeyed, holding the stone out in front of her. It projected a luminous halo onto the dwarf. Then the light faded and the stone spoke, this time in a voice they could all hear: "Aie, aie, aie! Fafnir eaten by Soul Ravager. It tried use me to flee. It tried use Fafnir also. No choice have you will."

"What do you mean?"

"Your friend kill have to will you. If Ravager eat Fafnir, then Ravager free and Ravager eat all peoples, then planet, then universe!"

"The universe, is that all?" exclaimed Cal, bug-eyed. "You know, you were right! Your problems *are* worse than mine!"

"If an evil spirit tried to possess me, my faithful axe would take my life and the Ravager's," Fafnir declared bitterly. "No one possesses a dwarf against her will!"

"He seize you how many?" asked the stone.

"Just once," answered Fafnir, who had figured out the stone's odd way of speaking. "Or, at least that's the only time I remember. I immediately left Hymlia for Lancovit to ask Master Chem for help, but he's still in Omois."

Cal chuckled. "I don't think the empress told our national dragon that we've disappeared. So, he must be flailing around to get me released without realizing that I'm already here."

"When I was traveling to Travia I had to fight a terrible impulse," the dwarf continued. "That *thing* wanted me to go to the Island of Black Roses. I think this Ravager guy must still be there. And he's trying to get me there so he can completely take me over."

"You right possibly," said the stone. "Maybe Ravager not succeed eat Fafnir good enough if Fafnir far away. Maybe Ravager need Fafnir on island. Fafnir must never go Black Roses Island, or Fafnir end up midnight snack!"

Tara could see the dwarf turning pale under her coppery tan and spoke up.

"Listen, Fafnir, here is what we're going to do. First we're going to get *The Forbidden Book*—or at least try—and put it in a safe place before the gnomes can steal it. Then we have to free the gnomes from Magister's control, assuming he's behind all this, and try to destroy his famous artifactum. That will allow us to get the antidote for Cal. In the meantime, you can go to Omois and discuss your problem with Master Chem. As soon as we finish our mission we'll take care of you. How's that?"

"I can wait," answered the dwarf proudly. "Now that I've been warned, that thing won't overcome my resistance so easily. And I'll help you steal the book. I can talk to Chem afterward."

Cal grimaced as he studied the massive dwarf.

"Er, for stealing the book, that won't be necessary," he said cautiously. "Sparrow and I can handle it. Right, Sparrow?"

He was answered with silence. The girl had fainted again.

Summoned by the panicked kids, Shaman Night Bird had Sparrow brought to the infirmary.

"The young princess has a concussion," he announced. "The Healus is working, but moving her is out of the question for the moment. I want to keep her in observation for a while. And I'll alert her parents right away."

"Can we see her?" asked Tara, who was very concerned.

"Sure, go ahead. She just woke up."

Sparrow was resting and looked as white as the infirmary canopy bed she was lying in.

"I'm so sorry," she said with a sigh. "I don't know what it is, but I can't keep my eyes open."

"Then close them," ordered Cal, who had disguised his appearance again. "You don't need to see in order to hear us. Listen, I'm going to go steal the book without you. Just repeat the instruction sequence, and I'll take care of everything."

The fact that Sparrow didn't object proved to them that she really wasn't well. To make sure there was no mistake, they all memorized the steps to get into the secret Book Room.

"Perfect!" said Cal, glancing at the accreditation card on his wrist. "I suggest we get a bite to eat and a few hours' sleep. At two thirty, when everybody should be asleep, we'll go into Master Chem's office."

"You can't!" objected Sparrow weakly.

"Why not?"

"My accredi-card was the only one programmed for access to the office, not yours. I have to come with you!"

"No way," said Fafnir, easing Sparrow back down. The pillows adjusted themselves to make her comfortable, the bed smoothed its wrinkled sheets, and the Living Castle sent a breeze to dry the sweat on the girl's feverish brow.

"I don't need an accreditation card," explained the dwarf. "My power lets me move through walls if I want. Once inside, I'll open the office door for the rest of you. And if I can't, I'll go steal the book in your place."

Despite their protests, Fafnir stuck to her guns. At dinner, Cal got a Soothsucker that read: "Unable to avoid the spell, you'll soon hurt a friend." He racked his brains, but couldn't understand the prediction. Blasted prophesicles! As for Tara, hers read: "If you're affected, you'll be unable to save someone." A shiver ran down her spine.

Lady Boudiou stopped by their table to ask about Sparrow's health and to check to see that they were all okay. Master Dragosh, who was presiding over the dinner with Lady Kalibris, ostentatiously ignored Tara and her friends. Manitou went over to chat with the other high wizards and was revelling in having his head patted by Lady Sirella, the beautiful mermaid. When he returned, he was drenched, but delighted.

"Cal's escape is still a secret," he announced, shaking himself. "And so is the fact that the empress imprisoned us."

"It wasn't the empress," protested Tara, who rather liked the young woman. "It was that horrible guard captain. And what about Master Chem? Hasn't he realized that we've disappeared? I find it weird that he hasn't done anything."

"Actually, I think he's afraid of Isabella," said the dog, grinning. "He's probably searching for us everywhere, while trying to think of some excuse for your grandmother. After all, this is the second time he's lost you. If he doesn't find you very soon, Isabella might turn him into a line of luxury suitcases."

Tara chuckled. "I'd be curious to know what outlandish explanation he's going to give her."

"Meanwhile," the Lab continued, "he could come back to Lancovit at any moment, so I suggest we act fast. That dragon has a bad habit of sleeping in his office."

With those words, they went to get some rest. Fafnir, Cal, Manitou, and Tara slept in her room. Like all elves, Robin preferred the open air, so he and Gallant went to perch on a comfortable branch of one of the steel giants on the castle grounds.

At two thirty in the morning, still sleepy, they gathered in front of High Wizard Chemnashaovirodaintrachivu's office. The tiny stone dragon and the unicorn were sleeping peacefully. The castle was projecting sand dunes and a sky glittering with stars. A gentle breeze wafted along the hall. Everything was still.

"Wait for me here," whispered Fafnir.

Taking care not to wake the little sentinels, she stretched out her hand, and it started to melt into the wall. Cal shuddered and turned his back. The sight of the dwarf slowly melting into stone always gave him the creeps.

A few moments later they were startled to see the wall opening up for them, and they hurried into the office.

"We're all set," Fafnir announced loudly when the wall had closed again. "No one outside can hear us. The door has an automatic latch, so I was able to open it for you. What do we do now?"

"Let's see if I can remember what Sparrow told me," said Cal.

He picked up the copy of *Comparative Anatomy of OtherWorld Fauna* and set it on the old wizard's terribly cluttered desk. He opened the book and tapped three times on page 3, then ten times on page 20. At that, the desk moved aside, revealing a beautiful glass staircase.

Tara spoke up then. "Listen, Cal, I didn't like what the Soothsucker said. I'm coming with you."

"If you insist. But try not to distract me, all right? I have to stay focused. Blondin, you're staying here. Chem said we have to act very fast once we've taken the book. Grab the flat stone hidden behind the pedestal and put it where the book was. Ready, Tara? Let's go."

Tara rolled her eyes and nodded, repressing the snippy remark on the tip of her tongue. When he was working, Cal was no fun at all. The little thief's personality changed completely. He didn't tell jokes; he scanned the darkness with rapt attention and was cold and concentrated.

Going down the staircase they skipped the fourth step, then the seventh, gradually disappearing from their anxious friends' view.

Down below, as expected, they came out into a huge room that lit up the moment they stepped on the white sand floor. Runes written on the black walls seemed like warnings: Do not enter, otherwise . . .

The Forbidden Book lay on a pedestal surrounded by six statues of fire snakes; the nearest two faced the staircase. Cal and Tara got down on their stomachs and began to crawl. They carefully watched to see if the stone reptiles reacted, but they remained still as statues. When the kids were able to stand again, the book was right in front of them, Cal gestured to Tara to go around the pedestal and get the flat stone so she could quickly put it in the book's place.

Suddenly Cal stumbled backward. The sand under his feet had begun to shift. Under their astonished eyes, a hole opened up at the base of the stone column supporting the book. Before they had time to react, a blue gnome jumped up, grabbed *The Forbidden Book,* and dove back down into the hole.

Cal screamed: "Nooooo!"

He tried to seize the gnome while Tara raced around the column and grabbed the flat stone behind the pedestal, but she was too late—much too late. The defensive spell protecting the book had already been activated. A terrible tongue of flame shot from the fire snakes' mouths and hit them. Tara and the stone resisted for a second longer than Cal, but then the pain was too intense, and the two spellbinders screamed in agony. That was all.

Up above, Manitou started. Gallant and Blondin had both screamed, then collapsed. Robin and Fafnir rushed down the glass staircase. The dog wizard moaned, hearing screams and terrible noises from underground. At last, the half-elf and the dwarf emerged, burned and pale, carrying their friends' lifeless bodies in their arms. When they reached the top of the staircase a strange light briefly flashed.

"What in God's name happened?" yelled Manitou.

"I . . . I don't know," stammered Robin, tears flowing from his crystalline eyes. "They were lying on the sand, and the book was gone. The fire snakes had been activated and tried to keep us from approaching. But that weird shield that protects Fafnir deflected their spells, and she was able to chop down the statues. Then we brought Cal and Tara up, and . . . Oh, Manitou! I can't feel their pulse! They're . . . they're dead!"

CHAPTER 8

THE DEADLY SPELL

An alarmed Manitou put his cold nose on Tara's neck, but got no reaction. Fafnir searched for Cal's pulse, then shook her head gravely.

"I can't find a pulse, either," muttered the Lab. "This is unbelievable! They were struck by the deadly spell that Chem placed. We have to contact him immediately!"

"That won't do any good!" yelled Robin, totally losing his cool. "*They're dead!* We aren't necromancers; we don't know how to bring back the dead. And even if we did, they wouldn't be our friends anymore, they'd be zombies!"

"By my pile of gold, what are you doing in my office?" roared a very familiar voice behind them. "Manitou, is that you?"

Master Chem had come in and was staring in astonishment at the glass staircase, the sprawled bodies of Tara, Cal, Gallant, and Blondin, and a despairing half-elf.

"Chem!" exclaimed Manitou. "Thank Demiderus, you're back! Cal and Tara were killed by your deadly spell! How could you put such a dangerous charm on *The Forbidden Book*?"

With surprising agility for his apparent age, the dragon wizard rushed to kneel by the two teenagers.

"There isn't a minute to lose!" he yelled. "Luckily for these two young fools, they triggered an alarm when they opened the secret entrance to the underground room. It alerted me, so I immediately came back from Omois. The spell that protects the book is just an Inanimus spell. But if the bodies are moved or taken out of the Book Room, it becomes a Destructus. I got the idea from the Bloodgrave who combined Rigidifus and Carbonus spells. But unless I can reverse the process in the kids right away, we'll be attending their funerals."

Robin was aghast. "Do you mean that by moving them, we killed them?"

"You killed them, yes, but they're not lost."

"Not lost?" he blurted, wiping his tear-streaked face. "But they're—"

"Dead? Yes, absolutely. But only for a very short time. All told, I have six minutes to revive them, and I figure that four minutes have already passed. After that, the brain is so starved of oxygen, it's too late. Hand me the kalorna powder on that shelf there. And give me some stridule drool and some powdered gambole."

Robin handed the powders to the wizard, who quickly drew a pentacle with them.

A very worried-looking Fafnir was fiddling with her axe, feeling totally lost.

"Stand back!" the old wizard ordered. "I have to revert to my natural body for this to work properly." He intoned: "Chalidonrainchi-vorachivu, god of dragons, I turn to you. Return me to my dragon form, vital healing to perform."

Chem's god must have been standing by, because silvery blue scales promptly replaced skin, monstrous claws grew from fingers, and dorsal spines shredded his unprepared robe. Soon a majestic blue dragon was looming over them.

Without wasting a second, Chem bent down to Tara and Cal and began to chant, while his huge scaly body pulsed with a bright white light: "By Resurrectus, I conjure you, may the Destructus cease! May life shine through and bring our friends peace!"

The white light flowed into the two motionless bodies and enveloped them in an iridescent halo.

Suddenly, one of them stirred.

With great difficulty, Tara raised her head, opened a bleary eye, and saw the dragon. The living stone was still linked to her mind. The last thing the two of them had seen before passing out was a stone snake shooting fire at them. So, when they saw a glowing blue dragon at close quarters, Tara and the stone instantly combined their magic and fired a powerful ray. It hit the dragon with incredible force, sending him crashing into a wall. The entire castle trembled under the impact, and the office lights briefly flickered.

Blasted by Tara's blazing riposte, the dragon didn't have a chance. His consciousness winked out like a candle being snuffed. First his head gently hit the ground, then the rest of his body crashed down, causing a small earthquake.

"By my ancestors!" screamed Manitou, appalled. "What do you think you're doing?"

Tara covered her ears, grimacing. "Stop yelling, Grandpa! And what do you mean, what are we doing? The snake fired a spell at us, so we fired back. What are you doing in the Book Room? This place is dangerous."

"For your information, we aren't in that room anymore," Robin announced cautiously. "And I'm pretty sure you just killed Chemnashaovirodaintrachivu."

Tara gaped to see the dragon's mass sprawled on the floor. She struggled to her feet, helped by Robin, who couldn't decide whether to yell at her for what she'd done, or to hug her because he was so glad she was alive. Gallant moved his wings as he gradually regained consciousness, and Blondin barked when he was back on his feet. The spell had caused Cal and Blondin to revert to their normal appearance, and the fox was pleased to see that his fur was red again.

Cal opened his eyes, but he was still dizzy. "Oh, my head! What the heck happened?"

Robin turned to him, while propping up a shaky Tara. "The fire snakes attacked you, the book seems to be gone—unless you've hidden it very well—and Tara just blasted Master Chem, who was trying to save you!"

"Nooooo!"

"Yesssss!"

"I mistook him for a fire snake," stammered Tara. "There was the light . . . I didn't do it on purpose. The gnomes . . . they stole the book. But I didn't have time to put the stone on the pedestal, so the snakes attacked us! I—"

A warm, humid breath of air abruptly cut her off, followed by a deep, low rumble. It was the dragon—and he was snoring!

"Okay, whew! Everything's fine!" exclaimed a very relieved Manitou. "Chem was just knocked out! I suggest we let him rest now. We can talk things over with him later."

"Isn't that a little cowardly?" asked Fafnir doubtfully.

"Absolutely," the Lab admitted. "But we can be brave some other day, can't we? Right now we have too much to do—you know, saving the world, not to mention the universe—and facing a very angry dragon isn't on the list."

With his muzzle, Manitou pointed to the way out.

In the hallway, they encountered the castle guards, who had come running to find out what had caused all the ruckus. In a lordly way, Manitou pointed at the dragon cave-office and told them that someone had broken the door and stolen something. Oh, and had knocked out the huge reptile in the process.

Before anyone could ask any awkward questions, the group hurried off to pick up Sparrow at the infirmary. The girl barely restrained a shout of surprise when they told her everything that had happened. She was feeling better and was able to quickly dress with Tara's help and go with them.

When a worried Cal asked about her concussion, Sparrow whispered, "It's fine. I just shape-shifted into the beast, and *poof!* it disappeared instantly. The shaman couldn't believe it. He kept me in the infirmary to be on the safe side, but believe me, I feel great! Let's leave before my parents show up and make me stay in bed for the next six months!"

They were silent as they made their way to the gnome embassy. OtherWorld's twin moons cast their silvery light on a world that except for the stridules' *cree-cree-cree!* chirping, seemed to be enjoying the sleep of the dead—except for those things that move in the night, of course.

They had nearly reached the embassy when Master Dragosh suddenly came stumbling out of a side alley, looking dazed. Clearly visible in the twin moonlight, the vampyr was wiping his mouth, and his red eyes looked wild. He didn't have time to hide his hand, which was spattered with blood!

"There's been . . . There's been a terrible accident," he explained shakily. "I have to go tell Their Majesties."

Then he caught sight of Tara and glared furiously at her.

"This is all because of you!" he blurted.

Then, before they had time to say a word, he ran off. Manitou and the five friends gaped at each other, speechless.

The Lab took a deep breath and said: "This alley reeks of death. Stay here, children; I'll go take a look."

"I'm not a child!" complained Fafnir, who was 250 years old, after all. "I'm coming with you."

When they returned a few minutes later, the dwarf was frowning and the dog looked ready to pass out.

"There's a guy in there who's been bled like a crouicc," Fafnir calmly informed them, "with two nice fang marks on his neck. I think our friend the vampyr has some explaining to do."

"I hate to say this," said Robin, whose elf hunting instincts were immediately roused by anything out of the ordinary, "but we just don't have time to deal with him right now."

Tara was feeling very uneasy. *What the heck is that blasted vampyr accusing me of now?* she wondered.

Cal shrugged, and said: "Dragosh said he had to talk to the king and queen. They can work it out. Ah, here's the embassy."

Despite the late hour, all the building's lights were lit, oddly enough. Gnomes on geometer moths guarded the embassy gardens, and praying mantises patrolled watchfully. Two large centipedes with poisonous mandibles flanked the entrance, so Manitou and his group were careful not to make any sudden movements.

Ambassador Bulul Bulbul was waiting and greeted them with urbane politeness. "Welcome back! Were you able to get everything you needed?"

"Yeah, and even more," grumbled Cal, rubbing his head, which still felt sore.

"A number of events have occurred that would justify a modification of our agreement," began Manitou very diplomatically, "and—"

"You stole *The Forbidden Book*!" yelled Fafnir, for whom the word "diplomacy" didn't mean much. "Give it back!"

Manitou glared at her.

Though startled by the harsh accusation, the imperturbable ambassador quickly recovered. "A dwarf! How interesting! I don't remember seeing her with you when you came through."

"She's one of the tools I need," Cal said quickly. "If she doesn't go, we don't go, worms or no worms."

"Tools?" began Fafnir indignantly. "What do you mean by—"

Fortunately, the gnome interrupted her.

"I am not authorized to discuss this," he said. "My government *and your friend* are waiting for you in Smallcountry. Let me show you the way to our portal."

Having none too subtly reminded them that the gnomes were still holding a hostage, Bulbul led them to the transfer tapestries.

The tapestries glowed, and the guardian mantises disappeared. In their place stood monstrous arachnes that clicked their mandibles and stared at the new arrivals with their large round eyes. Sparrow and Tara shuddered with revulsion, and Fafnir gripped her axe. One of the arachnes bowed, gracefully bending her eight legs.

"Our government awaits you, and in good time, too," she said in the melodious voice that had so startled Tara when she first heard it.

They followed the giant arachnid to a large hall. Whereas most gnome facilities are underground, official Smallcountry buildings are erected on the surface. In addition to the gnomes, this is also the land of the P'abo imps and the Lilliputian fairies. It's said that other fairies live in the far north, near the border with Gandis, the land of giants. These are evil fairies, who feed on travelers heedless enough to cross their lands, but no one has ever returned to confirm or rebut that.

The group of friends silently crossed a hall that was as elaborately decorated as the facilities underground. The walls displayed a good cross-section of OtherWorld's flora and fauna: fantastically colored flowers, birds, insects, and animals. The floor was not stone but covered with soft blue grass from the Mentalir plains.

The inhabitants of Smallcountry apparently hadn't always lived harmoniously together. Dozens of tapestries portrayed the bloody wars that had preceded the three races' surprising alliance.

Parti-colored fairies perched comfortably on floating bleachers and gossiped shrilly as they watched the arriving guests. Lemon-yellow imps, dressed all in green, also observed the meeting. Suddenly one of them yelped. A huge, hairy wart had just appeared on the tip of his nose. The other imps laughed, and he scowled at them as he made it disappear with an irritated wave. Then one of those laughing almost choked when a pair of wings sprouted on his back and flew him zigzagging through the air. His howls of protest only made the other scamps laugh all the harder. A third imp suddenly found himself with a mooouuu head on his shoulders and started bugling in terror—to general hilarity.

Tara couldn't help but laugh. So, these were the famous playful P'abo imps.

Glul Buglul was present, accompanied by a half-dozen other gnomes whose pale skin and nearly white quiffs revealed their great age. Next to them lay *The Forbidden Book*, carefully guarded by two enormous arachnes. Cal frowned and Sparrow nodded. *Fine,* she thought, *at least everything's out in the open.*

An arachne scuttled over to an enormous gong and rang it with a mallet. Sparrow grimaced when the sound hit her ears, but the imps immediately fell silent and the fairies stopped chattering.

"This noble council is now in session," the arachne announced. "May wisdom attend each intercession!"

Tara studied Buglul, who was sitting on a chair a little more ornate than the others. Partly hidden by his orange quiff, a gold crown rested on the gnome's head. *Let's see what happens if I take the initiative,* she thought.

"Thank you for receiving us so promptly, Your Majesty," said Tara in a clear voice, bowing to the gnome.

Buglul smiled slightly at being thus unmasked. Cal's eyes widened. So, the gnome who had infected him was a king.

"I see you retrieved *The Forbidden Book*," she continued, avoiding an argument that might erupt over a less diplomatic term.

"Yes, we decided to put it in a safe place," he answered smoothly. "Pul Pupul, who borrowed it, as it were, told us of your presence in the underground room. What do you have to tell us about that?"

Tara repressed a very disrespectful shrug, but again avoided an argument.

"Nothing at all. All we have left to do is to find out where your wives and children are held prisoner and to destroy your enemy's power, if we can. You will then give Cal the antidote and we will bring the book back to Master Chem in Lancovit."

On his throne, King Buglul bowed slightly in homage to the girl's skill.

"We would be delighted to give the book back to you," he said in a silky voice. "The antidote too, just as soon as our wives and children are out of danger. Does your dwarf friend know the entire story?"

He clearly wanted to know if the spellbinders had told Fafnir the blue gnomes' secret.

"Only the essential points, Your Majesty. Your struggle against the wizard who kidnapped your families and our participation in that honorable fight. As well as the means you are using to make us help you."

The king shrugged, appearing not to feel in the least ashamed of his methods. His people would always come first. Still, he nodded, relieved by Tara's discretion. Fafnir glanced at her friend with curiosity, sensing that she had hidden something from her.

"Well, then, let's go right to your enemy's palace," said Manitou, taking over the conversation. "With our friend Fabrice, of course, whom I don't see here in the hall."

Tara reddened. She had completely forgotten about Fabrice being held prisoner by the gnomes.

"Of course," said the king. "He is feeding his mammoth and will be with us in a few moments. We had a hard time finding red bananas and popping peanuts, and an even harder time dragging the animal away from his meals!"

At that, Fabrice and Barune walked into the hall. The reunion with their friends was somewhat noisy, with the little mammoth trumpeting in every direction.

When Fabrice learned what Tara had done to Master Chem, he nearly fainted. And he looked at *The Forbidden Book* with obvious disgust. Barune accidentally trod on one of the arachne's legs, and she clicked her poisonous mandibles with indignation. Fabrice sighed. Since he and the mammoth had become linked, he'd learned that his new companion was absolutely adorable—and incredibly clumsy. Shrinking had made Barune quite light, and his coordination was terrible. He kept bumping into creatures or things. When it was things, that was okay. But creatures didn't much like it.

They all agreed that a gnome would accompany the little expedition as a guide. When the king announced that he would be the one, the elders protested loudly, but he rebuffed them. If he didn't go along, he said, there would be no expedition, period. Tara smiled. The gnome was just like her grandmother: stubborn. She better understood the reason for his attitude when she learned that the king's fiancée, the beautiful Mul Mulmul, was among the prisoners. Tara didn't like the gnome's methods, but his courage appealed to her. This king didn't hesitate to run risks to rescue his beloved.

"Romantic, isn't it?" Sparrow sighed.

"I would do the same thing," said Robin stiffly.

"For me or for Tara?" asked Sparrow teasingly, who hadn't failed to notice that the half-elf had a serious weakness for the young earthling.

Robin turned as red as a ripe tomato.

"For both of you, of course!" he exclaimed.

Fabrice noticed his embarrassment and bit his lip when Tara flashed the half-elf her beautiful smile. Robin promptly turned purple.

Fortunately for him, Manitou signaled their departure. Though they hadn't slept much that night, they had to immediately head back to Omois, where the wizard's palace was located. Because of the time difference between the two continents, it was already night in Tingapore. The gnomes had been spying on their enemy and knew the wizard would be away from his palace for several hours. It was now or never.

The portal was activated and the arachnes left behind. On arrival in Tingapore, Cal disguised himself again, and they followed the gnome king through the streets of the capital. As on her first visit, Tara marveled at the city's beauty and effervescence. Silver, gold, and purple houses alternated with palaces with gleaming roofs. The eight levels of traffic created an incredible tumult. Everywhere flying carpets, armchairs, and beds encountered pegasi, ifrits, and winged bulls, not to mention spellbinders who were levitating their way home.

Their little group didn't go unnoticed. Robin's bow generated a lot of comments—much more than his half-breed looks—which seemed to surprise him. Elves saluted the new master of Lillandril's bow, dwarves called out to Fafnir, and gnomes bowed to their king until he signaled that he was traveling incognito. Delicious aromas set Manitou's sensitive nose a-quiver, and he had to restrain himself from jumping on the roasts, stews, and other marvels cooking in the open. Magic made the air shimmer everywhere.

They stepped aside for a troop of fierce-looking centaurs, their flanks emblazoned with clan markings. Tatris nodded their two heads, mermaids floated gracefully along in their water bubbles, and Salterians, the fearsome white-swathed desert felines, watched for potential victims to kidnap for their ravening, deadly mines. A group of chimera chatting with some unicorns was careful to turn their heads aside, so their flaming breath wouldn't scorch their interlocutors. Two dragons, one green and the other a deep, handsome red, were making a herd of mooouuu very nervous; the cattle could feel their life expectancy falling precipitously. All of OtherWorld's people seem to have decided to meet in Tingapore.

"It's normal," said Glul Buglul when Tara mentioned how surprised she was. "The Seventh Season Carnival will be starting soon and the mask makers have a tremendous amount of work right now. Ah, here is Gelina's house. The tunnel to the wizard's palace starts from here."

They were greeted at the door not by a gnome, but by a human, one of the mask makers Buglul mentioned. The store was full of feathers, furs, carapaces, silks, black, blue, white and pink pearls, jewels, and precious metals, along with cotton, organza, muslin, and every other kind of stiff or sheer fabric. Sparrow and Tara examined with delight at the masks hanging from the ceiling. They almost looked alive. Tara was reaching for one when a sharp command stopped her: "No! Don't touch it!"

Sheepishly, she pulled her hand back, then stared. The woman in front of her was blind! Like her hair, her eyes were completely white. Yet, she seemed able to move around as if she could see perfectly.

"Each of my masks is for a certain person," explained Gelina with a sweet smile. "If you touch one, I will no longer be able to sell it."

"Please excuse me," Tara said, feeling intimidated. "I didn't know."

"Come. The tunnel is over here."

The white-haired woman entered a completely dark room, then said, "It's right there."

"Er, it would be nice to have some light," hazarded Cal.

"Oh, sorry!" she chuckled. "I always forget. One second; I must have something around here . . . Ah, here we go."

A soft glow lit up the cluttered room. In her hand, Gelina held an illuminated globe, whose light didn't seem to affect her any more than the darkness had a moment earlier.

Before her was the dark entrance of a tunnel that sloped gently downward. Cal flashed a wicked smile.

"Cool, it slopes down! We can wheel-board again!"

Buglul turned a paler shade of blue.

Luckily for him, the tunnel didn't have enough of a slope for Cal to use his skateboard. Gelina wished them good luck and gave them a couple of light globes.

After walking for about an OtherWorld hour, they emerged at an exit hidden by a tangle of bushes.

"We are in the gardens of the wizard's castle," the blue gnome whispered. "I wanted to show you the building from the outside, before you start searching the interior."

Cal nodded without answering. The place was more a palace than a castle. And the architectural style was pure Omoisian: over-the-top ornate.

Purple- and gold-tiled roofs covered various parts of the building. Ridge lines curved upward slightly, reminding Tara of the palaces she had seen in documentaries about Asia. Downspouts were sculpted into fantastic animals, a pattern repeated in the gardens. Animated plants shaped like white vrrirs snapped harmless leaf teeth, and furious brrraaa bushes, pulling on their roots, threatened to stampede, but never would. Gorgeous banks of flowers waved their petals to attract pollinators, whether insects or Lilliputian fairies. As the dwelling for an evil wizard, it was surprisingly harmonious. Being a monster of cruelty apparently didn't keep one from having good taste.

Then Tara drew the group's attention to something. The gardens were patrolled by guards.

Worse, they were *imperial* guards!

Sparrow turned to the gnome. "What are imperial guards doing in these gardens? They usually only protect the imperial family."

"Oh, I forgot to tell you," exclaimed the gnome. "The wizard who kidnapped our families—"

"Well, what about him?" she asked curtly, already anticipating problems ahead.

"—is the empress's uncle."

CHAPTER 9

DESTINATION UNKNOWN

The news left them speechless.

Sparrow was the first to react. "You mean Prince Bandiou, the empress's uncle? The man who served as her tutor after her mother died? *Are you kidding?*"

The gnome turned a serious face to them.

"That was also the empress's reaction when I told her about our terrible predicament. I also imagine that the hunter-elves were not very thorough because of their respect for the prince. But that is not the case with you, is it?"

You could hear terrible anguish in Buglul's voice.

But Manitou didn't like being manipulated.

"We're citizens of Lancovit," he said coldly. "If we're caught snooping around Prince Bandiou's house or grounds, we could be executed as spies. You were very careful not to tell us this minor detail—that the wizard was Bandiou."

Fabrice gulped, but Cal whistled derisively. "Well, we'll just have to not get caught, that's all. There are only two guards outside, and probably not many more inside. Given the prince's personality, he must not be the kind of guy to have many people around him."

"You're right," agreed the gnome. "With too many servants, someone might discover what he was up to and tell the empress. And he would be immediately executed, uncle or no uncle. So he compensates by using magic as much as possible: he has cleaning spells, maintenance spells, anti-pest and anti-insect spells, and spells for food and drink. His staff amounts to a team of six guards who work in rotation, a cook, two maids, and two handymen, one of whom mainly looks after the garden and the prince's ball orchid greenhouse. So you are not likely to run into many people. In addition, when searching his palace, we were able to steal copies of his accreditation cards and forged new ones. Which means that the spells will 'see' you only as ordinary servants going about their work."

"Okay, got it," said Cal. "I have a pretty good idea of the palace's general layout. Let's go!"

While they were talking, Tara was thinking. There was something in all this that didn't add up, but she couldn't put her finger on it.

With the accredi-cards affixed to their clothes, fur, or feathers, they went back up the tunnel and took the branch that led to the house itself. They emerged in one of the palace cellars, where they were able to prepare their search discreetly.

Cal held a very handy crystal that could display the building's layout in three dimensions. It could also show the location of all sentient beings within a hundred-yard radius. Their little group appeared in blue, and the palace servants and guards showed up in yellow. This made it easy to keep track of where both groups were—and to make sure they didn't meet!

Cal was the only one with the skills to locate the hidden portal. Since the others couldn't share the task, they obediently followed him around. When the coast was clear, the little thief would slip into a room while they stood watch outside. He would measure, touch, look, touch again, smell, and then come out as quickly as possible.

It got late, and the servants eventually went to bed. The guards' patrols outside the building were pretty casual, which offended Robin.

"That's really no way to guard a place," he griped. "You need soldiers in teams of two inside and out, on irregular schedules to throw off possible attackers, and constant communication between the teams!"

"Well, if you don't mind I'm just glad the guards are incompetent," whispered Sparrow. "In fact, if they wanted to go to sleep I would be even happier. So there!"

"What I'd like," interrupted Cal, who had just sifted through a half ton of dust in the library, "is for somebody to tell me how to find that blasted portal. This is the twentieth room I've been in, and I'm getting the depressing feeling that the gnomes were right. It isn't here!"

Suddenly Tara stopped in her tracks. "What did you just say, Cal?"

"That the portal isn't here?"

"No, not that. Before that."

Cal looked at her with concern. "All right, what part of this sentence don't you understand? 'I'd like somebody to tell me how to find that blasted portal. This is the twentieth room—'"

"*Yessss!*" she interrupted, barely stifling a shout of glee. "That's it! Because we *do* have someone who can tell us how to find that blasted portal. Someone who can show us the way!"

Under the incredulous and somewhat dubious eyes of her friends and the gnome king, Tara bowed gracefully, put her hand a pocket of her robe, and pulled out the magic map.

"Well, it's about time!" the parchment snapped as Tara unfolded it. "I was beginning to feel positively musty, deep in that pocket. So, where do you want to go this time?"

Tara put on her friendliest manner and crossed her fingers. "Hello, map. I'd like to ask you something, but I don't know if you can do it."

"What you mean, can I do it?" asked the map huffily. "What kind of snippy remark is that? You just tell me where you want to go, and I'll tell you how to get there in less time that it takes to say, 'Here it is.'"

"All right, fine. We're in a palace. Every palace has a Transfer Portal. We'd like to know if you can locate a second one."

"The only portal in this palace is the one on the third floor," answered the map in a tone of disdain.

Tara grabbed her white forelock and chewed on it savagely. *Okay, that wasn't the answer I was hoping for. So, if the second portal isn't in the palace . . .*

"Show us the way to the portal that isn't *in* the palace, but near it."

"Hmpf! What kind of challenge is that?" said the map. "You could've asked for something more complicated. It's here!"

The parchment displayed the palace, the guards patrolling outside, Tara's little group, and a dotted line that led across the garden to a big blue cross—smack in the middle of the ball orchid greenhouse!

Fabrice, who had been holding his breath like the others, put an arm around Tara's shoulders and gave her a resounding kiss on the cheek.

"Bravo!" he exclaimed as she blushed. "You're a genius!"

Then he grinned at Robin, who was looking daggers at him.

Score, 1-1, Fabrice thought.

Like tropical flowers on Earth, ball orchids need warmth and humidity, and they're delicate. They can't handle Tingapore's occasional temperature extremes and the drought that can hit despite the weather wizards' spells, so the prince had a greenhouse built to house his passion. Constant humidity and ideal temperature had produced a riot of colors and shapes. The ball orchids' fleshy petals emerging from the large green-and-yellow root balls that give the plant its name glowed in the shadows. Flowers hung from the ceiling in voluptuous cascades of heavy pink, blue, black, and red clusters. The air was so full of perfume and pollen that the group had trouble breathing.

Like most Omoisian buildings, the greenhouse was vast, and it took them a good hour to completely explore it. But they didn't find Transfer tapestries anywhere.

Fafnir, who like all dwarfs wasn't especially patient except when it came to blacksmithing, began showing signs of annoyance.

"There isn't anything in this lousy greenhouse," she grumbled. "It's hot and damp, and there's nothing here except these stupid flowers dangling everywhere."

Robin, who is still smarting over Fabrice kissing Tara, scanned his surroundings very carefully, using his elf senses to probe the invisible. Suddenly he smiled. The wizard was clever—very clever—but not as clever as an elf, even a half human one.

Robin cleared his throat loudly, attracting his friends' attention.

"I think I found it!" he said, trying to look modest.

Buglul stared at him, full of hope.

"You found the portal?" he asked eagerly.

"Yes. It's all around us."

"What do you mean, all around us?" snapped Cal, who was supposed to be the expert. "What're you talking about?"

"You see these flowers?" asked Robin.

"Yeah," said Fabrice. "What about them?"

"Look at the patterns they make."

"By my ancestors, you're right!" exclaimed Manitou. "I can see unicorns and gnomes, giants and spellbinders!"

Delighted, Sparrow and Tara both kissed Robin on the cheek, which annoyed Fabrice no end. *Rats!* he thought. *Two points for the half-elf.*

It was true. The orchids around them formed the patterns of Transfer Portal tapestries. It was like a giant Arcimboldo, that sixteenth century Earth painter who composed portraits by arranging images of fruits, flowers, and other objects. Here a vine formed a unicorn's head, there a flower represented a spellbinder's body, and the plants as a whole faithfully reproduced the five tapestries.

Just then Sheeba growled and emerged from a bush with something in her mouth.

"The Transfer scepter!" cried Sparrow. "Sheeba, you're the best!"

The panther received their joyful caresses with dignity.

Fafnir set the scepter on its vegetable image, the greenhouse lit up . . . and the group suddenly had a problem on its hands.

"What do I say?" asked the dwarf.

"What you mean, what do you say?" asked Cal with annoyance, still irritated at not having found the portal himself.

"Where do we want to go? This is a Transfer Portal; it can take us wherever there are other portals. So the question is, what destination do I give it?"

"Good grief," muttered Manitou, "I haven't the slightest idea."

"Oh?" said the dwarf. "In that case, let's try this." She shouted: "To the places where the gnomes are being held prisoner!"

Cal snickered. "That'll never wor—"

The blinding light seized them, and they found themselves somewhere else.

Somewhere that seemed strikingly familiar to Fabrice and Tara. On seeing an astonished face, the two shouted:

"Dad?"

"Count Besois-Giron?"

Standing in front of them was the count, holding a watering can in one hand and pruning shears in the other.

"Fabrice? Tara? What in the world are you doing in my rose garden?" he asked. "Are you back from OtherWorld? Where you went without my permission, I might add."

Fabrice, who could feel a huge headache and a huge punishment coming on, suddenly felt awful.

Seeing the count's impressive eyebrows frowning and Fabrice turning to jelly, Manitou intervened.

"We're on a secret mission," he said quickly. "We can't tell you about it, but as soon as it is over, you'll get all the details. In the meantime, we need your help."

Then he waited, trying to look as self-confident as possible, given the fact that he was only two feet high, and a dog. Fortunately, the count had too much respect for high wizards to argue when one of them asked for his help. He bowed to the black Labrador.

"With pleasure, High Wizard Manitou. I'll do anything in my power for you, and I can wait to get the explanation later."

"Thank you, Guardian. I have a question: Does Prince Bandiou visit you from time to time?"

"Yes, he does," said the Guardian with a smile. "A delightful man, who has developed some very effective cutting techniques. He has one of OtherWorld's most beautiful collections of ball orchids, in fact. He often comes to look at my roses, and thanks to him I have achieved results I couldn't have dreamed of."

"I understand. Is he in the habit of visiting any other places when he's here?" asked Manitou casually.

"He's also an ardent fisherman. He often wets a line in the river down by the dock. He finds our fish less aggressive than those on OtherWorld."

The friends exchanged looks. A river? What did a river have to do with anything?

"Very well," said the Lab. "We'll go take a look at those fish too. Goodbye for now, Guardian. Lead the way, Fabrice."

With the count looking on suspiciously, they left the rose garden. Fabrice sighed. "I think I'm going to spend the next century locked in my room!"

"I'll tell your father what happened," said Manitou. "What we're doing is important, and he'll be very proud of you if we succeed."

"Yeah, but his being proud won't keep him from punishing me because I disobeyed him."

"You didn't disobey him," remarked Cal. "He didn't *specifically* forbid you from going to OtherWorld."

This didn't seem to console Fabrice, and they walked on in silence. Barune was quite surprised by the rather monochrome color of earthly vegetation and tried to sample everything. He eventually swallowed a big clump of nettles and got prickles in his tongue, and they had to cast a Healus to fix him up. From then on, he wouldn't touch anything and followed Fabrice so closely he kept stepping on his heels.

Fabrice sighed again. Between his too-strict father and his overly affectionate familiar, the coming months were going to be pretty lively. And he dreaded the prospect of their inevitable meeting.

"Here we are," he said. "There's the dock."

Silhouetted against the blue of the river, a long brown dock extended out over the water. Fabrice and Tara had enjoyed good times there, jumping into the chilly water. Having left sleeping Tingapore and now standing in the hot afternoon sun, they had trouble associating the image of the monstrous wizard with this peaceful landscape.

"You see any gnomes around?" asked Cal sarcastically.

They searched the vicinity with a fine-tooth comb, but found no secret entrances and no hidden dungeons.

A despairing Glul Buglul fell to his knees, blue tears in his eyes. "My sweet Mul, my beautiful love! I'll never see you again!"

Manitou put his head down and started sniffing carefully, walking up and down the dock.

"I smell *sniff* . . . I smell him *sniff, sniff.* . . . I can tell that he came here. Yes, for sure. His scent is strong. But he didn't stay very long."

Robin was scanning the river with his elf vision.

"I wouldn't swear to it, but there seems to be something in the water," he said.

The others gathered around, peering into the depths.

"Yes," agreed Sparrow. "I can see something too."

"I'm the thief here, so I guess I'm elected," said Cal with a sigh. "Too bad; we already have a dwarf and a gnome, we're just missing a mermaid. Good thing I can breathe underwater!"

Tara gaped at him. "What? You can breathe underwater?"

"It's dangerous to use magic in an unknown environment," said Cal loftily. He pulled off his spellbinder robe, revealing a T-shirt and underpants in a matching camouflage pattern. "At best, it warns the potential victim that you're robbing them. At worst, it activates defenses that are often disagreeably deadly. So I try to avoid doing it. And no, don't look at me as if I'm about to grow gills. I just kept the oxygenator King Buglul gave me. I figured it might come in handy."

"I'm going with you," the gnome broke in. "I actually *can* breathe underwater, and I'm not leaving the job of freeing my people to anyone else."

"Oh, great, now he's on a hero kick," grumbled Manitou. "We're off to a bad start."

"By the way," murmured Sparrow to Cal, her hands joined in a pose of total admiration, "speaking of heroism . . ."

"Yes?" he said, puffing out his chest.

"Your camouflage underwear, is that for nighttime attacks on your teddy bears?"

Cal made a face at her, and Tara and Sparrow burst out laughing. Out of male solidarity, Fabrice and Robin kept from laughing, but their eyes shone with amusement just the same.

Cal rolled his eyes. He put the oxygenator on his face and winced at the twinge he felt when the little animal began to feed.

"We're just going on a scouting trip," he explained in a slightly muffled voice. "See you soon."

He jumped into the water, followed by Glul, whose greater density made him sink right away. The two gradually vanished into the depths.

Cal had no trouble swimming. Glancing up, he could see his friends anxiously watching him. He waved and concentrated on going deeper. Luckily the river was shallow there, just a few yards deep.

Glul started waving excitedly. He had spotted a large rectangular outline on the riverbed, a shape much too regular to be natural. Swimming over to it, Cal realized that it was shaped like a door. They had found the portal! He signaled to Glul to go back up, but the gnome refused, preferring to stay on the river bottom. Opening a gigantic mouth to take in oxygen from the water, he seemed completely at ease.

Cal was about to swim up when he felt a slight current press against his mask and push it sideways. Somewhat surprised, he put it back in place, but the current pushed it again, harder this time. Frowning, Cal jammed the oxygenator back in position.

At that, the water became demented. Out of nowhere, seemingly solid tendrils of water attacked, trying to rip his mask off. Buglul was swimming over to help when other tendrils grabbed his throat and began to squeeze. Buglul struggled and Cal screamed with terror in his mask. Something was trying to kill them!

Above them, Tara and the others were scanning the water and quickly guessed something abnormal was going on. The water had become like a living thing and seemed to be attacking the two swimmers.

With no time to cast a spell, Tara cut to the chase.

"Bring my friends back here!" she commanded her power, stretching her hands toward Cal and Buglul.

The spell shot out, but the water merely glittered and absorbed the magic harmlessly. Then Sparrow tried with Robin's help, but was no more successful.

Suddenly, a loud *splash!* was heard. Axe in hand, Fafnir had leaped into the water to go save Cal and Buglul. Unfortunately her steel blade had no effect on the water, which let it slip harmlessly by, the better to attack again.

Despite all their efforts, their friends were drowning!

The way the water was behaving reminded Tara of something, and it suddenly came to her. The last time she'd seen a normally inanimate element come to life was when a fire elemental nearly burned down her grandmother's manor house. *So this one must be . . .*

"By the Elementus you are hereby bidden to let us see those forces hidden!" she screamed.

The water immediately gathered itself into a huge water elemental. A good fifteen feet tall, its body glittered in the sun, crowned with a wavy green thatch of weeds. On either side of the elemental the river stopped flowing, to the great surprise of a bunch of trout who bumped into an invisible barrier.

"Well, I'll be splashed!" thundered the elemental. "A little spellbinder! What can I do for you, cutie?"

"Good morning, Mister Water Elemental," said Tara with a polite bow, unfazed to be chatting with an entity made entirely of H_2O. "Would you mind not drowning my friends, please?"

"Sorry, but I agreed to guard this section of the river in exchange for a nice thunderstorm that fed me and helped me grow," the elemental gurgled with a touch of regret. "Drowning intruders is part of the agreement."

With that, it started to flow back, threatening Cal, Fafnir, and Buglul, who were on the dry river bottom, helplessly gasping for breath.

"Wait!" shouted Tara. "We mean you no harm. Why don't you help us instead of fighting us?"

The elemental heaved a deep sigh. "I'm terribly sorry, but a deal is a deal. If we water, wind, fire, and earth elementals don't keep our word, no one would ever call on us."

"If I can prove that my power is greater than yours, would you let us pass?"

"What can you do against me, little girl, given how much more powerful I am?"

"That's not the issue. Here's the deal I'm suggesting. If I can defeat you, you will let us pass and hold back the river long enough for us to free the wizard's prisoners. If you win, I promise to create a beautiful thunderstorm that will have you overflowing your banks."

"Hey!" protested Fabrice. "This is my father's land! Don't be so quick to make such a high school dance + start of Istanbul = prom + is = promise!"

"Fabrice, shut up!" cried Sparrow and Tara together.

"Prisoners?" The elemental's foam brows knitted in a frown. "He didn't say anything about prisoners. I was just to keep intruders from diving here, and if they persisted, to drown them. That's all."

Buglul, who had gotten his breath back after being choked by the water tendrils, yelled up from the river bottom: "I am Glul Buglul, King of Gnomes, Compensator of the Imperial Court of Omois, and representative of the Truth Tellers. The wizard with whom you made your agreement kidnapped my people. I came here to free them."

The elemental seemed to be thinking this over. Then it shrugged its wavy shoulders.

"All right, I accept the new agreement: my power against the little spellbinder's. But if you try the slightest dirty trick, I'll drown you without pity. Is that clear?"

"As clear as spring water," Tara said.

The elemental smiled, its teeth of solidified water gleaming like so many diamond daggers in its huge mouth. Then it moved aside, so the three victims could climb back up the bank.

Cal glowered at the elemental, spit out a final mouthful of water, and struggled to his feet on the muddy river bottom, leaning on Fafnir. The dwarf grabbed Buglul by the collar and lifted both of them onto the dock.

Everyone cautiously backed away, and the duel began.

The elemental filled its cheeks and squirted a waterspout at Tara. Anticipating this, she conjured a strong wall that easily deflected the jet of water.

The wall disappeared, and Tara now shot a blast of fire. The elemental avoided it by making a hole in its body through which the fire passed harmlessly.

First set. Score 0-0.

The elemental then created a gigantic tsunami wave high enough to overtop any wall. Tara countered by conjuring a huge funnel that sent it flooding back at its creator. The elemental didn't have the time to dodge, but stumbled and fell, hit by its own wave. When it arose, it was clearly displeased.

With a gesture, it raised an enormous hammer that came crashing down on Tara. To her friends' distress, she didn't budge. The hammer splashed apart when it hit the waterproof protection bubble she had improvised.

Tara was now thinking furiously. *My first jet of flame wasn't enough, but if . . .*

Giving her opponent no time to react, she skillfully conjured a gigantic magnifying glass that focused the sun's rays on the elemental. Taken by surprise, it started to evaporate in the burning heat. It countered by splitting its body to avoid the glass's hot beam. But as it did, icy rays shot from Tara's hands, freezing it under the rays of the sun. It was trapped! Concentrated by the magnifying glass, the sunlight was so strong that the elemental started to sublimate, going directly from a solid to a gas without passing through the liquid state. Under those conditions it was unable to launch any kind of attack.

With a gesture, Tara suspended the action of the magnifying glass, but without making it disappear. The sublimation stopped for a moment, long enough for the elemental to melt a little, and its face and mouth to reform.

"Do you admit defeat?" Tara asked harshly.

"Yes, yes, but stop that torture!"

"Do you agree to let us pass?"

"Yes! I swear it by the Great Elemental of the Four Elements. And may my spirit return to the Great Ocean if I'm lying. But please, release me!"

Tara glanced questioningly at Manitou, who nodded. The formula was correct. She made the magnifying glasses disappear and unfroze the elemental. Half of it had evaporated and its attitude was now much more accommodating.

"Ow," it lamented, "I'm back to my original weight! I should never have made that deal!"

Cal grinned. "Good! Let's go open that door on the river bottom."

Fafnir kept a wary eye on the elemental as they clambered down the slippery banks. Prince Bandiou clearly hadn't imagined that anyone would find the portal, much less open it, because Cal located the lock without any trouble. It wasn't a magic seal, and he was able to pick it using his tools like any earthly lock. The door opened with a creak of rusty hinges, and they found themselves in an airlock from which the water was draining. A second door also yielded to Cal's skilled fingers.

The opening led to a row of jail cells in which King Buglul's people were imprisoned. He rushed to them with a joyous shout. But the moment he touched the bars, a brilliant spark crackled, and he was flung against the opposite wall, unconscious.

A pretty blue gnome cried: "Don't touch the bars! They're protected by a magic spell! Glul! Glul! Answer me!"

"He's okay," Robin informed her. "He's just been knocked out and burned a little. I'll take care of him."

"We've got to hurry," said Sparrow anxiously. "The wizard could come back at any moment! Let me try something."

Shape-shifting into the beast, she grasped the bars. She resisted the pain as long as she could, but it became too strong, and she let them go with a howl of suffering. When she opened her paws, they could see they were badly burned. Tara immediately chanted: "By Healus, let the pain be gone, and Sparrow's wound be cured anon!" The burns disappeared.

"It won't do any good to cast a spell, either," explained the pretty gnome. "Bandiou has made the whole prison magic proof."

"All right!" huffed Fafnir. "None of that blasted magic, eh? In that case, make way for a pro!"

Ignoring the walls, she lay down on the ground and promptly melted into the soil without tripping the protection spell. In a few seconds she had vanished.

Fafnir reappeared inside the cell, popping up among the astonished gnomes. Cal stared at her, angry at himself not to have thought of that. Obviously, the spell protecting the ground had to be different. Otherwise the gnomes wouldn't be able to stand on it. The wizard was so confident of his defenses that he'd simply cast a spell to make the stones too hard for the gnomes to eat—but nothing that would stop a dwarf!

"All right, gnomes, let's go!" ordered Fafnir. "Grab hold of me. Whatever you do, don't let go! By touching me, we'll be able to melt into ground together. But if you let go you'll die instantly and your body will be stuck forever. Got that?"

The gnomes understood perfectly. Fearfully clinging to her, they heaved a sigh of relief when they emerged on the other side of the bars.

It took Fafnir only a few minutes to empty the first cell. In half an hour they freed 233 imprisoned gnomes and their children. They crowded around their king, who was still a bit groggy, but thrilled to have found his people. The pretty blue gnome hugged him lovingly, and they figured she must be Mul, his fiancée.

"Let's get out of here!" ordered Manitou. "We'll celebrate when we're beyond that sinister individual's reach."

In single file, they all followed the dog to the open air. The elemental was astonished when it saw them emerging onto the river bottom.

"By my birth waters, where did all these people come from?" it breathed.

"I told you," Buglul explained proudly, "that monstrous wizard imprisoned my people. And he made you their jailer!"

The elemental's foam eyebrows came together fiercely.

"Hey, that's not right at all! And I won't stand for it! Spellbinders aren't supposed to use us to do their dirty work."

The elemental seemed honestly outraged. Buglul asked if it would be willing to bear witness before the empress, and it said it would. An elemental can't be "read" by the Truth Tellers, but it could testify against Prince Bandiou.

After promising to meet them on OtherWorld whenever they called, the elemental returned to the river, which resumed its peaceful flow.

Very quickly, the group headed for the Transfer Portal. Not Bandiou's secret portal, but the official one in the castle tower. As they were passing by the rose garden, they heard a sudden howl of fury.

Standing in front of them was Count Besois-Giron and a small, skinny man, stooped with years. A gold band held his long gray hair, which was carefully gathered in a complicated braid that lay across his right shoulder. He was dressed in an elegant white robe with a repeating pattern of the purple hundred-eyed peacock. It perfectly matched his white and purple sandals.

"By all the demons of Limbo!" the man roared, as his hands lit up with a dangerous purple glow. "How did you scum manage to get free?"

As the astonished count looked on, Glul Buglul proudly stepped forward, heedless of the danger.

"We do not fear you, Prince Bandiou, and will never obey you again! Our friends have enough power to protect us. Face the fury of the powerful Tara'tylanhnem Duncan!"

"The powerful who?" murmured Tara. *What is he saying? He's crazy!*

Fabrice shot a dark look at the gnome, signaling to Tara that he agreed with her.

"You aren't Magister!" she said to the wizard, putting her finger on what had been bothering her since the beginning. "You don't have his stature, or his style."

"And you're the little girl spellbinder who managed to stand up to him," cackled the prince. "You should have seen him! I thought he was going to blow a gasket. I practically died laughing." Bandiou paused. "And speaking of dying, I'm sorry to be doing him this favor, but your time has come." With a lightning-quick gesture he fired a Destructus at them.

Tara and the living stone were ready, raising a shield that brutally deflected the spell, sending it to shatter the rose garden greenhouse.

The count started to complain, but suddenly realized he was in the middle of a spellbinder duel and dove behind the edge of the well.

The prince screamed with fury. While keeping pressure on Tara's shield, he raised one of his hands above his head.

Down in the well a powerful glow began to pulsate. Suddenly something burst out of it, in a kind of black halo: a hideous statue representing a demon that had seen too many science-fiction movies about unnatural mutations. It was a monstrous mix of hyena, octopus, and moray eel. The friends shuddered just to look at it.

"The artifactum!" murmured Buglul. "The repository of his power. We must destroy it!"

"Leave that to me," whispered Fafnir, hefting her axe. "Try to distract him, Tara."

Tara was finding it hard to maintain the shield protecting everyone. She merely nodded, as she drew power from the depths of her being.

Seeing that the girl was struggling, Buglul yelled to his people: "Gnomes, into the earth! Dig your way clear!"

Within seconds, the gnomes had dug themselves out of sight. This relieved Tara of some of the effort she was expending. It greatly displeased Bandiou, who saw his prey escaping.

Suddenly, he tottered. A huge hole had just opened beneath his feet, pulling him off balance. Dozens of gnomes emerged from it and grabbed at his clothes.

Grimacing at the contact with the little creatures, he tried to brush them off, but without stopping his assault on Tara.

Suddenly, she had a brilliant idea of how to unnerve him.

"Vomit!" she yelled to the gnomes. "Vomit dirt onto him, quick!"

The gnomes obeyed. All together, they spat up what they had swallowed in digging. Howling with indignation, the wizard was submerged by a flood of sticky mud and rocks. His attack faltered. Quick as lightning, Tara dissipated her protective shield, and Fafnir rushed forward. She reached the artifactum in a few steps and raised her axe. Bandiou looked over just as Fafnir was bringing her axe down, and his scream mixed with the *thonk!* of the blade hitting the statue.

To the dwarf's great surprise, the artifactum didn't shatter. Instead, Fafnir felt as if she had struck a steel anvil, as the vibrations shook her from head to foot. Then the black light climbed up along her axe and enveloped her hand. In a few moments it covered her completely, and Fafnir disappeared from her anguished friends' sight. Meanwhile, the gnomes were facing bolts flashing from the wizard's fingers and had to let go and seek refuge underground.

Tara seized the opportunity to attack savagely, casting a paralyzing Pocus at Bandiou. But the black light surged forward, and her sparkling spell was stopped and dissipated.

The wizard's mud-spattered face then emerged from the black cloud, looking jubilant. "You and your friends don't measure up against my power. Yield or die!"

Cal answered him with a gesture. It wasn't an especially elegant one, but it meant the same thing on all worlds. The wizard cursed and his black light rolled over the little group like a monstrous cloud.

Tara and her friends battled with all their might. They created a terrible thunderstorm that lashed the cloud, but couldn't dissipate it. They conjured rain and hail that pounded the ground, but the wizard was able to protect himself. Neither fire nor lightning seemed to affect him.

The evil cloud approached and touched them, ripping through their shield with a sharp screech. In spite of her beast strength, Sparrow was the first to succumb, smothered as she tried to protect Sheeba. Cal collapsed in turn, followed by Manitou and Blondin. Fabrice clung to Barune, who was unable to fight. The cloud slammed into Gallant, who crashed in a cloud of feathers. Robin was the last to yield.

Seeing her friends fall one after the other, Tara unleashed all her power. Her eyes turned completely blue and she rose majestically into the air, calling on the living stone to help her. Speechless, Prince Bandiou felt a spasm of fear. This wasn't some girl spellbinder facing him, but power, raw power. And when she spoke, her voice hummed with magic: "Stop this instant, wizard! Our patience is at an end. We won't allow you to hurt our friends."

"Give up! Give up, or I'll kill your allies right now!" he screamed. "I have their hearts in the palm of my hand. Look!"

Like unconscious puppets, Manitou, Robin, Sparrow, Sheeba, Cal, Blondin, Fabrice, and Barune emerged from the cloud, carried by its black tendrils. A black filament was stuck in each of their chests, right over their hearts. The wizard wasn't lying. He literally held the life of Tara's friends in his immaterial hands.

Tara hesitated, and Bandiou used the chance. His cloud struck like a snake, swallowing her. When it retreated, seemingly with regret, Tara lay on the ground, defeated.

A deathly silence permeated the battlefield. It was over.

CHAPTER 10

THE SPIRIT OF THE BLACK ROSES

In the shadowy depths of the black cloud, Fafnir was struggling, desperately trying to hit the artifactum with her axe. The cloud was seeping into her skin, gradually suffocating her. But then something in her body suddenly changed. The Ravager of Souls sensed that another power was trying to invade his host—and wasn't going to stand for it. *I can't let the Ravager possess my body*, she thought at first. *I've got to resist.* But that wasn't right . . . No, she actually was going to help her ravaging enemy . . . So she surrendered to the Ravager. When she did, her skin turned purple and her green eyes black, and she erupted from the black cloud like a missile.

"Bow before my power!" she screamed. "I am the Ravager of Souls! Kneel and worship your god!"

For a moment, Prince Bandiou was speechless. Having just overcome the young spellbinders, he was about to take their lives when the curiously transformed dwarf burst in front of him. Then he recovered.

"What god?" he sneered. "All I see is a dwarf, in an interesting shade of purple!"

"I am the Ravager, the master of the cursed island!" roared Fafnir. "I am the god of destruction, rapine, and death!"

"I beg your pardon, but that is a role I reserve for myself," said the wizard very politely.

"I am alpha and omega, the beginning and the end," thundered Fafnir, ignoring him. "I am terror, I am horror. Only those who worship me will be spared. Kneel, you wretch! Kneel before your god!"

"You're really hung up on that, aren't you?" said the prince, who found all this quite amusing. "I'm sorry, but my knees are a little stiff. I've forgotten how to kneel. Maybe you could show me how."

He pointed at the dwarf and the black cloud obediently settled on Fafnir's broad shoulders. She suddenly felt as if hundreds of pounds had been loaded on her back, forcing her down. Enraged, she resisted. The prince frowned and doubled the weight. Drops of sweat were now coursing down her face, but she continued to struggle. Suddenly the Ravager burst out of her body in a red mist. It confronted the black cloud, and the two powers clashed in an apocalyptic collision.

Now free, Fafnir immediately rushed at the prince and punched him in the face. Unprepared for a physical attack, Bandiou was caught completely by surprise. The punch snapped his head back. He slammed against the edge of the well and toppled in, screaming with rage. The well wasn't very deep, and Bandiou had no time to cast a spell to break his fall.

Also, he had dried the well, the better to store his artifactum—a mistake that would cost him dearly.

No splash was heard, just an awful *crack!*

The black cloud dissipated instantly, sweeping back into the artifactum, which also fell into the well.

Now greatly weakened, the red mist flowed back toward Fafnir. Despite her efforts to keep clear, it managed to touch her again. But the mist had lost its power. Struggling mightily, Fafnir was able to reject the attempt at possession. Gradually her skin regained its deep tan, and her eyes once again shone emerald green. She grunted with satisfaction.

Then, without a glance at her friends, she drew a rope from her jerkin and lowered herself down the well.

As Tara was coming to, she first heard a terrible crack, followed by a scream of rage. She felt bone-weary and didn't quite know where she was. Then it all came back to her: the prince, the cloud, the attack. Around her, Manitou, Gallant, Sparrow, Sheeba, Cal, Blondin, Fabrice, Barune, and Robin were all regaining consciousness too.

Fafnir climbed out of the well holding two things: the artifactum, now broken and powerless, and the equally broken body of the empress's uncle.

"Is . . . is he dead?" asked Sparrow.

"Dead as a doornail," answered the dwarf with satisfaction.

"And were you the one who—?" Cal made the gesture of drawing his hand across his throat.

"Nope, it wasn't me. He fell into the well and broke his neck. No more wicked wizard. Just good for the scrap heap!"

"Would someone kindly tell me what happened?" asked Manitou, who was having trouble gathering his wits.

"The Ravager picked a great time to manifest himself," Fafnir explained succinctly. "He and the prince fought over who would conquer the universe, they had a little spat, I took advantage of it, and that's all she wrote."

"You mean the Ravager *possessed* you?" exclaimed Tara. "And you're all right?"

"I managed to control him," answered the dwarf with a bright smile. "He was weakened from fighting the artifactum. So he's lying low for now. But that's enough talk. What we do now?"

"There's been an accident," said Count Besois-Giron, stepping from behind the well and dusting off his pants. "An accident that resulted in an unfortunate death. It also wrecked my greenhouse and my roses."

He sounded more upset about his rosebushes than about the dead prince.

"A storm came up unexpectedly while Prince Bandiou was fishing," the count declared firmly. "He slipped off the dock, fell on a boat, and broke his neck. That's the story I'll tell the empress and the rest of OtherWorld. And to think I welcomed that piece of garbage as a friend!"

The count looked bitterly at the prince's corpse, and Tara felt he was itching to kick it in the ribs. Tara rolled her eyes, thinking, *Adult politics are just too complicated!*

She cupped her hands and shouted: "King Glul Buglul!"

His small blue head popped out of the ground.

"Yes?"

"Everything's all right, you can come out now. Fafnir did a number on Prince Bandiou, so you have nothing to fear anymore."

The gnomes emerged shouting with joy and did a frenetic dance around the wizard's body.

With blue tears in his eyes, the king bowed to Tara's group. "My people owe you a great debt. We will give you whatever you desire. Just ask, and we will obey."

"Obeying that monster Bandiou didn't work out very well for you," remarked Manitou severely. "So just cure Cal, give us *The Forbidden Book*, and return the magic objects you stole. Then we'll be even."

"And if you feel like tossing in a few jewels, that would be perfect!" said the smiling thief.

"Cal!" shouted Tara and Sparrow.

"Hey, what? I deserve them, don't I?"

They left the count to handle any remaining problems—including facing an empress who certainly wouldn't be pleased that someone had killed her favorite uncle—and raced upstairs to the Transfer Portal before he started asking too many questions. They activated the scepter, and in a few seconds they were back in Smallcountry.

News of the rescue had preceded them, and an honor guard escorted them to the Throne Room. The hall's floor was strewn with luminous confetti, the beams were laden with flowers and hanging lamps, and fairies and imps scampered around celebrating their friends, the gnomes.

When she saw that the two arachnes were still carefully guarding *The Forbidden Book*, Tara heaved a sigh of relief.

"It's not that I don't like worms," said Cal nervously, "but it would be nice if I could take the antidote right now."

Sitting on his pink metal throne, the king smiled. "Of course. I will have it brought immediately."

He gestured to one of the arachnes. The giant arachnid squeezed a glittering crystal vial up out of its gizzard and handed it to the king.

"Here you are," he said. "Drink it, and the t'sil eggs will be immediately destroyed."

Cal reached out to take the vial. But just then Barune, who'd been frightened by a huge arachne, tripped on his trunk and bumped into Fabrice, who stumbled into Cal. The little thief dropped the vial, which shattered against the base of the throne, its precious contents soaking into the thick grass.

King Buglul instantly went from blue to an unusual color somewhere between white and green.

"By my ancestors," he muttered, "the vial is broken!"

"No big deal," said Cal with a smile. "Just give me another one."

"You don't understand. That is the only one we had!"

Now it was Cal's turn to turn pale. Very quickly he recited: "By Repairus, take these shattered bits and assemble them so each one fits."

The crystal vial reformed and hovered obediently in front of them, but it was empty! The liquid had soaked into the grassy floor, and they had no way to retrieve it.

Buglul stared at Cal in dismay. "You are doomed. You only have a few more hours to live. There is no more t'sil antidote."

Though emotions were running high, Manitou was thinking hard.

"How long ago did you infect Cal?" he asked.

"Three days and twelve hours. Which means the t'sil will become active in eight hours. And he absolutely must take the antidote two hours beforehand, otherwise it won't do any good. So, he only has six hours left."

Tara could feel herself starting to panic.

"Where can we find it?" she cried. "You must have bought that critter and the antidote from someone. Where is he?"

"It was a Salterian merchant," said Buglul quickly, his voice thick with tension. "We ordered a shipment of birds from him, and he threw in the t'sil as a bonus. The only way to find him is to go to Sala, the capital of Salterens. Our ambassador there, Tul Tultul, will help you. I will immediately dispatch a messenger to alert him."

"Don't bother," said Manitou firmly. "You're coming with us. We don't know what this merchant looks like. And since your people do business with the Salterians, you'll be our safe-conduct in case they get any weird ideas, like turning us into slaves."

"But—" began the king.

"No buts!" snapped Sparrow angrily. "You've manipulated us, lied to us, and infected our friend, who might die because of your scheming! You don't have any choice in the matter."

The king's pretty fiancée Mul Mulmul had been watching the exchange and was floored to see these strangers talking to her future royal husband this way. Suddenly, she frowned.

"Just a second, Glul," she said in her melodious voice. "What did you do to this boy that he should be in danger of dying? I thought you engaged him to help free us. You have been talking about t'sil worms and an antidote. Why?"

The gnome king suddenly looked very ill at ease.

"You were in danger, darling," he said very quickly. "Helping you escape called for somewhat expeditious methods. I will explain everything later."

It didn't work. Mul Mulmul was no fool, and she quickly understood what steps her future husband had taken to force Cal to free them. When she let Buglul know what she thought of that, the gloves came off.

The discussion quickly rose to a distinctly higher decibel level.

"Her voice is very . . . " commented Manitou, who wasn't able to put his paws over his ears.

"Yes, very . . ." agreed Robin, who was following the discussion with rapt attention. "Now *there's* an expression I didn't know!"

Buglul soon realized that it was wiser not to argue. His "But I's" very quickly became, "I am sorry, I am sorry, I am sorry." Which eventually did the trick, but only after he had sworn to the furious little gnome that he would personally do his utmost to cure the boy.

With a sigh of resignation, King Buglul stepped down from his throne and headed to the Transfer Portal Room. Tara and her friends followed him in total silence. There was no chuckling, no comments. Even Fafnir behaved herself.

Though he was scared to death, Cal finally cracked. "So, you're planning to marry that young gnome?"

The king looked at him wearily. "Yes, of course. We are engaged."

"I see . . . If I were you, I'd seriously consider the 'running away' option."

"I have loved her ever since I was old enough to tell the difference between boys and girls," Buglul said with a helpless shrug. "And she is right. I should have found another way. What I did was perfectly contemptible. I behaved like our enemy. For me, the end justified the means. I am sorry."

"Yeah, we got that," remarked Manitou sarcastically. "I think you told her at least a thousand times in the Throne Room. All right, can we get a move on here? You have a girlfriend to get back to, and Cal is carrying some undesirables around that we'd like to help him get rid of."

As they walked, Tara was thinking. She had the annoying feeling that she was missing something. Something that Cal had told them. Something important. *Rats! I just can't think of it!*

Also, she was feeling a bit overwhelmed. Fafnir, Cal, the mysterious killer who was trying to get rid of her, Magister, the Hunter . . . too many events and too much pressure were weighing on her. She had the unpleasant feeling of somehow being manipulated. Someone was burying her under these problems, to keep her from having time to think. Her brain was working at top speed, but it came up with solutions too late. She sighed, feeling a major headache coming on.

Which didn't improve when they reached Salterens.

The gnome embassy was cooled by an air-conditioning spell, but outside, the city felt like an oven on its self-clean setting.

The sun beat down like a hammer on a glittering anvil. The buildings were all a blinding white, and the spellbinders and their familiars quickly activated the ocular protection spell provided by the gnomes at the embassy. It turned their eyes completely black and filtered the light. That way, they could begin their search without going half blind.

The Salterians were large, two-legged felines with flowing golden manes. Their amber eyes glowed under their hoods, and they seem to view each passerby as a potential prey. Elaborate white camelin robes protected them from the sun. Spellbinders were shaded by discs floating overhead. Nonspells used parasols.

Tara and her friends rode giant slugs like the one that attacked her in Lancovit. Their thick hides made an unpleasant screeching as they slid over the sand-strewn cobbled streets.

Tul Tultul told them where the Salterian merchant's shop was located, but they also tried their luck in other stores along the way. The feline merchants treated them suspiciously when they explained they were looking for the antidote to a t'sil infestation. In Salterens, the only people interested in getting rid of t'sil worms were runaway salt mine slaves.

To overcome their reluctance, Glul Buglul displayed his crown, after which the merchants became much more cooperative.

The problem was, they didn't have any antidote. Not a shadow of a drop.

After more than two hours of vainly walking and searching, they finally reached the store of the merchant that the gnome had told them about. And gasped in dismay.

The place was closed.

A sign—which Manitou was able to make out because he knew some Salterian—read: "I am traveling in the deep desert. I will return in three days. For information or complaints, see the central administration." Deeply concerned, the dog shook his head. They turned around and headed for Sala's central administration, which was housed in a large white building they'd passed a few minutes earlier.

Like all bureaucracy headquarters, it was three times as big as the palace. The Salterians were ruled not by a king, but by a tribal chief called the Great Cacha. His vizier Iznogud greeted the friends suspiciously.

Unlike his fellow Salterians, who looked like a sleek mix of lion and leopard, Iznogud was a fat slob whose tangled mane and stained clothes testified to a distinct aversion to cleanliness. He was accompanied by his secretary, Satir, who had a profile like a knife.

A sharp one.

Ambition burned in Satir's amber eyes, and the way he watched Iznogud's every move suggested that the vizier would do well to avoid dark hallways and poorly lit staircases.

"Welcome, King Buglul," said Iznogud, sprawled in an armchair. "To what do we owe the honor of your presence in our beautiful capital?"

Satir remained standing behind him, watching the visitors closely.

"I want to buy some t'sil antidote from you," answered the gnome king. "This young spellbinder has been infected and the worms will become active in less than four hours. He has done Smallcountry invaluable service, and I owe it to him to save his life."

The fat Salterian scratched his head with a claw and yawned, revealing impressive fangs.

"I'd be delighted to sell you the antidote," he said amicably. "Problem is, I don't know where to find any. Infecting slaves with t'sil is going out of fashion. Too expensive. Even with the antidote, half the time the worms develop anyway, and we lose a good worker needlessly."

Cal glared at the gnome king, who was writhing in embarrassment.

"We've bought much more efficient anti-escape spells," continued the Salterian. "So we don't need to stock the antidote anymore. Look around town; one of our merchants must have some left over. Otherwise you'll have to go into the deep desert to get some. But even with sand slugs, it would take you a day and a half. I'm very sorry. Your friend's going to die."

Tara didn't much like the Salterians to begin with. Slavery was a monstrous practice, and OtherWorld's inhabitants didn't seem especially anxious to stop it. So the Salterian's casual condemnation of Cal made her act rashly.

"Making slaves of people is bad enough," she spat. "Infecting them with deadly worms to make sure they don't escape is even more monstrous. What kind of people are you?"

Satir's beautiful amber eyes narrowed, and he hissed like an angry tomcat.

"Insulting the vizier could cost you dearly, young lady," he snarled. "We aren't in the habit of discussing with humans what we can and can't do. One more word, and you'll wind up in our mines, where you can feed your fine speeches to the members of your chain gang."

Tara opened her mouth, but Manitou spoke first, which caught the two cats by surprise.

"I am High Wizard Manitou Duncan of Lancovit," he declared, "and I officially demand the unrestricted assistance due to high wizards. Under the Treaty of 5042 signed among the peoples of OtherWorld, you are obligated to help us in our search."

"Tsk, tsk, tsk!" exclaimed a surprised Satir. "A talking dog—amazing! Who claims to be a high wizard, which I don't believe for a second."

Iznogud was studying Cal when he abruptly adopted his hunting vision. The boy's neck snapped into sharp focus; everything was a blur. What he saw startled him. *Hmm, just as I thought.*

"Come here, young spellbinder," he ordered, silencing Satir.

Cal approached, uncomfortable at being so close to the big cat's fangs. Iznogud seized him with his large paw and shoved his mass of black hair away from his neck.

"I have good news and bad news," he growled. "Which would you like first?"

"I hate this," said Manitou with a sigh. "But go ahead and give us the good news first."

Iznogud smiled, revealing an impressive, if slightly yellowed, set of teeth.

"Your friend was bitten by a golden t'sil," he explained. "When it paralyzed him, its stinger made this small golden mark in his flesh."

With a claw, he pointed to a tiny spot on Cal's neck.

"So, the good news is that no other t'sil will bite your friend. That mark protects him. The bad news is that golden t'sil are the most virulent of the worms. There's no antidote against them!"

"But the merchant said . . ." stammered the blue gnome, his heart in his mouth.

"What the merchant told you was nonsense. Either because he didn't know, or he didn't care. Golden t'sil are *never* used on slaves. We only use them in cases of vengeance, or when we're executing someone and want to make sure they don't survive. So I'm very sorry, but there's nothing we can do for you.

"Oh, one more thing. Golden t'sil reproduce faster than other parasite worms. So you probably don't have more than a few minutes to live, young man. And if you'd kindly go die somewhere else, I'd appreciate it. This place is enough of a mess as it is."

Before they could protest, he signaled the guards to escort them out.

Tara was so furious she felt like blowing up the place—a project the living stone approved enthusiastically.

After considering the idea for a few seconds and seeing her hands start to glow from the rush of magic, Tara decided to calm down before she lost all control of her power.

And destroyed the building.

Not to mention the city and part of the continent.

Sparrow had tears in her eyes, and she wasn't alone. "Oh, Cal, what are we going to do?"

Cal didn't answer. He was pale and his eyes were empty.

"We're gonna turn this town upside down and find the antidote!" shouted Fafnir. She'd kept quiet during the exchange, and it had taken all her restraint not to sink her axe into the arrogant Salterian's head.

"Fafnir's right," said Fabrice, who'd been feeling terribly guilty since the incident with Barune. "We'll split up into groups and use our crystal balls to communicate. That way we can cover more ground."

Though she was weeping, Tara again had the momentary thought that she was overlooking something.

Cal pulled himself together and said, "No, we aren't. I want to go back to Lancovit. I want to be with my mother and father when I die."

His voice broke on the last word, and Tara thought her own heart would break. Robin put an affectionate arm around her.

"But you—" Fabrice protested.

"Fabrice, I only have a few minutes to live," said Cal with dignity. "And stop feeling bad. You and Barune aren't to blame. This is my fate, that's all. Let's go now. I don't have much time left."

With heavy hearts, they followed him out. The walk to the embassy cheated them of time they no longer had. They rematerialized directly in the Living Castle. Cal appeared in his real identity, having decided there was no point in disguising himself. Shyblossomonthebanko-faclearstream, the tall one-eyed steward, sensed that something terrible was happening and gestured to them to step out of the Transfer Circle.

The guards raised their spears. Seeing the group's look of desperation led them not to ask any questions. Cal radiated so much maturity and sober dignity that they instinctively saluted.

"We need to see Master Chem," said Manitou quickly. "Is he here?"

"Yes, Master Duncan," answered the steward. "He's in his office, recovering from his concussion. The shaman advised him not to use any portals for the time being."

"Shoot," murmured the dog. "I'd forgotten that Tara knocked him out. Well, let's go. We don't have a second to lose."

"Can you also alert my parents?" asked Cal. "Tell them that I've been hurt and don't have long to live. I want them here so they can say goodbye to me."

The Cyclops was very surprised, because the young thief looked fit as a fiddle. But he agreed without arguing.

As they hesitated at the entrance to Master Chem's office-cave, the little stone dragon guard challenged them.

"Stop right there!" he roared. "Identify yourselves, or get lost!"

"Wow! He doesn't seem in a very good mood," whispered Fabrice.

"Now, now, is that any way to greet visitors?" the stone unicorn, Chem's other office guard, said kindly. "Just because thieves broke into the office is no reason for you to be rude to everybody."

The little dragon sniffed contemptuously without answering. They gave him their identities and he crossed through the wall to alert Master Chem.

The roar that could be heard through said wall made them tremble. "By my pile of gold! Get those wretches in here right away!"

The stone dragon came back looking very pleased with himself.

"You may go in," he announced. "I think my master is quite eager to see you."

Cal was so wrapped up in his troubles that he was the only one among them who didn't dread the confrontation. The others were feeling shaky around the knees and had a heart rate much too high for comfort.

When the stone wall disappeared they could see the dragon stretched out on a big pile of gold and jewels. From the flames he was spouting, he seemed furious.

Chem opened his great jaws to bellow at them, but Cal was faster.

"I've been bitten by a golden t'sil," he said. "If you don't have the antidote or a cure for me in the next few minutes, I'm going to . . . I'm going to die."

His voice broke and he staggered.

The astonished dragon closed his jaws with a loud snap. Then he got up, cast a spell, and shape-shifted back into old Master Chem.

"Show me," he ordered, all thought of punishment forgotten.

Cal lifted his hair to show the t'sil's mark. Chem quizzed him about the circumstances of the infection and the time that had passed since then. They saw the old wizard go pale when he realized how many days Cal had been carrying the t'sil eggs.

"We have to isolate you," he said quickly. "As soon as the t'sil emerge from your body, they'll jump onto the nearest thing that moves. I'm very sorry, but we don't have any choice."

Before Cal could protest he cast a spell, enveloping the boy in a plastic bubble that let air, light, and sound through, but not matter.

"Chem!" protested Manitou. "Isn't there anything we can do?"

The dragon turned on him furiously.

"If you hadn't decided to go off to save the world all by yourselves, then yes, I could've saved him!" he thundered, as the Lab backed away. "But with *The Forbidden Book* stolen, I don't have the spell I need to destroy the t'sil without killing Cal!"

"*The Forbidden Book?*" cried Tara. "We have it! It's in Small-country!"

The dragon wasted no time on questions.

"So get a move on!" he roared. "Why are you still here? Bring me that book right away!"

Tara grabbed the gnome king by the collar and rushed out of the office so fast she almost hit the wall. The castle, which didn't like people running in its hallways because it tickled, quivered with indignation, but Tara raced along, ignoring Buglul's demand to be put down. Gallant flew behind her at top speed.

She was gasping when she reached the Transfer Portal Room, where a majestic matron with two giggling, fidgety babies was waiting for the portal to be available. Tara didn't mess around. Ignoring the matron and the Cyclops's outraged cries she shoved them aside, took their place in the middle of the room, and screamed, "Smallcountry!"

The moment she reached the land of the blue gnomes, she restored Gallant to his normal size and leaped on his back. They reached the Throne Room in minutes. Before Tara could toss him off, the gnome king slipped down from the pegasus and ordered his arachnes to give him *The Forbidden Book*. Then he jumped onto Gallant's back. The magnificent stallion beat all speed records racing back to the portal. Once at the Living Castle they flew directly from the Portal Room to Chem's office.

When they entered, they were greeted by a terrible scene.

Under his father, mother, the dragon, and his friends' horrified eyes, Cal was rolling on the ground, tortured by the itching of the worms that were eating him alive.

CHAPTER 11

THE LIMBO JUDGE

During the transfer from Smallcountry, *The Forbidden Book* almost seemed to struggle in Tara's grasp. She quickly handed it to Master Chem, praying that they weren't too late. Touching the book as little as possible, the old wizard set it on his desk and started turning pages at top speed.

Suddenly Manitou's voice broke through Cal's groaning. "There's something I don't understand. They should have come out long ago."

Cal's mother and father, eyes wide and faces wet with tears, stared at him in dismay.

"I mean the t'sil worms," he explained. "It usually takes them just a few seconds to emerge from their host's body. And here . . . nothing!"

"Of course!" Tara's yell made them all jump. "They aren't going to come out! That's the thing I wasn't able to remember!"

She turned feverishly to the gnome king.

"That merchant of yours—he told you that t'sil never infect dead bodies, right?"

Buglul blinked in surprise, then answered: "Er, that is right. If the heart of the infected organism is not beating, the eggs die immediately for lack of oxygen."

"And that's exactly what happened to us!" she exulted. "We *died!* Grandpa, after the Inanimus and the Destructus hit us, you said it took Master Chem four minutes to get back to his office and that he was just barely able to save us, right?"

"Right," said Manitou, who was beginning to understand. "But your hearts . . . your hearts hadn't been beating since Robin and Fafnir carried you out of the Book Room."

"*That* was the thing that was always in the back of my mind!" said Tara. "The eggs couldn't survive. The itching Cal is feeling now is probably caused by his body getting rid of them."

"Good grief, couldn't you have thought of this sooner?" cried Fabrice, who had to sit down because his legs were shaking so hard. "My own heart is going to fail if I get another scare like that."

Robin, Sparrow, and Fafnir burst out laughing, soon followed by everyone else. They had come so close to disaster that the laughter had a slightly hysterical edge, and they pounded each other on the back in congratulations. The friendly tap that Fafnir gave Fabrice practically knocked his lungs out. After that, he kept a safe distance from her for the rest of the celebration.

Cal, who was still being driven crazy by the itching, finally opened an eye. He felt tense and a bit annoyed.

"Could I have a little peace and quiet so I can die?" he grumbled. "What's all the racket about?"

"I have good news and bad news," said Robin with a smile, seizing the occasion.

"Oh no, not again!"

"The good news is that you're not going to die," continued the jubilant half-elf. "The bad news is that we're going to have to continue putting up with you."

At that, Cal opened his other eye. "I'm not going to die?"

"No, you already did that."

Catching Cal by surprise wasn't easy, but this time it was a complete success. He opened his mouth, closed it again, and growled: "Well, if this is heaven, I'm going to have a little chat with the owner. Because you don't look at all like an angel."

He suddenly caught on. "Hey, wait a minute! It's true, I already died once! So the eggs—"

He wasn't able to continue. Master Chem had canceled the isolation bubble and his mother and father were burying him with hugs. They were shouting, "Good Lord, Cal, don't you *ever* do something like this again!" and, "I was so frightened, Cal! Never, ever, again—okay?" When his tousled head eventually emerged, he looked a little embarrassed.

Wiping away her tears of joy, Cal's mother spoke: "I don't understand everything about your adventures, but you're all right, and that's the main thing. What's supposed to happen now?"

"Er, we can't tell you everything, Mom; it's a little complicated," said Cal, feeling a little awkward. "But when it's all done I promise you'll get the whole story."

Cal's mother said nothing, but from the way she looked at him, Tara got the idea that the story better be worthwhile. She hadn't much liked the t'sil trick, but her sharp political instincts told her that the friends needed to talk without anyone else around. When she was sure that everything really was fine, she made Cal promise to stop by later and then went home with her husband.

As soon as they left, Fafnir told Master Chem about her partial possession by the Ravager. He had heard something about the story, but he hadn't been part of the group that imprisoned the Ravager on the Island of Black Roses five thousand years earlier, so it was hard for him to gauge the danger. He offered to research the best way to help Fafnir.

"Very well," he said. "Now that I'm up to date on your initiatives, I'm going to put the book back in place and—"

"No!" cried Tara in alarm. "As Cal explained, we absolutely must consult the Judge of Souls in the demonic world. And we need *The Forbidden Book* to gain access to Limbo."

"Don't you think you've done enough harebrained things already?"

"Oh, cut it out, Chem!" snapped Manitou. "The only reason you're complaining is that you would've liked to be with us. We all know that you dragons fear boredom more than anything. So don't give me your offended patriarch nonsense. Tara's right. Cal can't remain a fugitive all his life. We have to prove he's innocent. And the only way to do that is to go to Limbo."

His argument torpedoed, the dragon shrugged.

"Give me a day or so to think about it," he said. "The bump on my head still hurts, and I need to weigh the pros and cons of the idea."

Hearing Chem mention that unfortunate incident made Tara grimace, but she didn't comment. At least he hadn't said no; he said he would think about it.

With a gesture to her friends, they quietly left the office.

"Whew, I'm exhausted!" said Sparrow. "Now that we've saved the world, and Cal's hide while we were at it, could we get a little sleep?"

The Living Castle obligingly added two rooms to Tara's suite. She, Fafnir, and Sparrow decided to sleep in one of them, so it provided two extra beds. Cal, Robin, and Fabrice chose a room with three beds. Manitou settled for the deep pile carpet.

For his part, Glul Buglul first checked to made sure that the young spellbinders didn't require his particular skills. (They turned down his idea of stealing *The Forbidden Book* from Master Chem, in case the wizard's answer was no.) He then explained that his kingdom needed him and left, after assuring them of his support for any enterprise that required digging or tunneling.

After a big dinner, the young friends gathered in the suite's living room before going to bed.

Robin had remembered their strange nighttime meeting with the bloody vampyr and went to see his father, the head of Lancovit's secret services. He now returned with incredible news.

"They've imprisoned Master Dragosh!" Robin said.

"No!" cried Fabrice. "You're kidding!"

"Nope. Dragosh was the only vampyr in Travia when the man we saw in the alley was killed. He's refused to open his mind to the Truth Tellers to establish his innocence, so he's been locked up. Nuts, isn't it?"

Manitou found this very surprising.

"No vampyr would ever drink human blood," he said. "It makes them crazy and cuts their life expectancy in half. They can't ever go out in sunlight without being burned to a crisp. Which means it would be easy to determine if Dragosh is guilty: just expose him to sunlight. If he burns, there won't be any doubt."

"That's the strangest part," said Robin. "He refuses to expose himself. He says that while he's in prison he can't hurt anybody, so he doesn't want to be released."

Tara just shook her head. She was so tired she couldn't think straight. Cal, who kept furiously scratching himself, was looking just as tired.

"Listen, I don't know about you, but I'm beat," Tara said. "We can talk about all this when I've slept. Okay?"

Nobody argued, and within a few minutes, Fafnir's and Sparrow's snores were punctuating a dreamless sleep.

When Tara awoke many hours later, she spent a few moments fighting the canopy bed for her sheets, which it kept trying to tuck in. She needed to shake up her little gray cells, and especially to try to understand what was going on with her. Ever since Cal had been jailed, she'd had the distinct impression that she was being controlled somehow. An invisible puppet master was pulling the strings, and instead of acting, all she was doing was reacting. After half an hour of intense cogitation, Tara had untangled some of the threads. She didn't reach a final conclusion, but she was beginning to discern a pattern. And she didn't like what she saw.

Eventually, she sighed and got out of bed. In the bathroom she waved at the mermaid singing on the rock in her vast bathtub. The hairbrush flew over to untangle her hair, then the shower heads hovered around spraying her while the soap and the sponge energetically scrubbed her. The accessories' agitation had the effect of soothing her, and Tara relaxed. She slipped into the warm water, listening to the mermaid's melancholy song.

Well, no point worrying about all this for the time being. Their first goal was to establish Cal innocence in the empress and the victim's parents' eyes. Then they had to rid Fafnir of her inconvenient host. Finally, Tara could look for—no, hunt down—whoever was trying to kill her and make him stop ruining her life.

One thing Tara enjoyed in this world was that being a teenager didn't mean being powerless. Against her enemy, Tara had a lot of power, though she always had to examine her conscience before using it, because of the blood oath. She'd never wanted to risk hurting her grandmother.

While Tara was soaking and pondering, Master Chem was also going over recent events in his office. *What a pleasure this all is,* he thought.

Dragons *love* unexpected developments. Once they had dealt with the demons' terrible threat to the universe, they'd been bored stiff. The adrenaline rush of danger, the anguish of defeat, the powerful thrill of victory—they missed all that.

The dragons had compensated by becoming deeply involved in the lives of OtherWorld's peoples. Politics was fascinating; something was always happening. For the dragons, who risked dying of boredom, any kind of action was necessary. Even wars, deadly as they are, were welcome. But that was something no one else could ever know. If the day came when the human and nonhuman peoples realized they were being manipulated, the dragons—for all their power—wouldn't be able to stand up to their anger.

Which was why the dragon conclave refused to participate in a special training exercise to increase one small group of spellbinders' powers. They feared, correctly, that their students might become more powerful than they were.

Obviously, Chem had disobeyed them.

And just as obviously, events had blown up in his face. Those spell-binders became the monstrous Bloodgraves, forged a pact with the demons, and tried to conquer OtherWorld and the rest of the universe.

Tara was Chem's favorite human. The little spellbinder had no idea what plans he had in store for her. She was probably the one he had been waiting centuries to find.

She *had to* like him. Chem had to become like the father she never had. He would do everything that was required for that. Once again he chuckled, rubbing his claws with joy. The years ahead would be completely fascinating!

By the time Tara and her friends entered Chem's office, they had rehearsed all the arguments they had to convince him. But that turned out to be completely unnecessary.

The dragon master greeted them with startling cheerfulness. "Good morning, good morning! Ready to take a little trip to Limbo?"

This left them flat-footed with astonishment, which made the big saurian chuckle. "What's the matter, cat got your tongue? No cries of enthusiasm? No jumps for joy? No, 'Thank you, thank you, oh wise High Wizard, for letting us risk our lives in those disgusting realms'? I'm very disappointed."

"Does this . . . does this mean you agree?" stammered Tara, who was having trouble believing her ears.

"Not only do I agree, but I'm coming with you!"

Manitou looked at him suspiciously. "You didn't seem especially convinced yesterday. What made you change your mind?"

"Ah, you're as stubborn as a mule. If I said no, you would just pester me to death. Besides, without me along the demons would tear you to pieces. That's messy, and it has consequences. So, I'd rather be there to protect you. Otherwise, you wouldn't stand a chance."

"Thanks," said Cal, who'd been apprehensive about the trip. "Your help will be very valuable."

"You can thank me when we get back. So, what exactly was your plan?"

"We have to appear before the statue of the Limbo Judge," said Sparrow. "He'll summon the dead boy's manes. We'll explain that Cal wasn't the one who caused his death. The Judge will confirm this, and we'll record his judgment with a taludi. With any luck, the boy will finger the *real* culprit this time. The Demon King played a dirty trick on Tara by infecting her with demonic magic on our last visit, so we thought we would transform ourselves so the demons wouldn't recognize us."

"Hmm, not bad," rumbled Chem. "Since I'm more powerful than you, I'll take charge of your transformation. And I have some experience with demons. I know what they like and what they don't. Manitou, you can keep your dog shape. You weren't with us on our last visit, so the demons don't know you. But the rest of you will have to leave your familiars behind."

Barune trumpeted indignantly, and the old dragon frowned.

"That mammoth isn't going to do anything stupid in my office while I'm away, will he?" he asked, sounding anxious.

"I'll give him some red bananas and let him out in the park," said Fabrice. "He'll be good. At least I hope so."

Robin looked bothered. "I don't suppose I can bring my bow, can I?"

"No, any more than Fafnir can bring her axe. Your weapons are too recognizable."

"The bow's not going to like that."

"See, that's the problem with magical weapons," said Fafnir. "When I put my axe down someplace, it stays there. I bet you'll have to negotiate with your little stick. It's ridiculous!"

The half-elf nodded his white head with its odd black streaks, but didn't answer. The dwarf was right, unfortunately. Robin could already hear the bow's outraged mental protests.

"I don't know how long we're going to be away," said the dragon. "In fact, I hope it's as short a time as possible. All right, take off your clothes."

"I beg your pardon?" asked Sparrow, suddenly blushing.

"I have to transform your bodies, and spellbinder robes aren't very common in Limbo," Chem patiently explained. "You'll have to change their color and pattern so they fit your new shapes. So just keep your underwear on while I transform you."

Fafnir looked at him strangely. "What underwear? I just have my shirt and my pants. I've never understood why you need to cover yourself with so many layers of clothes, anyway."

"Oh, all right," said the embarrassed dragon. "I'll make do."

The transformation experience wasn't very pleasant. When spellbinders want to change their appearance, they usually cast a light spell that doesn't involve major morphological modifications. In this case, the dragon had to add lots of extra fangs, eyes, legs, and tentacles. The results were pretty striking.

Tara shrank to an irregular ball dotted with dark purple blotches and covered with tentacles. When she put her robe on, it first strained to adapt to the new shape and then, to her great surprise, turned into a mustard yellow jacket and Bermuda shorts. Robin, whose head looked like a big asparagus, was now black and white all over and had acquired an extra mouth and a half-dozen legs. Knowing how touchy Fafnir could be, Chem had been cautious with her. He merely turned her skin a handsome gray, gave her a long tail with a stinger, and sprinkled her head with hissing snakes. Overall, it was quite exotic. (The dwarf complained loudly, though, when the tail burst through her fancy red leather pants.)

Fabrice was given a set of sharp chitinous insect arms, and eight spider legs. Cal grew to the size of a powerful demon with leathery skin and the ears and trunk of an elephant, which Barune found very unsettling. Sparrow looked like a half-peeled zucchini married to a snail. Manitou was allowed to keep his dog body, but the dragon added fifty eyes to it. Chem himself grew two extra heads, shrank to a quarter of his size, and traded his scaly skin for that of a slimy slug.

It was a total success.

They couldn't carry weapons to Demonic Limbo, but the dragon outfitted them with enough sharp claws and fangs to cut to ribbons anyone who bothered them. Tiny ribbons.

The first trouble came when Fabrice and Robin tried to walk. Their extra legs got tangled up, and the boys promptly tripped and crashed to the floor.

"Good grief, couldn't you remove a couple of these legs?" groused Fabrice, pushing Barune aside, who was licking his face with delight. "I'll never learn to use them all at the same time."

"You've got to practice!" said the dragon severely. "Our disguises must be perfect. One slip-up and we're dead."

"That's a pretty compelling argument," said Robin, who was trying to untangle his limbs. "Let's see if they work this way . . ."

Two chairs and a table became the innocent victims of their uncontrolled lurching, but the boys eventually managed to remain upright. The dragon taught them all how to use their various appendages. Fafnir's tail proved particularly lethal, which delighted her.

After a couple hours of practice they were more or less comfortable in their new bodies.

"Good; now for the details," said Chem. "I can maintain these new appearances for several days, if needed. The bodies are perfectly adapted to Limbo, and of course much stronger than your normal ones. But maintaining your disguises this way reduces my magical capacities a lot. So, if we have to fight or defend ourselves, be prepared to revert to your initial shape, which, I remind you, is much more vulnerable. So please, don't try anything fancy."

"Let's go over the etiquette rules for life in the infernal worlds. Politeness aside, it's wise to let a bigger demon go ahead of you. Be respectful of the strong and contemptuous of the weak. Don't be surprised, shout, or get upset if you see one demon devouring another. Those people are complete cannibals. We'll be in a group, so they shouldn't bother us. But stick together, and don't ever leave my side. Got that?"

Now looking a bit pale, the friends nodded silently.

"I made a mistake last time by transporting you to Limbo mentally but not physically," Chem continued. "This time everything should work fine. Step inside this circle of powdered gambole I just drew, and close your eyes."

They obeyed, but Chem spoke again: "Manitou!"

"What?"

"I said close your eyes!"

"You think it's easy?" grumbled the dog, who was struggling to close his four dozen eyes all at the same time.

He finally managed, and the dragon cried, "Sparidam!"

The next instant, they were in Limbo.

They rematerialized in a city swarming with demons. Which was logical, since it was a demonic city, though that didn't make it any more pleasant.

The houses had no windows. Or doors either. Demons passed right through the garishly painted walls with joyful casualness.

"Aren't we out on the plain anymore?" asked a surprised Tara, who remembered a gloomy gray expanse from which colors had been banished.

"The palace is traveling around," answered Chem. "I focused my mind on the place where it ought to be, so I'm guessing it's in this city now. We just have to find it."

They carefully stowed *The Forbidden Book* and their taludi in a slug saddlebag on Chem's back and started walking.

The black suns of this strange dimension were shining in the dark sky. Those suns had the bad habit of sparking monstrous storms, so the houses were built only to protect the demons from getting a sunburn. They never stayed inside for long. They didn't need to eat solid food, but they couldn't live without the energy from those evil suns.

There were trees too. Well, things that looked like trees. They were a vivid white to resist the burning sunlight, and bore large, dirty brown flowers, visited by enormous insects with black, green, and gray stripes.

When a demon came too close, a furious swarm of insects would attack, stinging him until he ran away screaming.

The other demons seemed to find this very funny.

As the friends passed a patch of white grass, they discovered that Limbo's plants could also eat them. Tough stalks were wrapped around the bones, insect parts, and paws littering the grass. No fool who stretched out on that lawn ever got up again.

A little farther they saw evidence that while the demons didn't need food, they still enjoyed eating, having discovered the sense of taste on other worlds. In exchange for services rendered, they were paid in food.

Living food. Which they ate raw.

"Yuck!" murmured Fabrice. "Don't they know how to use fire?"

"Yeah, but they feel it spoils the taste."

Demon merchants stood by their stalls, hawking their merchandise. The friends noticed that exchanges between sellers and buyers were fairly muscular.

The most common exchange currency was, "Gimme that thing or I'll rip your arm off." A popular comeback was, "Just try, and you'll get this axe in your face." Most transactions ended badly for the weaker of the two, which explained why demon merchants were especially husky and well armed.

Among demons, it was extremely difficult to tell females from males. Tara guessed that those who were wearing ornaments, decorations, or jewels, or who had painted their skins, were the female element.

The streets were laid out in no logical pattern, and since Chem's group lacked the others' power to pass through walls, their progress was fairly complicated. But he suddenly lifted one of his heads, and his three muzzles smiled. "Follow me. I think I've found the palace."

He was right. The Demon King's castle could be seen perched on its gigantic legs on a hill overlooking the city. The castle, too, had changed since their last visit. It was totally, definitely, absolutely . . . pink. A delicious, bizarre baby pink.

"Uh-oh!" muttered Chem. "This doesn't bode well."

"Why not?" asked Cal. "It's kind of pretty, isn't it? Even if putting the roof on the side makes it look a little odd. And having the doors up above and the windows down below isn't super practical."

"When the king's in a good mood, the palace is black," said the dragon soberly, sounding very worried. "When he's in a bad mood, it's pink. And the pinker it is, the worse his mood."

"Well, in that case let's avoid the dear old king, shall we?" said Cal. "I'm not too crazy about demons in general, so angry demons . . ."

"According to *The Forbidden Book*, the Limbo Judge will be in the Hall of Truth, Lies, and Betrayal."

"That's a weird name."

"The demons named the Judgment Hall that after their first hearings. The accused were supposed to tell the truth, but naturally they told lies, and they were betrayed by the Judge, who told the truth."

"A regular trifecta! So, how do we avoid the guards?"

"There aren't any guards," said the dragon. "Who would be crazy enough to threaten the Demon King in his own castle?"

"Yeah, right," muttered Cal. "You really have to wonder."

"By the way, how do you fight demons?" asked Robin. "Can you hurt them? Do they die?"

"They're subject to the same physical laws as humans," said Master Chem. "They're just stronger, faster, and much better armed with claws and fangs. Beyond that, stick a sword in their body and they'll do like everyone else."

"Oh, good. You mean they'll say 'Arrrgh, that hurts!'" suggested Cal, who since his resurrection was being relentlessly cheerful.

Chem glared at him from one of his slug eyes. "No, they'll *die*. At least they will if you hit a vital organ, which isn't necessarily the heart. But we aren't planning to do any fighting, are we? We just want to record Brandis's judgment and prove Cal's innocence. So we're going to be discreet. Very, very discreet."

The dragon was right: there weren't any guards watching at the palace windows, and they just walked in—to be greeted by a stench of rotting meat so revolting it nearly gagged them.

"Agh!" Sparrow choked. "What's that smell? It's unbearable!"

"It's coming from those things," said Tara, who was trying to breathe only through her mouth.

Scattered on short columns along the palace hallways were chunks of meat and pitchers of blood swarming with maggots and flies.

Tara suddenly understood. "They're like room fresheners! They put them out to create an atmosphere!"

Coupled with the warm pink walls, she had an awful feeling of being in a gigantic intestine.

"Well, it's a big success," breathed Cal, who could smell through his trunk more acutely than usual. "Let's try to find a place that stinks a little less."

They didn't find one, of course. The palace steward clearly took this sort of thing to heart, because the same horrible stench was everywhere.

Oddly enough, they were able to walk wherever they pleased, without anyone bothering them. Tara didn't know if her magic map worked on this world, but they needed a guide to find the Judgment Hall, so she gave it a try.

"No idea!" hissed the map, mortified at having to admit ignorance. "This sector hasn't been mapped, so I don't know where this hall of yours is. You'll have to figure it out yourselves."

Tara peered around. From the outside, the palace hadn't looked that big. But inside, it was an absurd labyrinth of corridors, halls, kitchens (what for? since demons apparently didn't cook), and rooms with strange, twisted furniture.

"We don't have any choice," she said, putting the map away. "We'll have to ask for directions."

"That's easy," chuckled Cal. "Watch and learn from the master."

Standing nearby was a little green demon looking enviously at some big ones. Which is why it was green, because demons change color according to their mood.

"We have to see the Limbo Judge," said Cal, flexing his impressive muscles. "Where's the Judgment Hall?"

"Everybody knows where that is! Get out of my space, pollen honey!"

Hearing the demon speaking to Cal, Tara almost burst out laughing. "Pollen honey" was quite an insult! Assuming that demons hated flowers, "pollen honey" in Limbo must be the equivalent of "traduc turds" on OtherWorld.

Cal was scowling, but Chem intervened.

"Leave this to me," said the dragon. "I think our little friend didn't quite understand the question. Maybe if we hang him by his toes he'll hear better. I happen to have just what we need to string him up."

Chem's slimy body produced a slew of sharp, hooked, and pointed things aimed at the green demon.

Wide-eyed, the little demon began to speak so quickly, it was as if his words were stuck together.

"Take the first door on the right, the second on the left, then you turn twice, and go straight ahead." It then cautiously added, "YourLordship."

"Thanks" the dragon answered politely. "Very kind of you."

Stowing all his weapons, Chem turned on his heel—or its slug equivalent—and followed the demon's directions. Which turned out to be perfectly accurate.

The only problem was that they weren't the only ones who wanted to talk to the Judge. At a glance, there must have been a thousand demons waiting before the enormous Judgment Hall. Unlike standard Limbo building practice, the Hall had a door, or rather an irregularly shaped opening like a hole in the pink wall. A creature with a head like an overcooked lobster flattened by a bulldozer announced the next litigants. They then went inside through the hole or sometimes passed directly through the wall, to lobster-head's loud complaints.

"Crap! It's going to take us a century to see the Judge," said Cal with dismay. "And we won't be able to appeal to him in front of all these demons."

"Who don't look especially satisfied with the sentences they're getting," remarked Sparrow, nodding toward the demons coming out through the wall.

To the extent that they could make out the emotions on the demons' faces, muzzles, or . . . facial things, they looked more appalled than pleased. And this was true of both plaintiffs and defendants. They were all being hustled along by members of what the Demon King considered his guard. These were sickly white bipeds with a revolting clutch of tentacles on their chests, spider mandibles protruding from their mouths, and a number of arms, which held the litigants.

The sentences were pretty straightforward. In fact, there were just two basic options. One: you lost a piece of your body, which was chopped off immediately, then and there. There was no possible appeal, though the demons protested loudly. Two: you were put to death. There again the demons argued a lot, but the Judge's verdict was final.

Heads, tentacles, and various unidentified body parts were hacked off, fell to the ground, and were immediately swept away.

Those demons who only suffered amputations ran away screaming and cursing the Judge.

It was fairly creative and extremely noisy. Reacting to the ambient savagery, Sparrow had to struggle mightily not to shape-shift into the beast, which would have given away her disguise.

Suddenly the group heard a blare of trumpets, or something about as loud, and the Demon King appeared. He hadn't changed much. His disgusting round body was still scattered with countless eyes, and his thick, spotted tongue drooled as he licked them.

It was all Fabrice could do not to gag. His enthusiasm for magic had been shaken the first time he met a demon. Now, he was faced with an infernal yelping and gesticulating cohort of them. *When you come right down to it*, he thought, *a calm, peaceful life on Earth without any magic is really super.* Tara was thinking exactly the same thing, and the two earthlings exchanged looks.

The others were just as nervous, including the dragon, who worried that the king might recognize them in spite of their disguises. Sparrow's knees began to knock. The snakes on Fafnir's head started hissing so wildly she was afraid they would attract attention, so she stunned them with a punch.

The Demon King passed without so much as glancing at them—quite a stroke of luck, given how many eyes he had. Yelling and swinging their truncheons, his bodyguards cleared the Judgment Hall when the king entered. Whatever he wanted to ask the Limbo Judge, he apparently wanted to do it in private.

Within minutes, the hall and corridor were both empty.

"This is perfect!" exclaimed Chem. "He's alone now. Let's go!"

Only two bodyguards remained, standing on either side of the opening that served as a door to the Judgment Hall.

Chem didn't fool around. He used his massive bulk to flatten the two demons like pancakes.

"Inside, quick!" said one of his heads while the other two kept watch.

Tara and her friends rushed in.

Once in the hall, they realized with horror that the demons who'd merely been amputated or executed had actually gotten off easy. Because the Limbo Judge could pronounce a third sentence.

Imprisonment.

For eternity.

A spell had been cast on the walls of the Judgment Hall, which displayed every convicted demon that had been imprisoned in the stone. The oldest ones, the ones who had been there the longest, no longer moved—they were statues forever. But the demons who had only recently been sentenced were still struggling, straining to free themselves. Imprisoned in the stone, they silently screamed with rage and fear.

The sight was so shocking that the friends instinctively drew together and kept their distance from the walls.

The Demon King was sitting on a throne directly across from an enormous statue of . . . nothing. Just a big, shapeless black mass, with a roughly carved eye, ear, and mouth.

The mouth was speaking and had the attention of the king, who didn't hear them enter the hall.

"He was lying," it said, in a resounding, brazen voice. "He knows where they are. You're no longer powerful enough to get the truth out of him. By giving him some of your power, you've created a real competitor for your race. Much more than the dragon standing right behind you, for that matter!"

Caught by surprise, Master Chem gasped at the same time as the king.

"What the—?" began the demon.

He didn't have time to finish his sentence. Rushing at the king like a runaway train, Chem used his enormous bulk to smother him. Tara didn't know if demons had lungs—though Limbo air was breathable—but when Chem slid off the king, he was out cold.

"Cursed judge!" snarled the old wizard. "This fake body of mine didn't fool him. Well, now that our cover is blown, I'm going to retransform you, so I can get all my magic power back."

"Ouch, that hurts!" complained Cal as he reverted to his normal body and his robe to its normal shape. "So, what do we do now?"

The dragon stretched its huge, scaly body with pleasure, then answered: "Not we—you. *You* have to ask the Limbo Judge for justice. Go sit on the throne, where the demon was."

Cal looked at the chair apprehensively. It exuded a viscous, blackish ooze, and its monstrous carved faces all seemed to be staring at him.

"Mom is going to scream bloody murder when she sees my clothes!" he muttered with a grimace of disgust and cautiously sat down.

The brazen voice rang out, filling the entire hall: "I'm listening, Caliban Dal Salan. Are you asking for my judgment?"

Sparrow had taken the taludi from the saddlebag, and it was now recording the whole scene.

"Yes, I am," Cal answered. "I've been unjustly accused of the murder of—"

"Brandis T'al Miga Ab Chantu. Yes, I know. And you want me to summon the boy's spirit so he can judge you again. And what will you do, Caliban Dal Salan, if he reiterates his judgment?"

"He won't," said Cal calmly. "The person responsible for Brandis's death is whoever tried to kill Tara."

"Ah, but it was Angelica Brandaud's cry of indignation, caused by your searching under her robe, that provoked the incident."

"Hey, I wasn't searching *under* her robe," he objected. "I was searching *in* her pocket. She had just sent a blood fly to sting Tara, to make her cause a catastrophe."

"And because your friends didn't believe you, you wanted to prove to them that you were right. Instead of waiting for the end of the two boys' demonstration, you immediately took action. Which led to the death of Brandis T'al Miga Ab Chantu . . . and would have sent your world into an infinite void if you hadn't found the power to close the vortex!"

Cal had gone deathly pale. The Limbo Judge was right. He'd only been thinking about himself—and his friends' admiration if he was able to prove Angelica's guilt.

He bowed his head.

"You're right," he admitted. "It was wrong of me to be so reckless."

"And so?" asked the Judge, who wasn't about to let him off the hook.

"It's my fault that Brandis is dead," he said with a sigh.

"Conclusion?" continued the Judge relentlessly.

"I'm going to turn myself in to the empress and go back to prison."

Tara and her friends were too stunned to react. But before they could protest, the judge started making an odd noise. It took Cal a moment to realize that the stone mass was . . . laughing. A full-throated, ironic laugh.

"Mmmm, you're a refreshing change from all those lying demons," chuckled the Judge. "You admit your guilt, and sincerely too! That's good. But I'm going to lift a weight off your shoulders. Your desire to get back at Angelica triggered the incident, but it should have been easy for the high wizards to close the vortex. So, the person who killed Brandis T'al Miga Ab Chantu while trying to kill your friend is indeed the culprit. I'm going to call the boy's spirit so you can ask for his forgiveness. Let this be a lesson to you. Every action has a reaction. You have to think before you act."

Still in shock, Cal was hanging on the judge's every word when Brandis's spirit materialized.

"Good," said the Judge. "I'll explain the situation to the victim. We'll see what he has to say about it."

The boy's ghost seemed more solid than it had at the Omois court. The exchange between Brandis and the Judge wasn't perceptible, but Cal and his friends could feel the boy's surprise. He turned to Cal and said: "So, you acted in that stupid way to protect your friend."

"Well, not exactly, but—"

"It's all right," the boy interrupted. "I probably would've done the same thing."

This was the second time that day that the young thief was taken by surprise. He opened his mouth, then closed it again, curious to hear what the ghost had to say. He wasn't disappointed.

"Just the same," Brandis continued firmly, "even if you aren't responsible for my death, you did give the real killer the chance to act. So I'm not going to sentence you to prison, but to help my parents when they're old and I'm not there to be with them. That's my sentence. I'm not asking you for money or blood. Just time. Does that strike you as fair?"

Cal had tears in his eyes. He hadn't thought of the pain of the parents whose child had died so young. He hadn't imagined their lonely old age.

"I swear it," he said solemnly. "I'll tell them about your wish, Brandis. You have my blood oath."

"That's not necessary. Your word is enough. On the other hand, I'd like to ask for a personal favor."

"Of course. What?"

"When you find the person who caused my death," snarled the ghost, suddenly angry, "make them pay for what they did to me. Make them really pay."

"You have my word on that too," said Cal with a fierce smile.

"Then I can leave in peace. Farewell."

And the colored figure disappeared.

"Well, that takes care of that," said the Judge. "Were you able to record everything, Princess?"

Sparrow started, unaccustomed to having people use her royal title.

"Yes, the taludi got it all. We just have to bring it to the empress."

Just then, a moan surprised them. The Demon King was coming to. His tentacles were twitching, and he was trying to open his dozens of eyes.

Master Chem acted promptly. Using his tail, he slammed the demon's weak point at the base of his tongue and sent him back to nightmare land. Then he said, "If we're finished here, I'll create a portal and we can leave."

With a claw, Chem delicately took *The Forbidden Book* from the saddlebag and was about to pick up the taludi when they all suddenly jumped. A second ghost had appeared before them. Panicked, Cal was afraid that Brandis wanted to change his judgment, but this ghost was taller than the boy and much older.

It was staring at them with equal astonishment.

Incredulous, Tara recognized its deep blue eyes, so like her own, and the mass of blond hair punctuated with the imperial white forelock. She knew its face for having gazed at it thousands of times in old photographs.

"*Dad?*" she exclaimed.

"Who . . . who are you?" asked the ghost, frowning.

"Dad! It's me, Tara!"

"Tara'tylanhnem? That's impossible! My daughter is only two years old."

"Dad, it *is* me. Look at me! Oh, Dad, I can't believe it! Is it really you?"

The ghost looked her over carefully, then smiled broadly.

"Tara! My baby!"

He rushed to take his daughter in his arms . . . and went right through her.

"Oh," he said, a note of bottomless sorrow in his voice. "I forgot that I can't touch you."

Tara's mind was in a whirl. *It's my father, my father!* It was almost physically painful not to be able to run into his arms. A pain they shared, because her father stammered: "My baby, I'm so sorry!"

Tara nodded and glanced at her friends, who were caught between laughter and surprise.

"Er, Dad?"

"What, baby?"

"I'm twelve years old, almost thirteen, so it would be nice if you could avoid the 'my baby.' Please?"

Danviou smiled at his daughter tenderly. "I'm sorry, darling. When I left, you were barely two, so it's something I'll have to get used to. No more 'baby,' I promise. Is 'my darling' okay?"

"That's perfect, Dad. I'm so happy to be able to see and talk to you! I've missed you so much—you and Mom. And to find both of you in such a short time, I can hardly believe it."

Danviou frowned. "Find *us*? Weren't you with your mother?"

"She was kidnapped, Dad, by the same monster who killed you. He calls himself Magister, and he's revived a clan that's taken the name Bloodgraves. They struck a deal with the demons and infected the apprentice spellbinders with demonic magic. Then Magister wanted to kidnap me because, thanks to you, I have Demiderus blood in my veins, so I can approach the demonic objects that the dragons hid after their war with the demons. My friends and I managed to defeat him and free Mom at the same time. She'd been his prisoner for ten years! That's about it. Oh, and my familiar is a pegasus. I also have a living stone who helps me when I need power. But she's become a friend because she has a conscience. We came here to prove Cal was innocent. He'd been accused of killing Brandis in the vortex, but he isn't responsible. The guilty one is the same person who's tried to get rid of me several times. I'm not sure I've been very clear. Did you understand all that?"

The ghost looked as stunned as if a brick wall had just crashed down on his head.

"To be honest, no. Someone's trying to kill you? And you have a familiar? But I made your grandmother swear that you would never be a wizard, to save you from this life on OtherWorld. Speaking of which . . . where are we?"

He looked around at the monstrous throne and the Judgment Hall.

"This looks like the high wizards' description of Demonic Limbo."

Master Chem stepped up, getting the ghost's attention. "I'm sorry to interrupt this touching reunion, but we are, in fact, in Limbo. And now would be the perfect time to leave."

The ghost's eyes narrowed, and he stiffened (well, to the extent that a ghost can stiffen).

"Master Dragon Chemnashaovirodaintrachivu? Are you responsible for all this?"

The dragon smiled coldly. He and Danviou clearly didn't like each other. "Actually, I'm not. Your daughter is perfectly capable of getting herself into worse trouble all by herself."

Suddenly the Limbo Judge spoke, startling everyone: "Can you guess why I had your father come here, Tara? I read in your mind that you're worried about your grandmother. I judge, of course, but my function is also to solve the problems of those who appear before me— if I can, that is. And this problem isn't very complicated. It's your move, young spellbinder."

Tara understood. She turned to her father.

"I try not to practice magic, but magic doesn't seem to agree. So, I wind up using it all the time. And the more I do, the closer I get to becoming a wizard. And if I become a wizard, it'll kill Grandma, because of your blood oath. Do you understand?"

"I didn't imagine for a moment that magic would take over your life, darling. I'm very sorry. I was trying to protect you from OtherWorld."

"Well, it's more like OtherWorld that needs to be protected from Tara," grumbled the dragon. "She sweeps across the planet like a natural disaster. Anyway, we really have to leave now. Tell us quickly what Isabella has to do so you can free her from the oath?"

"You have to bring her here," said the ghost. "In front of me. And I'll release her."

"Here? In Limbo?" Tara was alarmed. "Are you kidding?"

"The Judge is the only one who can bring the dead back more than once," Chem answered for Danviou. "But coming back here with Isabella is out of the question. It's even out of the question for us to come back at all. I think it's time for you to say goodbye. We won't be able to invoke your father's spirit a second time without the help of the statue, Tara. I'm very sorry."

If fact, Chem didn't look sorry at all. Tara shot him a sharp glance, noticing a hint of satisfaction that the dragon was unable to hide. He didn't want her talking with her father. But why?

Cal spoke up: "Er, I hate to bother you, but I can think of an approach that doesn't involve risking our lives to come back to Limbo. I already died once this week and I'd like to not repeat the experience for the next hundred years or so."

The ghost gave him a look of surprise. "And you are?"

"Caliban Dal Salan, the son of Aliana Dal Salan."

"The master thief? Yes, I know her. My sister cursed her up and down the block when she managed to swipe the Sailibo parchments from us. What's your plan?"

"We just steal the statue!"

The ghost gave a quizzical glance at the gigantic statue of the Judge. "Are you serious?"

"Completely! I'm not saying I could manage it all by myself. And Master Chem has to save his energy to get us back to Lancovit. But Tara's wicked powerful when she puts her mind to it. I'm sure she has enough magic to shrink that big chunk of masonry. Once it's shrunk, I'll slip it into my pocket and away we go!"

"I could even follow you without losing the link," said Danviou. "An excellent idea, young thief—worthy of your famous mother! Go ahead Tara, give it a try."

Tara sighed. She knew it would be up to her, sooner or later. And good grief, how big that thing was!

She raised her arms, mentally alerting the living stone. *I'm going to need your help to shrink that statue. Not just in size but also in weight. Also, the less I use my own magic, the less I risk hurting my grandma. Okay?*

Your father you found? Your family you completed? It's for your grandmother help? My magic you take!

Aloud, Tara said, "By Miniaturus, shrink that statue judicious, to make our transfer expeditious."

When the Limbo Judge felt the spell hitting him, he shouted loudly.

Alerted, the demons outside the hall sprang into action. Hoofs, feet, horns, and . . . other things could be heard pounding on the ground.

"Hurry up and keep shrinking the statue," said Chem. "I'll cast a spell to protect the hall. Everybody else, deal with any demons who manage to get through the barrier. And be careful; the ones who break through will be the most powerful."

Fafnir was grumbling that she couldn't do much without her faithful axe, so Robin promptly conjured one for her.

"Hmpf!" snorted the dwarf. "More of your stupid magic! And what if you faint or die? Your magic stops working and I'm without an axe."

Robin shrugged. "As Cal says, I'll try to avoid dying. And I have to create a bow for myself—"

He never got to add "—as well," because Lillandril's bow suddenly materialized in his hand. Followed by its quiver. Its arrows. And his arm guard.

The expression on the half-elf's face was indescribable. Despite the fear knotting his gut, Fabrice burst out laughing.

"Holy smokes!" exclaimed Robin. "It found me!"

"Well, you can tell it I'm very happy it did," said Cal. "Because I have a hunch we're gonna need it."

The screams of the demons who had slammed into the spell blocking the hole and sealing the wall confirmed his prediction. Fafnir readied her axe, Robin nocked an arrow, Fabrice and Cal cast a Destructus that they restrained with difficulty, Sparrow shape-shifted into the beast and popped her claws, and Manitou bared his fangs, ready to attack the first demon to get through.

Meanwhile, Chem had opened a Transfer Portal. On the way to Limbo, invoking the Demon King's name had been enough to get them here. But for the trip back, because of the Demiderus protection spell, they had to create the equivalent of a portal that would redirect them to Lancovit.

Encouraged by her father, Tara struggled to keep shrinking the statue. She tried not to let herself be distracted from what she was doing, but it wasn't easy. She was so happy. Within the space of a few weeks she had found first her mother, and now her father. *Okay, Dad's a ghost,* she thought, *but I can deal with that.*

Fortunately for Tara's personal survival, the magic continued to act while her thoughts wandered. The Judge twisted and moaned under the burning lash of the spell and continued to shrink.

When he was the size of a fat hamster, Tara interrupted the action. She scooped up the little statue and the taludi and quickly stuffed them into the dragon's saddlebag.

And none too soon. Two demons, smarter or more powerful than the others, had managed to break through the dragon's spell. Cal and Fabrice's Destructus cut down the first one, but the second was fighting fiercely. He looked like a cross between a shark and a centipede, with a whole set of legs, claws, and teeth. One of them wounded Fabrice on the arm, so Sparrow snatched the young earthling out of the demon's reach and shielded him with her body. Cal, who had been half knocked out by one of the legs, took revenge by paralyzing them one at a time, slowly but surely immobilizing the creature.

For her part, Fafnir was chopping off anything that stuck out of the demon. One of the Demon King's bodyguards, who managed to push his head through the protective force field, screamed with rage to see his king unconscious, the portal activated, and the Judge gone.

On Tara's signal, they all retreated toward the portal, fending off the attacks now coming from all sides as best they could.

"Go!" yelled Chem, as he shifted back into his wizard shape. "Quick!"

They all leaped through the Transfer Portal.

And found themselves in Lancovit.

With Master Chem in his underwear.

And one very surprised demon.

The demon felt a little lost at first. Caught up in the fighting, he hadn't hesitated to follow the impostors through the portal. He now realized that he had been teleported to OtherWorld and was surrounded by a slew of Lancovit guards, all eager to chop him to bits.

He wisely dropped Fafnir, whom he had grabbed, raised his legs in the air, and quickly retracted his claws and fangs.

The furious dwarf very nearly lopped off another of those legs, but Chem stopped her. "That's enough, Fafnir. He surrendered. Leave him alone."

Then the old wizard noticed he was in his long johns.

"By my ancestors, this simply won't do! By Fashionistus, silver and blue, enrobe me now and quickly too!"

Chem's blue and silver spellbinder robe, which hadn't traveled with him to Limbo, immediately materialized.

Fafnir was staring with dismay at the hole her scorpion tail had punched in her second pair of handsome, red leather pants.

"Stupid magic!" she raged. "Those pants cost me a fortune!"

"Guards!" roared the wizard.

"Yes, Master Chem?" answered one.

"Send for Shaman Night Bird. We have two wounded and a demon, and our beneficent magic doesn't work very well on demons."

"Very well, Master Chem."

The guard ran off.

"You aren't going to treat him, are you?" Fafnir thundered.

Chem turned to her in surprise. "Of course we are. Why wouldn't we treat him?"

Fafnir was practically speechless. "But he attacked us!" she blurted.

"Well, not exactly. We entered Demon Limbo, we knocked out their king, and we kidnapped their judge. From their standpoint, *we're* the ones who attacked *them*. All they did was defend themselves."

The dwarf was silent. She'd hadn't considered the situation from that point of view.

Something had been hovering under Tara's nose, and when it caught her eye, she stared at it in panic.

She had shrunk the Judge. The problem was, she had also shrunk her father! Now the size of a mouse, Danviou's ghost floated in front of his daughter, looking perplexed.

"Well, I'll be . . ." he said in a tiny high-pitched voice. "What happened to me?"

"Dad, are you all right? Oh boy, I am *so* sorry. I didn't expect this."

"So, you're the one who . . ." Then he understood. "I must say, your magic really is powerful. But don't worry. As soon as the Judge is restored to his normal size, I will be too. At least I hope so."

Deeply embarrassed, Tara smiled faintly and nodded. Her stupid power was running away with her again.

The Living Castle was delighted to have its favorite spellbinders home again, but didn't quite know how to deal with the demon. So it projected a burning desert, to suit the prisoner's centipede side, and a blue sea on the ceiling, for his shark side. The effect was pretty unnerving.

"Do you understand our language?" Chem asked the prisoner.

"Understand I," he reluctantly answered.

"Don't worry. We're going to treat you, and then send you home."

The demon raised what served as his head and asked hopefully: "You keep Judge?"

"You'd like that, wouldn't you?" chuckled the wizard. "No more verdicts, no more sentences! Sorry, but no. For the stability of your kingdoms the Judge must be restored to his position. I will return him to your king."

The demon shot him a look of hate, but obediently followed the guards to the infirmary.

Master Chem then turned to Fabrice, who was cradling his arm and grimacing. Robin's Healus spell had dulled the pain, but the wound was deep. The demon's spines were poisonous, and they had to immediately counter the effect of the venom, so they took Fabrice to the infirmary as well. The young earthling didn't enjoy having a shark-headed centipede as a roommate.

The moment the friends rematerialized in Lancovit, Barune, Blondin, and Gallant immediately sensed their presence and came running. Barune was now giving Fabrice worried little taps with his trunk.

"It's okay, Barune," Fabrice reassured his mammoth. "It's nothing; just a scratch."

"No, it isn't," said a deep voice behind him. "It's a deep wound caused by a demon on an evil world," Shaman Night Bird continued. "It will take time to heal."

"Time?" Fabrice's voice quavered. "How much time?"

"We'll see. My remedies need time to work. And no visitors. You're going to suffer, and it won't be especially pleasant."

Fabrice almost passed out.

"I'm . . . I'm going to suffer?" he stammered. "But—"

"You have to suffer if you want to get well. Drink this," said the shaman, commanding a glass to float over to his patient. The bubbling mixture it contained seemed to be trying to escape from the glass.

Cal, who hated the infirmary, spoke up quickly: "Okay then, we'll leave you to it. See you tomorrow."

"Farm animal + difficult," grumbled the patient, looking apprehensively at the roiling potion.

"What?" exclaimed Cal, who didn't understand what he was saying.

"Cow + hard = coward!" translated Tara, giving Fabrice a sympathetic smile.

As they left, they heard a loud "Yuck!" behind them, confirming that the mixture's taste perfectly matched its revolting appearance.

"Poor Fabrice," said Sparrow with a grin. "Master Night Bird's potions are known far and wide."

"For their effectiveness?" asked Tara.

"That too, but mainly for their awful taste. I suspect our master healer of making them especially revolting to encourage people to get well as fast as possible."

Tara smiled . . . and swore never to get sick on this crazy planet.

They had barely stepped out of the infirmary when a familiar voice made Manitou put his ears down, Master Chem back away, and Tara tremble. She turned around and said the only thing she could: "Grandma?"

CHAPTER 12

A ROYAL AUDIENCE

Tara's grandmother wasn't known for her sense of diplomacy. At court, it was said that her ancestors must have had dwarf blood, because like them, she tended to strike first and ask questions later.

Isabella gave a vigorous demonstration of this by yelling at Tara for a good ten minutes. "Ingrate!" was the kindest of all the words she used.

At first Tara tried to defend herself, but eventually gave up, fascinated by her grandmother's breath control.

I've only met Dad very recently but . . . Yes! She could feel him reacting.

Danviou popped out from behind Tara's shoulder and planted himself in front of Isabella. Forcing his tiny voice, he remarked coldly: "You haven't changed, dear mother-in-law. I see you're as direct as ever."

Isabella, who was halfway through her tirade, abruptly closed her mouth and stopped in midsentence. Her green eyes widened in astonishment, and a welcome silence fell on the assembly.

Tara grinned. Seeing her grandmother mute with amazement was worth all the bawling out in the world.

"Danviou?" Isabella stammered. "But . . ."

"It's a long story," snapped the ghost, to save time. "Stay where you are and stretch out your arms."

Fascinated, Isabella obeyed. The red glyphs could be seen on her wrists, living testimony to Tara's growing power.

"By the blood spilled, by the word given, I free you from your oath," the ghost recited. "The Blood Oath is ended."

The crowd turned to stare at Isabella's wrists. Nothing happened. The glyphs continued to slowly pulse on her white skin.

"I don't understand!" he cried in surprise. "They should disappear!"

Still unnerved at finding herself facing the tiny ghost of her son-in-law, Isabella rolled down her sleeves.

"I have no idea why it didn't work," she said. "And Danviou, why are you so . . . small? And how do you happen to be here? I don't understand."

Just then a trumpet blast rang through the castle, which quivered with outrage. Access to the Transfer Room had been requested from the demonic realms, which tripped the alarm. Magically amplified, the king's voice summoned all high wizards to the Council Chamber.

"Drat! I have to go," said Master Chem, shaking his head in annoyance. "Isabella, you should come with me; it's been a long time since you've been to a council meeting. Children, the session is open to the public. Come and sit in the stands. I want you to follow the discussion, in case it concerns you. Manitou, please make sure they don't take any unusual . . . initiatives."

A note of pleading could clearly be heard in the dragon's voice.

The Council Chamber was used for administrative functions. It was smaller than the Throne Room, but just as elaborately decorated. The lacy open work on the marble and granite columns hardly seemed strong enough to support the room's vaulted blue-and-silver ceiling.

Here, too, the banners of Lancovit's counts, dukes, and barons brightened the walls. Tara was surprised to notice a catwalk of carved blond wood that ran around the room above the stands. It was for the archers. Holdovers of a more tumultuous past, the bowmen stood with bows drawn and arrows nocked, ready to skewer anyone who made a threatening move toward the king or queen.

Just in case.

The high wizards were floating near the thrones. Isabella's appearance was unexpected, and it generated a murmur of surprise.

Finally, King Bear and Queen Titania, who were both powerful spellbinders, entered. They were short and, like their niece Sparrow, had brown hair and eyes. The king seemed as irritated as his first counselor, Salatar, who was breathing tiny flames of indignation.

"Oyez, oyez," yelled the marshal, a redheaded Cyclops. "Our kingdom has just received an ultimatum of war!"

An anxious murmur rose from the crowd of courtiers. *What? An ultimatum?*

"It is claimed that the Empire of Limbo, in the Union of Demonic Worlds, was invaded by a Lancovit wizard and spellbinders. This wizard brutalized the Demon King and caused the death of several of his guards. He then absconded with a relic of inestimable value that is vital to the maintenance of peace in those realms. The Demon King states that if the relic is not returned to him immediately, he will abrogate the Demiderus Treaty and attack the rift and the spells protecting Earth, dragons or no dragons. He further states that the Lancovit kingdom will be his second objective."

King Bear leaned close to his counselor. "Can he really do that, Salatar? I thought our wizards and the dragons had sealed off access to the demonic planets, so demons couldn't come to our worlds unless they had been sent for."

The chimera breathed a jet of fire, then answered: "That is correct, sire. Normally, they can't. But when the peace treaty was signed, the demons demanded an amendment to the agreement. If they were attacked and were not the aggressors, and something essential to their survival was taken from them, then the spell would no longer stop them from entering our worlds. At the time, the wizards and dragons agreed, because the war had cost so many lives, and the clause was considered a minor problem."

The king then leaned toward the queen, and the assembly respectfully waited for him to speak again.

From where Tara and her friends were sitting, they could see Master Chem pacing around in midair, looking deeply worried.

"Good grief!" muttered Manitou. "Chem and I completely forgot about that clause! We should never have taken the Judge. We just gave the demons a perfect excuse for invading us."

Sparrow had the saddlebag containing the Judge, the taludi, and *The Forbidden Book*. She opened it and took out the statuette.

"We have a problem," she whispered to the Judge.

"No kidding!" snapped the tiny brazen voice angrily. "Whatever possessed you to drag me away like that? Do you really want to plunge the universe into war?"

"We didn't have any choice," said Tara. "We had to try to help my grandmother." Then, because she knew the Judge wouldn't miss it, she added: "And I couldn't pass up the chance to spend a little more time with my father."

"Yeah, sure!" spat the statuette. "That'll be great consolation for all the people who will die because of you! Anyway, enough of this. Send me back to the demons before things really go bad."

"We tried to release Isabella from her blood oath, and it didn't work," said Tara's father quickly. "Do you know why?"

"For two reasons," the Judge explained. "First, because I was stuck in a bag like some cheap knickknack. Second, because you weren't your normal size. The spell didn't recognize you as the original Danviou. You have to do it again."

While they were talking, Master Chem was working to bring the council around to his way of thinking. With sweeping gestures, he pointed first at Isabella and then at the glyphs on her arms. He reminded the assembly that she was the mainstay of their Earthly Surveillance program. No other wizard of her stature ever agreed to go live on a planet so devoid of magic, he said. He explained the effects of the blood oath and how important it was to free her from it.

A murmur of compassion for Tara rose when Chem mentioned her father. And the crowd's attention was at its height when he ended by telling about Cal's arrest and sentence.

To Tara's great surprise, who considered his arguments rather lame, the old dragon was able to get the council to see the rightness of what they had done.

Quite an accomplishment.

By the end of the session, the king and queen were practically thanking him for risking his life to save Cal and Isabella.

Hmm, thought Tara. *So the dragon can make people swallow practically anything.* She carefully stored that fact in her memory. Fine. But he wouldn't take her in, ever.

Robin's faint smile confirmed that he shared her opinion.

Master Chem finished his heartrending homily, then gestured to Sparrow to bring out the Judge.

Chem didn't need Tara's power to restore the statue's normal size this time. It did it just fine on its own, and soon the Judge's impressive dark mass was looming over them.

"Whew! That feels a lot better!" he said.

The crowd stirred. Though the Judge had existed for centuries, no one had ever seen actually him. People were curious, fascinated, enthralled . . . right up until the moment when the statue started doing what it did best.

Judging.

Before they realized what was happening, two counts and a baron were accused of embezzling tax money, which came as a surprise to Salatar. Guards promptly hauled the indignant noblemen away. The Judge had already taken up the case of a voluptuous marquise when Master Chem interrupted him. "Er, we didn't bring you here to do that. And time is short; we must send you back to Limbo. We just need to—"

"Spoil my fun, right?" interrupted the Judge. "Very well. I understand. Danviou Ab—"

"Just plain Danviou," said the dragon quickly. Chem had no desire for the ghost's real identity as the empress's brother and heir of the Empire of Omois to be revealed in open council.

The statue's carved mouth pursed ironically.

"As I was saying," he continued. "Danviou, father of Tara, do you wish to release your mother-in-law from her blood oath?"

The ghost seemed to hesitate for a moment, but then nodded.

"By the blood spilled, by the word given, I free you from your oath," the ghost recited. "The Blood Oath is ended."

This time, the formula worked. The red glyphs on Isabella's outstretched forearms faded, then disappeared.

The blood oath had finally been canceled!

Tara and her father exchanged radiant smiles.

Isabella examined her arms, which were finally bare of all marks. Then she turned her green eyes to the ghost. "Thank you, Danviou. I'm glad to see that you accept your daughter's heritage. She will become a powerful spellbinder."

"She's *already* a powerful spellbinder," he said proudly. "And I regret with all my heart that I can't stay with her."

"Dad! What do you mean?" Tara's cry drew the king and queen's attention.

"You *have* to stay!" she continued. "I don't want to lose you, not now. Not again!"

"I'm sorry, darling, but it isn't up to me!" Danviou answered, sounding terribly sad. "My place is no longer among the living. We have to part now. I'm grateful that fate gave us a chance to see each other one last time. Tell your mother that I love her and that I always will."

There was no longer a dry eye in the crowd. The women were weeping into handkerchiefs that materialized here and there; the men were rubbing their eyes; and even gruff old Salatar shed a fiery tear. It ran down his lion's face and fell hissing to the ground.

Tara was about to speak when the Judge abruptly sent the ghost away. "*Dad!*" she screamed, as her father's figure slowly vanished. "No! Dad!"

And before she could stop him, Master Chem and the other spell-binders seized the Judge and sent him back to Limbo.

Tara was furious and wheeled on the old dragon.

"Why did you do that? I had so many things to tell him! Bring both of them back, right now!"

Queen Titania intervened.

"Tara, darling, we didn't have any choice," she said gently. "If it had been in our power to keep your father, we would've done so without hesitation. But the demons left us very little time. A few more minutes, and it would have been war. What would you have done in that situation?"

Tara opened her mouth, then closed it again. Though heartsick, she had to admit that the queen was right. She obviously couldn't keep the judge for her own personal use.

The king could tell that the girl was terribly affected by the loss of her father and felt deeply concerned.

Tara's friends all gathered around, hugging her. Even Fafnir, who wasn't much given to affectionate demonstrations, put her arms around them all.

"Ouch," Cal finally said with a grimace. "You don't need to break my ribs, Fafnir. I love her too."

Despite her tears, Tara couldn't help but laugh when she saw the dwarf's outraged expression. Tara wiped her eyes and turned back to the king and queen.

"We have another problem," she said in a voice that still quivered. "Fafnir tried to get rid of her magical power by drinking a brew of black roses a while ago."

Her statement was greeted by murmur of horror, and the spellbinders nearest them moved away slightly.

Master Chem shot Tara an irritated glance, because this was an announcement he'd planned to make himself. He continued: "Unfortunately, it seems Fafnir has been infected by a kind of evil entity, the Ravager. Each time he possesses her, she loses all control. If he succeeds in taking her over completely, he could contaminate anyone around her for years. Like a virus that can't be stopped, he could infect our world, other worlds, even the universe!"

"What kind of outlandish story is that?" growled Salatar, who had long resented the dragon's influence over the kingdom. "We just barely avoided a bloody war with the demons, a war we weren't at all sure of winning. And now you're serving up some ridiculous tale of possession? If memory serves, the only place where black roses are found is in the Swamps of Desolation, in Gandis. That's the land of giants—our allies! Your Majesties, this is nonsense. I suggest we wrap up the council session and focus on more pressing concerns. Our time is precious!"

Annoyed by the chimera's skepticism, Tara whispered to Fafnir: "Do you think you could you loosen your control over the Ravager a little? I think the First Counselor needs a little demonstration."

"I could, but are you sure about doing that?" the dwarf asked worriedly. "This thing wants my body, and it might attack and hurt you. By my axe, if I'm possessed there'll be nothing I can do about it."

"The living stone tells me the Ravager doesn't have all his power, because part of him is still imprisoned on the Island of Black Roses. We should be able to control him. At least I hope so."

"Hmpf, blasted magic! Okay, you guys ready?"

"Go ahead," said Sparrow with a grin. "I think my uncle and my aunt also need to know what they're dealing with."

The dwarf concentrated and slowly yielded control over her body. The courtiers stared at her, unsure of what to expect. The Lilliputian fairies stopped flitting about, the imps quit their pranks, and the unicorns postponed their discussions. A deathly silence fell on the assembly.

They waited.

And waited.

And waited some more.

Nothing happened. The Ravager was no fool. Fafnir alone knew what he was capable of. The Ravager was well aware that he couldn't resist an onslaught by dozens of high wizards and dragons. His only chance was to remain hidden. Overcoming Fafnir was very tempting, but he resisted it at this moment.

After a few minutes, Salatar spoke up.

"Well?" he thundered.

Fafnir hesitantly opened her eyes.

"I don't get it," she muttered. "The darn thing doesn't want to come back."

The chimera stared at her, his amber eyes focused on Fafnir's head.

"Your aura is blue," he finally announced.

The dwarf's eyes widened. "My *what* is *what?*"

"Your aura. It's blue. Which means you practice magic. We chimera are sensitive to magic; we can see it. But dwarves don't like magic, I believe. In fact, doesn't your people banish those individuals affected by it?"

"Yeah, but I don't see the connec—"

"I see the connection very clearly. You've been driven out. You have no place to go."

Salatar stood up smoothly and went to stand in front of the dwarf, his dragon tail twitching nervously. "You decided that you'd get Lancovit to take you in. So, you come to us with this story of possession. But there's no need to lie to gain our sympathy. We're very glad to welcome you among us. Powerful spellbinders like you are always welcome in Lancovit!"

The dwarf was practically speechless, but not quite.

"Grachiia!" she hissed in Dwarvish.

From the look on Sparrow's face, it must have been an especially ugly curse.

Then Fafnir took a deep breath, and when she spoke, Salatar was buffeted by the power of her voice.

"By my mother!" she yelled. "By all the gold in the world, I wouldn't want to be a spellbinder. Give me a sword, give me a collar, give me some metal, and keep your blasted magic! I drank that brew to get rid of it. And not only did the magic remain, but I picked up some sort of a parasite! Since you're too stupid to realize it, don't come running to me when the Ravager has your guts for garters!"

Red-faced with anger, Fafnir turned her back on the chimera and began to force her way through the crowd. She wasn't very tall, but it was easy to follow her progress, which was punctuated with the courtiers' reactions: Ow! Ouch! Hey!

She didn't get far, though.

The king cast a spell, and instantly Fafnir was hanging in midair.

"Let me go!" she roared. "Let me down, or I'll . . . I'll . . ."

The king's voice was calm, but it rang throughout the chamber: "Take it easy, Miss Dwarf. Our counselor wasn't trying to insult you. He was merely testing a hypothesis to gauge your reaction. That reaction was, shall we say, energetic enough to convince us. We hereby appoint Master Patin and Master Chanfrein to accompany you to the Swamps of Desolation to evaluate the danger this creature represents. If the Ravager exists and wants to possess you, he won't be able to resist attempting it, knowing you are so near. Masters Patin and Chanfrein can protect you, while judging the Ravager's power to do mischief. They're both powerful spellbinders and will help you. Is that acceptable, Miss Dwarf?"

Fafnir had stopped struggling. She now simply folded her muscular arms to show how little it bothered her to be floating ten feet off the ground.

But Tara, who knew her well, was sure she was extremely uncomfortable. Dwarves were very afraid of heights!

"That suits me fine . . . Your Majesty," she said through gritted teeth. "We can leave right away. If your wizards are ready, that is."

From her tone, Tara felt that Fafnir greatly doubted the Lancovians' ability to hurry.

Master Patin, a cahmboum who looked like a big pat of yellow butter with two bulging red eyes, frowned as best he could without having real eyebrows.

"Give us a few minutes to get our equipment together, Miss," he said politely, "and we'll follow you to the ends of the earth."

The dwarf blushed and bowed, still suspended in midair.

The king released the levitation spell, letting Fafnir land as gently as a feather on the shiny marble floor.

The Living Castle, which didn't usually project its illusory landscapes on sculpted surfaces, decided to give Fafnir a little present. To the courtier's surprise, it projected Hymlia.

The dwarves' houses appeared, with their forges and metal shops, shooting sparks and glowing fires. Dwarves like nature, too, and amid the stone and metal, flowers, trees, and grass softened the rough angles of their dwellings. The scene was full of vigorous energy.

And then a miracle happened. Fafnir smiled!

The courtiers applauded the dwarf's pleasure and the castle's sagacity.

Tara and her friends only had a few minutes to say goodbye. As the council wrapped up its business, they crowded round and wished Fafnir good luck, heartsick at being apart from her again.

"The king's right," said Cal. "Patin and Chanfrein are very good. And you're in no danger if you don't get too close to the island."

Fafnir was doubtful.

"We dwarves don't like asking for favors," she whispered as the wizards headed her way, trailed by two big floating bundles. "But I'd like you to find out more about the Ravager. Like, what he is, and where he's from. I don't think the court realizes what it's dealing with. If anything happened, you'd be my last hope!"

Sparrow shuddered. "Don't say that! Everything will be fine. I'm sure the two wizards will find a way to cure you. Come back to Lancovit quickly. We'll be waiting."

"It's a promise. May your hammers ring clear, my friends."

"May your anvil resound," they chorused.

After a last goodbye, Fafnir headed for the Transfer Portal with a wizard on either side. Destination: the Gray Fortress.

Meanwhile, Chem and Isabella were deep in conversation, with the dragon bringing her up to date on Tara's latest adventures. From the expression on Isabella's face, Tara felt it might be a good idea to a quickly leave the room.

The chamber emptied amid an excited ruckus. It had been a very lively council session!

Tara, Cal, Sparrow, Manitou, and Robin headed for their room. The castle displayed a variety of landscapes along the way. Tara kept her eyes peeled, but it didn't play any tricks on her. What happened last time had clearly inhibited it. In fact, the castle had created an addition to Tara's suite: a believable replica of the Chateau of Versailles.

Tara sat cross-legged on her bed. The pillows arranged themselves to cushion her back, and the blue bed grumbled because she hadn't taken off her sneakers. As her friends gathered around, Manitou leaped up onto the bed next to her and said: "I just learned some wonderful news!"

"The high wizards are giving us a year's vacation?" hazarded Cal.

"Better yet!" exclaimed the dog. "There's going to be a feast! A sublime, marvelous, succulent feast! To celebrate Isabella's freedom from her oath, the king and queen have decided to throw a party!"

"But we're supposed to be on vacation!" Cal moaned.

"So what?" asked Manitou, surprised.

"The apprentice spellbinders often have kitchen duty when there's a feast. We have to replicate the dishes the chefs make."

"Yes, I know," said the dog. "When I was young, I hated working in the kitchen. But as I've gotten older, I find it's a comforting, delicious, aromatic place. I'd be happy to spend the rest of my days there."

Cal rolled his eyes. "And you'd get so fat we wouldn't even to be able to move you. At least with us you always have lots to keep you busy."

"Yeah, and it wouldn't hurt if we had a little less to do. Okay, Tara, I suppose your priority is to gather as much information as you can on the Ravager."

Tara blinked, surprised at seeming so transparent.

"Oh," she exclaimed. "Is it that obvious?"

"As plain as the nose on your face," said Manitou. "And I think it's a very bad idea, just as I know you won't listen to a single word I have to say. So, go ahead. I await with impatience the horribly dangerous and totally deadly plan you've probably concocted."

His tone made Tara laugh. "I have to admit I don't have anything very definite right now. Fafnir just asked us to do some research in case things turn out badly for her."

The dog licked his chops thoughtfully. "And you think that—"

"They'll turn out badly? I've noticed that events in this crazy world do one of two things: they turn out well, or they turn out badly. Guess which one happens most often?"

"They turn out badly?" suggested the Labrador.

"Exactly! You win the Golden Chew Toy! How much do you want to bet that Fafnir will have problems?"

"Forget it, I'm not betting with you," said Manitou. "So, all we have to do is go to the library, and that's that."

Sparrow, who appeared to be thinking hard, cleared her throat: "If we have to look through all the books, parchments, and journals in that library, it's gonna take us months."

"Months? You've got to be kidding!" said Cal, who didn't especially care for reading.

"The Discussarium!" Tara shouted, making them all jump. "It's been in the back of my mind. Sparrow, you remember the first time we went to Omois; that boy Damien asked a question about one of your ancestors."

The pretty brunette blinked in confusion, then suddenly remembered.

"Yes, of course! He wanted to know the first name of Beauty's daughter, the one who passed the beast curse on me. And you think that—"

"Absolutely!" Tara interrupted joyfully. "When we went to the Discussarium, Damien asked the question, and this thing called the Voice immediately answered him. It's supposed to know everything about everything. It should be able to give us information about the Ravager!"

Manitou approved. "We have to go to Omois anyway, to give Empress Lisbeth the taludi and to get Cal's verdict overturned."

"So that's settled," said Cal. "Let's go."

"Yeah, let's," said Tara, "before my grandmother drags me back to Earth and locks me in a dungeon for the next two hundred years."

"We're all agreed?" asked Cal. "We'll pick up Fabrice and head for Omois."

"What about my feast?" moaned Manitou.

"You can stay here, Grandpa," said Tara kindly. "After all, we're just gonna do a little research."

"Yeah, right! Every time you go somewhere, something happens. I'd rather cheat my stomach than let you out of my sight."

Tara kissed him, both touched and annoyed by his concern.

Before they left, Cal decided to transform himself so he wouldn't be arrested the moment they reached Tingapore.

Fafnir had recognized him pretty easily, so he chose a very different look this time. He made himself taller—the metamorphosis wasn't pleasant—lightened his hair, broadened his shoulders, and aged his body about fifteen years.

"Heyyyy!" whistled Sparrow. "Cute guy!"

"Thenk yew, thenk yew," Cal said, bowing.

But just as they were about to leave, a black streak appeared in Cal's hair, one of his legs suddenly shortened, making him fall, and an eye reverted from blue to gray. The overall effect was pretty slapdash.

"Crap!" said the little thief. "I'm too tired to maintain my appearance. It must be an aftereffect of the t'sil worms. I'm going to need your help, Tara."

"Sure," she said, though a little surprised. "What do I have to do?"

"Really powerful spellbinders like Master Chem can modify other people's bodies for a certain length of time. That's what he did for us when we went to Limbo. But it takes lots of energy. He has to constantly hold every detail of the transformations in his mind, so they don't vary."

"So what?"

"It might be hard for you to manipulate my body that way, so that's not what I'm going to ask you."

"To be honest, it's just as well, because you might wind up missing an arm or a leg."

Cal smiled at her. "My mother has had all kinds of adventures, and she told me about them because she figured they might be useful some day. And she told me that it's possible to lend your power to another spellbinder."

"*No!*" Sparrow's outburst startled them.

"Don't do it, Tara. It's too dangerous!" she said, looking upset. "If you aren't in control of the flux when you're transferring your power, you can die!"

Tara was taken aback by her friend's forcefulness.

"Don't worry, the living stone will help me control my magic," she said. "Besides, Cal doesn't need much power—just enough to stabilize his transformation."

Sparrow took a deep breath and smiled weakly. "I'm sorry, but I've heard about some horrible accidents. So be very careful, okay?"

Tara hugged her.

"I won't take any chances," she whispered reassuringly. "And if I feel Cal's grabbing too much power, you have my permission to shift into the beast and punch his lights out. All right?"

"All right," Sparrow said with a chuckle.

"Tara, I'd knock myself out before I'd hurt a hair on your head," said Cal. "So, are we ready?"

"We're ready."

Living stone? Tara mentally inquired.

Heard I did, answered the stone. *Power you need for nice Cal? Power I give.*

Tara only intended to give Cal the look he'd chosen initially: a tall man of twenty-five with brown hair and blue eyes. But the stone's magic was hard to control, and its notion of what the young man should look like was very different from Tara's.

251

Its great power seized Cal and whipped up a howling whirlwind around him. When it subsided, Robin and Manitou both whistled in surprise.

Standing before them was the handsomest man they had ever seen. His eyes were sparkling green. A thick head of golden hair fell to his broad shoulders. He had a gladiator's chin and a Roman emperor's nose. Everything about him embodied nobility, strength, and honor. His spellbinder robe had disappeared, replaced by a kind of jewel-studded loincloth that set off his beautifully muscled legs and a glittering jerkin that molded incredible abs and left his enormous biceps free. A white cape, held by a golden clasp, fell gracefully down his back.

He was . . . amazing.

"Wow!" yelped Sparrow, agape.

"Yeah, like, wow!" agreed Tara.

"So, does it look all right?" asked the apparition in a resonant voice.

Sparrow giggled. Pointing at one of the suite's walls, she said, "By Reflectus, a mirror I now require, the better cute Cal for us to admire."

The wall turned into a mirror, and Cal was able to see his reflection in it.

Seeing his eyes widen and his manly jaw drop, the girls practically died laughing.

"Holy smokes! What the heck is *that?*"

"That's you," said Manitou simply, with a hint of envy.

"But it's awful! Everyone's gonna notice me!"

"No duh!" said Robin, laughing. "You're right, it's going be hard to avoid attracting attention. But don't worry. We'll protect you from the hordes of crazed fans who'll rush you the moment you stick your nose outside."

Cal gulped.

"Tara?" asked Sparrow, sounding quite serious. "Next time the court holds a ball, will you lend me a little of your power?"

"Sure!"

Tara was glad to see that Cal's astonishing transformation had eased Sparrow's fears. She was circling him wearing a huge smile, while the poor boy writhed in embarrassment.

Blondin barked to get Cal's attention.

"Crap! I almost forgot," he said in his thrilling, resonant voice. "Everyone knows my familiar is a fox. We'll have to disguise him too."

"All right, what kind of familiar would you like?" asked Tara. "How about a hydra, like Toto?"

He scowled at her.

"Very funny. No, an Arctic fox, like the last time. That would be fine."

Tara sent the image to the living stone, and they combined their magic.

The whirlwind spun around the fox, and when it subsided, a magnificent red lion stood in his place.

I asked for a white fox, said Tara mentally.

Pfft! answered the living stone. *Not big, fox. Lion better. Go good with gorgeous, pretty new Cal.*

"You know, Tara," he said, "this isn't quite what we agreed on."

"I'm sorry," she muttered, "but I still can't control my power very well."

"That's all right. I'll just look outside to make sure your grand-mother isn't hanging around, okay?"

"Go ahead, Cal. We'll follow you."

"Sure," said Robin, "just as soon as we find some cotton."

"Cotton?"

"To plug our ears when the girls see you and start screaming."

"Idiot!"

Shrugging his broad shoulders, Cal walked to the door with a majestic stride.

He took a peek outside, ignoring the waves of giggles shaking his friends. Suddenly the Council Chamber popped up, and he jumped backward. Blondin meant to bark, but, forgetting that he was a lion, let out a mighty roar, which made his irritated master jump again. Master Chem, Isabella, King Bear, Queen Titania, and Counselor Salatar were meeting, and they looked so real, you'd swear they were in the same room.

Cal slowed his pounding heart. Then he realized that the Living Castle was trying to be helpful.

"Thanks a lot," he said, speaking to the wall. "What you just did was really neat. But next time, warn me, all right? I'm too young to die of a heart attack!"

Amused, the castle projected a unicorn, which bowed graciously to him. Cal bowed in turn, at which point the unicorn bowed again . . . This would've gone on for a long time if Tara, Robin, Manitou, and Sparrow hadn't come out of the room.

"What in heaven's name are you doing?" asked the latter, seeing their friend bowing to nothingness.

"I'm thanking the castle," he answered with dignity. "It just showed me a image of the Council Chamber. Your grandmother's still there, so we can leave."

But their progress to the portal didn't go unnoticed.

The first two women they encountered would have bumped into a statue and knocked themselves out if the statute hadn't quickly moved out of their way.

Serving girls jostled each other as they backed off, the better to see the manly apparition. An old witch fainted, unable to stand the sight of so much splendor. A dozen girl spellbinders giggled when they passed, then began following Cal, unwilling to abandon their prey. Ladies-in-waiting fell into step with them, and the friends were soon followed by a whole mob of women. The whispering was the worst.

"Tara, can't you dial back your power a little, please?" moaned Cal. "Otherwise these looky-looks are gonna follow us to the ends of the earth."

"Hey, this was your idea! And in any case, there's nothing I can do. I just gave you my power. It's not my fault the living stone did whatever she felt like. Personally, I prefer boys with dark hair."

Robin glanced at his white locks and looked glum.

"Is that so? asked Cal, suddenly very interested.

"Nah, I'm just teasing you," said Tara with a chuckle. "I don't have a preference."

Robin sighed with relief.

Amused by Cal's glorious appearance, the castle arranged itself so that a ray of sunshine constantly illuminated him, and it created splendid landscapes to show his impressive physique off to all. He strode by hills lit by a glowing red sunset, with a gentle wind billowing his cape and ruffling his red lion's mane. It was spectacular.

Followed by their little troop of panting admirers, the friends went to the infirmary to see how Fabrice was doing. The centipede + shark demon was no longer there; Master Chem had probably returned it to Limbo. But neither was Fabrice.

They jumped when he suddenly spoke from behind them: "Ah, I was looking for you! I was told you were in the Council Chamber."

Turning, they saw Fabrice looking bright-eyed and bushy-tailed, with Barune at his side.

"Weren't you supposed to stay in bed?" asked Robin.

"That shaman!" grumbled Fabrice. "He scared me out of my wits talking about infections, gangrene, intoxications, and poisonings. Then, when he was sure I was good and terrified, he cured my wound just like that, *poof!*, I must have drunk a hundred gallons of that awful brew of his, and then he kicked me out of the infirmary!" He paused. "So, what's been happening while I was laid up?"

Fabrice suddenly noticed the presence of the extraordinary Cal.

"I don't think I know this gentleman," he said.

"Stop kidding, Fabrice. It's me, Cal."

"*Cal?* What in the world—"

"It's just something that didn't work quite the way we expected. Anyway, we have lots to tell you, and then we've got to get the heck out of here before they close in."

Fabrice suddenly burst out laughing. "They? Oh, you mean that crowd of girls outside is after you? Man, oh man!"

"Tell me about it!"

The friends brought Fabrice up to date on the recent developments. When he learned that the king had sent two high wizards off with Fafnir, he whistled in surprise.

"Fafnir's got a pretty difficult personality," he chuckled. "And when she's possessed, she must be a total drag. I wish the two wizards luck!"

"Speaking of that, she asked us to do some research on the Ravager, and we're heading for Omois. Want to come along?"

"Of course," said Fabrice, rolling his shoulders. "Otherwise, who'd protect you from those nasty monsters, mam'zelle?"

Tara grinned at him, and Robin frowned.

Apparently, not having gorgeous Cal right under their eyes helped the female spellbinders and ladies-in-waiting come to their senses, because the hallway was empty when the friends stepped out, to Cal's great relief.

But they didn't get ten yards when seemingly from nowhere, a covey of giggling and blushing women, teenagers, and little girls emerged and again started following them.

Cal picked up the pace.

The crowd sped up.

Cal walked even faster.

So did they.

"Hey, why are we running?" asked Fabrice, who, with Barune, was having trouble keeping up.

"We're running," muttered Cal through gritted teeth, "because I've become so handsome that all the women in the country have decided to pursue me."

"Gee, I think that's kind of nice."

"Well, I don't," said Cal in a tone that was melodious, but final.

The Living Castle decided to lend its friend a hand and created a violent storm in the hallways, which slowed the pursuers. The female courtiers were plastered against the walls, but the spellbinders used magic to free themselves.

The group arrived at the Transfer Portal out of breath, and in Cal's case, disheveled—but still elegant!

Luckily for them, the Cyclops couldn't be bribed. He categorically refused to tell the gaggle of smitten spellbinders where the incredible apparition had transferred to. Then he sighed. *That guy was too handsome to be real,* he thought sadly. *Why can't I have girl Cyclopes chasing after me like that?*

The five friends, their familiars, and Manitou rematerialized at Tingapore in a palace that was completely black. The marble walls, the gold statues, the imperial guards' uniforms—everything was black. Lady Kali, the head of housekeeping, greeted them graciously, draped in a long dress that was . . . terribly black.

"Have you come for the Dilution?" she asked, wringing her six hands. "What a terrible misfortune! To break one's neck in the prime of life. There wasn't a thing our shamans could do. The ceremony is tomorrow afternoon. Damien will show you to your rooms. The empress warned us that you would be coming, and we've kept your suite available in spite of the crowds."

Now the group was completely at a loss. Who had died? And how did the empress know they were coming? Also, Tara and Fabrice didn't have the slightest idea what a Dilution was.

Suddenly a figure they immediately recognized appeared in front of them. Prince Bandiou! The empress's uncle, whom Fafnir had destroyed.

Sparrow shape-shifted, and Tara activated her power, her hands glowing bright blue.

"Taxes are necessary to pay for public services," Price Bandiou declaimed persuasively. "On Earth, our planet of origin, they pay for our civil servants, schools, hospitals and their expensive supplies, trains, roads, public buildings, garbage collection, and much more. Here on OtherWorld, the government needs taxes to pay civil servants, who are found on all planets"—the figure smiled sardonically—"but also our army, spells necessary for our defense, improvements in our lifestyle, and scientific and magical research. Citizens of Omois, remember that the greatness of our empire rests on your shoulders. Pay your taxes!"

The figure bowed and vanished.

Kali wiped away a tear.

"What a great man!" she exclaimed. "Each time the empress has one of his speeches projected I can't help but weep."

Very discreetly, Sparrow drew in her fangs and claws, then shape-shifted back. Her robe groaned as it regained its normal proportions.

Tara extinguished the blue glow from her hands. With an effort, the two girls managed to look angelic and contrite.

"Yes, indeed," muttered Cal, his head bowed. "Such a tragic loss! Thank you for your hospitality, Lady Kali. What time will the Dilution take place?"

Catching sight of Cal's splendor, the head housekeeper's eyes widened imperceptibly.

"At three o'clock tomorrow afternoon," she purred. "The empress has reserved seats for you next to her—a distinct honor. We will see each other again, which will give me *great* pleasure. In the meantime, I must ask you to check your weapons. You'll be given a receipt so you can pick them up when you leave."

Robin sighed when he handed in his bow, which wasn't pleased in the least.

Though Cal's clothes fit him quite snugly, they hid an impressive number of knives and other sharp weapons, which he checked with regret. Tara strongly suspected that a fair number remained, but Kali didn't insist on a body search—though Tara felt she was dying to perform one.

"I don't believe I know you," she meltingly murmured to Cal. "I'll need your name for . . . for . . . for tomorrow's ceremony."

Cal, who loved Earth movies, didn't hesitate.

"Bond," he said in his velvety voice, bending to kiss one of the young woman's many hands. "James Bond."

Fabrice and Tara had to bite the inside of their cheeks so as not to burst out laughing.

Lady Kali flushed, and her smile widened. "Very well, er, Mister Bond. I hope to . . . see you soon."

Catching Sparrow's mocking gaze, she pulled herself together. "Damien, please show our friends to their suite."

"Yes, my lady."

Fabrice and Tara were annoyed at Cal. Bursting out laughing in a palace that was in mourning was hardly recommended, and they had a hard time not doing it. A very hard time.

They had barely taken their first steps when Robin suddenly stopped, then carefully turned his back away from Damien. Lillandril's bow, with all its accessories, had just rematerialized in his hand. Since they didn't hear any shouts from the Transfer Portal, they concluded that the elf's private rearmament hadn't been noticed.

"Man, that thing of yours is really handy," muttered Cal admiringly. "Still, make sure Damien doesn't see it."

"Yes, Mister Bond," Robin answered. This drew a glare from Tara, who was struggling to control her hysterics and couldn't repress a small chuckle.

Their trip through the palace calmed her down. The best way to describe the reigning atmosphere was morbid. The trees in the hallways had lost their leaves. The firebirds gazed sorrowfully at their black feathers. The big drago-tyrannosauruses were so depressed, they didn't even consider munching on Fabrice when the group crossed the black jungle. Pterodactyls soaring in the distance croaked anxiously, like birds of ill omen. The vrrrirs couldn't understand why their white fur had suddenly turned dark.

The filtered light from the bay windows was cold and gloomy, and a lugubrious moaning echoed throughout the palace.

"Brrr," said Fabrice, who no longer felt any urge to laugh. "It's very . . ."

"Yeah, very . . ." agreed Cal. "Especially since they are mourning a guy who was crazy for power and killed lots of people. If people knew the truth, they'd toss him in a cesspool and have a party instead!"

Gallant, Sheeba, and Blondin stood out vividly against all the black. The courtiers, some of whom had darkened their skin in mourning, looked disapprovingly at the white pegasus, silver panther, and red lion.

The female courtiers certainly admired Cal, but because of mourning, they simply gazed at him in awe and walked off, whispering.

"I know that you are Her Imperial Majesty's guests," began their guide Damien delicately, "but I think it might be appropriate if you changed your familiars' colors. We wouldn't want to offend the sensibility of our sovereign, who has been deeply affected by the loss of her uncle. Don't you agree?"

Tara smiled. The boy was very careful with them, since the previous visit.

"We'll take care of it," she said kindly.

Damien seemed relieved. "Thank you, Miss."

"But before we do, we need some information. Would it be possible to visit your Discussarium?"

Relieved that Tara had agreed to deal with the familiars, Damien was happy to oblige. "Of course. Follow me, please."

There weren't many people in the vast wood-paneled hall dedicated to the pursuit of knowledge. Though the walls were lined with manuscripts, books, journals, and travel logs, most spellbinders preferred to use the voice-activated Discussarium system.

Suddenly Fabrice stopped. Protruding from behind a table was a long, hairy, gray leg that ended in a very sharp claw.

"Good grief!" he hissed furiously, "there's an arachne here!"

Cal looked, then whispered, "Oh, that's Drrr! You know, the arachne who was being treated for her allergy problem. I got to know her when I was in jail. She's very nice."

"Well, she can stay right where she is," said Fabrice, as he searched for the table farthest from the spider.

Robin and Cal merely shrugged. To them, the arachne was just a citizen like any other.

They sat at Fabrice's chosen table, and Damien went back to the Transfer Portal to welcome other arriving guests.

A sphere of silence promptly isolated them.

"Voice!" cried Sparrow, who knew how the Discussarium worked.

"Princess Gloria?" answered Voice.

Sparrow grimaced. She was so accustomed to her nickname that it always sounded odd when someone used her true title.

"We're looking for information about an entity called the Ravager of Souls."

"I'm very sorry," Voice answered immediately, "but that information is classified. I can't give you access to it. Only the high wizards have the authorization. Can I do something else for you?"

"I am High Wizard Manitou Duncan," said Tara's grandfather, "though I may not look it at the moment. Give us the information, please!"

"My apologies, High Wizard," Voice responded, this time with a touch of asperity. "Authorization is only given to *Omois* high wizards."

"Crap!" said Cal. "The one time that we aren't being crushed, boiled, or kidnapped to get information, it doesn't work."

Thinking fast, Tara got an idea. "Voice?"

"Miss Duncan?"

"The empress has access to that information, doesn't she?"

This time Voice's tone was a bit scornful. "Yes, Miss, of course. As a member of the ruling family, the empress has access to all information."

"Fine," said Tara with a smile. "I just wanted to make sure that access didn't depend on the emperor."

To her friends' surprise, Tara got up and signaled them to follow her out of the Discussarium.

"I know what we're going to do," she announced when they were in the corridor.

"Oh man, I hate it when you talk that way," groaned Fabrice. "It usually means we're in for big trouble, probably involving serious, if not crippling, injuries."

"Actually, if my plan doesn't work, I don't think we'd be convicted of any crime more serious than lèse-majesté!"

Fabrice could hardly breathe.

"Treason against the sovereign?" he croaked. "What—"

"What are we going to do?" guessed Tara. "Oh, nothing special. We're just going to blackmail the Empress of Omois."

CHAPTER 13

IMPERIAL DISHONOR

This time, Fabrice groaned so audibly that everyone could hear him. Loud trumpeting from Barune showed that the little mammoth shared his dismay.

Other spellbinders turned to look at them, shocked.

"Shhh!" hissed Manitou. "Relax, Fabrice. You know how much Tara likes to joke."

"Trouble is, I have an awful feeling she's not joking at all," said Cal. "Come on, Tara. Are you serious?"

"You're right, I wasn't joking," snapped Tara. "I have to speak to the empress—right away. Anyone have an idea how to do that?"

"Easy. You request a private audience," said Robin. "Since there are maybe a million people who want the same thing, and they're adult citizens of Omois, I'm sure your request will be granted in a couple of centuries."

"I don't think we'll have to wait that long," said Tara thoughtfully. "The empress knew we were coming. She even saved us a space for the Dilution tomorrow, whatever the heck that is."

"A Dilution," Robin said, "is the ceremony by which the body is diluted and flows into the soil of the park, returning to the wellsprings of OtherWorld."

"Yuck!" said Fabrice. "You mean that when I walk in the park I'm walking on dead people from Tingapore?"

"No, of course not!" answered Robin, sounding offended.

"Well, that's reassuring."

"Just on the members of the imperial family," he said with a sly grin.

"Double yuck! That's really disgusting."

Tara brought them back to the topic at hand. "So, as I was saying, we have to see the empress fast, not only to get the information we need for Fafnir, but also to give her the taludi to prove Cal's innocence. In spite of his magnificent disguise, 'Mr. Bond' here risks being arrested again."

"Yeah," said Cal. "I'd kind of like to skip the time in jail this time."

Sparrow laughed.

"If you keep looking the way you do," she said, "the empress won't ever lock you up, at least not in a prison."

"Har-dee-har-har—very funny. I'm going to submit a request to prove my innocence and ask an ifrit to bring it to the empress. After that, we'll see what happens."

"Hey, time's a-wasting!" announced Manitou.

"Really? Aside from the risk of my being arrested, we don't have any other irons in the fire, do we? Fafnir doesn't need the information about the Ravager until she comes back from the Swamps of Desolation."

"I wasn't thinking about Fafnir," the Labrador said quietly. "I had some other folks in mind. Chem will be attending the funeral, probably accompanied by Isabella. I wouldn't be surprised if Sparrow's parents came to represent the Lancovit government as well. Not to mention Fabrice's father, who is sure to be invited as a friend of the late prince."

Fabrice turned an intense shade of green.

"You've got to be kidding!" he stammered. "My father and Isabella—at the same time? After the Bandiou episode, the smashing of Dad's greenhouse, and the trips to OtherWorld without Isabella's permission, I can't even imagine what punishment they'll slap on me. In fact, I was seriously thinking of going into exile on some other planet!"

"Oh, stop talking nonsense!" said Robin, giving him a friendly pat on the back. "Your father saw that we saved the Earth and OtherWorld from a brutal tyrant. He'll probably complain a bit, but that's all."

"Robin, my father will skin me alive and nail my hide to the living room wall. And Isabella will take what's left and make a doormat for the manor house. At least that way, I'll be useful."

Cal tried to cheer up Fabrice, but without success, and they walked on toward Tara's suite in silence. The palace was huge, and they had to ask an ifrit for directions. Noticing that courtiers were frowning at them along the way, Tara remembered that she wanted to change their familiars' colors.

Suddenly, shrieks of consternation rang out throughout the palace.

Drat! My blasted magic must have gotten away from me again! Tara realized. She had been looking at Cal and idly thought he would look even more handsome dressed in red.

Her magic struck instantly, and the entire palace turned red. Spell binder robes, statues, walls, curtains, animals—all red. The effect was pretty spectacular.

Horrified, Tara watched as frantic courtiers stared at their clothes in amazement.

Sparrow chuckled. "Just exactly what were you thinking, anyway?"

Tara blushed, a color that went nicely with her crimson robe, then canceled the spell. Robin took over and cautiously turned their robes a blue so dark they it looked black, then darkened the animals' coats.

Fabrice sighed again. Tara had so much power. And she manipulated it so easily. He wasn't jealous but . . . Well, actually he *was* jealous. Why didn't *he* have that kind of power? But then he remembered about the Bloodgrave who was trying to kill her for some mysterious reason. And Magister, who considered her the key to demonic power. All in all, maybe having less power was just fine. *Besides,* he thought, *I have Barune!* He looked down at the mammoth affectionately and stroked his head, while keeping his toes safely out of range. Barune was much smaller now, but he was still awfully heavy.

Robin was wondering what would happen when all this was finished. He knew that Tara would have to go back to Earth. He also knew that he couldn't accompany her. A half-elf on Earth—how ridiculous! His magic wasn't powerful enough to disguise his strange crystalline eyes, with their cat-like vertical pupils, and his odd, black-streaked white hair.

Besides, elves were hunters and warriors. Joining Tara on Earth would mean giving up that heritage. That was something he couldn't do, and the idea caused him almost physical pain. So for the moment, he was grateful for the problems they kept running into, which forced Tara to stay on OtherWorld.

As for Cal, he was thinking that he would soon have the murder charge dismissed. Then he had a few things to tell his professors at the University of Licensed Thievery about their grading. With a touch of sadness, he remembered that he would have to visit Brandis's parents and tell them their son's last wishes. More than anything, he wanted to be back in his own, real body. This one was just too much!

Sparrow was worried, but not for herself—for Tara. Sparrow had always been a solitary child because her parents traveled so much. Then Tara showed up and in a few weeks they had become like twins—better yet, they were confidantes. But Tara kept a lot secret, as if she had trouble expressing herself or didn't know how her displays of friendship would be received. And Sparrow knew how heavily the future weighed on her friend's shoulders.

In fact, they all had some idea of what they would do later on. Robin wanted to enter the royal Lancovit elf services, like his father. Cal was already a licensed thief, even though he didn't have the official title yet. Fabrice was in the apprentice training program and would become a high wizard. Sparrow was considering going into her mother's field—working with the dwarf tribes on OtherWorld's sources of magic. And if she didn't like that, she could study in Lancovit and also become a high wizard.

But Tara had no choice. She was the heir to an empire, the hope of an entire nation. Plus, she was also a key to demonic power, the target of a killer, and the center of a tangle of plots and dangers. She would never be a normal girl living a normal childhood.

Unaware of all this, Tara was lost in thoughts of her parents. She would have to tell her mother that she had seen her father again without her. Tara knew Selena wouldn't be angry. They'd had to act fast. But she regretted with all her heart that she hadn't been able to bring her father's back to her mother. Oddly enough, though she'd only known Selena for a few days, she missed her terribly. Isabella, too, even though she absolutely had to avoid her grandmother for the time being, so as not to find herself stuck on Earth forever.

In a remote corner of her consciousness, Tara worried about what Magister might be up to. Gallant mentally protested, telling her in his own way not to worry. If Magister bothered them, they would just ship him off to Demonic Limbo. The pegasus sent her an image of a frantic Magister dangling from his claws, surrounded by a horde of cackling demons. Tara couldn't help but chuckle. Pleased that he'd made her laugh, Gallant landed next to her and gave her an affectionate shove with his head. Sparrow shot Tara a questioning look and was reassured when her friend responded with a bright smile.

Once back in their suite, Manitou moaned that he was dying of hunger and begged them to order something to eat. An ifrit brought food, and they savored such bizarre dishes as brrraaa ribs in slurp sauce, kalorna purée, and brill shoots, accompanied by Tzinpaf, chocolate cake with bizzz honey, and Soothsuckers.

Tara looked suspiciously at the heart of her caramel/banana/pimento prophesicle. Its message was: "She will be here soon. There is no danger in her words, but the truth must be deserved." *As usual, not much to go on*, she thought.

Sparrow gave the ifrit their message for the empress, stressing that it involved new information proving Caliban Dal Salan's innocence. Then they waited.

By one o'clock in the morning, it was obvious that the empress wouldn't be summoning them, and they went to bed.

But a very sleepy Cal practically had a heart attack when an ifrit appeared at the foot of his bed and yelped: "Wake up! A visitor is coming! Get up!"

He found himself in the living room in his pajamas before he quite understood what was happening. Roused by the messenger, the others came in as well, rubbing their eyes and feeling equally baffled.

Suddenly the door swung open without their authorization and in walked Xandiar, the captain of the guards.

"Oh no," groaned Cal. "Not him!"

But Xandiar didn't pay the little thief any attention—most likely since Tara's magic was still working and Cal was as gorgeous as ever.

The guard captain first scrutinized the room, then waved in the slim, hooded figure behind him, and nervously slammed the door. He was red in the face and sweating heavily.

Seeing Xandiar so panicked, Tara immediately guessed who was under the hood. Her hunch was confirmed when it was pushed back to reveal the beautiful face of the empress. She had tied her lovely hair in a double braid that brushed the ground and wore a simple white robe cinched at the waist with a gold belt.

Despite his agitation, Xandiar snapped to attention and loudly declared: "Her Imperial Majesty Lisbeth'tyl—"

"That will do, Xandiar. They know who I am. Guard the door. If someone finds out I was here without an escort, the secret services will never let us hear the end of it."

From the anxiety with which he was wringing his four hands, the poor captain seemed to agree with them. Being solely responsible for his sovereign's safety was clearly too much for his nerves. He went to stand by the door, looking very unhappy.

The empress gracefully sat down and invited the friends to do the same. They obeyed, staring at her in astonishment.

She studied Cal for a moment and then nodded, as if she had just gotten the answer to an enigma. "Caliban Dal Salan, I presume?"

Gorgeous Cal bowed with unbearable grace. "At your service, Your Imperial Majesty."

"A beautiful disguise. Very original."

"Thank you, Your Majesty." Cal gave her a smile so brilliant, the empress blinked and couldn't help but smile back. Then, with visible effort, she got a grip on herself. While carefully avoiding Cal's eye so as not to be distracted, she asked in a clear voice: "What reward could I give to the killers of my uncle?"

Out of the corner of his eye, Robin saw Xandiar start. Fabrice gulped audibly.

This time, Sparrow jumped in.

"Your Majesty," she said cautiously, "the choice is yours."

"That is, to the extent that you're *also* responsible for his death," said Tara.

Manitou caught his breath, and horrible images of prison bars and dry bread began to flash before his eyes.

The empress didn't react, but merely studied Tara carefully. You could practically hear the gears going around in her head. Finally, she spoke: "How did you know?"

Manitou started breathing again. The bars and the dry bread receded.

"A couple of clues put me on the trail," answered Tara, whose heart was pounding. "In spite of my being attacked, you didn't call me in, because at the same time the gnomes had come to ask for your help. For the third time in a month. That's what was being whispered in the hallways. You sent hunter-elves to search Prince Bandiou's palace, and they didn't find anything. But courtiers were whispering the word 'scandal.' I think you'd already been suspicious of your uncle for some time. And when Glul Buglul introduced himself to us, he said that you'd insisted that he be Cal's compensator. You knew that his fiancée was among the prisoners; he'd told you. You guessed that he would turn to Cal to try to find evidence against your uncle. And I'll bet ten to one that you were the person who cast the Mentus Interruptus on Cal and Angelica to keep the Tellers from 'reading' them. And then got them thrown in jail. When Cal escaped, you prevented anyone from following him. In Lancovit, people didn't even know he had disappeared, which made no sense. That's when I finally understood that you were using us as detectives . . . or bloodhounds."

Manitou and the others were stunned. They stared in turn at Tara and at the empress, who remained perfectly calm.

'Your Majesty!" shouted Xandiar angrily. "Let me teach this impertinent girl manners. She is—"

"—quite correct," the empress said. "Though I'm very surprised that such a young spellbinder could have seen through my strategy."

"And this was the only solution you could come up with?" exclaimed Tara, angry at having her suspicions confirmed. "To convict an innocent person? To make us risk our lives?"

"No, that was *not* the only solution we came up with," answered the empress coldly. "We had no evidence to present to the court, so we couldn't formally charge Bandiou. Before Caliban was accused by Brandis's parents—which we had nothing to do with, by the way—we'd settled on another plan. A much simpler one."

She paused, challenging the friends to question her. Tara didn't hesitate: "And your plan was?"

"We tried to assassinate him," she answered simply.

"Wow!" exclaimed Fabrice. "Wonderful family relationships in this world of yours."

"When it's a matter of power, there's no family, and no friends," said the empress with a sigh. "Anyway, it didn't work. Bandiou had become too powerful. He sent our assassin back to us. In little packages."

Her statement was followed by a heavy silence. But it was quickly broken by Tara, who was still angry. "So, you put together this whole complicated plan so we would get rid of your uncle! What if it hadn't worked?"

"I wasn't trying to get you to rid me of my uncle," protested the empress. "Once the gnomes were free and the evidence of his crime presented, my high wizards would have made short work of him. But the five of you are a kind of uncontrollable weapon, and it turned out to be quite fatal to him."

"How did you know that we would be so . . . effective?" Cal dared to ask. "After all, we're just kids. As plans go, wasn't that one a little risky?"

"All OtherWorld knows that you caused the fall of the very powerful Magister, whom neither the dragons nor the high wizards had managed to locate. And you freed our apprentice spellbinders. So, when Brandis's parents accused Caliban Dal Salan, we seized the opportunity. Together, the emperor and I cast a Mentus Interruptus. And there, we got a surprise."

"A surprise?" asked Sparrow, who was fascinated.

"There was already an extremely powerful Mentus on Caliban and on Miss Brandaud."

"That's incredible," murmured Manitou, reflecting the general feeling. "So, you were interfering with someone else's plans. But when you asked for Brandis's manes to be called back, weren't you afraid he would declare Cal and Angelica innocent?"

The empress's smile became mocking. "There was a second spell on the ghost. A very subtle one that made him do exactly as we wished. We didn't intervene. So Caliban and Miss Brandaud were convicted. When Xandiar came to tell me that Caliban had disappeared, the emperor and I suspected that the gnomes had helped him escape. The rest of you clearly hadn't been informed, since you went and put half my palace to sleep. Then you disappeared in turn. I stopped Xandiar from pursuing you. That's the reason I asked him to accompany me this evening—so he could understand."

She gave the tall guard captain a kind smile, and he nodded gratefully.

"Finally, Guardian Besois-Giron showed up with my uncle's body and a fantastic story about a storm, a fall from a dock, and a broken neck. To his great relief, we pretended to believe him, and we declared a period of mourning. So, here we are."

"Crap! That means we went to Limbo for nothing!" exclaimed Cal angrily.

"Limbo?" asked Empress Lisbeth, surprised. "I don't understand."

"I wasn't absolutely positive about your role in this business," explained Tara. "I was only going on a hunch. So, we traveled to Limbo to call Brandis's manes back and have him judge Cal again. It's all recorded on a taludi."

"Oh, but there was no need of that," exclaimed the empress. "I pardoned Caliban and Miss Brandaud when mourning was declared. Didn't you get the official announcement in Lancovit?"

Up to then, Cal had remained standing, unconsciously displaying his impressive physique to best advantage. He now flopped into an armchair.

"By my ancestors!" he muttered. "I can't believe it. Nobody told us!"

"So let me repeat my question," she said. "What reward can I give to the people who just saved my empire?"

The six friends were too stunned to answer, so the empress went on. "To Caliban, I offer the Salendourivor estate in the north of Omois. Its livestock and fields bring in about a hundred thousand immutacredits a year. It will be a place to retire to after his exploits as a licensed thief."

Looking elegantly world-weary, Cal just stared at her.

"For Princess Gloria," she continued, "because you belong to the royal house of Lancovit, I imagine that an estate in our country could be misinterpreted. However, I understand that you would like to pursue research with the dwarves on the sources of OtherWorld magic. I own parchments and documents that are unique in the world. They are yours."

Sparrow stood up and bowed deeply, too moved to speak.

"High Wizard Manitou, the Imitanchivor estate awaits you. It is identical to Salendourivor and comes with every comfort, including the personal services of the famous chef François, one of the best in OtherWorld."

"Your Majesty . . . that's too great an honor," stammered the dog, who was already drooling.

"Robin, I believe your dearest wish is to enter the Lancovit secret services, like your father. I'd like to offer you a position as an officer in mine, effective immediately. It would make you our youngest officer, but your experience is undeniable. I won't offer you a piece of property. I know that you elves don't like to live outside of your country, and that you return to Selenda whenever you can. Lest you feel shortchanged, I will have a bank account opened in your name with a sum that matches the income from the other properties."

"Majesty, your generosity is boundless! The money will be welcome in Selenda. But I must decline your invitation to join your secret services. My father feels he isn't finished training me. I thank you nonetheless."

"As you wish. But my offer remains open if you decide not to stay with your father."

Lisbeth then turned to Fabrice.

"Young Besois-Giron, you're the only one on whom I don't have much information. Would you also like an estate?"

"Thank you, Your Imperial Majesty, but I have my father's. Serving you is reward enough."

"Hmm, an elegant answer. But elegance doesn't put food on the table. I will create an account for you under the same conditions as for your friend Robin. Does that suit you?"

"Marvelously, Your Imperial Majesty."

"As for you, young Tara'tylanhnem—"

"I know what I want," interrupted Tara as politely as possible. She was annoyed to see her friends rapt with admiration for the empress, when she had just blatantly manipulated them. "I would like access to the classified information in your Discussarium."

The empress stiffened.

"What classified information?" she asked cautiously.

"About the Ravager of Souls. We're having some problems with him."

The empress whistled through her teeth. "By my ancestors! You know how to choose your enemies, young lady. The Ravager—is that all? I know he was imprisoned by Demiderus himself, because he betrayed the human cause by allying himself with the demons in the Great Rifts Battle. He is extremely dangerous, because he can't be destroyed. Your request is granted. You can access the information in the Discussarium. I will give the order when I leave here. And though you probably won't want it, I am also giving you Sevendareve in Tarvenchir, an estate near mine."

Tara was about to refuse, but the empress stopped her with a gesture. "Wait. Go see the property before you turn my gift down. If you really don't like it, then I will withdraw the offer and replace it with immuta-credits."

Tara bowed her head obediently. She had gotten what she wanted, and there was no point in annoying the powerful sovereign.

"As you wish, Your Imperial Majesty."

"Very well."

The young woman smoothly got to her feet and drew the hooded cape around her.

"Let's go, Xandiar. We still have a lot to do. I'm counting on you all later for the Dilution."

The empress left, followed by her extremely nervous guard.

"Tara!" exclaimed Sparrow. "Enough is enough!"

Tara looked up, surprised by the girl's tone.

"We're friends, aren't we?" Sparrow asked firmly. "Much more than that, actually. After everything we've been through, we absolutely trust each other, right?"

"Er, of course," said Tara, who had no idea what she was getting at.

"Then the next time you have doubts, hunches, or suspicions, don't just keep them to yourself, understand? You have to share everything with your friends, even at the risk of looking like a complete idiot. I hate it when you hide things from us!"

"I'm sorry," Tara said with a sheepish smile. "It's just I didn't want to bother you with my stupid ideas. The plan seemed so complicated and so unlikely. In the beginning I figured Magister was behind everything. I didn't think of the empress at all! Besides, my grandmother taught me not to annoy her with my problems, so I tend to work them out by myself."

"Well, I'm not your grandmother! And problems we solve together. Okay?"

"Okay."

They spent the next hour discussing the empress's lavish gifts. Eventually, excitement gave way to fatigue and they went back to bed.

Cal was still gorgeous the next morning and as tall and muscular as ever—to his dismay.

"How long is this blasted spell gonna last, for Pete's sake?" he grumbled into his breakfast bowl.

Sparrow looked up from her slice of whaloon buttered bread.

"Considering how powerful Tara's magic is, it might last your whole life," she said teasingly.

Cal stared at her in horror.

"You think so?" he quavered. "You think I'm stuck in this fat body?"

"Hey!" protested Tara. "You're not fat."

"Nope," agreed Sparrow. "I think you're beautifully proportioned. You did a great job, Tara."

"But I'm a *thief*, for crying out loud! I have to be small and agile and able to slip into places without being noticed. How do you expect me to do my work looking like this?"

"Well, you'll just be a high-profile thief," suggested Fabrice. "Very high-profile."

For a moment, they thought Cal would start weeping. Instead, he just glowered at them.

"All right," he said. "What do we do now?"

"We're going to the Discussarium to get information about the Ravager," said Tara, trying to hide a smile. "That way, if Isabella and Fabrice's father come here for the Dilution and we get grounded for the next fifty years, Sparrow and Robin will still be able to give Fafnir the information."

This jolted Fabrice back to reality.

"Yeah, and I hope you'll visit us from time to time," he said. "If Isabella doesn't turn us into toads for disobeying her first, that is."

As they headed for the Discussarium, Tara and Sparrow couldn't help but laugh each time a female spellbinder bumped into a wall or a tree—or fainted—on catching sight of gorgeous Cal. He picked up the pace until they practically sprinted to the Discussarium.

Entering the big hall, they sat at a table in a sphere of silence. Cal, who was in no mood to be trifled with, barked at the Voice: "All right, we're authorized now. So give us the information about the Ravager, and make it snappy!"

"Ohhhh, with pleasure, handsome spellbinder," cooed the Voice.

Cal groaned. Tara and Sparrow chuckled.

"The Ravager is an enemy of OtherWorld who allied himself with the demons and was taken prisoner by Demiderus after the Great Rifts Battle. The only entity that can fight him is the White Soul, an extremely powerful magic artifactum. After Demiderus imprisoned the Ravager on the Island of Black Roses, a knight whose family had been killed because of him wanted revenge. He took the White Soul and went to the Swamps of Desolation."

Tara was fascinated. "So what happened?" she asked.

"He was killed. The Ravager set a trap with the help of the Mud Eaters, and the knight never reached the island."

"That means the White Soul can't be very far from it!" exclaimed Sparrow. "We have to talk to the Mud Eaters."

Tara wasn't too crazy about that approach. After all, the Mud Eaters were Magister's minions.

"Er, I'm not sure that's such a hot idea," she began. "Fafnir is fine for the time being. And even though the Ravager managed to possess her a couple of times, she pulled through all right, didn't she?"

"Are you saying the Ravager touched one of your friends?" asked the Voice, sounding incredulous.

"Yes, a dwarf named Fafnir. She was partly possessed after drinking a brew made from black roses."

"Ye gods!" exclaimed the Voice, all cooing forgotten. "That information must be immediately shared with the empress and the emperor. If the Ravager gets free, all life on the planet will be in danger!"

"King Bear and Queen Titania have sent two high wizards with her on a scouting trip to find out what's happening on the Island of Black Roses."

"*What*? They're out of their minds!" The Voice now sounded completely panicked. "Without the White Soul, no power on earth can defeat the Ravager. And sending the dwarf near the island is the best way for her to become totally possessed. By my creators, they don't teach you *anything* in those books of yours!"

"That information was classified!" Cal reminded him firmly. "You even refused to give it to us yesterday. So how could the king and queen possibly know it? Unlike your empress, they aren't descended from Demiderus."

"That's no reason," said the Voice angrily. "You don't realize—"

"That's just it, we don't," Cal interrupted. "So, what should we do?"

"You're a magnificent specimen of a spellbinder," the Voice answered quite seriously. "So I would advise you not to get close to the Ravager. It would be a pity to spoil so much beauty."

Cal gritted his teeth and continued: "All right. What else?"

"Find the White Soul. That's the only solution."

"What does this White Soul look like?"

"It's a statuette of a woman with her arms raised in supplication. It's white and luminous."

The Voice projected an image of a statue about a foot tall and began to rotate it. The expression on the woman's face was of indescribable sadness.

"And once we find it?"

"You have to put it on the Island of Black Roses, that's all I know."

"And this thing could be in the hands of the Mud Eaters, right? Who are allied with our worst enemy and who tried to lock us up?"

"I would've been tempted to lock you up myself," said the Voice with a chuckle, "so I understand them very well. When you come right down to it, those crude creatures have pretty good taste."

Cal ground his teeth and got up without comment. The others followed him, and—to the Voice's disappointment—left the Discussarium.

Out in the corridor, Fabrice couldn't resist. Gazing at Cal adoringly, he purred: "So, handsome spellbinder, what do we do now?"

"Oh, shove it!" Cal barked. "For the time being, there's no way to warn Fafnir; she must already be in the Swamps of Desolation. All we can do is wait for her to come back. And since the empress ordered us to attend the Dilution, we really don't have any choice."

In fact, they would have gladly skipped it, but a glance at the portal Room quickly convinced them there was no point in trying to leave Omois. The guards, already quite numerous in normal times, had been reinforced for the mourning period and the arrival of many foreign dignitaries. Kings, queens, presidents, ministers, and counselors from all over OtherWorld and the other planets arrived in a steady stream, and poor Kali was looking a bit haggard. King Bear had to preside over a trial and hadn't been able to come, so only Queen Titania was present. Master Chemnashaovirodaintrachivu showed up with a whole delegation of dragons, but Isabella wasn't along, to Tara's great relief.

Fabrice wasn't so lucky. Damien confirmed that the young earthling's father was indeed there and watched curiously as Fabrice turned white and green at the same time.

From then on Fabrice shut himself away in their rooms, trembling each time the door opened. He did have to leave the suite for lunch, but luckily the sovereigns and their guests ate their meals in another part of the palace. Tara's little group wasn't invited, which allowed Fabrice to avoid his father for a little longer.

The empress had prepared a spectacular feast. Meat and fowl from OtherWorld, hot spices from Dranvouglispenchir, the dragon planet, grains, sprouts, tubercles, semolina, breads, pasta, and other delights from Santivor, the Truth Tellers' planet, cheeses from Earth, and sweet wines from Tadix, OtherWorld's larger moon. The desserts were prepared by the greatest pastry chefs, and included an amazing fountain of white and dark chocolate mousse, pastries filled with sweet whaloon cream, and OtherWorld fruit tarts—blackberry, strawberry, cherry, apple, vlir, mrmoum, and gandari—not to mention the candies and marshmallows served with coffee, tea, and the soothing brew called kax.

Manitou was so happy, he forgot he was human—psychically human, that is—and wagged his tail while tasting everything. The silverware had some trouble feeding him, and the fork finally gave up after the Lab's powerful jaws twice nearly bent its tines.

After two hours at the table, Manitou had eaten so much, he could hardly walk. Tara couldn't help but chuckle when he gave a resounding *burp!* She didn't know that dogs could belch like humans. She drank a bit of Tzinpaf, the delicious apple-orange cola drink, while looking warily at the Soothsuckers. But she couldn't resist, and soon found herself reading another message: "You must save him, he doesn't deserve it." *Save who? From what?* Tara sighed. She was getting a little fed up being the masked avenger, supposedly because she had some sort of really big power. Besides, in movies it was usually the boys who rescued the girls. Well, usually.

A loud gong roused Tara from her thoughts. The Dilution was about to begin. The spellbinders and courtiers all left the dining rooms and headed to the imperial park.

The thrones had been set out on a pedestal, surrounded by the guests and the high wizards. Tara, Cal, Fabrice, Manitou, Sparrow, and Robin found out that they had been seated next to the two sovereigns!

Empress Lisbeth looked stunning in a black robe studded with rubies in a golden-eyed peacock pattern. Her mass of hair, colored black for the occasion, set off her blue eyes and white skin with almost painful intensity. A simple black gold band set with black diamonds encircled her brow. She was thoroughly imperial, and the courtiers looked awed.

When Cal sat down next to her, he felt very embarrassed to be in the guest of honor's seat. Whistling with surprise, the crystalists started feverishly writing headlines for the newsrystals: "Empress Finds New Suitor" and "Mysterious Stranger: A New Prince Consort?"

Emperor Sandor wasn't enjoying any of this. His black armor made him look small, he was in a foul mood, and his half-sister was being far too friendly with the handsome stranger. So he lent an attentive ear when the majordomo signaled the herald to announce the guests. The herald was a wrinkled creature whose mouth was shaped like a bull-horn, and his task was to introduce the guests to the imperial couple. When their name was called, each stood and bowed to the twin thrones. The Omois sovereigns nodded politely in response.

The herald soon came to the following name: "Count Salendou-rivor."

All eyes swung toward the two thrones, but nobody stood up.

The herald, feeling a little awkward, said, "Count Caliban Dal Salan of Salendourivor."

Sparrow was the first to get it, and she poked Cal in the ribs.

"That's you," she whispered. "Stand up and bow!"

"What?" he exclaimed, completely lost.

The empress leaned over and murmured: "Sorry, I forgot to tell you. The estate I gave you is a county, so you are now the Count of Salendourivor."

Cal leaped to his feet and bowed with unbearable grace. Smiling happily, the empress returned his greeting. The emperor followed with a curt nod, while scowling at the young man.

Kali turned to Fabrice, who was seated next to her.

"I don't understand," she whispered. "Isn't your friend's name Bond? James Bond?"

It was a tough moment for Fabrice, since bursting out laughing in the middle of a funeral ceremony wasn't quite proper. Kali must have thought him very rude because he seemed unable to answer her. When she saw him turning red, she gave up.

Funeral orations to the late prince followed, and Fabrice was able to compose himself. Bandiou's body floated peacefully in and landed gently on the black lawn.

Contrary to Tara's expectations, the ceremony was quite short. The empress clearly didn't want her uncle praised too much. As soon as the speeches were over, the body began to sink into the ground. And as it liquefied a curious phenomenon happened. The grass became blue again, the black trees regained their vivid colors, the birds their bright plumage, the flowers their blazing hues. The empress's robe and the emperor's armor were the last to change, going from black to shining white.

The spellbinders immediately followed their example, and the crowd broke up without further ado.

"Uh-oh," muttered Sparrow. "Here come Count Besois-Giron and Master Chem!"

Fabrice looked totally panicked. But he realized there was no way out, so he settled down to face the music.

On the right, the count was reading the riot act to his son, while on the left the dragon did the same for Tara. She had gone off again without telling him, and Chem found that truly exasperating.

Tara wanted to come to Fabrice's rescue, so she simply apologized to Master Chem and promised—with her fingers crossed behind her back—never to do it again. Or, at least not without warning him first.

Fabrice was sweating under the barrage of questions from his father, notably about a certain theft of keys and an unauthorized transfer. The boy was bravely trying to explain the chain of circumstances that involved them in Bandiou's death while trashing his father's greenhouse, roses, well, and half his garden. The count had seen the result but didn't know why or how it had happened.

The empress was eavesdropping without being obvious about it, and she finally intervened. Without revealing all the ins and outs of the affair, she let the count know that his son had been very helpful to the empire, and that his actions as a temporary secret agent had earned him a beautiful estate or its equivalent in immuta-credits. Besois-Giron was speechless with surprise.

Empress Lisbeth took advantage of this to again compliment Fabrice, and that did the trick. He would not be grounded for the next fifty years. He just had to swear not to do it again, which he did, perspiring with relief.

The empress would have gladly kept Tara's little group under her benevolent surveillance, but Master Chem firmly turned her down. He wanted the them all to return to Lancovit on urgent business, and she had to yield.

She left after a last, regretful glance at Cal, and the group headed to the Transfer Room with the dragon.

"Is everything all right?" asked Tara, worried. "Any news of Fafnir?"

"No, she isn't back yet," Chem answered. "About Caliban: isn't his disguise a little showy?"

"Tell me about it!" said gorgeous Cal, sighing. "I just wanted to change my appearance a bit for little while. I borrowed some of Tara's power, and this is the result."

Master Chem was impressed. "I see. And how long has this lasted?"

"Since yesterday," said Cal very unhappily.

"Oh! Well, it's quite a demonstration! All right, let's hurry up. We've got to get back to Lancovit as quickly as possible."

"Why? Is there a problem?" asked Fabrice, noticing the distress in the dragon's voice.

"Yes. A very big problem, you might say. Safir Dragosh has confessed to murder!"

CHAPTER 14

THE
VAMPYR'S
MURDER

"What? That's impossible!" exclaimed Sparrow, who knew Master Dragosh well.

"No, it isn't," said Cal, who didn't like the vampyr at all. "When we ran into him at the alley his mouth was bloody, and the guy Manitou and Fafnir saw was lying there dead."

Tara had read enough Agatha Christie mysteries to know that things weren't always as they seemed. Like Christie's detective hero Hercule Poirot, she could feel her brain getting busy.

"He said that something terrible had happened," Tara said aloud. "And that he had to notify Their Majesties. We were kind of in a hurry just then, so we didn't try to figure it out. What happened after that?"

"He returned to the castle and told Robin's father that a murder had been committed," said Chem. "When the elves examined the body, they found the man died from loss of blood due to a deep bite in the jugular vein."

"And the secret services say Dragosh was the only vampyr present in Lancovit at the time of the attack," said Robin.

"The only vampyr *officially* present," said Tara. "What's to prove that another vampyr wasn't around?"

"That's impossible," said Sparrow. "Vampyrs have to notify the authorities when they go anywhere. Ever since the great Starlings War, when they were allies of the Edrakins and ravaged the continent's countries, they can't travel without registering."

"But I thought human blood was harmful to vampyrs."

"Very harmful," Chem confirmed. "It cuts their life expectancy in half, they can't stand sunlight anymore, and their bite becomes poisonous. That's how they enslave humans."

"Yuck!" said Fabrice. "I like this world, but your monsters are a little too aggressive for my taste."

"We haven't had any problem with vampyrs for years," said Chem. "And I'm absolutely sure Dragosh isn't guilty. That's why I want to attend the trial. I'd like to understand what's going on."

Having reached the Portal Room, they had to interrupt their conversation. Kali looked displeased that Mr. Bond was leaving so soon. When the shaft of golden light hit him, bathing Cal's body in a flaming glow, she couldn't repress a deep sigh of disappointment.

In a few short seconds they were back in Lancovit.

"You should go back to your mother and grandmother, Tara," announced Chem after greeting the Cyclops who oversaw the portal. "You're not safe here on OtherWorld. Also, your mother said something about classes, and school, and late registration."

"Are they still hung up on that stupid idea? What's the point of going to school if I can learn a book by heart just by casting a spell?"

The dragon shrugged helplessly. "I have no idea what they want you to do, but I agree with them. Whoever wants to kill you certainly hasn't given up."

Tara studied the dragon wizard carefully. She hadn't forgotten the mysterious killer, of course. In fact, when she reached the Living Castle, she'd instinctively scanned her surroundings for signs of an animatrap. The castle could sense her anxiety and projected lovely, inoffensive landscapes: blue hills, trees in bloom, and frolicking animals. Its good intentions were a little spoiled when a peacefully grazing mooouuu was suddenly swallowed whole by a passing snaptooth. Tara had to look away, gagging. Snapteeth would make the most demented Earth tigers jealous.

Her thoughts returned to Master Chem. Tara sensed there was something that he wanted. And he said she "should" go back to Earth, not she "must." *Maybe playing on the big saurian's heartstrings will give him a reason to keep me here.*

"Master, I understand that my mother and grandmother are worried," she began, smiling sweetly. "And to be honest I'm not exactly at ease on your planet, either. But my friends and I have spent a lot of time dealing with Cal's problems and then Fafnir's. We haven't had any real vacation time together. I'd really like to be able to spend a few more days with my friends. May I, please?"

She batted her eyes at him, looking as angelic as she could.

The old wizard gave a snort of derisive laughter. "Tara, you really remind me of a dragon. I think your soul made a mistake when it incarnated in the body of a little girl. I know perfectly well that you want to stay because you're dying to know what happens to Fafnir. So don't try to fool me by playing innocent. Let's make a deal. You can stay two more days—"

"A week," countered Tara, suddenly enjoying herself.

"Three days. I don't want Isabella skinning me alive," grumbled the old wizard.

"Six days, and I'll be your apprentice again for two of those days. That way you can keep an eye on me, and I'll be under your mighty protection. You're a dragon! Who better to teach me to defend myself against my enemies? You're a lot more powerful than they are."

Tara had put her finger on the wizard's weak spot. Out of vanity, he couldn't refuse to protect her. And having worked for Chem before, she knew how forgetful he was and how much help he needed to find his things.

Chem's eyes narrowed, making him look like a crafty old mandarin. "Hmm, your arguments are pretty compelling, but no: six days is too much. Four should be enough."

"Five days, and I'll also straighten your office."

"Done!" he said, shaking her hand. "You'll be my apprentice spellbinder for two days, *plus* you'll straighten my office. You're free today, but I want to see you tomorrow morning first thing."

Tara's smile was so bright, it practically made Chem blink.

"Sir, yes, sir!" she snapped, clicking her heels like a perfect little soldier.

The old wizard walked off, laughing and shaking his head. *That little spellbinder is as stubborn as a whole pack of mules!*

Robin, Fabrice, gorgeous Cal, Sparrow, and Manitou had watched the exchange with great interest.

Sparrow ran over to give Tara a hug.

"Wow! Remind me never to argue with you!" she said.

Tara happily hugged her back. Then she stepped away, suddenly serious.

"Master Chem must still have some plan," she said. "I've never seen him do something without a good reason. In fact, I actually argued with him because I felt that he wanted me to stay. I didn't know for how long, which is why I left that option open. But we know now that something's going to happen in the next five days, and that he wants me to be on OtherWorld for it."

Fabrice was amazed. "What? You mean the two of you were play-acting? Why?"

"I think Chem hasn't given up on catching Magister," said Tara, who after Sparrow's rebuke had resolved to share her hunches with her friends. "He might be dangling me under the Bloodgrave Master's nose as bait. The question is, who's going to wind up on the hook, the fisher or the fish?"

A worried Robin shook his head. "We just barely survived Magister's attacks. I can't believe Master Chem would make you run such a risk a second time."

"You might be right," she admitted. "I guess I'm just a little suspicious of him. Anyway, we'll see."

They had left the Transfer Room and were heading to the Great Hall when the sharp ringing of a bell was heard. A loud voice echoed through the hallways: "The trial of Master Safir Dragosh, vampyr, is about to begin!"

The crystal screens brightened, showing an image of the hearing room.

"C'mon!" said Sparrow. "Follow me!"

Barune wasn't able to run as fast as Sheeba and Blondin, so Fabrice levitated him, which he hated. The friends arrived out of breath just as the day's session was starting.

The vampyr hadn't changed, at least in appearance. He was still tall and sinister, and still had red eyes, black hair, and white fangs. But his shoulders were slumped despondently and his former arrogance had vanished.

Dragosh's eyes blazed momentarily when he saw Tara enter the hearing room, then he lapsed back into apathy. He had already confessed his crime, so the Truth Tellers weren't present. The hearing room was full, however, because the courtiers and spellbinders hadn't seen a trial like this in centuries.

Tara and her friends made their way as far to the front as they could.

King Bear and Queen Titania were presiding over the trial. The initial sessions had taken place in previous days. By the time the group arrived, First Counselor Salatar was questioning Dragosh. The vampyr answered in a dull, weary monotone.

"Yes, after shifting into wolf shape I grabbed Mr. Carlit by the shoulders," he said in a flat voice. "That's why they found hairs on his clothes. I drank his blood and he died."

The chimera looked doubtful—at least that was Tara's best guess at the expression on his lion face—but he was doing an effective job. It took him just half an hour to spin out the entire course of events. The vampyr hadn't eaten for days, he said, and he'd gone downtown and gotten drunk. He was starving, and when a warm human unfortunately crossed his path, he hadn't been able to resist.

"Master Dragosh is protecting someone," Robin whispered to Tara. "It's obvious to me."

"I suspect everyone thinks so too," she said. "But who, and why?"

The sentence was clear. Since the death penalty had been abolished in Lancovit, Dragosh was sentenced to life in prison.

The vampyr didn't react when the sentence was pronounced. He followed his guards without complaint, closely watched by the crystalists and the public. People stood up, landed (those who were hovering), stretched or straightened, and left the court room exchanging excited comments. What a strange business this was!

Still looking unbearably handsome, Cal decided to go home to see his parents. He would come back to the castle later to warn Master Sardouin that he wouldn't be available for a few more days. As Lady Boudious's apprentice spellbinder, Sparrow went to let her know that she was back, and to also ask for a few extra vacation days to spend with Tara. Robin visited his father to talk over recent events, and in particular, the trial. As Master Chanfrein's apprentice, Fabrice was automatically free of any obligations, since his master had gone with Fafnir to the Swamps of Desolation.

Tara, who didn't need to ask anyone's permission, roamed the Living Castle with her mind working overtime. She was sure the dragon wizard was up to something, but what? And did it have anything to do with Master Dragosh's trial?

Flying ahead, Gallant attracted her attention and sent her a message: The weather was beautiful and they hadn't flown together in the longest time. What was she waiting for?

Tara didn't need to be asked twice. A few moments later, they were soaring, free as air, chasing the puffy little clouds scattered across the sky. It was a rush of boundless freedom to feel Gallant's powerful muscles working under his skin and see his white wings cut through the air. They frightened a herd of baaa grazing in a meadow and did loop-the-loops. Well, sort of. The first one was perfect, and it was during the second that things went wrong and Tara almost fell to the ground.

In other words, they had a long, wonderful time together, and Tara felt completely relaxed when she slipped off her pegasus's back. She rubbed him down and curried him, made sure he had everything he needed for the night, and settled him comfortably in the royal stables. Then she returned to the castle. Gallant was a little surprised not to be sleeping in her bedroom, but Tara wanted to be alone.

She told her friends the same thing. They weren't too happy about it, but she insisted. Feeling somewhat hurt, Sparrow went to sleep in her own room, Robin left with his father to see his mother in Selenda, and Cal, instead of staying in the apprentice spellbinders' dormitory, decided to sleep at home. ("With Toto?" asked Sparrow teasingly.) Manitou went to see some old friends and spent the night with them. They all ate dinner together, and then went their separate ways.

Tara took a quick shower, then got dressed again but without her shoes, so as not annoy the bed. The pillows immediately positioned themselves behind her back, and she waited.

It took a long time. In fact, she was half asleep when he arrived.

He seemed surprised to see that she was waiting for him. And his red eyes widened when she spoke to him calmly, or at least in a voice that quavered only slightly. "Hello, Master Dragosh. Or, good evening, I should say."

He folded his long wings. The air trembled for a moment and the dark bat grew once again into the familiar shape of the vampyr.

"I expected to frighten you," he announced.

Tara swallowed the "no such luck" on the tip of her tongue. She knew she didn't want to use sarcasm with a guy with teeth to put a German shepherd to shame.

"In fact, you don't even seem particularly surprised."

"That's right, I'm not," Tara answered calmly. "I asked my friends not to stay with me tonight, and you may have noticed that Gallant is in the stables. I wanted us to be alone."

The vampyr stiffened, then bared his fangs in a threatening rictus. "How?"

Tara guessed that his laconic "How" really meant, "By my ancestors, how did your brilliant intelligence manage to weave together such random hints to know that I would escape from my prison with the sole aim of coming to see you? I'm astonished." Or, something like that.

"You can shape-shift at will," she remarked, "and without using magic, so you don't trip the spell detectors."

"That's not quite true," the vampyr said. "Knowing that I have that ability, they put a protective charm in place."

"Obviously a really effective one," snorted Tara. "I suspect that the prison that can hold you hasn't been built yet. When we ran into you in the alley the night of the murder, you looked at me and said, 'This is all because of you!' I concluded you were still angry at me for some unknown reason and would enjoy coming here to tell me. What I didn't know was whether it would be tonight or tomorrow night. It's nice of you to come so soon; it spares me some sleepless nights."

The vampyr suddenly looked terribly tired. He glanced at a chair, and it raced over to catch him as he sat down.

"Talking with you is like walking on quicksand," Dragosh said with a sigh. "You know you're going to sink in at some point, but it's never when you expect. Very well. I've come to tell you that a . . . let's say 'a thing' is after you. And that thing mustn't find you."

Tara appreciated the heft of the phrase. A *thing*, then. "So?"

The vampyr rubbed his eyes. "So . . . I don't have to give an explanation to some girl of . . . whatever age you are. You just have to leave, that's all."

"I'll be thirteen in a few days," Tara said. She was starting to enjoy the vampyr's discomfort. She intended to keep him off balance to get as much information as she could. "And I'm not planning on going anywhere, at least not without a very good explanation."

"Miss Duncan, I think I just put my finger on what irritates me the most about you," he growled.

Tara looked at him in surprise.

"It's the fact that you aren't able to do anything without arguing. You always have to know the whys and the wherefores. You have to save your life, and you'll only do that by leaving here. Isn't that reason enough?"

Tara shrugged. "Master Dragosh, since discovering OtherWorld, my life has been like those nightmares that kids have when they've gone overboard on ice cream and horror movies, with their parents out, and they're all alone in a dark, gloomy house, on a stormy night. At this point, I find it a bit hard to be frightened."

Dragosh hadn't completely lost his meager sense of humor. The corners of his lips lifted a tiny fraction. "It's true that a surprising number of people on the planet dislike you. Can I conclude that you're not going to pack your bags and return to Earth tonight?"

"That's right!" Tara exclaimed cheerfully. But she could tell that the vampyr felt sincerely upset, so she softened her tone. "I'm due to leave in a few days anyway, four to be exact. I'll be spending most of my time with Master Chem or with my friends. Does that make you feel better?"

The vampyr got to his feet. "In that case I'll be going, and I hope my warning will have been useful."

Before he could shape-shift, Tara spoke: "Just one more thing. You don't like me. You're afraid that Magister will imprison me and use me to open Limbo and free the demons, who could then overrun the universe. You've made it clear that you're prepared to kill me with your own hands, or claws, or whatever, rather than let the demons get here. Yet, now you come in the middle of the night to tell me that I'm in danger and that I've got to run away. I don't understand you."

"At least we have that in common, Miss Duncan."

Great; now the vampyr was being funny. Sensing that it could be a long night, Tara sighed. "So?"

This time she was treated to a broad, toothy smile.

"The only thing I can be sure of," Dragosh said somewhat sadistically, "is that you're going to ask yourself a lot of questions about my visit this evening and probably not sleep very well because of your insatiable, irrepressible, and dangerous curiosity. Whereas I plan to rest peacefully in my prison."

"That's a very childish thing to say," she said indignantly, crossing her arms. "And very small minded."

"Yes, isn't it?" he agreed, looking pleased. "We get our compensations where we can."

He bowed. "I hope to have the pleasure of not seeing you again, Miss Duncan."

Tara could hardly believe her ears, but she recovered, and bowed in turn.

"Believe me, Master, the feeling is mutual."

Elegantly, the vampyr had let her have the last word. He shifted into bat shape, opened the door quietly, and vanished down the hallway.

Tara ordered the castle not to open the door to anyone without her permission. Then she got undressed and slipped into bed, feeling troubled.

She tossed and turned for a while, her head full of questions. Since the vampyr could get out of prison, why didn't he just run away? Had he really killed that man and drunk his blood? And if so, why? That story of being hungry in the middle of the night just didn't make sense.

Darn! The vampyr was right. She *hated* not understanding things.

The next morning, Gallant, Sparrow, Robin, Cal, Fabrice, and Manitou came to get Tara so they could have breakfast together before she started work with Master Chem. So they were very surprised when the door to her suite refused to open. They waited for a few minutes, calling to her, but she didn't appear.

"You think she's not in her room?" asked Sparrow, who was starting to get worried.

"Let's try the main dining room," suggested Cal. "Maybe she went down for breakfast. C'mon, I'm famished!"

Gallant refused to leave his post, however. The pegasus stood in front of the bedroom door, his body tense with anxiety. The others went downstairs and looked around, but didn't find Tara. Cal grabbed a croissant and a roll and headed back up to try the room again. To his surprise, he met Angelica on the way. The tall brunette had been released after being pardoned by the empress. She didn't recognize Cal in his gorgeous persona, of course, and stopped in her tracks. He was about to say something nasty when she smiled at him.

"Hello," she purred. "I don't believe we've met."

He snatched a piece of croissant from his mouth, brushed off his crumb-spattered jerkin, and bowed.

"Bond," he murmured in a velvety voice, as Fabrice and Robin rolled their eyes. "James Bond. And you are . . . ?"

"Angelica. Angelica Brandaud, apprentice spellbinder to Master Dragosh, the vampyr. Or, I was, because I've been reassigned to Lady Boudiou." (Sparrow, who was Boudiou's apprentice, jumped.) "Or, at least I will be until another high wizard comes to take his place. Could you possibly be that person?"

Cal couldn't resist.

"Absolutely," he said firmly. "I am High Wizard Bond and I would be deliiiighted to work with such a voluptuous beauty."

He again bowed over the girl's hand. Before she swooned, he said:

"Unfortunately I have to leave you, beautiful. Duty calls! See you soon!"

Angelica looked at him the way a cat looks at a particularly appetizing canary. "Oh yes, soon! Very soon!"

Cal flung his cape across his broad shoulders and manfully strode off. Angelica was so captivated that she didn't notice that Sparrow was choking with laughter.

Robin and Fabrice managed to keep a straight face—and Manitou a straight muzzle—as they passed Angelica, who hadn't yet come down from her little cloud.

When they were in front of Tara's suite, however, they grew serious again. They knocked and called, but nothing worked. Gallant was going crazy pounding the door, first with his wings, then his claws, and Sheeba and Blondin had to calm him down before he hurt himself. When the castle refused even Cal's entreaties to open up, they finally went to get Lady Kalibris.

Dana and Clara, the tatris's twin heads, together ordered the door opened, and the castle had to obey.

A terrifying scene awaited them: Blind eyes staring at the ceiling, Tara lay on her bed with a stream of dried blood across her cheek.

And a crossbow arrow was lodged in her heart.

CHAPTER 15

THE RAVAGER OF SOULS

obin gave an anguished cry and raced over to the body.

"Watch out!" shouted Manitou. "It's a—"

Too late. The half-elf was moaning with despair as he went to clutch Tara . . . and his hands passed right through her body!

"—shadow!" the Labrador finished.

"A shadow?" croaked Fabrice, sobbing. "You mean Tara's dead, and this is her ghost?"

"No, no, not at all," said Manitou reassuringly. "It's an illusion. The spitting image of her, down to the smallest detail. Unless you touch it, you can't tell the difference."

"But how—?"

"How did I know? An illusion has no odor. I didn't smell anything, so it wasn't Tara."

Sparrow had already recovered and was watching Gallant. Far from seeming upset, the pegasus was carefully sniffing at the walls like an overgrown bloodhound.

All right, I've got it, Sparrow thought. She shouted, making the others jump: "Tara! Where are you?"

"In here!" answered the "dead" girl. "I'll be right out."

A section of the wall behind them suddenly pivoted and Tara stepped through it, covered with dust.

"Whew!" she said. "I had a pretty busy night."

That was all she was able to say, because Robin had grabbed her and was hugging her so tight that she could hardly breathe. This immediately raised another cloud of dust and made the half-elf cough, but he didn't let her go.

Tara could feel his heart thudding.

"Er, are you okay?" she asked him.

"I thought you were dead!" Robin stepped away, and Gallant immediately took his place.

"So did I," said Fabrice tearfully, hugging her in turn. "What's this set-up on the bed about?"

Tara felt bad that she had frightened her friends. "I'm sorry," she said, stroking her pegasus's soft hair. "I thought I'd be back before you got here, but I lost track of time. I asked the castle not to open my door."

Lady Kalibris, who was trying to calm down, jumped on the opening.

"The castle was only obeying us," began Dana sharply. "Could someone—"

"— please explain—" continued Clara.

"— what's going on here—" said Dana.

"—for chrissakes!" Clara's curse drew a shocked look from her twin head.

Tara asked for a moment to wash off the dust and ran into the bathroom. When she came back out, she was a lot cleaner. While they were gathering around, she made the image of the bloody corpse disappear. All that remained was the crossbow arrow sunk deep in the bed, which quivered in indignation.

Stifling a yawn, she explained: "Someone tried to kill me, and I thought it might be smart to make them think they'd succeeded. I was dozing off last night when it occurred to me that the killer might well try again. So I decided to sleep on the floor with a blanket. The castle helped with the trick, by hiding me under an illusion, and I forbade it to open the door. But the killer used a secret passage instead of the door. The opening in the wall was completely invisible. I had put my substitute image on the bed. Two hands emerged from the passageway, holding an armed crossbow. They aimed at the fake Tara and fired."

Even though they knew she had survived, Tara's friends were hanging on her every word.

"I made my ghost body writhe as if I were dying, produced some fake blood, and waited until the opening swung shut. Then I walked over to the wall and figured out how to open the passage, and I followed it. There's a whole maze of corridors and rooms back there! With lots of cobwebs and dust. I followed the killer's tracks, and the footprints led to . . ."

Like a skilled storyteller, she paused to heighten the suspense.

"So, where did they lead?" blurted Robin impatiently, his elf blood crying for vengeance.

"To Master Chem's office!"

Seven exclamations burst out at once, as Tara's friends and Lady Kalibris reacted with disbelief, fury, and astonishment.

"That's impossible!" the two heads roared. "Chemnashaovirodain-trachivu couldn't ever—"

"I didn't say that it was Master Chem who tried to kill me," Tara interrupted. "Just that the footprints in the dust led to his office, that's all. Actually, when I went in, he was snoring on his bed of diamonds and didn't move a scale. I went over and made some noise, but he didn't stir. If somebody had gone out of the office, the stone dragon and unicorn would've sounded the alarm. So, I figured there must be a second passageway."

"Our old dragon is going to be happy to find out that his security system is riddled with holes," said Cal, chuckling.

"I knew what I was looking for, so it didn't take long to find it."

"What then?" asked Fabrice, who couldn't stand the suspense.

"The passageway had a number of branches. Some led to the big Throne Room, others to the prisons, and still others to various rooms I've never seen. I didn't explore all of them. But in spite of all my efforts, I wasn't able to find the killer."

"I will immediately tell the castle—" snapped Clara.

"— to seal off those passages," ended Dana, furiously.

"It can't do that," said Tara. "Some areas aren't enchanted, and the castle has no control over them. They're especially hard to find because the castle projects its illusions everywhere. Not to mention that it has some secret passages of its own that it doesn't necessarily want everyone to know about."

"I'm going to put this castle on a diet, starting right now," grumbled Clara.

"No more illusions for three days—" agreed Dana.

"—while we find and close off those passageways—" said Clara.

"— right away!" Dana concluded.

"That's all very well, but what do we do now?" asked Sparrow. "Tara is supposed to be dead."

"We mourn her," suggested Fabrice. "We cry our eyes out, because we've lost our friend. If we don't show sadness, the killer will know they've been fooled, and will try again."

"Tara, you have to transform yourself," said Cal, with a touch of irony, "into something that the killer is sure to notice."

"An elf!" exclaimed Robin. "A warrior elf . . . in charge of an investigation!"

"That's an excellent idea," approved Dana.

"We could even say that she had been engaged to find the killer," suggested Clara, picking up on the game.

"That wouldn't surprise anyone," continued Dana. "After all, the hunter-elves are OtherWorld's detectives. Yes, an excellent idea. Go ahead, Tara. Transform yourself quickly before someone starts looking for me. I have a castle to run!"

Tara obeyed. Her and the living stone's combined magic caused her to grow taller. Her hair turned white and grew into a complicated braid held in a springy metal clasp. Her eyes became crystalline, her eyebrows angled up to her temples, and her ears lengthened. Like all warrior elves, she wore a white, gold-embossed keltril breastplate over a fine white silk tunic. She carried a number of knives; a sword hung by her side, and a beautiful bow was slung across her back.

The living stone gave her an elf's inhuman speed, and Tara was surprised to notice how heavy and clumsy the others now seemed. All her senses were heightened. She could see the smallest grain of dust, hear the slightest sound, and feel her entire body with an intensity that was almost painful. She wrinkled her pretty nose. Smells were very intense as well.

Fabrice grimaced. Tara looked stunning, and she and Cal now made a perfect couple.

Cal bowed to her.

"Wow! Great transformation job!" he said admiringly. "Er, while you're at it, do you feel like giving me my old appearance back? Even Angelica fell for my look, and I'm sick and tired of it."

Tara laughed. "You don't mean Angelica—"

"Yes, she did," said Sparrow, her eyes sparkling with amusement. "Cal did his 'James Bond' number. He told her he was the next high wizard she would be working with."

Tara whistled. "Oh, she's gonna be so disappointed!"

"No kidding," said Cal with a laugh, who didn't feel guilty in the least. "So, can you do something about my looks?"

"You already asked me that," answered Tara. "I have no idea how to do it without maybe giving you five extra noses or putting green hair all over your body. Be patient. It's got to wear off sometime."

She smiled at him, but Cal didn't exactly looked convinced.

"All right, since you like transformations, it's Gallant's turn now," he said. "Not many elves have familiars, and none of them has a pegasus. You'd be recognized immediately."

At that, Sheeba growled softly, and Sparrow informed them that her panther suggested that Gallant be turned into a white tiger. He already had claws, so it wouldn't feel like that much of a change. The suggestion was adopted and in moments the magnificent stallion had become a giant cat. He didn't much like walking, and asked Tara if he could have wings. But since there aren't a lot of flying tigers in Other-World, she turned him down.

The friends refined their plan and split up. Fabrice, Barune, Sparrow, Sheeba, and Manitou began by casting Lamentatus spells on themselves. They were disheveled and in tears when they emerged from the suite to announce that their friend Tara had been killed. To complete the illusion, Tara put her macabre corpse back on the bed, and Lady Kalibris sealed the room.

For their part, Cal, Blondin, Robin, Tara, and Gallant went underground to try to find the tracks of whoever had fired the crossbow at her. Blondin sniffed about, while mentally complaining of lions' poor sense of smell.

Thanks to her heightened elf senses, Tara's progression into the tunnel was very different from her first time. She was now able to make out the unknown person's movements, easily visualizing the least of his actions. He had leaned against the stone, maybe to draw the crossbow. He had kneeled down at one point, possibly having dropped something. Further on, he'd hesitated where two passages divided.

Tara was startled to realize that her blood was boiling with rage against the monstrous killer, and she had to control herself to keep from screaming in fury.

"It isn't easy, is it?" murmured Robin, well aware of his friend's agitation.

"Man! Do you feel this way all the time? This urge to fight and smash everything when you get angry?"

"Not as much as full-blooded elves, but yes," he said. "We're a very turbulent people. Our elders have sort of loaned us out to other races for their armies and police forces. Otherwise we'd spend all our time fighting each other over nothing."

"I get it now," said Tara with a smile. "I didn't realize how much you have to constantly control yourself. All right, you're a better detective than I am. What do you make of these tracks?"

"With spellbinders, it's hard to tell," he said. "Going by the stride, I'd say it's a man. The steps are long and powerful. And given the depth of the footprints, he's pretty heavy. But he could well have transformed himself, so none of that means much."

"Can you determine where he went?"

"No, I can't. Do you see that cloud of glitter?"

Now that he mentioned it, Tara could see golden particles floating in the air.

"Your killer's clever. He cast a Dislocus behind himself, a spell that confuses elf senses. We can only hope that he left enough footprints."

It was a little like tracking Tom Thumb. The winding steps led to a door in the wall. They opened it and found themselves facing a wall of flame.

The footprints had indeed led to Master Chem's office. Startled by their interruption, the dragon very nearly barbecued them.

Recognizing Cal, he stopped instantly.

"I'll be darned!" Chem roared. "What are you doing here, Caliban? Robin? And who are you, Miss Elf?"

Tara smiled at him. "I see that my disguise is working, Master. Didn't you recognize me?"

"Tara?" The dragon's eyes were round with astonishment. "What're you doing, looking like that?"

"Somebody tried to kill her again, Master Chem," explained Robin. "Last night. So we thought a little mystification might be in order. The killer will be sure he succeeded."

The dragon drew his enormous eyebrows together in a frown. "But how did you get to my office?"

Cal explained. When the dragon wizard learned there were unknown tunnels in the castle—where he'd been living for many hundreds of years, after all—he was amazed.

"Er, Master Chem, could you please change yourself back to normal size?" asked Tara, who was getting a crick in her neck from looking up at him.

"Oh, yes, of course."

In the place of the imposing dragon appeared wizened old Chem, who muttered, "This changes everything!"

"What changes everything?" asked Tara innocently.

Master Chem gave her a sharp glance and continued: "I think hiring you, in your elf shape, is a very good idea. I'll announce that the warrior elf Manludil T'aril has come to the castle to investigate not Tara's killing, which we'd have no way of anticipating, but the murder committed by the vampyr. Then, when your death is officially announced, we'll put you in charge of that investigation as well. Does that suit you? And in four days you'll go back home to Earth, as agreed. Show me your accreditation card; I'm going to modify it."

He passed his hand over Tara's wrist, changing her name and picture.

"My name is Manludil T'aril, and I'm an investigator," she read from her accredi-card. "That suits me fine. But I can't sleep in my usual room, it would look strange. Where do elves live in the castle?"

"We have rooms in the guest wing and in the quarters reserved for Lancovit secret service agents," Robin answered with a little smile. "But we elves usually prefer to sleep out in the park. We don't like being shut in."

"Well, I prefer a bed, if you don't mind," she announced firmly. "Sleeping in trees—no thanks. They've already tried to kill me, and I'm not going to make the job easier by falling out of a tree in my sleep and smashing my skull."

Robin looked disappointed, but he didn't argue.

Leaving the dragon to arrange Tara's cover story, they left by the second secret passage. (Master Chem had looked shaken when he learned there wasn't just one but *two* passages in his own office!)

"You were right," whispered Cal once they were in the tunnel.

"About what?" asked Tara.

"Our national dragon really wants you to stay a little while longer on OtherWorld. Here you almost got killed again, but he didn't immediately ship you back to Earth. Very odd."

The other tunnels led to the high wizards' quarters, then descended to the dungeons and eventually to the passage they'd taken when they discreetly entered the castle the last time. By then, the friends had run out of time, so they decided to resume their search in the coming days.

Everyone in Lancovit accepted their story, and Tara was impressed to learn how respected elves were in the kingdom. Whenever she asked questions she got prompt, deferential answers.

Tara's new identity opened many doors for her, and she took advantage of that to make a complete tour of the castle. This included zones that had been off limits to her as a spellbinder, but which the king and queen had opened to the elf investigator.

She learned that the former royal chambers that the passages led to had been given to the high wizards when the castle was enlarged in the twenty-second century. *All right, that limits the field of research a little,* she thought. The killer had to be a high wizard living in one of those chambers who knew about the passages and could easily access them. So who? Lady Boudiou? No, the old lady seemed genuinely fond of her. Besides, Tara couldn't quite imagine her running around drawing a crossbow. Lady Sirella? She hadn't had much contact with the beautiful mermaid, so it was hard to tell. Master Den'maril? Elves were warriors, as she was now in a position to know. Could she have accidentally offended him? No. Elves preferred formal confrontations; he would have challenged her directly. It couldn't be Master Chanfrein or Master Patin, since the most recent attack happened while they were away in the Swamps of Desolation. Master Sardoin, the spatial mathematics specialist who was Cal's master, didn't look brave enough to swat a fly. And what about Master Dragosh?

Tara had a lot of questions, but not a single answer yet.

In addition, she was becoming more and more concerned about Fafnir and the two high wizards. They hadn't given any sign of life since their departure.

During the somewhat calm days that followed, Tara's friends talked about recent events and congratulated themselves on the ruse they had devised. No one had tried to kill, strangle, broil, or skewer Tara in her persona as an investigating elf. They hadn't made any progress in finding the killer, but at least they'd been left alone.

The mock corpse had been discreetly shipped to Earth, where Master Chem paid a quick visit to explain the situation to Isabella and Selena. Tara was afraid her grandmother would come haul her off by the scruff of the neck, but Isabella was apparently satisfied with Chem's promise to send her granddaughter back soon.

On the fourth day, on the eve of her return to Earth, Tara, Robin, Gallant, Cal, and Blondin were snooping around the secret passage, where they had discovered several dusty, unused rooms. Tara hadn't said anything about it, but she was now very worried about Fafnir's continued absence.

They were struggling to control their sneezes when they suddenly heard an odd noise, something like a giant foghorn choking on a cat. They listened carefully, and Tara suddenly recognized the sound.

"It's Fafnir!" she exclaimed. "She's . . . singing!"

One of the passages led to a hallway close to the Transfer Portal Room. They ran to it and emerged to witness an incredible scene.

There was Fafnir, accompanied by Master Chanfrein and Master Patin, singing her lungs out.

For a moment they thought she was singing for joy. But the dwarf's beautiful green eyes were filled with horror and her two companions' skins were turned completely purple! A cloud of black smoke was rising from the two wizards' bodies and drifting inexorably toward the stupefied guards and the Cyclops. Fafnir roared:

After the battle of the canyonnns,
The dwarves and all their brave companionnns
Made the enemies bend their kneees
Say their prayers and shout their pleeeas
Submit to the valiant rulers of the gorrrge
The great clan of the Fireforrrge!

The black smoke seemed to be carefully keeping its distance from her. Suddenly, Fafnir started yelling in a voice hoarse with exhaustion: "Run away! As long as I'm singing it can't completely possess me, but I can't hold out much longer! I've been singing for the last five days!"

The moment she started talking, the black smoke drew closer, and Fafnir desperately began singing again:

Lovely Talnir, blacksmith fairrr
Had a lover dark of hairrr
His forge was new, his hammer truuue
The sparks that flew between the twooo

Inspired songs quite beautifulll
From their village of Tanderulll!

As if repulsed, the black smoke again moved away from her. Instead, fast as a striking cobra, it leapt at the retreating guards. Their skin immediately turned purple, and their eyes glassy. Seeing that, the spellbinders put up protection shields, but the smoke wafted through them as if they didn't exist.

Tara was paralyzed with astonishment, but Robin leapt into action. With inhuman speed he dodged an approaching smoky tentacle, grabbed Cal and Tara by their arms, and dragged them off, running fast. "Quick, to the passageway! We've got to get out of here!"

"What about the others?" yelled Tara, now panicked. "Sparrow, my great-grandfather, Fab—"

"No time!" interrupted Robin, pulling her along.

They reached the passage just in time. With the door closed behind them, they were safely hidden. It became apparent that the Ravager was using Fafnir's memories to invade the Living Castle, but since she didn't know about the secret tunnels, they were out of danger for the time being.

In the dark, Cal started to say something, but Robin instantly clapped his hand over his mouth.

With her cat-like elf vision, Tara could see him gesturing at them to keep quiet. They moved away from the door and entered one of abandoned rooms.

"This should be okay," whispered Robin. "Nobody should be able to hear us here."

"It's the Ravager, isn't it?" gasped Tara. "He managed to possess the two wizards and force Fafnir to come back here so he could seize the

Castle. And he seems to be able to contaminate other people very easily."

"I think it's even worse than that," murmured Cal. "Did you notice that Fafnir was wearing different clothes? She wasn't coming back from the Gray Fortress. I think the Ravager has already taken Hymlia!"

Robin and Tara stared at each other, deeply dismayed.

"After elves, dwarves are the fiercest warriors on this planet," said Robin. "If the Ravager has overcome the dwarves, then humans won't be able to hold out very long."

"We've got to leave," said Cal. "The Voice was very specific. It said the only way to defeat the Ravager is to attack the source of his power, the Island of Black Roses, with the help of the White Soul."

"But what if we can't find it?" asked Tara.

For the first time, she felt discouraged. In a strange way, she could face the fact of someone trying to kidnap or kill her. But, if they went after her friends, it sapped her strength and made her feel unable to fight.

In the darkness, Cal shrugged, saying, "I'm sure I'll be as handsome as ever with purple skin, but it's going to clash terribly with my blond hair!"

Tara couldn't help chuckling. Cal had his own way of dispelling anxiety.

"So, what do we do?" she asked.

"First, we get out of here," said Cal. "The Transfer Portal will almost certainly be guarded. So we'll take the passage the Castle showed me, the one we used to come in the last time. Once we're outside, we'll decide what to do next. All right?"

"Okay. Let's go."

It was quiet in the tunnels, and Tara realized with a shiver that the dwarf's voice could no longer be heard. Fafnir had fallen silent.

The secret passages that the killer had used connected with the Living Castle's tunnels, so they soon reached the dungeons below. They quickly realized that the guards there had also been infected. With glassy eyes and purple skin, they were walking around like zombies.

Cal went first, in a foul mood because his new body greatly impaired his natural agility and secrecy. Then Robin waved Tara ahead.

She ran forward and had almost reached the exit when a dark mass crashed down on her, half knocking her out. Her reaction was lightning fast. In a single motion, she let herself fall, rolled on her shoulder, and drew her sword. She only stopped her blade when it was a hair's breadth of the throat of a vampyr!

It was a good thing her reflexes were equally fast, because she'd almost slit Master Dragosh's throat.

"Good grief!" she hissed. "You can't go around jumping on people like that! I nearly killed you!"

The bat tried to answer, but produced only a squeaking gibber. Then Dragosh remembered that he couldn't speak in that form, and he shape-shifted.

Tara, Robin, and Cal examined him very carefully. Red eyes, white fangs, black hair, and nice pale skin—not the slightest trace of purple. All right, everything was fine. For the time being, anyway.

"Miss Duncan?" breathed the incredulous vampyr. "What are you doing here, disguised as an elf?"

"It's a long story," she whispered quickly, "and this isn't exactly the place to tell it. How did you recognize me?"

"By your smell. I was about to neutralize you when I recognized your smell. Elf blood isn't harmful to us, but human blood is, terribly. If I had bitten you, I would have been contaminated!"

Tara frowned. Contaminated? She stared at the vampyr, who was shaking with anxiety. Her brain was working at top speed. *But in that case . . .*

Cal's voice interrupted her thoughts. "Hey, this is no time to slow down! Let's get out of here before we're spotted."

The Living Castle opened the secret passage to the street behind the building, and they soon found themselves outside. On the streets of Travia, nobody seemed aware of what was happening in the castle. People were going about their business without realizing the terrible danger threatening them from within.

Once the group was far away from the castle, the vampyr explained that he'd seen the cloud of black smoke making its way into the prison. The prisoners had their own tubs, hot and cold, and he happened to be soaking in the hot one. As soon as he saw the smoke, he let himself sink to the bottom and held his breath for half an hour. Underwater and in the darkness, he was invisible. The black smoke eventually withdrew, and Dragosh was able to get out. He shape-shifted into a rat to explore the castle. To his horror, he saw that nearly everyone had been possessed and they were all obeying Fafnir. He then shifted into bat shape to fly out a window, only to find all the doors and windows locked. He had just returned to the dungeons to think the situation over when Tara and her friends had burst in. He thought he'd been spotted, so he attacked her.

Tara quickly told him everything she knew about the Ravager, who she believed was invading the castle.

The vampyr was naturally pale, but as he listened, he went dead white, with a hint of green on his cheekbones.

"We have to combine our forces," he said anxiously. "I'm going to immediately leave for Urla, our capital, and gather other vampyrs to help you find the White Soul. The Mud Eaters fear us, so it shouldn't be hard to get information from them. The problem is the Transfer Portal.

We don't yet have a vampyr embassy in Travia, like in Tingapore. The only available portal is the castle's."

"Not exactly," said Cal. "We can use the gnomes' portal. Their king owes me a ton of favors."

Dragosh looked intrigued but didn't pursue the matter. "In that case, let's go quickly. There isn't a moment to lose!"

They cautiously moved through the streets. People were dressed in hide, hair, and feathers of every possible color, but purple was generally absent, except for an occasional decorative touch. They reached the Transfer Portal and were soon at the gnome embassy. But once there, they encountered a slight problem.

When they requested a meeting with Ambassador Tul Tultul, the guards mounted on their giant praying mantises refused to let them in. The guards told that that since they didn't have an appointment, they couldn't just show up this way. It simply wasn't done.

Cal grabbed one of the mantises by its mandible, ignored its squeaks of protest, and forced the giant insect's head down. Then, displaying his rippling muscles, Cal stared the little blue gnome nervously gripping the reins right in the eye.

"You've got a choice," he growled. "You can either call the ambassador immediately to tell him that Thief Caliban Dal Salan, who saved your king's butt, is waiting, or I'll beat you and your beastie to a pulp. Is that clear?"

The gnome gulped and nodded. Wheeling his mount, he raced off to inform His Excellency of their presence.

When the latter finally appeared, he was wearing an elegant bathrobe and seemed annoyed. His mood grew even worse when he didn't recognize Cal.

"Well, well, well," he said sarcastically, studying the two elves, the vampyr, and the gorgeous human. "The last time I saw Sir Caliban Dal Salan, he stood about five foot three. Have you had a sudden growth spurt?"

"Very funny," grumbled Cal. "It's a disguise. There's been a huge problem at the castle and you and your gnomes better get the heck out of here before it spreads. The Ravager of Souls has overcome everybody there. We need to borrow your Transfer Portal so we can go to the Gray Fortress and then to the Island of Black Roses. We have to stop the Ravager before he takes over the entire planet."

Ambassador Tultul looked at him, then sighed. "The mental health clinic is just two streets farther on. My guards will show you the way."

He gestured to his guards to encircle the little group. The green mantis that Cal had grabbed squeaked with satisfaction and clicked its mandibles.

Cal glared at Tultul and stood his ground. He opened his mouth, but Robin spoke first.

"Look at his neck," he said, pointing to his friend. "Our little adventure in the service of your King Glul Buglul left Cal with a souvenir. Something you will find easy to identify. Because he's probably the only person still alive to carry this mark."

The gnome raised an eyebrow in surprise, but obeyed. And when he saw the small, golden scar on Cal's neck, he turned bluer.

"By my ancestors!" he muttered. "The mark of a golden t'sil!"

He straightened and waved them into the embassy, to the mantis's great disappointment.

"Explain exactly what happened," Tultul ordered, once they were all comfortably seated in the conference room.

Tara jumped right in, with Cal and Robin adding details from time to time. By the time they finished their story, the gnome had turned a very dark blue.

"This is a disaster! I'm going to immediately order the evacuation of the embassy. To escape the Ravager, our people will take refuge underground."

"Send messages to all the countries," said the vampyr. "We have to prepare our world for what it's facing."

"Yes, yes," said the ambassador, jumping from his chair in a great hurry. "I'll take you to the portal immediately. I'll leave two volunteers here to greet you if case you need it again later. Good luck! May the spirit of Demiderus protect you!"

In seconds, the Transfer Portal was activated and Dragosh was on his way to his native Krasalvia. Before the others departed, they turned their skin color purple, to be on the safe side. Tara restored Gallant to his pegasus shape. Then, along with Cal, Blondin, and Robin, they transferred to the Gray Fortress.

Located in Gandis, the land of giants, the Fortress had been Magister's old headquarters. The terrible Bloodgrave clan used it to imprison OtherWorld's apprentice spellbinders, whom they'd kidnapped and infected with demonic magic. After the stinging defeat of the Bloodgraves at the hands of Tara and her allies, Master Chem had suggested that the giants turn the Fortress into a treatment center for giants who were infected by magic despite their natural immunity, and for infected dwarves, who despised magic but whose members occasionally exhibited it. Spellbinders from all the other nations were there to help the patients as well. So Tara and her group expected to be welcomed by one of the representatives of those communities.

But when they rematerialized, no one greeted them—neither giant, dwarf, nor spellbinder. They looked around curiously. Built of gray spellblock stone, the Gray Fortress hadn't changed much. It was still huge, cold, and massive.

Tara, Gallant, Robin, Cal, and Blondin walked from the Transfer Room to the landing at the top of the stairs. There, they found themselves nose to nose with a giant. Under his blue and gray breeches and gray jerkin, he was purple from head to foot.

CHAPTER 16

THE WHITE SOUL

"What are you doing here?" thundered the giant in a voice so low it seemed to be coming from some deep cave.

Cal's pulse was racing about two hundred miles an hour, but he managed to keep his tone flat and cold.

"Our master ordered us to go to the Fortress," he said. Then—because lying is always dangerous when you don't know the situation—he added, "We don't know why. We're waiting for his instructions."

"I see," said the giant, shifting the gigantic axe resting on his shoulder. "I'll go check. Wait here."

He strode off heavily, his steps shaking the Fortress.

"We better get out of sight," whispered Tara. Despite having her powerful new elf body, she'd practically choked when she saw the huge axe.

"The main gate is guarded," said Robin, leaning over the banister. "There are two giants and two dwarves downstairs."

"Crap! I didn't imagine we'd get trapped right away," grumbled Cal. "What about the tunnel that Fafnir dug when we escaped? You think it's been filled in?"

"Can't hurt to check. It's probably the only way for us to get out of the Fortress without being chopped to pieces."

They discreetly made their way down to the cellar. To their great relief, the storeroom shelves hiding the mouth of Fafnir's tunnel were still in place, though the bottles on them were gone.

"All right, let's just pray that the other end hasn't been blocked," said Tara.

Luckily for them, this wasn't the case. The high wizard in charge of the Fortress apparently hadn't had time to deal with the tunnel, and it was intact.

They emerged at the same spot as during their first flight through the forest, but the situation now was very different. This time they could use their magic fully; no Bloodgrave was hunting them. And Tara was no longer constrained by the fear of killing her grandmother because of the blood oath.

"We can't take as much time getting to the island as before," she announced. "Three days is too long. Who knows what the Ravager will do while we're walking. I'm going to shape-shift."

"Shape-shift?" asked Cal, who didn't understand. "Into what?"

"Into a dragon, to fly us to the Island of Black Roses."

"Oh, no you don't! No way! The last time we climbed onto your back, you almost killed us. I'll do my own shape-shifting."

"Come on, Cal, be reasonable!" said Tara with annoyance. "After the effort you've put out these last few days, you don't have enough power to maintain the same shape for long. What if you shifted into a hawk, but reverted to your human form when you were half a mile high? Can you imagine what you'd look like when you hit the ground? *Splat!* Flat as a pancake!"

But Cal was stubborn. "Look, I'm not climbing on your back—period. You can just use the same process you did to create this stupid show-off body of mine. Give me some of your power and I'll change myself into a bird."

This time, it was Robin's turn to get annoyed. "No way! Tara's going to need all her power to fight the Ravager. Each time she gives you some of it, she needs time to compensate for what she's lost. And what if you're not able to shift back? I don't think you've got a choice, Cal. You're not gonna get your way this time."

Tara spoke up before Cal could change his mind: "Let's find some place out in the open. I'll need a lot of space."

They moved from the Gray Fortress toward the plain, where they would have plenty of room. To show Cal that he had nothing to worry about, Tara quickly shape-shifted. Helped by the living stone, it was pretty easy. Within moments the young she-elf was replaced by a magnificent, blue-eyed, golden dragon with the living stone set in its forehead like some fantastic jewel.

Cal was facing her, so he didn't realize that Tara had neglected to grow herself a tail.

A tail is essential, because it counterbalances the front of a dragon's body—a fact brought home when Tara decided to test her forelegs. She made a slight move and suddenly felt herself tipping forward. Instinctively, she realized she was missing something. Seeing her enormous bulk toppling toward him, Cal began to back away. She created her caudal appendage in the nick of time, restoring her balance before she crushed him. The tail appeared with a loud *pop*!

"What was that popping sound?" asked Cal suspiciously.

"What was what?" she asked, in her deep dragon voice.

"That sound, that *pop*?"

"I didn't hear anything. Did you, Robin?"

"Not a thing," he said, limp with laughter. "All right, I'll climb aboard first. Have Blondin follow me. That way, we can wedge him between us."

"You overlooked one minor detail," noted Cal sarcastically. "My familiar isn't a fox anymore; he's a big lion."

"Just shrink him! It's easy. You say, 'By Miniaturus, make the lion shrink to a smaller size, quick as a wink.'"

Having run out of objections, Cal finally obeyed and shrank his lion to the size of a large dog. When Robin suggested making him even smaller, Tara said:

"That'll do, Cal. My back is broad enough to carry him. And I'm going to create a passenger basket for the three of you. It will make the ride safer."

Tara remembered seeing a picture of a howdah, a riding box on an elephant on Earth. With an ease that somewhat reassured Cal, she made one appear on her back. It was a strong wicker basket held down with wide cinch straps in front of and behind her wings.

Gallant mentally informed Tara that he planned to fly too and took off immediately. He knew that she was much more powerful than he was, and therefore faster.

Tara waited patiently for Cal, Robin, and Blondin to be securely seated before starting her takeoff. She had observed Gallant's technique and copied it exactly.

To get underway, she began running, which tossed her passengers about.

"Whaaa . . . t . . . aaa . . . ar . . . e yyy . . . ou . . . ddd . . . ooing?" screamed Cal.

"I'm running so I can take off," she yelled.

"Yyy ou're . . . a . . . ddd . . . dragon. You . . . dd . . . don't nn . . . eed tto . . . run! Jjj . . . j . . . just . . . flap . . . yyy . . . your . . . wi . . . wings!"

"Oh? Just my wings?" Tara stopped in her tracks, nearly pitching her passengers overboard. Then she flapped her wings, raising a huge cloud of dust.

"Let me down!" screamed Cal, trying to fight free of Robin, who was holding him. "Let me down! She's going to kill us all!"

Cal had one leg outside the howdah when Tara finally managed to get airborne. The takeoff was so abrupt that he fell out backward and wound up dangling from the basket by his hands.

"Pull me up," he cried, terrified. "Pull me up!"

Because of the wind roar, Tara didn't understand him. She thought he was telling her to pull up, so she did, climbing straight up into the sky.

Cal closed his eyes and screamed: "Ahhhhhhhhhhhh!"

Robin grabbed him and used his elf strength to haul him back into the basket.

"Man, are you heavy!" he complained. "I liked you better as a skinny runt."

Cal said nothing. He was too busy trying to get his breath back.

"Why me?" he finally moaned. "Life used to be so easy. Apprentice spellbinder, future licensed thief, settled nice and cozy at the castle. I worked a little, ate a lot, and drove Angelica out of her mind. The good life. But since meeting Tara, I've almost died a half-dozen times, the world is constantly on the brink of disaster, and I spend all my time trying to save it, along with my own skin!"

"That's true, isn't it?" said Robin, looking delighted. "You're never bored with her! I wouldn't miss this for all the immuta-creds in Other-World! Tara's the best thing that's ever happened to me. Thanks to her,

I've acquired Lillandril's bow and earned the respect of elves. She's faithful, loyal, sensitive, funny, elegant, subtle, smart—"

Cal cut his lamentations short and gave his friend a sideways glance.

"And so pretty," he added craftily. "She's really beautiful, with those lovely deep blue eyes in that pretty face."

Robin jumped into Cal's trap with both feet.

"Oh, yes!" he agreed, an ecstatic smile on his face. "Even that white strand in her blond hair is the perfect beauty mark."

Cal's suspicions were confirmed.

"I can't believe it" he chortled. "You're in love!"

The young elf reddened. "Who, me? Of course not!"

"Oh yes, you are," Cal insisted. "I can tell. You're in love with Tara."

For a moment, he thought that Robin would protest, but instead, he bent his head and his shoulders slumped.

"Is it that obvious?"

"About as plain as the nose on your face," answered Cal, not at all kindly. "As for her . . ."

"She's too young," sighed Robin. "Besides, we're her best friends. And—"

"And her birthday is in three days. She'll be thirteen."

"Her birthday? I don't have a present for her!"

Robin stood up so quickly he rocked the howdah, and Cal clutched the rim in alarm.

"Heyyyy," he hissed through gritted teeth. "Stop jumping around like that!"

Robin's excitement collapsed as quickly as it had soared.

"Even thirteen's much too young," he moaned. "At that age you're interested in dolls, not in some miserable half-elf."

Man, this love stuff really turns your brains to mush, thought Cal.

"Tara? Tara and *dolls*, did you say?" he sneered sarcastically. "I dunno . . . the two just don't go together. Tara and swords, yeah, I can see that. Or Tara and battles, bruises, fistfights, murders . . . I can see that too. But Tara and dolls, nah, that definitely doesn't work."

"She doesn't even know what I'm feeling," lamented Robin, who hadn't heard a single word of his friend's speech.

"Well, just tell her," said Cal, who didn't see what the problem was.

The elf stood up again, and Cal grabbed the rail, determined not to make any more friendly suggestions.

"Certainly not!" Robin declared. "I'm keeping my secret to myself. No one will ever know what I'm enduring. I'll wait. I'll wait until she notices me. And then, and only then, I'll tell Tara how much I—"

"I heard my name. Are you talking about me?" asked Tara with great interest.

She had bent her long dragon neck back and was giving them a wide, toothy grin. While flying full speed ahead.

Cal turned pale.

"Tara!" he screamed. "Look where you're going!"

"It's okay," she answered calmly. "There's nothing in front of me, so I don't need to see what—"

"*You* may not think you do," he interrupted, "but I sure do! Look in front of you and stop doing that weird thing with your neck, all right? I'm too young to die of a heart attack."

Tara gave a deep sigh, but obeyed.

Cal watched her carefully for a few moments, then turned back to Robin.

"So, what were we talking about?"

"Oh, nothing important," said the half-elf, feeling he'd revealed enough. "Let's discuss our plan to find the White Soul."

"Hoo-hoo, he's in love! He's in love!" hooted Cal, determined not to let his friend off the hook. "And he's afraid to say so!"

But Robin knew how to put the little thief in his place. The formerly little thief, that is.

"If you keep on pestering me," he said calmly, "I'll make this basket disappear."

"No! You wouldn't really do that, would you?"

"In a heartbeat! I'm an elf, see? I'm not afraid of heights."

Cal gulped. And gave in. "All right, this White Soul. Where do you think we'll find it?"

"What would you do if you were a Mud Eater?"

"I'd buy a razor and some deodorant."

Robin rolled his eyes.

"I mean what would you do if you came across a thing like the White Soul?"

"As a Mud Eater? I'd hide it, so I'd have something to decorate my stinking hole with. Or else I'd show it to the other Eaters and tell them that it was the statue of a goddess and that I was her high priest. Then I'd create a new religion where I was the only person able to communicate with this so-called goddess. I'd make the others work for me and spend the rest of my days stuffing myself while gazing at my Mud Eater toes."

Robin looked at him in dismay. "You know, I hope the Eaters don't have minds as twisted as yours."

"I am *not* twisted," corrected Cal, pleased with himself. "I'm lazy. There's a difference."

"We're above the Swamps of Desolation," Tara informed them, interrupting their conversation. "What should I do, land?"

"Go ahead," said Cal, gritting his teeth. "We're ready."

Once they'd gotten out of the mud, wiped off their clothes, bandaged their bruises, and gotten their breath back, they took a look at the long trench dug by Tara's landing. And agreed that, all things considered, it hadn't been that bad.

Gallant, who flew in just as Tara was landing, was caught between hearty laughter and a legitimate concern for the state of his mistress.

Tara was spattered with mud from claws to muzzle, and her ears were ringing from having clipped a tree growing by mischance at the end of her landing skid. She went looking for a lake big enough to wash herself. She scrubbed off her golden scales as best she could, helped by Gallant, who had trouble muffling a few sarcastic whinnies.

"Oh, can it!" Tara snapped. "I wasn't born with wings, so stop making fun of me. Cal?"

"Yeah, what?"

"I'm going to stay in my dragon shape for a while," she announced, shaking the water off. "That way if the Mud Eaters attack, the way they did last time, I'll be able to defend us."

Cal looked at her hesitantly. "Actually, I think you'll scare them so much they won't come out of their holes."

"That's no problem," said a chilly voice behind them. "We know how to get them out."

Cal spun around, and Blondin gathered himself to leap.

Twenty huge black wolves had just stepped out of the bushes.

Tara was already filling her lungs to carbonize the new arrivals when she noticed that the wolves had red eyes. *Vampyrs!* Frying your allies wasn't such a good idea, so she held her breath. But that caused another problem. Not being a natural-born dragon, Tara didn't know how to get rid of the burning blast rising in her throat.

She raised a sharp-clawed arm to her muzzle and mumbled a strangled "Excuse me." Then she quickly turned toward the lake and fired a long jet of flame.

The swimming glurps were distinctly unhappy at suddenly finding themselves in a steam bath. Screaming bloody murder, they erupted from the lake and raced up its banks, the ends of their tails bright red from the boiling water.

"Ah, that's better!" said a relieved Tara.

One of the vampyrs was looking at her suspiciously. His eyes went to the glurps in the mud desperately waving their legs, then came back to the enormous golden dragon awkwardly shifting from foot to foot.

"You sure she's one of our allies, chief?"

Master Dragosh sighed. "Yes, unfortunately. All right, you all know the drill. Locate the Mud Eaters and try to find out what happened to the White Soul."

The first wolf practically snapped off a salute. "Yes, chief! All right guys, on the double. Let's go! Hut, hut, hut!" The vampyrs charged off enthusiastically.

Dragosh rolled his eyes and sighed again.

"They shouldn't let so many Earth movies be shown on Other-World," he grumbled.

By unspoken assent, they avoided getting too close to the island. The Ravager's center of power was located in its heart, and they had to find the White Soul first.

With their incredibly acute sense of smell, the vampyr-wolves quickly located the first Mud Eaters. They tried to put up a fight, but weren't able to resist for long.

Tara had seen Mud Eaters up close—uncomfortably close, in fact—during their last battle, but without enough time to examine them in detail.

They were big balls of earth-colored hair with outsized jaws that allowed them to swallow mud, their main food. They used their curved, very sharp claws to dig and their webbed feet to swim. Tara knew they could speak, though that wasn't obvious at first glance.

When they caught sight of the great golden dragon, the Mud Eaters all crouched and intoned: "Nice dragon, handsome dragon, not eat Eaters, nice dragon, not roast Eaters. Eaters did nothing. Eaters quiet, nice."

"I don't want to hurt you," murmured Tara, lowering her voice so as not to frighten them further. "We just need some information. You know there is an evil entity on the island, right?"

The Mud Eaters didn't react.

She tried again: "On island Black Roses, not nice, nasty black cloud, yes?"

That did the trick. They immediately understood what she meant.

"Black cloud eat Mud Eaters," they lamented. "Black cloud also want eat dwarf, but dwarf sing, so cloud not eat dwarf. Eat wizards instead."

"Us kill black cloud," she announced. "Us eat black cloud!"

The Mud Eaters lifted eyes full of hope to her. At least she supposed that's what they were doing, because with all their hair, she couldn't see their eyes.

"Dragon eat cloud?" they pleaded.

Tara didn't hesitate. "Yes. Dragon eat cloud."

The Mud Eaters began to leap about. The news clearly made them happy.

"So they don't like the Ravager; that's helpful," said Cal. "Hey, guys!"

The Mud Eaters stared at gorgeous Cal, dazzled by his magnificence.

"We need you to give us a hand, okay? Eaters help dragon, handsome dragon, all right? The weapon against the black cloud is a statuette. A shiny white thing about this high." Cal held his hands about a foot apart. "It represents a human woman with her arms up. Seen anything like that?"

Great silence greeted his statement.

"All right," he said with a sigh, "let's translate that into a language you can understand. Nice, pretty piece of white stone, us find, us take, us eat cloud. Got that?"

Re-silence. The Mud Eaters were actually so attentive and focused that they didn't move a hair—which was quite an accomplishment.

One of the vampyrs fixed his glowing red eyes on the Eaters. "Maybe our friends need a translation that's a little more . . . forceful."

"Master Dragosh?" called Tara.

"Miss Duncan?"

"Would you explain to your hothead here that we need allies, and that torturing people doesn't cut it?"

Dragosh glared at his lieutenant, who had the grace to look embarrassed.

"Robin," Tara continued, "you once told me that the Mud Eaters have a system of clans, right?"

"Yeah, so what?"

"If the members of this clan don't know where the White Soul is, maybe another clan will."

"Good idea," said Master Dragosh. "Let's put it into practice. These Eaters can spread the word. Were looking for the clan that knows where the White Soul is."

Their search unfortunately took much longer than expected. Soon night fell and beasts of all sizes were angrily whining around Robin and Cal, frustrated at not being able to penetrate the insect-repellant barrier. And the tireless vampyrs kept bringing new Mud Eaters in. Well, not exactly *new* Eaters, because the balls of hair all looked alike.

By the time they had gotten rid of the same Eater four times in a row—a little more frightened each time—they decided they had to somehow identify the ones that had already been questioned. So they started magically putting a glowing circle on the Eaters' greasy fur. Strangely enough, this delighted them. So much so that very quickly a crowd of Mud Eaters arrived, not to help in the search for the White Soul, but to get their own glowing circles.

After some hours, the disgusted vampyrs decided to stop for the night. Cal and Robin used Tara's wing to make a comfortable tent and spent a warm, cozy night under it.

The next day the search continued. All day long, they kept repeating the same question in vain.

The third day, when Tara felt she would go crazy imagining Fabrice, Sparrow, Fafnir, and Manitou caught in the Ravager's grasp, she awoke to see a parcel floating in front of her.

"Happy birthday, Tara!" cried Robin, looking very pleased with himself. Cal sang "Happy birthday" with great enthusiasm, and way off key.

"Oh!" she breathed with delight. "I'd completely forgotten!"

"But we didn't," said the boys. Clearly delighted with the impression they'd made, they shook hands, congratulating each other.

"You'll have to wait for the cake and candles until we get back to Lancovit, though," said Cal.

Very delicately, Tara open the parcel with a claw, surrounded by the curious Mud Eaters and vampyrs. Together, Cal and Robin had worked to create a lovely piece of jewelry: a beautifully carved bracelet studded with dazzling jewels that Cal had sort of picked up here and there while he was with the gnomes.

The bracelet was gorgeous. Sorry that she couldn't put it on right away, Tara slipped it into her ventral pouch for safekeeping.

For their part, the Mud Eaters were all very excited. They apparently understood the concept of "present" very well. Now convinced that Tara was the kind of superior being they should play up to, they started depositing all sorts of odd gifts at her feet: flowers, rotting swamp fruits, small animals living and dead, piles of stones, pieces of wood, bone fragments—whatever they thought might be a proper gift for the great golden dragon.

Early that afternoon, a very, very old Mud Eater with gray fur and worn claws approached her.

"Handsome dragon, nice dragon," he said. "Present for gold dragon."

It made Tara feel bad to see the Mud Eaters giving away their miserable treasures for her.

"Thanks, but I really don't need it," she said kindly. "You can keep your . . ." But she stopped abruptly when she saw what he was holding out to her.

In his paw, the Mud Eater held a small, luminous statuette of a woman, her arms raised beseechingly to the sky.

"Not want you?" he asked, sounding terribly disappointed.

"Oh yes, I want!" she said very quickly, terrified that he might take it back. "Very beautiful present, very nice Eater, very, very beautiful present!"

The Eater bowed again and went to add his treasure to the pile. Before he shuffled off to his den, a grateful Tara made sure he was given a beautiful glowing circle, bigger and brighter than anyone else's.

Cal was dozing, but opened his bleary eyes when he saw what was before him.

"I can't believe it!" he yelled, leaping to his feet and startling the vampyrs. "The White Soul!"

"It was thanks to you!" shouted Tara, mad with joy. "If you hadn't given me a present for my birthday, that Mud Eater would never have given me the statuette! You've saved OtherWorld!"

Cal examined the statuette, turning it this way and that.

"There's no inscription or anything," he observed, sounding annoyed. "Where's the manual? Every weapon comes with an instruction manual!"

Tara's enthusiasm began to ebb a little.

"Darn! I don't remember what the Voice said. Just that we had to put the statue on the island, right?"

"That's right," said Robin. "Do you want to go there now, or wait until morning? It's almost dark."

Tara hesitated, then—realizing that their enemy's power was growing by the minute—decided to act.

"Let's go now. The island's just a minute's flight away. Master Dragosh, what would you like to do?"

"I'll come with you to the island, but my fellows will stay on shore," answered the vampyr. "If we carry the day, there's no problem. If we fail, they can go warn the rest of the world."

The hotheaded vampyr protested that he didn't want to leave his chief, but Dragosh stood firm.

For such a short hop, Cal and Robin climbed onto Gallant. The vampyrs and Blondin, who didn't like to fly, would go on the ground. Tara was no longer worried about carrying passengers and only knocked down two trees when she took off. Master Dragosh shape-shifted into a bat and followed, a bit surprised by Tara's energetic takeoff style.

Flying over the island, they saw that the rosebushes had grown a lot since their last visit, but the island still looked deserted.

Suddenly the living stone came to life in Tara's mind.

Afraid I am.

Don't be! answered Tara mentally. *We have the weapon that will destroy him. Don't worry, I won't let him take you prisoner again.*

The stone heaved a deep, anguished sigh, but said nothing. How could she explain to Tara that the Ravager's power was multiplied here?

When Blondin reached the shore, Cal shrank him so he could climb on the pegasus's back, and they took off.

Tara was making a final pass above the water near the island when a monstrous black smoke tentacle suddenly wrapped around her neck, choking off her cry. The Ravager must have sensed the living stone's presence, because a second tentacle grabbed at the dragon's forehead, ripped off the stone, and heaved it into the water.

Tara screamed with pain.

And shape-shifted back. She lost her wings and tried in vain to stay in the air. She fell into the water at the same time as the White Soul and the bracelet, both of which shot out of her lost ventral pouch.

Coming to the surface, Tara activated her power to free herself. She imagined an enormous pair of scissors cutting the tentacles, and they fell away, their stumps retreating to the center of the island. The Ravager screamed with rage, and dozens of new tentacles came twisting toward her like monstrous black worms.

"Keep away from them!" Tara yelled to her friends. "Don't let them touch you!"

Unfortunately, a tentacle had wrapped itself around one of Gallant's hoofs. Despite his fierce resistance, it dragged him toward the center of the island. Robin cast a spell and cut the tentacle, but ten others rushed to the attack.

Tara was totally unable to help her friends. She surrounded herself with an impenetrable force field that immediately stopped the other attacks and allowed her to float on the lake surface.

Tentacles were lashing at her bubble, and to her horror she realized that it was starting to weaken. The tentacles stuck to its surface were sucking at its power like horrible mouths. She knew that she wouldn't be able to resist for very long. Using all her power, she reinforced the bubble and with a terrible effort burned the attacking tentacles to ash. This time the Ravager screamed, not with rage but with pain. She had hurt him, maybe enough to make him leave her alone.

Tara directed her bubble toward Gallant, but as soon as she got close some of the tentacles pursuing the pegasus turned and attacked her. This time they were too many, and her magic began to wane. Exhausted, she had to admit defeat. She had lost the White Soul and could no longer move. Sensing that she was weakening, the tentacles shoved her toward the island along with Gallant, Cal, Robin, and Blondin. Master Dragosh and the other vampyrs had disappeared. Had they managed to escape? That tiny ray of hope cheered Tara and she saved her strength, determined not to give up.

Carrying their prize, the tentacles soon reached solid ground. There they moved slowly, as if bothered by the black roses. Tara noticed that they avoided them as much as possible. The dark flowers were swaying along the tentacles' way, as if wanting to spear them with their thorns. *That's strange!* After all, it was by drinking the brew of those roses that Fafnir had been possessed. She was still thinking when they finally reached the center of the island.

That's when she noticed it had changed horribly.

A blackish, bubbling magma now filled a vast pit from which the tentacles emerged. For a moment Tara thought they would be tossed into the abyss at the island's center, but the tentacles seemed to have something else in mind. A huge black Transfer Portal suddenly opened in front of them, and the tentacles threw them into it.

Screaming in fear, they fell through empty, terrifying darkness.

CHAPTER 17

CAPTURED!

Gasping for breath, Tara landed in front of a pair of feet.

Feet that looked familiar.

Looking up, she realized that she was back in the Living Castle, flat on her stomach in front of Fafnir! But this wasn't the stubborn, grumpy, affectionate dwarf she knew. Her skin was purple, her eyes shone black instead of green, and she was wearing a horrible smile.

"Well, well, well, if it isn't our dear little Tara!" Fafnir said in the Ravager's voice. "What a pleasant surprise! Well, more or less. When I finally managed to possess the little dwarf I read in her mind that she was counting on you to save her. Did you find it?"

His voice carried a hint of concern.

Tara glanced toward Cal, Blondin, Robin, and Gallant, who were trying to untangle themselves. To her relief, they all looked more or less intact. She dusted herself off and looked back at Fafnir.

"Did we find what?" Tara asked, though she knew perfectly well what he meant.

"Did you find the White Soul?"

"No, we didn't," she answered dismissively. "Those stupid Mud Eaters couldn't understand what we were asking. We were flying over the island looking for it when your trap caught us."

She paused and looked Fafnir—or rather the entity controlling her—right in the eye, and added: "Which was pretty stupid, if you think about it."

"Stupid? I don't see why!" snarled the Ravager.

"You've been looking for the White Soul for a long time, right?"

"No, not especially. I knew the Mud Eaters had it. But now that you're aware of my existence, I have to destroy it before it destroys me!"

"Well, you should've just waited until we found it, and *then* grabbed it."

That shut him up.

Fafnir's eyes narrowed, and the Ravager's voice said: "Who's to say you don't have it now?"

"Search us," answered Tara, shrugging. "You'll see. We don't have a thing."

"This dwarf's brain tells me you're clever," he said. "But don't think for a second that you'll be able to fool me."

The Ravager had the purple-skinned guards search Tara and her companions roughly and very thoroughly. Naturally, they didn't find anything—aside from a few jewels, lots of strange tools, and an assortment of various weapons. Gallant went to stand next to Tara, glowering at the Ravager.

"So you were telling the truth," he said, sounding a little surprised. "I'm sorry I'm not able to absorb you right away. Each time I absorb a new soul, my mind must integrate it before I can control it. I've been a bit of a glutton lately, and my mind is tired. So I don't want to risk absorbing any more souls before tomorrow. By my ancestors, I didn't realize that conquering the world would be so much work!"

A miracle—and none too soon! thought Tara, grateful for a few hours' respite.

The Ravager ordered the guards to surround the young spellbinders, the lion, and the pegasus, and to take them to jail.

"Ow! I'm, sore all over!" said Robin, who hadn't liked being manhandled during the search. Quick as a flash, he rushed the nearest guard and grabbed his dagger. Then he leaped at Fafnir and set the blade on her jugular.

"You're gonna let us leave nice and easy now, or I'll slit her throat!"

"By my black roses, what bravery!" gushed the Ravager, ignoring the knife.

The half-elf gritted his teeth and pressed. A thin trickle of blood began to run down Fafnir's neck.

"Ouch, that hurts!" said the Ravager. "But if it's so important to you, go ahead! I've contaminated so many people I don't need the dwarf anymore. I'd rather keep her alive; I have a soft spot for her. But if you really want to cut her throat, I won't stop you. Better yet, I'll leave her body. That way you'll be able to experience her death in real time."

As Robin looked in amazement, the black smoke left the dwarf's body. She regained her deep, coppery tan, and her dark eyes reverted to their familiar green.

"By my ancestors!" Fafnir spat when she was able to use her own voice again, "I'm gonna tear that Ravager limb from limb!"

Then she realized that Robin still had the knife to her throat and froze.

"He's telling the truth," she said regretfully. "He needed me as a way to get off the island, but now he's possessed enough people to maintain his power here, even if you kill me."

Robin still refused to remove his knife. The black smoke chuckled and summoned another of its zombies. When Tara heard the footsteps shaking the castle, she was filled with momentary hope until a dragon appeared in the hall. It was completely purple. And her hope died. Robin dropped the knife.

"Master Chem!" Cal murmured in dismay. "Okay, now we have a problem. A very big problem."

"Did you think I was lying?" roared the Ravager through the dragon. "So, half-elf, you want to cut the dragon's throat too? It won't be a knife you'll need, but an axe. And what about your friends? They're possessed too; do you want to kill them? How about killing everybody in the castle? Or the city? Believe me, that won't change the situation one bit."

Tara started. *He's already conquered the whole city? Cal's right. We have a big problem on our hands.*

Just how big Tara realized when her friends, obeying a silent order, filed into the hall. Standing ten feet tall, Sparrow was in her beast shape for some reason. Fabrice was possessed, but not Barune. Manitou was now a purple Labrador retriever. His unusual color would make him very popular on Earth, but when he stared coldly at Tara, it broke her heart.

She was startled to see that Angelica and her parents were also with them. Surprisingly, they were dressed in court robes and were wearing the royal Lancovit crowns! Another thing: their skin was just as purple as the others', but their eyes weren't completely black, and they seemed to be able to move independently.

"Oh, Master, you finally captured them!" exclaimed the tall brunette. "Congratulations, you're the best! This little bitch and her friends could have caused you a ton of problems. And thanks again for letting me have these three as my servants. It's been a lot of fun."

"Yes, Master," said her father unctuously. "And asking us to run Lancovit for you was an excellent idea. King Bear and Queen Titania certainly haven't been very cooperative."

Tara was flabbergasted. Angelica and her parents were speaking with their own voices, not the Ravager's, and they didn't seem completely possessed. *How can that be?*

She soon got the awful answer.

"You're more than welcome," the Ravager said with a touch of contempt. "Your ambition has been very useful to me. Souls as greedy as yours don't really need to be controlled; giving you a little power is enough. As for the king and queen of this two-bit country, it's just a matter of days. They won't be able to resist me much longer."

"You haven't been able to . . . possess my uncle and my aunt . . . You couldn't do it!"

With an enormous effort, Sparrow had spoken. She was clenching her paws so hard that her claws dug into her flesh, leaving a stream of red blood on her purple fur.

"That's not important!" exclaimed the Ravager, furious at Sparrow for rubbing his nose in his failure. "I don't understand how that family can resist possession when the supposedly powerful dragon succumbed right away."

"You won't be able to ever possess them," managed Sparrow, straining with all her might and drawing the strength to resist from her lacerated palms. "They're too strong for you!"

"Shut up, you idiot!" cried Angelica's mother, clearly afraid that the Ravager would lose his temper. She even ordered a black tentacle to wrap itself around Sparrow's mouth, muzzling her.

"Angelica is the one whose throat I should've slit!" said Robin angrily to Fafnir. "I wouldn't have hesitated for a second, believe me!"

The tall girl's attention suddenly came to rest on gorgeous Cal.

"Mister Bond!" she cried with delight. "What are you doing with this group of losers?"

Suppressing an urge to wring Angelica's neck, Cal gave her a charming bow.

"Miss, your skin is the color of the heart of a rose," he purred, gazing deep into her eyes. "Amazing, how it sets off your beauty. I find it quite captivating."

Angelica gave Cal a huge smile and took his hand. "Master, there must be some mistake. This one doesn't belong with those other people. May I have him?"

Speaking through the dragon, the Ravager chuckled nastily. "If you want him, you can have him. I'll make him your servant as well, as soon as I've possessed him."

Cal quickly spoke up: "I'm not sure I could survive in prison even for a second without you. I can't endure not having your beautiful face before me."

"Master, please!" cried Angelica, mesmerized by gorgeous Cal batting his long eyelashes at her. "Don't send him to jail. Give him to me now. I'll watch him, I promise!"

"Very well," said the Ravager, who obviously didn't care one way or another. "You can put him with the others."

Cal bowed and ran over to stand by Fabrice, who showed no reaction.

Robin wondered what was happening with the little thief, and Tara frowned. *Is Cal joining the winning side to save his skin?* She shook her head, uncertain. Then she turned back to Fafnir, who was standing motionless and staring anxiously at the black smoke.

"Fafnir, I'd like you to tell me exactly what happened," Tara said, ignoring Angelica, her parents, and the Ravager.

The black smoke hung motionless in the air, giving the dwarf a chance to answer.

"We got close to the island," said Fafnir, absentmindedly tugging on a strand of her red hair. "Too close. The black roses had grown tremendously since we were there last. Except for the center, the island's practically covered with them. The Ravager didn't give me a chance. He grabbed me, then the two wizards. I yelled, and I saw that my yelling kept the Ravager at bay. He didn't release me, but he couldn't get more of a hold on me. So I started to sing."

"You sang for five days without stopping?" asked Robin, astonished at her endurance.

"We dwarves have lots of songs, and we're stubborn. Hanging on was the only way to warn you, so I hung on. At least that gave you a chance to get away!"

"Fat lot of good it did you!" cackled the Ravager by way of Shyblossomonthebankofaclearstream, the Cyclops. "You've only gotten a short stay of execution, my pretties. By tomorrow I should have digested my most recent possessions, and I'll take care of you. And now, off to jail you go!"

The last thing Tara and her friends saw was the monstrous black smoke swirling around Fafnir, and the look of despair in her beautiful green eyes.

The Ravager had been cautious. The cells were surrounded by a dense fog of black smoke, its tendrils drifting along the prison hallways.

Guards opened the cells and shoved Tara, Gallant, and Robin in. The heavy, magical Hymlia iron gates slammed shut behind them with a sinister clang. The guards resumed their monotonous rounds, walking through the pools of smoke as if they didn't exist.

Tara examined the cell, then stifled a shout of surprise. In the cell next to hers were King Bear and Queen Titania!

They looked very pale, and the queen seemed to be breathing with difficulty. Every so often a black tentacle came to touch them, as if to test their resistance. They tried hard not to react, but you sensed it cost them a lot of pain. Though they had been stripped of their court robes and their crowns, they remained the king and queen. Showing the Ravager their distress was out of the question.

The king could see that Tara and her friends hadn't been possessed, since they were being locked up and their skin wasn't purple. He smiled weakly, both happy and unhappy to see his apprentice spellbinders.

"Tara! Robin!" he exclaimed. "I'd like to say it's a pleasure to see you again, but that's not exactly the case. I thought you managed to get away and had taken refuge far from this castle."

"Well, that's exactly what we did," answered Tara, who was trying not to cry, "at least in the beginning. Until the Ravager captured us."

She took a deep breath, struggling with her emotions. In despair, she decided to try humor as a last resort.

"And this is the second time in ten days I've been thrown in jail," she said, sighing comically. "Granted, these were imperial and royal jails, but I'd like it not to become a habit!"

"I hate jails," muttered Robin. "They stink, and they're cramped, dusty, and skuzzy."

He was exaggerating. Aside from the fact that the Lancovit cells had bars, unlike the ones in Omois, they were quite comfortable, dry, and spacious. There was no dust, and thanks to spells, no bugs. The king and queen didn't approve of substandard prisons, it appeared.

"Do you know what's going on upstairs?" asked the king. "We haven't gotten much information these last days."

"What's happening," said a voice they knew all too well, "is that idiot dwarf freed the Ravager, and he's slowly but surely conquering the world. He's already sent infected agents to Omois and Selenda."

"Angelica!" exclaimed Robin, leaping up and grabbing the bars. "Did you come down to taunt us?"

"No, to save your miserable hides," answered the tall girl with purple skin, keeping a safe distance from the angry elf. "Obviously, I don't much like it but if you have the White Soul, then you absolutely have to destroy the Ravager."

The royal couple was confused. Whatever was she talking about?

"How are you able to do that, Miss Brandaud?" asked the king. "Aren't you under that monster's control?"

"My parents and I are just pretending to cooperate," she explained contemptuously. "When the Ravager saw that we were prepared to help him, he loosened his grip on us, so he isn't constantly in our minds. This leaves him free to possess other people faster. And it gives us a big advantage: we can control the tentacles without being controlled by them."

And in fact, in response to her silent order, the black cloud drifted away and the purple guards disappeared. They were now alone in the prison.

"There! Now we can talk at our ease," Angelica said with satisfaction. "Tara, you have to tell me where the White Soul is."

Robin was opening his mouth to explain the situation when Tara cut him off.

"We don't know, unfortunately," she lied. "We've heard it's in Hymlia, in the Tador Mountain mine."

"What mine?" asked Angelica nervously. "There are hundreds of them! That mountain's like Swiss cheese!"

"I'm telling you, we don't have any more information than that," said Tara. "We were captured by the Ravager before we had time to locate it."

The tall girl chewed her fist, visibly torn. "You don't understand! He's like gangrene, slowly spreading. If somebody doesn't stop him, he'll conquer the whole planet within a year!"

Since the tentacles had disappeared, Queen Titania was breathing a little more easily. In a weak voice she asked: "What can you do to help us? We can't find this famous White Soul as long as we're in prison. In fact, I'd like someone to explain to me what it is."

"It's a weapon, Your Majesty," answered Robin. "A small white statuette of a woman. It's said to be the only thing that can destroy the Ravager. We were searching for it, as you've no doubt figured out, when he captured us."

"In that case you must free us, Miss Brandaud," said the king firmly.

At that, Angelica seemed to completely lose her composure.

"That's impossible!" she moaned. "If I free you, he'll kill my parents as punishment. I can't do it."

And before they had time to react, she turned and ran off.

Robin released the bars and fell back on his cot looking discouraged. Tara did the same. She felt pretty low, and Gallant came to stand beside her, stroking her with his wing to console her.

After a while the half-elf raised his head and saw how upset Tara was. Their cells were next to each other, so he could reach out and touch her hand.

"Don't worry," he said tenderly. "I'm sure we'll figure something out."

"You're right," said Tara, abruptly sitting up. "Can we practice magic here, or is it like in Omois?"

"You can use magic inside the prison," the king answered, "but if you change shape, for example, you can't go through the bars. The whole building is built of magic iron from the Hymlia Mountains, and it's impervious to magic, like the dwarves and giants."

"Okay, got it," said Tara. "We'll have to try something else. This iron, can it be melted?"

The king rubbed his head, then shrugged. "Melt it? I suppose so, since the dwarves were able to shape it in their forges."

"Perfect!" said Tara with a little grin. "Let's see how it stands up to dragon fire!"

"Are you going to shape-shift?" Robin asked in alarm. "You don't have the living stone anymore."

"I know it, but we don't have any choice. You have any other ideas?"

"No, it's just that this castle is fragile," he said. "The city too; the whole continent, in fact. So be careful!"

The king assumed Robin was joking.

"I doubt Miss Duncan has enough power to endanger the castle. My ancestors built it to be very strong."

"Don't speak too soon, Your Majesty. Tara's power is way beyond anything you're accustomed to. And when the time comes that she can control it, the Ravager will look like a little boy by comparison."

"You're exaggerating," said Tara, nervously touching her white forelock. "All right, let's do it before the black smoke and the guards come back."

"This'll certainly be the first time we can thank Angelica for helping us," said Robin darkly.

Estimating the size of her cell, Tara figured she could change into dragon shape without any problem. She took a deep breath and summoned her magic.

In the adjoining cell, the king and queen stiffened. They were extremely sensitive to magic, and when Tara's power hit them like a burning wave, they exchanged astonished glances.

Tara could feel the transformation about to occur when an angry yell stopped it cold.

The next moment Angelica burst into the prison, screaming with rage. Behind her, tentacles were hissing like poisonous snakes.

"I'm going to kill you!" she screamed.

CHAPTER 18

THE RAVAGER REVEALED

Tara struggled to breathe as Angelica tightened the tentacles around her throat. Gallant reared and tried to slash them with his claws, but in vain.

Thanks to his elf agility, Robin was able to avoid the ones grabbing for him.

"Angelica, stop!" he yelled. "If you kill her, the Ravager will make you eat your own heart!"

He had found the only argument that might make the tall girl yield. The red haze of fury lifted from her eyes. She made a gesture, and the tentacles released Tara, who fell to her knees, clutching her throat and gasping.

"You're lucky!" spat Angelica. "Very lucky. As soon as the Master is finished with you, I'll ask him to make you my servants as well. You'll be cleaning my things and living on your knees for the rest of your days!"

Like a fury, she spun or her heel and stormed up the stairs.

A few moments later the guards opened another cell and tossed in Cal and his red fox.

Gone was gorgeous Cal's manly beauty, his shock of blond hair, his brawn and his pectorals. Cal the little thief was back, but he looked pale, and for some reason kept wiping his mouth.

"Cal!" exclaimed an astonished Robin. "What happened to you?"

"Yuck! Yuck! Yuck!" he cried, wiping harder than ever. "Angelica *kissed* me!"

Tara started to laugh, choked, and had a coughing fit instead.

"What are you talking about?" asked Robin.

"I was in her rooms, wondering how I could knock her out and come free you, when she walked in. Before I knew it she grabbed me and kissed me. It was such a shock that I shape-shifted, and instantly reverted to my old body. At exactly the wrong moment, of course!"

"So you weren't the only one to get a shock," said Robin with a chuckle, who could well imagine the scene. "She must have been really surprised!"

The little thief finished wiping his mouth and nodded.

"She was actually so surprised that she thought she was hallucinating. I guess I spoiled the illusion by spitting."

This time Tara managed to laugh without choking. Robin chortled to imagine Angelica jumping gorgeous Cal, passionately kissing him, and winding up with the little thief in her arms. His laughter got to Cal, and within seconds they were all on the ground howling with laughter under the somewhat surprised eyes of the king and queen.

"Ooooh! That feels so good!" said Tara, wiping away her tears.

Robin and Cal nodded in agreement. They were still in prison, and they were still threatened with a horrible fate, but they felt a lot better in that moment.

The soreness in Tara's neck brought her back to reality, though. She fingered her throat gingerly and swallowed.

"Why the heck is everybody always trying to strangle me? First the Ravager, and now Angelica. What have I done to her now?"

"Who knows?" said Cal, shrugging. "When I reverted to my normal shape she first screamed with surprise, and then she got angry. She muttered something like, 'It's her! It's another of her tricks! I'm gonna kill her!' Then the guards grabbed me while Angelica raced off to the prison, head down like an angry brrraaa. You know the rest."

"Angelica must have suspected you didn't have enough power to change your appearance that much," he said. "She figured that Tara was the only one of us able to turn you into an Adonis."

"I'm sorry, Tara," said Cal with a chuckle. "If your spell had lasted just a few more minutes, I would've knocked her out and come to free you."

Tara was about to warn him not to reveal too many details in the presence of the black smoke when she looked around in surprise.

"That's weird; the Ravager's smoke is gone!"

She was right. They could still hear the guards pacing like watchful zombies, but the terrifying smoke had disappeared.

"So much the better," said the queen with a shudder. "Those horrible tentacles kept probing us, trying to possess us. And the less they succeeded, the harder they tried."

"Do you have any idea why the Ravager wasn't able to overcome you, Your Majesty?" asked Robin.

"No," sighed the king. "By the time we were aware of the danger, it was too late. We fought back, Titania and I, but without result. His tentacles seemed to suck our power, even though they couldn't possess us. And we're not the only ones. Salatar and Lady Kalibris were able to resist too. We think they managed to escape."

"We ought to take advantage of the smoke's disappearing to do the same," said Cal soberly. "I was able to walk around the castle a little before getting to Angelica's rooms. It wasn't a pretty sight."

Tara chose not to ask for details.

"Before Angelica decided to strangle me," she said, "I was wondering if dragon fire could melt these bars."

"Afraid not," said Cal. "They're forged of magical iron, which makes them immune to magic, but they've also been surrounded by a protection spell. The only thing you'd melt would be yourself. The way the spell works, any violence done to the bars bounces back against the attacker."

"The prison's very well protected," remarked the king approvingly.

"Darling, for once I wish Salatar had been a little less efficient," said the queen. "What are we going to do?"

"You? You aren't going to do a thing," said a voice like liquid velvet. "*We*, on the other hand, are going to set you free."

Emerging from the darkness like a masked demon was Magister.

Tara reacted without thinking, firing a Destructus at the figure in black.

"Tara, no!" screamed Cal.

The spell had barely touched the bars when it ricocheted back at her. Warned by Cal's shout, she barely had enough time to erect a protective shield.

Magister hadn't stirred.

"Tut, tut, tut!" he said, shaking his head. "What impetuousness! What anger! And here I was coming to save you. That wasn't a very nice welcome."

For a moment, Tara was speechless. Then she exploded.

"I'd rather be possessed by the Ravager!" she screamed. "How did you find me? I'm warning you, I'm not gonna let you manipulate me so you can appropriate the evil power of the demonic objects—even if it's to use them against him!"

Magister was silent for a moment, then his mask turned blue. Tara knew this meant the Bloodgrave was amused, which made her even angrier.

"That's an excellent idea, Miss Duncan. I admit it hadn't occurred to me. And we found you thanks to a simple locator spell. In fact the only reason for our presence was to bring you . . . this!"

With a magician's sweep of his arm, he revealed the White Soul!

Cal ran over to the bars.

"How in the world—"

"I brought it to him," interrupted Master Dragosh, materializing like a silent shadow behind Magister.

"Everything's set," said the vampyr, pointing at the stairs. "The guards have all been knocked out, and I took their keys. Let's go!"

"Very well, let's free them," said Magister.

But just as Dragosh was about to unlock the cells, Magister said, "Wait a second!" Turning to Tara, he said, "I want your word that you won't try anything against me while we're fighting the Ravager together."

Tara could hardly believe her ears. *Is Magister offering to be my ally?*

Cal and Robin were just as surprised, and Master Dragosh enlightened them in a bitter tone.

"I didn't have any choice," he explained. "This Bloodgrave is the only person able to fight the Ravager. So I sent him a message by way of one of his acolytes. We retrieved the White Soul and also these."

In his hand, glittering with a thousand points of light, was Tara's bracelet and the living stone!

Tara was overjoyed to see her luminous friend again.

Living stone, she asked mentally, *how do you feel?*

Tara, pretty Tara, nice Tara! Was afraid, very afraid. But vampyr swim and pick up. Whee! Back with Tara!

What the living stone didn't say was how completely lost she'd felt when the Ravager tore her away from Tara. Falling into the water, she'd almost accepted that the lake would be her tomb forever. Sensing her friend's anxiety, Tara tried to comfort her.

She then gave the vampyr one of her famous smiles, and he reeled a little under its impact.

"Thank you," she breathed gratefully. Then she turned to Magister.

"Very well, I agree to a truce," she said curtly. "But at the slightest sign of sneakiness on your part, I'll send you to join your ancestors. Got that?"

Magister nodded and his mask turned red. He clearly didn't like threats, but that was just too bad.

The left corner of the vampyr's lip curled—his version of a smile. He didn't like Magister very much either. In fact, he had much more cause to hate him than Tara did. Proposing an alliance to the Bloodgrave had been the worst moment of Dragosh's existence.

"We better get out of here fast," he announced. "The Ravager will soon start to sense our presence."

The king, queen, Tara, and her friends were the only prisoners, so it didn't take long to open the cells. They used the Living Castle's tunnels to reach the hidden exit. The castle's spirit, or soul, or whatever served as its brain and gave it consciousness, had escaped possession. It projected scenes of crowds silently applauding along their way, to wish them good luck and to give them courage.

Once outside, they were still far from safe. Many of Travia's inhabitants were under the Ravager's spell, and the few who weren't kept a low profile and stayed out of sight. Tara and her friends did the same. Gallant scouted ahead and let them know when it was safe to move.

Tara observed Magister closely, straining to figure out who he really was. There was something in the Bloodgrave's current attitude she found unsettling, but what? Suddenly, it became clear. He was afraid! For the first time in a long time he was facing a power much greater than his own. So he actually hadn't only come to free them; he'd come to ask for their help. *Perfect.*

Magister must have felt Tara's eyes on him, because he abruptly turned around. "Miss Duncan, I would guess that it's taking you quite an effort not to carbonize me, right? Believe me, I'm also fighting the urge to kidnap you. I would take you to my new fortress, since you conquered the old one. Unfortunately, our friend the Ravager would soon get his red claws on it, so I don't think we have any choice. We *have* to cooperate."

Tara's eyes narrowed, but she didn't reply. Magister waited a moment for her to answer. When she didn't, he resumed his cautious progression through the town.

Tara smiled to see his back rigid with apprehension. *He must imagine I'm cooking up some sort of scheme.* Which wasn't entirely wrong.

The gnome embassy seemed completely deserted, but Cal quickly ran into one of the two gnomes who had volunteered to stay behind.

"We have to leave right away," he said.

The blue gnome bowed. "For what destination, sir?"

"The Gray Fortress, same as before."

The king and queen spoke: "We'll come with you. You're going to need all the help you can get to fight the Ravager."

"No," said Magister shortly. "You have to go to Omois and warn the emperor and empress of what is happening here. Tell them to prepare the planet's defenses against the Ravager."

Dragosh agreed.

"He's right, Your Majesties" he said. "You will be much more useful to us there."

"But what if you aren't able to defeat him?" asked the queen anxiously.

Cal couldn't resist. "If everyone around you suddenly starts turning red, it won't be from a sunburn."

"Cal!" exclaimed Tara.

"What? What did I say now?"

The queen shuddered and hugged the kids tightly. Then the portal transferred the two sovereigns to Omois.

As a precaution, the others colored their skin purple before leaving for the Gray Fortress. Busy with the transformation, they didn't notice what was happening behind them. A tentacle carefully hidden in the gnome's body emerged and touched Robin. The half-elf stiffened very slightly as he fought the possession, then slumped in defeat. As the portal transferred Tara's group, they also didn't notice the gnome turn completely purple and laugh sarcastically.

They rematerialized in the Gray Fortress prepared to do battle, but curiously, there was no one there.

They left the Fortress very easily, again by way of Fafnir's tunnel.

Once they were beyond the walls, Magister spoke.

"Something's odd here," he said, frowning. "That Transfer Portal is the only one that gives access to the center of the Ravager's power. Why isn't it better guarded?"

Cal shrugged. "Hey, dude, the guy's busy conquering the world. He doesn't have time to worry about some little portal out in the boonies."

"Sir Dal Salan?"

"Yes?"

"Let's avoid familiarity, if you don't mind. I am Magister, the Blood-grave Master. So 'Master' or 'Magister' is fine. 'Dude' is not."

Cal grimaced and said nothing.

"What say we make our skin normal again?" suggested Tara, who thought purple looked better on flowers.

"No!" cried Robin.

They turned, surprised by the abruptness of his reaction.

"I mean . . . that's not a good idea. If the Ravager has overcome the Mud Eaters, it's best if they think we've been possessed too. It'll spare us having to fight them."

They agreed that he had a point.

"How are we going to get close to the island?" asked Tara.

The masked Bloodgrave turned to her, and she repressed an instinctive urge to back away.

"It's not far," he said. "I've prepared a Transmitus. Kindly stand in a circle, with the familiars in the center. You must all be touching each other, please."

Magister went to stand between Tara and Cal and took their hands. The glove he wore was so thin that Tara could feel calluses on his palm.

In this world, such calluses were usually the sign of a warrior. Was the Bloodgrave a mercenary? A fighter?

Interesting . . . very interesting. Tara tucked this new clue away in a corner of her mind.

Magister cast his Transmitus. The forest disappeared in a flash of bright light, and the next moment they were in the Swamps of Desolation.

Ko-axes croaked enthusiastically, huge blue-green dragonflies chased yellow flies, lots of the plants looked like insects, and lots of insects looked like plants. The dominant color palette ranged from gray to black to dark black. The air reeked revoltingly of stagnant water, outsized snakes slithered nearby, and glurps quarreled over a chunk of some poor animal who had gotten up too early. In short, they were back in the good old Swamps of Desolation.

It was nighttime, though hardly pitch-black dark. The silvery light from OtherWorld's moons made the landscape almost as bright as day.

The Ravager apparently hadn't yet extended his power to the swamp, because the Mud Eaters were their usual color, a crushed taupe. *This is the first time I've almost liked that shade*, thought Tara. *Just goes to show how tastes can change with circumstances.* Right now, she was seriously allergic to anything purple.

Magister pulled the White Soul from his pocket. When he did, Robin shuddered.

Cal noticed, and he frowned. Something very strange was going on. He'd better check on it and fast.

"Your Transmitus is a darned practical transportation system," he told Magister, stretching. "It would have saved us lot of problems if we'd had it when we escaped from you the last time."

Magister's mask turned brown. "Don't be so sure, Caliban. The Transmitus doesn't always work right, and the arrivals are, shall we say, fragmentary."

"Oh, really? You mean people come one after another? That's not so bad!"

"Well, not exactly," said Bloodgrave. "The *pieces* arrive one after another."

It took a moment for Cal to get the picture.

"Yuck!"

"Yes, it can be messy," said Magister. "That's why I use Transmitus spells very cautiously."

Cal thought this over for a moment. Then he said, "Anyway, now that we're safe and sound and the Mud Eaters aren't possessed, why don't we go back to our normal colors? I don't much like walking around looking like a yummm."

An image of a red cherry the size of a peach popped into Tara's mind. When there was no Earth equivalent for an OtherWorld word, or the reverse, the Interpretus spell put weird images in her head. *All right, got it: yummm = big cherry.*

"Why would we do that?" Robin immediately exclaimed. "Doing magic here might attract the Ravager."

"No, it won't," said Magister. "The Ravager isn't especially sensitive to magic."

With that, they transformed themselves back to normal. Robin had some trouble restoring his translucent white skin and apologized for being slow. Probably because he was tired, he said.

Cal, who had been watching him closely, relaxed. *I guess it was stupid to be suspicious,* he thought, *but just for a moment there . . .* Now that they had the White Soul, they had to be very careful.

"I found out some things about the Ravager," Magister said. "He was one of the high wizards who fought with Demiderus against the demons. His real name is Drexus Vlani Gampra. One day a group of demons managed to get through Demiderus's barriers and cast an evil spell on the wizards. Drexus was fighting alongside his wife, the beautiful Deselea. When the demons cast their spell, the wizards they hit turned into terrifying demons. Deselea and her children were among those affected, and they started to massacre Demiderus's wizards and their allies. The others realized they had no choice but to eliminate this new menace.

"Drexus begged Demiderus not to kill his wife and children. He pleaded for time to find an incantation, a potion, something, anything that might save them. But time was exactly what Demiderus didn't have. Thanks to their monstrous spell, the demons were now winning. So he destroyed Deselea. After his confrontation with Demiderus, Drexus disappeared. The threat from the demons was put down. Then a curious rumor began making the rounds on Earth. An insidious purple sickness had started to attack and kill women and children, but not men. It became known as the Purple Plague. Hunter-elves were sent to Earth to investigate and quickly discovered that Drexus was back. He had turned into the Ravager of Souls. Since he'd been deprived of his reason for living, he was now determined to do the same to others."

Cal was horrified. "Do you mean to say that he—"

"He killed women and children, thousands of them," said Magister. "He spread this awful sickness across the whole planet. Drexus nearly wiped out the human race, because without women or children, mankind would perish. The five surviving high wizards came to Earth to hunt him down, but he fled to OtherWorld and started killing again. That's when Demiderus set a trap for him. He announced publicly that he was going to get married. OtherWorld was delighted, because he was the great hero who had saved the universe. When he introduced his future wife to the public, the Ravager wasn't able to resist his thirst for vengeance. But despite all the precautions they took, he managed to break into the castle and kill her. This enraged Demiderus. His power, which was already enormous, grew to unprecedented strength."

Cal glanced at Tara, who was chewing on her poor white forelock, completely engrossed. She was fascinated by her distant ancestor's exploits.

He returned his focus to Magister as the Bloodgrave went on with the story.

"At the time, the Imperial Palace didn't exist. It was just an ordinary castle that the giants had built for the humans at the dragons' request. Demiderus's anger was so great that he blew the castle down like a piece of straw. Some of the debris landed ten miles away. Needless to say, the Ravager was defeated. But to OtherWorld's great surprise, Demiderus didn't kill him. Instead, he decided to imprison him on the Island of Black Roses. Then he spent several years perfecting the White Soul, which was the only thing that could destroy him. Unfortunately, a knight from Earth managed to reach OtherWorld and steal it. He wanted to kill the Ravager for wiping out his family. He died before getting the Soul to the island, and the statuette was lost for a very long time. Fortunately, you found it."

One detail had been bothering Tara throughout the story. "What are the black roses for, exactly? Fafnir apparently became possessed because of them, yet they seem to defend the island against all intruders."

"The black roses were there to guard the Ravager," explained Magister, who seemed very well informed, "and they're still aware of their function. But the Ravager managed to corrupt some of the bushes during the last five thousand years. It was just bad luck that your dwarf friend made her brew from the very roses that are under his control. Also, one of you made those roses grow so dramatically that they've overwhelmed the bushes that are still faithful to their original mission, namely keeping the Ravager locked up."

"That was me," said Robin with a rueful sigh. "I used the living tree's magic to make the roses grow. I didn't know—"

"The Ravager has apparently changed tactics," interrupted Master Dragosh, who wasn't interested in the ins and outs of past events. "He has stopped killing people. Now he possesses them."

"It amounts to the same thing," said Magister sharply, who didn't want his allies pitying their enemy. "His victims are prisoners, subject to his every whim. Who would want to live as a slave for the rest of their days?"

"I sure wouldn't," said Cal. "Anyway, since Master Dragosh went to get you, it means he figured you're able to defeat the Ravager. What's your plan?"

"I don't have one," the Bloodgrave admitted. "I never expected him to seize power. In fact, I didn't even know the Ravager existed until our vampyr friend contacted me. We'll have to put our heads together and come up with a solution."

Master Dragosh spoke: "From what I've been able to tell, you and Miss Duncan are the most powerful among us, even if her power is subject to . . . fluctuations."

Tara scowled at him. Sharing information with her worst enemy wasn't exactly a great idea.

Unaware of her irritation, the vampyr continued. "I saw the Ravager's tentacles attack everyone who approached the island. To protect herself, Miss Duncan created a shield, but it eventually failed. Why, do you suppose?"

"The tentacles seemed to suck the power out of it," said Tara with a shudder. "After a while I just couldn't maintain it."

"But it might be possible to create a series of nesting shields," said Magister. "I could set up the first one, for example, and Miss Duncan could create a second one inside it. When mine collapsed, hers could take over. When hers failed, I could create a third, and so forth until we reached the center of the island."

"Hmm, that might work," said Tara thoughtfully. "But the first shield would have to be very big—big enough to surround both of us, 'cause our available space will gradually shrink."

"You held out for about a minute before your shield collapsed," observed the vampyr. "How long would it take you to reach the island?"

"If the tentacles attack us over the water, like the first time, it shouldn't take us more than a couple of minutes," she said. "It's not far to the island, but we'll have to fight our way there."

"And we can't set down the statuette just anywhere," said Magister. "In his notes, Demiderus wrote that the statuette must be placed in the center of the island."

"Really? That's a little trickier. That should take us . . . I dunno, two to three minutes, maybe."

"Which means you'll have to create three or four shields," said the vampyr. "Do you think you'll be able to hang on?"

"I've never fought this thing, so I don't know," said Magister. "But do we really have a choice?"

"Not really," said Dragosh. "My vampyrs and I will launch an attack to distract the Ravager. While he's coming after us, you get as close as you can. We'll try to hold on until you're able to set the statuette in place."

Cal spoke up. "Excuse me, but does anybody have any idea what happens after that?"

"Well, the Ravager will be destroyed," answered Magister.

"Yeah, I got that," he said sarcastically. "But how, exactly? Because if he goes *boom!* while you're in the neighborhood, won't you also go *boom!*?"

A thoughtful silence greeted Cal's question.

"You're right," admitted Magister. "I hadn't thought of that."

"We'll have to set the White Soul down and get out of there as fast as we can," said Tara. "We'll make our shields as strong as possible."

Suddenly Cal started. Here Tara would be risking her life, yet Robin hadn't reacted. *That's totally abnormal,* thought Cal, taking a deep breath. *And it confirms my worst suspicions.* But before he could do anything, Robin caught him looking and made his move. With inhuman speed, he slammed into Magister, knocked the White Soul out of his hand, and scooped it up in a cloth. Then he spun around and raced off into the swamp.

Tara immediately understood what had happened.

"Gallant!" she screamed. "Stop him! The Ravager's possessed him. Master Dragosh, follow them!"

Without waiting to see if she'd been obeyed, she went over to Magister. The Bloodgrave was gingerly cradling his head. It was an odd sight, with his hands sticking through the part of the mask that was only an illusion, even though its protection was real.

"Wha . . . what happened?" he mumbled.

"Robin was possessed," answered Cal darkly. "It must have happened during the transfer. It did occur to me that we escaped very easily, and there wasn't anybody in the Fortress. You were right. It wasn't normal."

"Are you all right?" Tara asked the Bloodgrave, who was still stunned.

"Don't worry, I can still fight," he said. "My mask cushioned the blow."

Tara rolled her eyes and swallowed the retort on the tip of her tongue. Showing compassion clearly wasn't the right approach with the Bloodgrave Master.

"Go on ahead," he continued. "I'll catch up with you as soon as the world stops spinning."

They hurried off in pursuit. The half-elf ran very fast, but the pegasus and bat flew faster. They caught up with him a few hundred yards away.

When Tara and Cal joined them, Robin had turned completely purple, and tentacles were erupting from his body, attacking Gallant and Dragosh. Having learned their lesson, the pegasus and the bat were nimbly avoiding them. The two weren't able to approach Robin, but he couldn't escape, either.

Cal was about to join the fray when Tara stopped him. "Wait, I have an idea. Look at Robin. He wrapped his hand so as not to touch the White Soul. What does that tell you?"

"That he's afraid of it?"

"Better yet, I think touching it will destroy the possession. Did you notice which direction he ran?"

Cal looked around.

"Oh, yeah," he murmured. "Away from the island, right?"

"Right. The tentacle possessing him must not have be directly linked to the Ravager. I bet he was trying to bring the White Soul to the Fortress so he could use the Transfer Portal."

Suddenly Robin dropped the statuette on the ground and picked up his bow and arrows.

"Hey, none of that!" Tara shouted, instantly casting a spell.

Her protection spell was faster than the arrows. Gallant blinked to see one hit an inch from his head, then whinnied his thanks to Tara before returning to the fight.

"Cal, try to get close to Robin and grab the statuette. Then you have to somehow touch his skin with it."

The little thief cast a Camouflagus spell, making himself practically invisible. He started quickly crawling toward Robin, and Tara lost him from sight almost immediately.

Robin had been surprised when his arrow didn't kill the pegasus. He now shot at the bat, but with no more success. He realized that someone, probably Tara, was protecting his attackers—and he started looking around for her.

Uh-oh! thought Tara. She leaped behind a tree and held her breath, hoping he wouldn't see her. But Robin's hyper-acute senses located her almost immediately, and he smiled evilly. Ignoring the White Soul on the ground, he nocked an arrow and tiptoed toward Tara, who couldn't see him coming. Gallant whinnied loudly, but the tentacles kept him from coming to the rescue.

The elf suddenly leaped and pointed his arrow at Tara at point-blank range.

"You're dead!" he cried.

When you're about to die, your entire life passes before your eyes, they say. But Tara didn't have time to see anything. Held by Cal's invisible hand, the White Soul flew up out of nowhere to slap against Robin's cheek.

The effect was immediate. He opened his mouth, but didn't have time to scream. Tara dove to the ground, but Robin had dropped his bow, and the arrow didn't fly.

The White Soul left a pale mark on the elf's cheek, and it now spread quickly, overwhelming the purple. The black tentacles quickly turned white as well, then vanished.

Robin crumpled to the ground, finally able to release the scream caught in his throat.

"Super!" exclaimed Cal as he canceled the Camouflagus spell. "Nothing went *boom!*"

Tara knelt down and pulled the unconscious elf's head onto her lap.

"It's okay," said Cal. "He's breathing."

The pegasus and the bat landed nearby moments later, joined by Magister, who staggered up.

"Is everything all right?" he asked, leaning against a tree for balance.

Then, seeing Robin lying on the ground, he exclaimed: "Isn't he possessed anymore?"

"No," said Tara. "Cal pressed the White Soul against his face and the Ravager was immediately driven out."

"So it works," said the Bloodgrave with satisfaction. "That's perfect."

When Robin opened his eyes, the first thing he saw were Tara's beautiful deep blue eyes, and he gazed into them with rapture.

"Am I in heaven?" he murmured. "Are you an angel?"

"Fortunately not," Tara said with a smile. "Those wings are very impractical when you're getting dressed. How do you feel?"

"As if a braaa trampled me. But the Ravager's gone, and that's the main thing. Did I hurt anybody?"

"You sort of knocked Magister out, but that's not real serious," answered Cal. "The rest of us are fine."

The Bloodgrave said nothing, but his mask turned an irritated red, suggesting he didn't much appreciate Cal's humor.

"The gnome was possessed," said Robin with a shiver, still feeling shaken. "It was a trap. The Ravager let us escape so he could see if we'd brought the White Soul back. He knew we would spot him because of the purple, so he didn't change the gnome's skin. In my case, when Cal suggested we go back to our normal color, he drained the purple from my hands and face. By the way, Cal, how did you guess I was possessed?"

"I wasn't sure, and when your skin turned white again I thought I'd made a mistake. It was only when Tara said she was going to risk her life and you didn't react that I got it."

As he spoke, the little thief gave Robin a sly look, who turned beet red.

Seeing Robin's embarrassment, Tara decided not to press the matter. No point in making the handsome half-elf feel more awkward, she thought. But she promised herself to have a serious conversation with Cal and maybe extract some vital information from him.

Magister grumbled: "The cursed elf hit my head so hard, I'm not sure I'm in any condition to fight."

Tara couldn't believe she would ever say what she said next: "Come over here. I'll treat you."

Magister raised his head and looked at her through his mask, seeming to hesitate.

"Oh, for crying out loud, I'm not going to hurt you!" she cried. "I understand the equation: you + me = dead Ravager. So c'mon, let's do it."

Magister came over and Tara reached out to him, her hand easily passing through the mask. Her fingers felt a wide forehead sticky with blood. She quickly cast a Healus and pulled her hand back.

Magister moved his head cautiously.

"That's perfect, Miss," he said approvingly. "I feel much better."

"It was a deep gash," said Tara, bending down to wash her hand in a small pond. "You better take it easy for a while."

"In that case, I'll leave you the task of raising the first shield," he suggested. He was moving slowly, so as not to revive a killer migraine.

Cal drew a rough sketch of the island and its surroundings.

"Robin and I will take the east shore of the lake," he said. "The vampyrs can take the west. The rosebushes are thickest in the north, so you should be out of sight until you're above the water. With a little luck the tentacles will be too busy fighting us to realize that you're attacking at the same time."

Tara carefully studied the sketch.

"That's fine," she said. "We'll ride Gallant, which will save us having to cast a levitation spell. He's able to carry us for as long as an hour, so a few minutes won't be anything for him."

"In that case, we're all set," said Magister.

They climbed onto the pegasus, who didn't flinch under the double weight. Master Dragosh shifted into wolf shape and called his pack. The vampyr wolves appeared in a few minutes. Half of them had gone back to Krasalvia to warn of the danger they faced, but there were still a dozen left—plenty for a diversion. Five of these shifted into bats. They agreed that the signal for the attack would be a wolf howl, and silently disappeared. The half-elf and the little thief left just as quietly. Soon only Magister, Tara, and Gallant were left.

"Your friends are very loyal," observed the Bloodgrave.

Great! Now he wants to talk. Tara was so afraid of Magister that she was struggling not to throw up, and he was feeling chatty. *Super.*

"Of course they are," she answered distractedly, praying that he would shut up. "They're friends."

Magister seemed to have trouble grasping the concept. "They're drawn to your power. That's why they're loyal to you."

For a moment, Tara wandered if the Bloodgrave was a complete idiot, or just pretending.

"No. I'd do the same thing for any of them. Wouldn't you?"

"I beg your pardon?"

"If one of your friends was in danger and needed your help, wouldn't you risk your life for them?"

"If it served my purposes, of course I would," he answered arrogantly.

Tara sighed. "No, I mean if you weren't getting anything out of it. You just help them, that's all."

Magister mulled this over.

"No," he admitted. "In that case I'd have no reason to risk my life."

"That's the main difference between you and me," Tara concluded. "I don't help people because I expect something in return. I help my friends because I love them. And love is a lot more powerful than greed."

"And you don't love me."

"Not in the least!" she exclaimed. "Why would I? You killed my father and you kidnapped my mother. You robbed me of ten years of life with her. Besides, you've been trying to kidnap me just to get your hands on a few powerful objects. You already have power. What more do you want?"

"I want to get rid of the dragons," he shot back. "And I won't be able to fight them until I have supreme power."

This came as a surprise. It had never occurred to Tara that Magister might want to seize demonic power for a specific reason.

"What have the dragons ever done to you that you should ally yourself with the demons to destroy them?" Tara asked.

"I have no intention of allying myself with demons," he said scornfully. "Once the demonic objects are in my possession, I'll seal the rift forever, and no demon will ever be able to enter our universe. That's what Demiderus should've done."

"But what about your hatred of the dragons?" Tara insisted. "Where does that come from? To me, they seem pretty benevolent toward the peoples of OtherWorld."

"They *control* us!" said Magister sharply. "There's no reason for humans to be controlled and directed by overgrown lizards, supposedly because of a battle between them and the demons. We're powerful. We don't need them!"

Tara didn't quite agree. "But the dragons saved our race, didn't they? I heard the demons had already invaded Earth when the dragons intervened."

"That's actually not clear. The archives don't spell out exactly whether the demons or the dragons invaded Earth first. It's commonly believed that it was the demons, but maybe history was rewritten by the winners."

"But the dragons are peaceful, and they don't enslave people, the way the demons do." She paused. "For the sake of argument, let's say that the dragons exercise some control over the peoples of OtherWorld and Earth. So what? Everyone here seems pretty happy. People are free, and the dragons don't ask for anything. In fact, aside from Master Chem, I don't know that there are dragons on the other nations' High Councils."

"Except for Omois, and among the dwarves and the giants, there are dragons everywhere," said Magister bitterly.

Tara was about to ask another question when they suddenly heard a wolf howl.

"Let's go," she whispered.

Tara activated the shield and cast a spell that combined a Protectus with the Camouflagus Cal had used, making them completely invisible. From the outside it looked as if a giant hand had erased the pegasus and its two riders.

Gallant took off, and within a few seconds they were over the lakeshore.

The battle was raging. The vampyrs had borrowed the Mud Eaters' rafts, crude craft that they used to harvest the lake's blue water lilies, whose root was a favorite food. The rafts had been launched, and a magic spell had peopled them with dark figures, one of whom was holding a white statuette! It was a very clever ploy. The tentacles immediately attacked the rafts, while carefully avoiding the one carrying the fake statuette. Meanwhile, Robin and Cal had done the same on the other side of the lake, and the tentacles didn't know which way to turn.

There was a lot of noise, splashing, and screams.

As a result, Tara, Magister, and Gallant flew over the lake and were able to reach the island's north shore undetected.

Magister took the White Soul from his pocket.

"We'll be over the center of the island in a minute," he said. "Is everything all right?"

"Yes," answered Tara. "As long as the tentacles don't touch the shield I can maintain it almost indefinitely."

Eventually, though, they were detected, but it was completely by accident. One of the tentacles was racing toward the attackers when it bumped into the cloaked bubble. The Ravager immediately realized that an invisible enemy had infiltrated his lines and gotten terribly close to the middle of the island.

A dozen tentacles immediately fastened onto the shield, and Tara began to struggle. She was joined by the living stone and its enormous power and this fried the tentacles like hot dogs on a grill, and they fell away. Gallant forged ahead, beating his wings with all his might. Then new tentacles gripped the shield and the struggle began again.

Tara and Magister had underestimated the Ravager's power. The tentacles were immobilizing them. They were inching ahead when Tara felt her shield about to collapse under the strain.

"Now!" she screamed.

Magister immediately created a shield a little smaller than the first, just in time. Tara's shield collapsed and the victorious tentacles closed in . . . only to slam into the second shield.

They clearly heard the Ravager's scream of fury.

Tara, who had stopped breathing in the thick of the struggle, began again. Magister seemed to be blocking the tentacles' attacks easily, but looking at his clenched hands and tense body, Tara knew he was actually struggling.

Gaining ground inch by inch despite the tentacles, they finally flew above the center of the island.

The blackish magma that filled the pit had doubled in volume. It was now blistered like some horrible boil oozing black, nauseating pus.

"Your turn, Tara!" Magister suddenly cried.

Feeling somewhat refreshed, Tara took over. By now, the tentacles had gone berserk and were sucking her power with all their might. It was an accomplishment just to hover over the pit.

"So, what do we do now?" asked Tara, gritting her teeth with the strain.

"Drop the shield! Now!"

Without thinking, Tara obeyed and Magister dove headlong toward the tentacles, which immediately reached for him. Screaming in horror, Tara instantly raised her shield again, in the process lopping off the tentacles stuck to Gallant. As she desperately strained to see what was happening in the furious bubbling around Magister's almost inert body, Tara could feel tears of despair running down her cheeks.

Now completely powerless, the Bloodgrave had stopped moving. They had lost.

Gallant, who was beating his wings furiously, gave a piercing whinny. They couldn't give up now! But the tentacles had surrounded them and were sucking Tara's power. She could feel her strength ebbing. If she'd been alone, she probably would've succumbed under their number. But the need to save her pegasus was stronger than her fear and her pain, and she reinforced her shield.

In the center of the blackish pit, Magister's body was gradually sinking out of sight.

Suddenly he waved, like a dying man in a final spasm, and Tara started.

His arm was holding something. Something shaped like a statuette!

The panicked tentacles tried to get clear, but it was too late. Magister firmly pressed the statuette into the magma.

And the White Soul made contact with the Ravager.

Amid something like an explosion of light, the Ravager's scream of pain practically shattered their eardrums.

With incredible speed, the tentacles turned white, and so did the roiling magma pit. The change spread outward to the entire island, and the black roses became white as well.

The tentacles surrounding Tara faded to white, then disappeared. The white magma sloshed furiously and for a moment Tara thought the Ravager had managed to resist the White Soul's power. Then, to her disbelief, the magma condensed into two pale clouds that gradually took human shape.

Tara cursed. Instead of a single Ravager, now there were *two* of them! Determined to fight, she gritted her teeth and reinforced her shield again. To her alarm, though, the two translucent shapes suddenly soared out of the center of the island. One had taken the form of a beautiful young woman, the other a stocky spellbinder with a somber gaze. They came to stand in front of Tara.

"Are you responsible for this?" growled the spellbinder figure.

Tara hesitated for an instant, then answered curtly: "Yes, and I'm prepared to fight you—"

The spellbinder interrupted her: "You have our deepest thanks, Miss. You've just accomplished what Demiderus undertook thousands of years ago. I never realized what he was up to, but now I understand. And I regret all the harm I've done."

Tara was wide-eyed for a moment. Then it dawned on her. "You're Drexus, right? And the White Soul is—"

"Deselea, my beloved wife. Demiderus was forced to kill my wife and our children during the battle against the demons. To counter his horrible but unavoidable action, he spent years trying to find a way to reunite us. The White Soul wasn't a weapon against me. It was my salvation!"

"You've always been so stubborn," said Deselea sweetly. "I tried to communicate with you during all the time I was held by the Mud Eaters, but you weren't listening!"

"I . . . I know. My hate and my thirst for vengeance were too great. Let's leave now. I don't want to remain in a place that has seen so much pain and sadness. Let's go find the children."

Under Tara's and Gallant's shocked eyes, the two figures joined in a sparkling whirlwind and disappeared.

She was speechless. *What? All that pain, all those deaths, all that destruction and fear, all that for . . . nothing? Just a thanks and goodbye!* She felt her anger rising, as great as the terror she had just experienced.

Cal, Blondin, and Robin soon joined them. They were accompanied by Master Dragosh, now in bat shape.

"Is everything okay, Tara?" cried Robin.

"No, it isn't!" she answered, still furious. "The Ravager turned into a ghost, he found his wife, and *poof!* they disappeared. They'll probably live together for eternity and have lots of little ghosts! It's unfair! They should have been punished!"

Cal stared at her, wide-eyed "Er, how do you intend to punish a ghost? By killing it?"

Tara opened her mouth, then closed it again. The little thief was right.

Then she remembered Magister. Gallant landed, and Tara ran toward the pit that the Bloodgrave master had dived into.

When she leaned over the rim, all she saw was an empty pit. Magister had disappeared!

CHAPTER 19

TRAPPING A SPELLBINDER

Suddenly Tara heard a muffled cry behind her. She turned around and stifled a shout of dismay.

Magister was standing before her, and Cal, Blondin, Robin, and Gallant were his prisoners. What looked like silver mittens were clamped around their hands and arms. They were gagged, and their legs were tied. Apparently, only Master Dragosh had escaped Magister's sudden attack. He must have quickly flown away as soon as the Bloodgrave started to cast a spell.

"Now that the Ravager is out of commission, let's get back to business," cried Magister. "Come here, Tara!"

"You're alive!" she said in astonishment. "I thought the tentacles had crushed you to death."

"Ho, ho! Do I hear a touch of relief in your voice, dear Tara? Were you afraid for me when I jumped out? Did you consider me . . . a friend? If that's the case, *friend*, I'd like us to have a chat about a certain demonic scepter I could use. Those-Who-Guard and Those-Who-Judge won't let me get to it, because they answer only to you. Will you kindly do me this little favor?"

Tara snorted with rage. Magister was turning her own arguments against her, using the fact that he had risked his life to save them to bargain with her. Seeing her expression, the Bloodgrave burst out laughing.

"No, I can tell that my proposal doesn't appeal to you. Well, too bad. We'll have to use stronger measures. Although to be honest, I would've been very disappointed if you had agreed."

"There was never any chance of that!" she said, mopping her sweaty brow.

Master Dragosh suddenly appeared, shape-shifted back, and stood next to her, his hatred for Magister reflected in his eyes.

"It's you and me, Bloodgrave!" the vampyr growled. "I'm finally going to pay you back for what you did to my fiancée!"

Tara gave Dragosh a perplexed look. *His fiancée? What was this all about?*

She would come to understand later on. For now, they had a fight on their hands. Tara turned her attention back to her enemy, ready to do battle. But the vampyr was way ahead of her and began the duel by firing a Carbonus at Magister.

Dragosh was powerful, but Magister was much more so. He protected himself with a shield that absorbed Dragosh's spell. Then, seeing that Tara was about to join the fray, he shot a Quakus at her. The resulting mini-earthquake shook the ground, and Tara lost her balance. The spell she'd just fired turned awry and missed its target. With his other hand, Magister shot an incredibly powerful Knockoutus. It slammed into the vampyr, and he crumpled to the ground.

When Tara was back to her feet, she was the Bloodgrave's only remaining opponent.

"Well, well, well," he chuckled from behind his mask. "We're face to face at last. But you have an advantage, Tara. I don't want to kill you."

"Which isn't the case for me," she said, trying to hide her fear. "I wouldn't hesitate for a second."

"You certainly are bloody-minded for such a little girl!"

"No, I'm not," she said, as a fresh spell lit up her hands. "I don't have any taste for fights, assassinations, or any of those OtherWorld pleasures. But with you, I really don't have any choice."

"Wait a minute!" said Magister. "Don't you want to hear about the trap?"

So Magister wants to talk—great! Tara was all for talking and for as long as possible. Hope and fear were contending in her head. She lowered her hands a little.

"What trap?" she asked innocently.

"The one you fell into, you and the dragon."

Tara had since figured it out, of course, but she played along, praying that Master Chem and the full pantheon of high wizards would make a magical, thundering, lifesaving appearance at any moment.

"Well, when we overheard the conversation between the two Bloodgraves, we suspected you were involved in that whole trial business."

Magister stiffened, clearly surprised. "When? Where? What conversation?"

"During the hearing, one of you Bloodgraves cast a spell on Manitou to read his mind, didn't you? We figured you wanted us to know about your plan to steal *The Forbidden Book*. I thought it was it a bit complicated, to be honest."

Magister's mask turned an irritated orange.

"I never cast a spell on that stupid dog!" he exploded. "And when I want to steal something, I don't usually tell the owner beforehand. I bewitched Brandis's parents to make you come to OtherWorld and keep the old dragon stuck in Omois. I was planning to kill Bandiou myself, who was taking too much power within the Bloodgraves, and have you accused of the crime. Then, after that, I was going to steal the book and kidnap you. I'm going to cure those two Bloodgraves for their habit of discussing my plans in public."

"Oh, so it was a coincidence?" exclaimed Tara, honestly surprised. "That's unbelievable! If Manitou hadn't left the hearing room—"

"You wouldn't have known I was behind that business. You wouldn't have tried to free Caliban," Magister continued, "and you wouldn't have escaped me. Unfortunately, you mysteriously disappeared before I could step in. After that, my spies sighted you in Lancovit, but you didn't stay there long enough. Later, I was pleased to hear that Bandiou had an accident, a fatal one. For which I must thank you, since I suppose that was your doing."

Tara nodded, shuddering as she remembered the horrible wizard.

"I suspected as much. So, thank you for ridding me of that troublesome prince. Then the Ravager showed up, and our little affairs no longer seemed that important."

Tara could feel that Magister was reaching the end of his speech, and so she reactivated her power. No one was showing up to lend her a hand, so she would have to take care of Magister herself.

Then Magister tried one final appeal: "Tara, we made a powerful team in the battle against the Ravager. We could work together! I'm begging you, don't make me force you, it really pains me."

She knew he was telling the truth. He needed her alive and healthy. She sighed. "I'm sorry, but I'll never join forces with you."

"Never say never," said Magister. "In that case, it's too bad, but I—"

Tara didn't give him time to finish his sentence. She activated a terrible Destructus spell.

Not to be outdone, Magister's hands glowed red and he activated a Defendus. A powerful shield appeared in front of him.

Cast at the same instant, the two spells collided with a deafening crash. Each was buttressed by a magic anchor deep in the island's soil, and the power of the impact shook them both.

"Stop, Tara!" cried Magister. "I don't want to hurt you! If you join with me, I'll make you a being of incredible strength. You'll have power!"

"I already have power!" she retorted, shaking her head to get rid of the sweat dipping into her eyes. "In fact, it's high time you got a taste of it."

Tara took a deep breath. She had never really unleashed all her power at once. In the back of her mind, she'd always been afraid of hurting her grandmother. But not anymore.

In the surge of energy, her eyes became completely blue, her white forelock began to blaze, and her terrifying blue ray hammered Magister's red shield mercilessly.

The Bloodgrave suddenly realized that she might defeat him. Which would mean death.

Magister then cast a spell he had sworn he would never use. The one that would force him to spend a year of his life in the service of the king of Limbo. The one he had obtained at the price of his soul—to the extent he still had a soul worth bargaining for, that is.

His shield became wreathed in a black glow, and from its heart a monstrous ray shot out that slowly, irresistibly repulsed Tara's pure light.

Without easing the pressure, Tara then did the impossible. She transformed herself.

In her place appeared the magnificent golden dragon with the living stone on its brow. She shone with the blue light that continued its tireless attack on Magister.

"Ha, ha! A dragon!" laughed the Bloodgrave sarcastically. "All right, we'll have a dragon!"

In the next moment, a terrifying black dragon appeared in front of Tara, roaring with hate and spitting hellfire.

Abruptly, Tara broke off the engagement. She leaped into the air so suddenly that the Bloodgrave's burning ray passed behind her, destroying some white rosebushes and part of the island, and vaporizing the lake water so suddenly that the glurps found themselves swimming in midair.

"We're of equal strength," she shouted. "Since you don't want to kill me, then face me in solo combat without any magic, if you dare."

The black dragon ran a red tongue over its fangs. "With or without magic, you don't measure up, sweetie. But if it amuses you, let's see what you can do."

If there was one thing Tara hated, it was being called "sweetie."

She studied the black dragon carefully. Magister was bigger than she was, but Tara had an advantage over him. On Earth, she had occasionally watched sumo wrestling matches. She'd been fascinated by the grace, agility, and speed of those masses of muscle and fat. And she noticed several times that the smaller wrestler wasn't necessarily at a disadvantage if he had mass.

So instead of making herself larger, she used her resources to increase her mass. The big black dragon noticed that something odd was going on when the ground around Tara slumped under her sudden weight, but he realized too late what that meant. Tara raced at Magister like a golden missile, and at the last moment, lowered her head and slammed into his belly.

The black dragon let out a "Whooof!" as he was tossed backward a dozen yards, half conscious. He'd had the breath knocked out of him and wasn't able to strike back, but reflexively activated a defensive spell to absorb any opposition from her while he was recovering.

But Tara didn't try to attack him. She had just gotten the few seconds that she needed. Then she did what spellbinders never do. The one thing Magister could never have imagined.

"*Bond, James Bond!*" she yelled, desperately hoping that Cal would understand.

Taking advantage of her opponent's semi-consciousness, she released all her power and projected it onto Cal. It flowed into the boy with such violence that the impact left him speechless. The magic shackles binding him exploded under the shock, and he instantly changed back into gorgeous Cal. Oddly enough, Blondin also recovered his huge red lion body.

The power transfer was so total that Tara was unable to stop the internal bleeding she'd suffered in the collision. She lost her dragon shape, and her vision clouded. All Tara saw now was a wavering, blurry image of Magister getting up, roaring with rage.

With her last ounce of strength, she cast a Destructus.

The big black dragon easily blocked the spell, and laughed. "Is that it? Is that the best you can do? That spell's so weak, a child could block it with its little finger. So, do you admit you're defeated? Give up?"

Tara glared at him.

"In your dreams!" she managed to say with effort.

Then with graceful slowness, she collapsed. Magister stared at the girl's inanimate body, puzzled. And that's when Cal attacked him using Tara's power.

Cal's spell pierced Magister's defenses as if they were paper, extinguishing his consciousness. Like Tara, he collapsed, but much less gracefully, and his brutal fall shook the island.

Cal removed Robin's gag.

"Good going!" the elf shouted. "You killed him!"

"I'm not positive about that," muttered Cal. "I'm going to give him another dose, just to be sure."

But Robin noticed that Tara was still sprawled on the ground, motionless.

"Tara's hurt!" he yelled. "Cal, do something, quick!"

Cal cast a quick spell that cut the bonds from Gallant and Robin, who immediately ran to Tara. Cal turned toward her and cast a spell: "By Healus, help Tara conquer strife, and fill her with the breath of life."

When the spell shot out, it encompassed everything in its path. It hit Tara, then Robin, who was holding her in his arms, then the white roses, the lake, the Mud Eaters' burrows, the Swamps . . . and then vanished from sight. Withered bushes suddenly bloomed, the parboiled glurps regained their green and brown scales, and Tara took a deep, ragged breath.

"Oops!" yelped Cal in surprise. "Hey, this power of hers isn't easy to control. Look at all that! The Healus must've affected half the continent!"

"Well, maybe not that much," said Tara with a weak smile, as she regained consciousness. "But thanks for reviving me. My heart had stopped beating and the living stone was about to give up. She thanks you, by the way. So, did it work?"

"For heaven's sake, next time tell me your plan before you do something like that!" he shouted. "Good thing I understood what you wanted to do. When you yelled 'Bond!' I was ready to receive your magic. Otherwise it would've been a real mess. And yeah, it worked. We got rid of the Bloodgrave before he had time to say boo!"

Tara gave him a brilliant smile.

"In that case, it was worth it," she breathed. And fainted again.

Robin checked Tara's pulse, but found it strong and regular. She just needed to rest. Relieved, he turned and smiled at Cal.

"Oh, boy! Have you seen that body of yours? You—"

"Yeah, I know," said Cal with resignation. "When she shouted 'Bond!' the image popped into my mind and *pow!* it changed me again. With the dose of magic she's stuck me with, it could last quite a while longer. I tell you, someone's out to get me. It's the only explanation!"

Robin couldn't help but laugh at his friend's comic despair.

"Okay," said Cal, "let's take care of this other jerk."

They turned to the motionless black dragon and got a surprise: Magister's body was floating in midair. Cal activated Tara's power, ready to strike again, when he realized that Magister wasn't conscious. Amazingly, it was being lifted by some invisible force. Before an astonished Cal had time to cast a spell, a sort of ripping sound was heard, two immense paws appeared out of the void, seized the black dragon's body in their claws, and disappeared.

Cal was dumbfounded. "What was *that*? Did you see the size of the paws that grabbed him?"

"The only time I've ever seen something like that was when a twisted spellbinder used a spell against our hunter-elves," said Robin, frowning. "He'd gotten it from the Demon King. My father managed to knock him out, but a pair of paws grabbed him, and we never saw him again. After that, we only heard rumors. Some ifrits told us that he was a slave in the kingdom of Limbo, for eternity. He had pledged his life to get the spell. I'm pretty sure Magister must have done the same thing."

Cal shivered. "Yikes! I don't want to know the details. Whether Magister is dead or a slave in Limbo, the important thing is that we're rid of him."

"You're right," said Robin. "In the meantime, we've got to take care of Tara and fast."

"No problem," said Cal with a satisfied smile. "I'll transform myself into a dragon and carry you all to the Fortress."

Robin couldn't help but groan.

"A pegasus would be nice too," he suggested hopefully.

"Nah, it doesn't fly fast enough," said Cal, drawing a scowl from Gallant.

Robin was desperately trying to think of other convincing arguments when a deep voice startled them.

"Ooh, my head! Is . . . is everything all right? Where's Magister? And what happened to Tara?"

They had forgotten about Master Dragosh! The vampyr grimaced as he got to his feet, still groggy.

"Tara's fine," answered Cal. "Well, she's sort of passed out, and I've got her power, but aside from that, everything's cool. Magister is either dead or alive in Limbo; right now we aren't sure. Naturally we're hoping for door number one."

The vampyr grimaced again, but not only because of his headache. "Then the fiend has managed to escape again!"

"Well, we can't be too sorry he's gone," said Cal with some annoyance. "Right now what I'd like is to get rid of Tara's power—or rather return it to her. And get my normal body back, which would be great. I don't even know what I really look like anymore!"

"She transferred her spellbinder power to you, is that it?" asked Dragosh in some amazement. "That's very unusual. Do you know how to reverse the process?"

"Er, not exactly, no."

Robin stepped in. "Master, for all of our safety, not to mention the planet's, you have to remove this power from Cal. Who knows what'll happen the next time he uses it? He has to get rid of it, now!"

"That's impossible. This power is frightening for such a young girl. Caliban can't hand it over to her just like that. If it goes wrong, the power might scatter in all directions and Tara would die. I'm going to need Master Chem's help in channeling it. Let's go back to Lancovit." Without waiting for Cal's assent, Dragosh shifted into bat.

Feeling a bit nervous, Robin waited for Cal to turn himself into a dragon.

At first, everything went pretty well. In the blink of an eye the handsome spellbinder became a handsome red and gold dragon—very elegant and matching his familiar's color.

Then Cal wanted to shrink Blondin so he would take up less room in the howdah.

"By Miniaturus," he chanted in his booming dragon voice, "shrink my fox down to my knees, so I can take him where I please."

Instantly, Robin was astonished to find himself in a forest of grass. The vampyr, now the size of a butterfly, was desperately dodging a ko-ax bent on eating him for dinner. All around them, little rosebushes furiously waved their tiny white flowers. Blondin gave a shrill, indignant yelp.

"Oops!" said Cal. "By Normalus, it would be wise if you all regained your normal size!"

With that, the ko-ax suddenly found itself with an enormous bat in his mouth that was looking at him with some annoyance. It immediately spat Master Dragosh out. In a fury, he turned on the frog, which wisely dove into the water. Robin and the rest of the island regained their usual dimensions. The bat said nothing in words, but its screeches sounded distinctly irritated.

Robin took charge of the miniaturization operation. He also created a wicker howdah for Cal's back and strapped Tara and Blondin in. Gallant took off, followed by the dragon.

Cal paid attention, and his takeoff was fairly smooth. He had watched Tara's maneuvers carefully and was beating his huge wings efficiently. Once airborne, he headed for the Gray Fortress. It was still dark and Robin suggested they gain some altitude so as not to smack into a mountain.

Then the sun rose.

Marveling at the beauty of OtherWorld as it slowly emerged from shadow, Cal looked down. Big mistake.

Suddenly, he felt terribly dizzy. His smooth flight turned chaotic, and he started flailing with his legs instead of slowly beating his wings. The howdah lurched from side to side.

"Hey! What are you up to?" cried Robin.

"I feel dizzy," moaned Cal. "I'm afraid I'm going to fall."

"You can't fall!" Robin screamed. "You're a dragon, you have wings!"

"But the ground is pulling at me! I'm falling!"

"No, you aren't! You aren't falling in the least! Look up, look anywhere you like, just don't look down."

But down was the only direction Cal was looking. His long neck followed his head, and of course so did the rest of him.

Now they really *were* falling. Cal was using his wings only to glide, since he was feeling too dizzy to beat them. This slowed his descent somewhat, but without stopping it.

The bat couldn't speak, but Dragosh was clearly upset by the dragon's behavior.

Robin looked over at the pegasus flying nearby.

"Gallant, come here, quick!"

The pegasus came alongside, clearly wondering why Cal was diving straight for the forest.

"You take Tara and Blondin," cried Robin. "I'll deal with Cal."

He immediately levitated the two over onto Gallant's sturdy back, who took the extra weight without batting an eyelash.

Just before the red dragon landed—or to be more precise, crashed noisily into the forest—Robin cast a cushioning spell to protect Cal, then a Levitatus for himself. The spell saved Cal from breaking his long dragon neck, though he cut a swath of devastation through the forest three-hundred-yards long.

"Ow, ow, ow!" he moaned, holding his muzzle in his claws and looking glassy eyed. "What happened?"

Robin was so incensed he could hardly speak. He floated around with Gallant at his side, glaring at Cal.

"Do you know how long it took those trees to grow?" he finally yelled. "I told you not to look down, you stupid idiot!"

Still groggy, Can nodded his dragon head.

"When I stared down before, this forest wasn't there," he muttered.

"It's been here for five million years," screamed Robin, out of his mind with rage. "Believe me, it didn't just appear all at once. But you glided down, and instead of landing in the plain you veered off into the forest. I *told* you not to look down!"

"Okay, okay, I got it. You don't need to keep repeating the same thing. When you're flying and you get dizzy, don't look down. Right!" Cal quickly changed the subject so his friend would stop yelling at him. "Is Tara okay?"

"She's doing better than this forest!" roared the half-elf, who was still outraged by the destruction of the trees. "She and Blondin are on Gallant. Listen, Cal, I can understand that having Tara's power is pretty heady stuff. But you're a little dangerous in your dragon shape. So if you don't mind, you, Blondin, and I are going to continue on foot. Tara and Gallant will fly directly to the Gray Fortress, and we'll meet them there."

"No, it's okay," answered Cal, gingerly feeling his muzzle. "I think I've got the hang of it now. I can do this."

"I don't want to take the chance," retorted Robin stubbornly.

"We have to get to Lancovit as fast as possible," said Cal. "I have Tara's power, and Chem and Dragosh are going to need me to give it back to her. Besides, I don't feel like walking for a whole day."

"Well I do, as it happens!" answered the half-elf. "In fact, I'm going to start right away." Robin gracefully floated to the ground, resolutely turned his back on his friend, and headed for the edge of the woods in the direction of the Gray Fortress.

Feeling annoyed, Cal watched him walk off as he thoughtfully sniffed a small flower he had plucked. Suddenly he felt a terrible sneeze rising in his muzzle. He stared at the little white flower in horror. Crap! It was a tatchoo, whose seeds are used as pepper on OtherWorld. He opened his mouth to warn Robin, but it was too late.

Cal's flaming breath missed his friend by less than a foot, sent him diving to the ground, and incinerated the trees that had survived his landing.

Robin whirled around, his elfin blood boiling.

"By my ancestors!" he yelled. "What the heck are you doing?"

"Oops, sorry," said Cal apologetically. "I just sneezed. You know, now that I think of it, I'm going to choose another shape. This one's a little too hard to control."

Robin stood up, pointed at the blazing trees, and quickly recited: "By Aquus, give me a drenching wave, and this poor charred forest save."

Then he turned back to his friend.

"Cal," he hissed," if you don't get out of this forest right away, I swear that Magister is going to look like a choirboy compared to what I'm going to do to you."

"All right, all right, I'll transform myself. You're such a spoilsport!"

"Wait a second!" cried Robin.

"What is it now? Make up your mind!"

"The basket must weigh a couple of hundred pounds. How much do you weigh, about one hundred and thirty pounds? Do you want to get crushed?"

Cal scowled at him and let him remove the howdah. Then he cast a spell to shift back to human shape.

There was a *poof!* and Cal disappeared!

Robin was searching for him everywhere when he heard a high-pitched little buzzing voice.

"I zzzhink I kinda screwed up herezzz!"

"Cal, where are you?"

An annoying bizzz was hovering around Robin's face, and he waved it away.

"Zzztop waving your hand like zzzat," buzzed the voice. "You're gonna flatten me!"

Robin's eyes widened. "Cal? Is that you?"

"I don't know whazzz happened!" spluttered the little voice. "I wazzz about to transform myself, I saw a bizzz out of the corner of my eye, and *bang!* I zzzuddenly felt a tremendouzzz hunger for pollen. You know, I'm zzztarting to underzzztand what Tara meant about her power."

"Cal, will you kindly shift back to human shape? We'll find a faster way to get to the Fortress, I promise."

A tiny *poof!* was heard, and gorgeous Cal reappeared in all his splendor.

"Oh, man!" he groaned, holding his head. "How does Tara manage it? I swear, I'm never using her magic again. It's too unpredictable."

"Great!" Robin's approved. "An excellent decision. All right, let's get going. We have a full day's walk ahead of us."

"But you said you were going to find a faster way to go!" cried Cal.

"I lied," said Robin, striding toward the edge of the poor forest. "I'll ask Master Dragosh to fly on ahead with Gallant and Tara. We'll join them later. It won't hurt her to wait a couple of hours before getting her power back. And it'll be less dangerous for this world than letting you use it."

For a moment, Cal was speechless.

"You lied!" Cal cried, running after Robin. "You can't do that!"

"Why not?" he asked with a shrug. "You do it all the time."

"That's no reason!" said Cal angrily. "You don't lie to your friends! And think about Tara for a moment. Imagine her being handicapped for life because we didn't hurry. Imagine if she weren't able to use her power anymore!"

Then he delivered his most potent argument, lowering his voice for dramatic effect. "Imagine if I'm not able to give her power back and wound up keeping it for life?"

At that, Robin shuddered.

"No! The world wouldn't survive!" he exclaimed. "Here's what I suggest: Tara often uses the living stone to control her power. The first time they merged, the stone took over and dominated Tara's mind, until she woke up—"

"Yeah, and nearly killed us," said Cal sarcastically. "I'll never forget that thrilling moment when she came to her senses six hundred feet in the air, with us riding on her back."

Robin smiled. "Okay, we know you get dizzy. But if the living stone is controlling you—"

"I won't be aware of what's happening, and the stone will do the flying for both of us. Perfect! That's an excellent idea. Let's do it."

Very carefully, they took the living stone from Tara's pocket. She and Robin had worked together to shape it from its native quartz, turning it into a luminous ball of crystal. They'd earned the stone's gratitude in the process. The stone was quite fond of Robin, so he hoped it would answer him.

"Living stone? Can you hear and answer me?"

Nice Robin, pretty Robin needs me? politely asked the stone, casting a halo of light on him.

Whew, she recognized me, Robin thought. He quickly summed up the situation and what he wanted from her. The stone understood very well. Her vocabulary was somewhat limited but her understanding was not, though she sometimes interpreted in her own way what Tara asked her for. Before Cal knew it, he was back in his dragon body, with the living stone set in his forehead.

Robin again strapped the howdah on his back, but left Tara and Blondin on Gallant for the time being. He wanted to see if Cal was able to master both takeoff and his dizziness. They walked for a few hundred yards to find an area open enough for him to take off. Robin thought it best that they be far from the forest in case of any mishap. Despite his fatigue, Robin levitated, the better to watch Cal as he began to flap his enormous wings.

With the living stone's help, she and Cal performed a perfect takeoff, as if they'd had wings all their life. Once airborne, they next flew over to Robin.

"Is everything all right, Cal?" he asked cautiously.

"We are fine," Cal answered in a melodious voice, a curious mix of the dragon and living stone's voices. "We are not afraid, and we love flying."

"Great!" Robin approved with satisfaction. "I suggest we fly high enough to have time to take action in case there's a problem. May I come onto your back?"

"Come ahead, half-elf friend of Tara. You are welcome!"

Robin carefully sat down in the wicker howdah, then retrieved Tara and Blondin.

The flight was smooth as silk and brought them within sight of the Gray Fortress in just a couple of hours. They landed and waited for Gallant and Master Dragosh to catch up. The two couldn't fly as fast, but had prudently declined the living stone's invitation to take them as well.

The Gray Fortress lookouts saw them arrive, and they were met by a loud trumpet fanfare. Master Chem, King Bear, Queen Titania, half the Lancovit court, and all their friends spilled out to greet them.

"Bravo! Bravo!" shouted Chem deliriously. "They saved us!"

"Hurray!" shouted Fafnir as loudly as she could—which was saying something. "Hurray!"

The courtiers started to shout, stamp their hoofs, neigh, roar—in short, to make a deafening racket.

Somewhat taken aback by the rousing ovation, Robin got down from the dragon carrying Tara, who was still unconscious.

Master Chem rushed over and gave a strangled cry of concern.

"Is Tara—" He couldn't bring himself to say the terrible word.

"Dead? No, she's just exhausted," said Robin with a smile.

He managed to stay upright when his friends ran to hug him, though Fafnir's resounding thump on his back almost bowled him over.

"Why's she out cold, then?" asked the dwarf worriedly.

Robin nodded toward the big red and gold dragon behind him. "She gave all her power to Cal to help him defeat Magister."

Chem frowned in puzzlement. "Magister? What does Magister have to do with all this? Weren't you battling the Ravager?"

"We were, Master," explained Cal in his deep dragon voice. "But it was Magister who managed to defeat him."

Chem's eyes widened, imitated by those of Manitou, Fafnir, Sparrow, and Fabrice.

"All right, I can see that we have a lot of things to talk about," the old wizard finally said. "Let's go into the Fortress. We'll be more comfortable there."

"Wait," said Robin. "We're still missing—"

Just then a beating of wings interrupted him, and the bat and the pegasus landed in their turn, exhausted from flying so fast.

Master Dragosh shape-shifted and offered no resistance when two guards recognized him and immediately took him into custody.

Robin tried to plead the vampyr's case.

"I know that Master Dragosh escaped from prison," he said, "but we would never have been able to defeat the Ravager and then Magister without him! You must pardon him."

The king felt deeply troubled. "Doing a good deed can't erase the horror of a crime, unfortunately. Master Dragosh must pay for his offense. Otherwise his entire race will suffer ill will."

The half-elf insisted. "But—"

"Don't worry about it, young Robin," interrupted the vampyr. "We have something urgent to accomplish before we go into the Fortress, and I go to jail. I think we're going to need plenty of room to do it."

Master Chem raised a questioning eyebrow.

"We have to give Tara her power back," Dragosh explained. "And for that I'm going to need you, Chemnashaovirodaintrachivu. Her power is too great for me."

"Oh? All right, no problem. I'll create a pentacle to protect everybody. Cal?"

"Yes, Master?" answered the red dragon in its curious melodious voice.

The old wizard frowned again. "Are you under the influence of something? You're talking strangely."

"We were suffering from dizziness," explained the dragon, "so we merged in order to control it. That is how we were able to get here safe and sound."

"*We?* Oh, I understand; you mean you and the livings stone, like with Tara. Very well. It is now time to break the connection, but with all our thanks to you, living stone."

You are welcome, Master.

With a claw, Cal delicately unseated the stone from his forehead.

He staggered for a moment, then brought his muzzle down to Robin, who was beginning to find Tara kind of heavy.

"Don't tell me I admitted being dizzy in front of everyone," Cal whispered.

"Well, yeah, that's exactly what you said."

"Darned stone! Didn't anybody explain the notion of *tact* to her?"

"You mean the notion of *lying*," he chuckled. "Hey, telling the truth will be a change for you. You see, it's a little hard in the beginning but you get used to it fast."

The dragon shot him a furious glance. On Master Chem's order, he then went to stand with Tara in the center of the immense pentacle the wizards had drawn on the ground. Fafnir, Sparrow, Manitou, and Fabrice were allowed to remain during the transfer operation, but forbidden to enter the pentacle under any circumstances. The rest of the court cautiously retreated to the Fortress. The courtiers didn't especially care to find themselves turned into toads because of a magical operation gone wrong.

For starters, Master Dragosh asked Cal to retake his human shape. He obeyed, and gorgeous Cal appeared. He scowled to hear the sigh of admiration that arose from the Fortress windows where the courtiers, king, and queen were gathered.

On Chem's order, Cal took Tara's hand, who was still unconscious. The two high wizards then levitated, conjuring fiercely: "By the Exchangus, the power from one body flows and to the proper body goes. By Confinus, it must not stray, but travel there straightaway. By the Exchangus, the power from one body flows and to the proper body goes."

At that, gorgeous Cal seemed to melt. As the power drained out of him, his physique changed and shrank, and he reverted to his boyish body.

Suddenly, an incredibly bright, glowing shape materialized above Tara. It attempted to penetrate her body, but encountered terrible resistance. Twice the power tried to "inhabit" the girl, and twice it was rejected. The magic flux then took the shape of a fiery pegasus that tried to break out of the pentacle and head for Fabrice. The boy stumbled backward and the two astonished wizards stopped their incantations.

"By my ancestors, she's refusing her power!" muttered Master Dragosh.

At the Fortress windows, murmurs of surprise greeted the pegasus's apparition. Then word began to spread: *Young Tara is rejecting her own power!*

"She's right to do it too!" said Fabrice, who disliked magic as much as ever. "In fact, it would be good if I could do the same thing!"

"It certainly looks as if she's trying to give it to young Besois-Giron," said Master Chem.

And in fact the fiery pegasus kept fighting to cross the invisible barrier to reach him. Deeply frightened, Fabrice continued to back away.

"Tara's unconscious," remarked Cal. "Magic has completely upset her life, it deprived her of her mother and father, and it's constantly putting her life in danger. So, unconsciously, she's trying to get rid of it. We have to wake her up, otherwise this will never get done."

"How can we wake her up?" asked Chem. "Except for returning Tara's power to her, we can't perform any magic within the pentacle. The fiery pegasus representing Tara's power wants to return to a body, any body, and she's refusing it. If we use magic, we'll be exposing ourselves. The pegasus might take the opportunity to penetrate us and the shock would kill her."

Cal smiled slyly. "I'd be happy to slap her a few times upside the head, but I don't want her to get mad at me. Not to mention that Robin would tear me to pieces. Fortunately, I have something that will revive her without magic. Take a look!"

He proudly held out a little flower with white petals and a mustard-colored center.

"A tatchoo?" exclaimed Master Chem. "How in the world did you happen . . . No, I don't want to know. Go ahead!"

Cal put the tatchoo under Tara's nose, but she didn't stir. For a moment he thought it wasn't going to work. Meanwhile the fiery pegasus continued struggling to reach Fabrice.

Then Tara's chest heaved, and she produced a magnificent, deafening, perfect sneeze!

She opened a bleary eye, absentmindedly wiped her nose, and spoke.

"What . . . what's going on?"

Then, seeing the fiery pegasus attacking the invisible barrier separating it from Fabrice, her eyes widened.

"And what's *that* thing?"

"That *thing* is your power," said Cal, laughing with relief. "For some mysterious reason you seem determined to give it to Fabrice."

"Who? Me? Of course not . . ."

"Of course yes," said Cal flatly. "So, if you don't mind, we'd really like it if you would fetch it back so we can go have lunch. I'm hungry!"

Tara frowned, then mentally called the immaterial pegasus. To Fabrice's great relief, it immediately obeyed. It stopped struggling to escape the pentacle and dove toward Tara. When it was right above her, it spread into a cloud, enveloped her, and disappeared.

"Whew! That's better!" said Cal, as he helped Tara to her feet. "And here's your living stone back too. Now can we go eat?"

The high wizards erased the pentacle. Fafnir was the first to give Tara a hug.

"May your hammer ring clear, Tara!" she cried, while nearly crushing her.

"May your anvil resound!" answered Tara, delighted to find her friends safe and sound. "Is everything all right?"

"Thanks to you, yes, everything's fine," said Fafnir. "Except that the blasted magic that caused all these problems is still in me. I thought the black roses brew would get rid of it, but not so. It's back. I'll have to find something else."

Cal gave her a sharp glance. "Listen, Fafnir, we just barely saved our skins and almost witnessed the end of the universe because of you, so please give us a bit of a break before you cause another apocalypse!"

The dwarf shrugged and didn't answer. After all, the little thief was right.

Though Sparrow was smiling at Tara, she seemed angry at something.

"You have no idea what Angelica put me through while I was possessed and forced to serve her!" she snapped. "Believe me, I would've a thousand times preferred to be with you fighting against Magister and the Ravager. Still, I'm eager to see her again," she added, her eyes glittering with evil glee. "She'll find out what it means to face the fury of the beast."

Tara nodded. If she were Angelica, she would already have left and gone to some galaxy far, far away. Sparrow looked as if she was ready to put her through a cement mixer.

Fabrice kissed Tara on the cheek at least a half-dozen times. And he made the kissing last, taking advantage of the fact that Robin had no excuse for doing the same thing.

Then they all went into the Gray Fortress. A little hop in the Transfer Portal followed, and they were back in Lancovit. The Living Castle greeted them by projecting scenes of happy crowds applauding the heroes. And the courtiers who hadn't been able to go to the Gray Fortress gave them a triumphant welcome.

Lady Boudiou hugged Tara so tightly that she nearly crushed her, followed by about a hundred other people, not a one of whom the girl recognized. The crystalists shouted into their crystal balls while writing headlines: "Adolescents Save OtherWorld!" "Brave Young Spellbinder Defeats Ravager!" The scoops jostled each other to film Tara and her friends, who felt a little overwhelmed by all the commotion.

That evening, the king and queen held a sumptuous feast and invited the entire city of Travia. The tables were set outside in the gentle late-summer warmth.

By the light of OtherWorld's two moons, the kids told about their exploits, their fears, and their doubts, while their voices were relayed to the whole city. A blushing little girl presented an enormous floral wreath to Cal, who immediately started to sneeze.

Flowered Burnsides, the lord mayor of Travia, gave them the city's heroism award.

After eating tons of sweets, Tara picked up a Soothsucker. As usual, the lollipop's message was cryptic: "Everything will soon be clear, because it's actually the father."

The father? What father? Though perplexed, she soon forgot the message.

At last, the friends were able to gather in Tara's suite to talk in peace. Fabrice, Sparrow, and Manitou described their adventures while possessed by the Ravager. Tara, Cal, and Robin told about their fights and other adventures.

The business with Cal and Angelica had them all howling with laughter. But Robin was the funniest when he described Cal's aerial acrobatics.

Exhausted but happy to be back together, they all retreated to their respective rooms after the banquet had ended. Manitou, who was never full, headed to the kitchen for a little nighttime reconnaissance.

It was the middle of the night, and they'd been asleep for several hours, when Tara was abruptly wakened by Sparrow, who was trembling from head to toe.

"Tara!" she whispered fiercely. "Tara! Wake up!"

She woke from a dream in which she was just about to lift Magister's mask and finally learn his identity. She was still half asleep when she looked at her friend. "Is it time to get up already?"

"No, there's a problem. It's Manitou!"

Hearing Sparrow's alarmed tone, Tara felt her heart sink. She jumped out of bed and fumbled in the dark for her spellbinder robe.

"What's happening?"

"I just got this taludi. Take a look. The soldier on guard outside our door said that a kid gave it to him. I wanted to watch it, but it's addressed to you."

Tara was completely confused. "A taludi? What does that have to do with Manitou?"

"Oh, Tara!" answered Sparrow. "I think your great-grandfather's been kidnapped!"

CHAPTER 20

THE VAMPYRESS

"What?" asked a baffled Tara.

"Quick! Put on the taludi," begged Sparrow. "Apparently the boy told the guard that if we want to see Manitou alive, you have to watch it right away! The guard was kind of out of it. I think he partied a little too hard last night, celebrating the kingdom's liberation. By the time he got what the kid was saying, he'd already run off."

Up to then, Tara's bedroom had been lit only by images of the planet's twin moons.

"Castle, give us some light, please," she requested.

The scented, peaceful night was promptly replaced by bright sunshine.

"Too bright!" said Tara, shading her eyes. "A little less, please. I just woke up!"

The castle immediately reduced the brightness. Tara slipped into her spellbinder robe and put the taludi on. In front of her she saw Manitou, trussed up like a Christmas turkey. With a crossbow aimed at his head.

In the taludi, a hoarse voice was heard. "I'd hate to kill your great-grandfather, sweetie, but you give me no choice. I thought Magister or the Ravager would get rid of you for me, but those losers failed, so I'll have to do it myself. And if you think I'd hesitate to kill your great-grandfather, you're mistaken."

The crossbow shifted a few inches and fired its arrow, which slammed into Manitou's hind leg.

The dog's howl was muffled by his gag, but Tara's scream woke all her friends up.

"He's going to bleed to death," the voice went on relentlessly, "but you might arrive in time to save him. Go to Master Chem's office, now!"

When she yanked off the taludi, Tara was white as a sheet. In a few words she described the horrible situation to her friends, who had come running when they heard her yell. They were still trying to grasp what she had said as Tara rushed for the door.

She was already at the threshold when Robin shouted: "Tara, wait! What are you doing?"

"I'm going to save my great-grandfather," she said, tears running down her face.

Leaping to Tara's side, he grabbed her. "It's a trap to kill you! What good will you be if you're dead?"

She raised haggard eyes to him. "So, what do you want me to do?"

"Think," said Cal very calmly. "He sent you that message so you'd rush there without using your head. That's exactly what he's hoping. You've got to act, not react."

Cal nodded toward the tall cabinet they'd used to block the secret entrance.

"Suppose we went that way? He won't be expecting it. With a little luck we may even be able to free Manitou without his realizing it."

"You should also transform yourself into an elf," Robin added. "Your body will be more powerful. Faster too."

With the living stone's help, Tara quickly assumed her she-elf identity.

"All right, let's go," said Robin, grabbing Lillandril's bow. "We'll see if that crossbow shoots arrows faster than I do!"

Tara smiled. Her friends were again prepared to risk their lives with her. Unbelievable!

"By my axe," growled Fafnir, "we'll teach that killer what you get when you mess with us!"

The dwarf contemplated her weapon for a few seconds, and grumbled.

"Our date's in the dragon's office, right? I hope that big lizard isn't behind all this, because if he is, I'm gonna need a larger model."

They silently slipped into the secret hallway and soon reached the hidden entrance to Master Chem's office. Tara activated her power, and blue fire danced on her slim elf fingertips. Sparrow shifted into the beast, barely avoiding bumping her head on the low ceiling. Cal readied his daggers, and Robin nocked an arrow.

Quietly, they swung the hidden door open.

The masked man clearly hadn't expected them to use his own passageway. He had put down his crossbow and was pacing in the dragon's office. When the friends burst into the room, he rushed for his weapon, but it was too late. Lillandril's bow was faster and shot an arrow through his hand. Screaming with pain, he raced to the main door and ran out.

The others ran after him while Tara untied Manitou. The poor Labrador had fainted from the pain of his wound.

She heard shouting. "Here he is! This way!" Then the sounds of a chase, and a loud *thwack!* followed by Fafnir's frustrated bellow: "Rats, I missed him!"

But Tara wasn't paying much attention. The crossbow arrow was still stuck in her great-grandfather's hind leg, and she didn't know what to do. Her elf blood was boiling, and she decided to shift back to her normal shape. Then she took a deep breath to settle her mind and cast a spell: "By Disintegratus, may this vicious arrow dissolve into healthy bone and marrow."

The spell worked perfectly. All that remained of the arrow was a wet spot on Manitou's leg. Tara immediately cast another spell: "By Healus, may this wound be mended, and Manitou's health forever defended!"

Not a perfect rhyme, she reflected, *but the best I could do under the circumstances.* As she watched, the torn flesh knitted, the hole closed, and black fur grew over the wound.

"Ouch," said Manitou, opening an eye. "I dreamed I was kidnapped and then someone shot me."

Still shaken by fear, Tara gave him a weak smile.

"The cavalry showed up in the nick of time," she said. "And I treated your wound. How do you feel?"

"I'm okay," said the dog, grimacing as he tried to stand up. "It almost doesn't hurt anymore."

The office door suddenly flew open, startling Tara. It wasn't her friends, but Lady Boudiou. The old wizard seemed surprised to find them there.

"Where's Master Chem? And what are you doing here in the middle of the night?"

Tara was about to answer when she noticed a red mark on the old lady's hand.

"It's her!" yelled Manitou at that same moment. "She's the one who attacked me! I recognize her smell."

But Tara didn't have time to act. Lady Boudiou grabbed her and aimed the crossbow at her head.

"Not a move, not a word," she said coldly. "If I detect the slightest spell or the tiniest bit of magic, I'll kill you. Understand? And you, pooch, don't move either. Otherwise . . ."

Tara was so petrified she practically stopped breathing; Manitou froze, his eyes locked on the woman, ready to pounce.

"I've got you at last, Tara!" the old woman exulted. "I was very disappointed that you didn't die earlier. I certainly set enough traps for you. But you've had the luck of the devil."

Tara was so astonished that she didn't know what to say. Half strangled by Boudiou's arm, she managed to choke out one word: "Why?"

The old woman stiffened and glared at Manitou.

"Don't you remember me?" she screamed at the Labrador. "I was one of your customers, back in the day. One of those vain, foolish girls who bought your eternal youth potion."

Manitou shuddered. "My eternal youth potion? But Chem told me that he cured all the spellbinders who had aged, except for—"

"Look at me! Look at my face! I'm thirty years old, Manitou!" the young-old wizard angrily interrupted him. "Your potion aged me fifty years in a matter of minutes, you filthy mutt! My husband left me. I became an object of ridicule in Omois, where I was living. My father and I have been consulting OtherWorld's greatest mages, including Master Chem, for the last year. But your accursed potion seems irreversible! The old dragon felt so bad that he suggested I come work in Lancovit, so he would have me close at hand while he looked for a cure. I was so mortified that I made him swear not to tell anyone.

"After his successive failures, I tried to find you. I wanted to make you pay for what you did to me. That's when I learned that you were on Earth and that you'd lost your magic and your memory. My father has been a Bloodgrave for a long time, so when Magister asked for a volunteer to kidnap Tara, he offered to do it. His plan was to kill you at the same time, Manitou. But my father failed and Tara wounded him horribly.

"I've tried to heal him. Demiderus knows how many remedies, potions, and spells we tried—all in vain. His face causes him constant agony, and there's no relief. He's even begged me to kill him. But I found a better solution. Tara is the one I'll kill, because her death will cure my father. And after her, it'll be your turn. That way you'll never be able to harm any more bird-brained spellbinders."

Tara remembered what her Soothsucker had foretold. The prophesicle had spoken of a father—it was Lady Boudiou's father! And she suddenly realized something else. "So the vortex attack . . ."

"That was me, of course," Boudiou confirmed. "And I tried to kill Manitou before too."

The Labrador opened wide, startled eyes. "Me? When, and how?"

"I hoped both of you would die in the vortex, but you didn't. Then I cast a Cerebelluboom on you during Caliban and Angelica's trial. But instead of exploding your brain, the way the spell was supposed to, for some reason it only made you leave the hall."

Tara started. So it was because of Lady Boudiou that they'd stumbled upon Magister's plot to acquire *The Forbidden Book*.

Lady Boudiou continued: "When I saw that your dog body wasn't reacting to the Cerebelluboom as expected, I decided to get rid of Tara first and to take care of you later. I attacked her in the empress's boudoir, but that stupid guard captain heard our fight and intervened. The next time, I followed her when she and her friends went out into the park, and I heard them talking about visiting the mammoth. So while they were admiring the firebirds in the hallways I went ahead of them and bewitched the animal. But that big hairy fool didn't do the job right. I was about to attack her when the empress suddenly appeared. I joined her retinue and canceled the counter-spell I'd put on the mammoth, so as not to leave any evidence behind.

"I also set an animatrap in Lancovit in case Tara went back, but she managed to escape my carnivorous slug. There, I was afraid I might have serious problems, because the trap could have been traced back to me. So I used the fact that Master Dragosh was angry at Tara. I cast a very light, undetectable spell that amplified his rage and caused him to destroy all evidence of the trap, thus putting me out of danger."

So that was it! thought Tara. She remembered the vampyr's baffled expression after he carbonized the slug. He'd seemed disconcerted by the intensity of his anger.

Boudiou turned to Tara. "I thought I'd finally succeeded when I shot you in your bed. You very nearly tricked me, but my father was still in as much pain as ever, which meant that you were still alive."

"What if Tara offers to heal your father?" suggested the dog.

"It won't work, and she's far too powerful for me to risk trusting her," cried the old wizard. "And now the time has come. When they find you, you'll both be dead, and no one will suspect me. Say goodbye to your great-grandfather, Tara."

But Tara had no intention of saying goodbye to anyone. She mentally called to the living stone. Their powerful magic combined, ready to neutralize the old lady. But just then, they all heard a sarcastic chuckle overhead.

They instinctively looked up to see a shadowy figure hanging from the beams and looking at them ironically. Lady Boudiou quickly raised her crossbow but the mysterious person was faster. He pounced on the old wizard, and a pale hand with claws snatched away the weapon before she could make a move. Lady Boudiou released Tara and seized a dagger, but the figure disarmed her with blinding speed and grabbed her by the throat. He casually held the woman at arm's length, paying no attention to her attempts to free herself.

Tara stared at the figure in fascination. He was very tall, entirely dressed in black leather, his face covered with a leather mask. He had white hair that fell to very broad shoulders and a surprisingly narrow waist. He looked powerful. Worse, he looked pitiless. And his strength was terrifying. When Lady Boudiou tried to cast a spell, he slapped her so hard that Tara actually felt sorry for her.

When he spoke his voice was both soft and cold. "So, this is the prey I have been hunting for so long."

The word "prey" reminded Tara of something, and she suddenly remembered.

"The Hunter!" she cried. "You're Magister's Hunter!"

He bowed, then pulled off the black hood hiding his face. Tara was shocked. It was a woman, a vampyress! As if carved from alabaster, her face had an unearthly beauty, and her perfection was almost painful. Her red eyes blazed with a hypnotic glow. But she was very different from Master Dragosh. Her skin, her hair, everything about her looked somehow faded, washed out. Except for her eyes.

"I'm pleased to see that my reputation has preceded me," said the vampyress. "My master asked me to find the person who was trying to kill you. That's done."

She turned on her heel and prepared to walk away, casually carrying the old woman with her.

Even though Boudiou had tried to kill her several times, Tara could understand the woman's love for her father and her desire to rid him of his pain.

"Wait!" Tara shouted. "What are you going to do with her?"

The vampyress looked at her with bloodshot eyes, and Tara shuddered. She smiled, as if enjoying the girl's terror. "I'll have her for dinner, I think—with the master's permission, of course. He doesn't much like people who interfere with his plans. I'm just the opposite. I love people who oppose him. They make delicious meals!"

Tara couldn't believe her ears.

"But I thought human blood was poison for vampyrs," she blurted.

"Poison?" She laughed. "For some of us, human blood is the sweetest nectar. We pay a price, but believe me, it's worth it! I'll show you."

Baring a pair of terrifying fangs, she bent to Lady Boudiou's throat, who was moaning feebly.

"Selenba! Stop!"

Startled by the shout, the vampyress abruptly straightened. Master Dragosh had just entered the office by way of the secret door. Pleadingly, he reached out to the beautiful young woman, as she studied him.

"What a pity," she sighed. "I really thought I'd succeeded this time."

The vampyr master grimaced. "No, you didn't. The mouthful of blood you spat in my face didn't contaminate me. I was able to wipe it off without swallowing any. So I didn't become like you. And you'll never enlist me under the orders of the monster who turned you into a renegade."

Tara, who had listened to this exchange without understanding, had a sudden flash of insight.

"You're the one!" she cried, pointing at the vampyress. "You're the one Master Dragosh was protecting by letting himself be put in prison. You're the one who killed the man in the alleyway. But why?"

"I was watching you, to try to learn who was trying to kill you," said Selenba. "And I got hungry," she added with a shrug.

Tara glanced at Dragosh, who seemed in despair.

"Why did you do it?" she asked gently. "Why protect her to the point of going to jail for her?"

"She's my . . . she *was* my fiancée," he said. "My kind hunts down creatures like her, who get addicted to human blood. If I had revealed her guilt, our vampyr-killers would have come immediately. And she refused to leave until she learned your attacker's identity. So I let myself be jailed. Once I was in the human justice system, my fellows couldn't come after me, and Selenba was out of danger."

"And thanks to you, I can now bring my prey back to the Master," she purred.

"I . . . I can't allow you to leave," said an anguished Dragosh. "You've done enough harm already. You manipulated me, using my love for you like a weapon. But that's all over. I won't let you take her away."

Selenba looked at him with annoyance.

"Oh, drat!" she said. "I hate doing this. It hurts. But too bad, I don't want to fight you."

As they looked in astonishment, the vampyress sank her teeth into her wrist. Using her blood, she made a circle in front of her and screamed: "Delanda Tir Vouch Transmir!"

A kind of portal appeared, and before Dragosh could grab her, Selenba leaped through it, dragging Lady Boudiou along. The opening closed with a sickening sucking sound, but not before they glimpsed the vampyress and her prey on the other side, blowing them a kiss with her free hand.

Tara slumped to the floor, exhausted. Manitou slipped his silky head under her arm and she absentmindedly stroked him, forgetting for a moment that he was her great-grandfather. Then she realized what she was doing. "Oops! Sorry, Grandpa!"

"No, no, don't stop!" protested the dog. "I'm in serious need of some petting. Everything's been happening a little too fast for me. Besides, I feel terribly guilty. It's because of my potion that all this began. By Demiderus, what have I done?"

Tara consoled him by reminding him that no one had asked Lady Boudiou's father to become a Bloodgrave or to try to kill Isabella and to kidnap her. It was terrible that the potion had side effects, but they couldn't have been anticipated. Manitou promised to start work on an antidote as soon as possible and to track down his former customers.

Tara's friends returned and were brought up to speed about what had just happened. To Tara's great surprise, Master Dragosh didn't try to hide anything, including the part about his bloodthirsty vampyress fiancée.

In turn, Robin and the others explained Lady Boudiou's ruse. While they were chasing her, she apparently created a shadow self, hiding the hand wounded by Robin's arrow. The trick worked, and they ran off in pursuit of the shadow.

Like Tara, the Lab felt bad about the fate facing the old woman.

Fafnir, on the other hand couldn't care less. They'd finally gotten rid of the mysterious killer and she understood why her faithful axe hadn't hurt the shadow they were chasing. She seemed relieved. The idea that her axe might have missed its target really bothered her.

The next day, Master Chem returned from his travels and learned about the events of the night before. It put him in a very bad mood.

A wanted poster for Selenba was broadcast on the crystal screens and plastered around Lancovit. Each time Tara saw the beautiful vampyress's bloody gaze, she shivered.

The murder charge against Master Dragosh was dismissed, but Counselor Salatar was furious at the vampyr wizard for misleading him and slapped him with a heavy fine. Only the fact that Dragosh had helped destroy the Ravager saved him from being sent back to prison.

In the days that followed, Angelica and her parents were brought to trial for temporarily usurping the Lancovit throne. They were given relatively light sentences, because it was obvious that the Ravager had a powerful hold on the psyches of the people he possessed. They had to pay the kingdom a large immuta-credit fine, but got no jail time. Master Brandaud was demoted from high to simple wizard, and Angelica from senior to ordinary spellbinder (which she found outrageous).

The trial was broadcast by the crystalists, and Cal was incensed when he heard the verdicts. He knew that the Brandauds had been the Ravager's accomplices, but didn't have any way to prove it. Sparrow, however, wasn't finished with Angelica. Each time she met the tall girl in a hallway, she would shift into the beast and start filing her claws. Angelica's nerves finally snapped, and she left for a long rest somewhere in the countryside.

Fafnir returned to Hymlia. The Ravager had infected nearly the entire dwarf nation. Because Fafnir had saved OtherWorld by resisting him for five days, the dwarves unanimously decided to welcome her back into the tribe, even though she was still cursed with magic. This was unprecedented in dwarf history and became the talk of all Other-World. Nations sent their crystalists to cover the ceremony.

To general astonishment, Fafnir refused. She announced to the crystalists that since the position of senior spellbinder previously held by Angelica was vacant, she had decided to go work in Lancovit. Nowhere else in OtherWorld would she find a better place for fights, deadly perils, and plots of all sorts, she said.

When Tara heard the news, she practically died laughing. She knew perfectly well that the dwarf hadn't given up on ridding herself of magic and that this was the only reason she'd refused her fellow dwarves' offer.

Meanwhile, Tara was getting ready to leave Lancovit and return to Earth. She and her friends were in a room chatting quietly with the king and queen when Master Chem suddenly burst in. "Hello, Your Majesties! Ah, Tara, children—there you are! I was looking for you. I have a taludi for you."

Tara shivered. The last message she'd received via taludi had been less than pleasant.

This time was different, however. The empress and emperor had officially requested their presence in Omois.

CHAPTER 21

HEIR TO THE EMPIRE

"Oh no!" cried Cal, rigid with alarm. "What have we done now?"

It turned out that Empress Lisbeth'tylanhnem was merely inviting them to two celebrations: one to recognize their heroism and the other to celebrate Tara's birthday.

Master Chem said he regrettably couldn't accompany them—he had to deal with a lot of problems related to Lady Boudiou's disappearance—but he gave them a large escort in his place.

When the young spellbinders rematerialized in the Omois Palace, they were received as special guests. The imperial guards snapped to attention, each with head held proudly up and his four fists over his heart. Two hundred heels clicked as one. Lady Kali, who'd been infected by the Ravager and still suffered from its aftereffects, thanked them at least a half-million times.

The kids were thrilled to be welcomed as heroes, and the feast given in their honor was so sumptuous that Cal nearly resigned from Lancovit to come live in Omois.

Two days later, the empress threw a birthday party for Tara. To their surprise, it wasn't held in one of the palace's vast reception halls, but in a charming salon that opened onto the interior garden, with about a hundred guests gathered around the empress and emperor. Tara loved roses, and the decoration theme for the room was rose, rose, and more rose. There were roses of every shape and color cascading down the walls, their scent dizzying.

As usual, Empress Lisbeth was nothing if not imperial. She was wearing a dress shaded from a pink so deep it was almost red, to one so pale it was almost white. She wore a simple crown of pink gold, and her long hair was colored to match her dress. The effect was stunning.

The smiling empress showed the young spellbinders to their seats, then sat down at their table, which greatly surprised the onlookers. Unruffled, Emperor Sandor did the same.

"I'm very happy that Tara is celebrating her thirteenth birthday in Omois," said the empress clearly, "even though it's a few days late. And frankly, I've had trouble choosing a present *for my heir*."

The emperor stared at his half-sister in astonishment. He wasn't alone. A dead silence settled on the happy crowd.

Tara's heart skipped a beat. She then bravely looked up, directly at the empress. "How did you find out?"

"There's a spy in your midst!" the empress innocently announced.

Tara could feel that the empress was testing her, so she kept calm, even though she felt like wringing her neck.

"A spy?"

"Yes, an unwitting one, I hasten to add," said the empress, very pleased with the effect she was having. "A taludi!"

Sparrow suddenly understood and turned pale.

"The taludi! The one that recorded our summoning Brandis's ghost in Limbo. When I put it down, it must have continued recording!"

"Exactly!" said Lisbeth gleefully. "I was curious to know how you managed to prove Caliban Dal Salan's innocence, so I put the taludi on. By my ancestors, the Limbo Judgment Hall is a real horror! And that Judge! I'm very happy he's staying there."

"I'll bet she is," muttered Cal under his breath. "He'd have lots to say if he started rummaging around in her brain."

"I was about to take the taludi off," she continued, "when I saw another ghost appear. I didn't recognize it right away, I have to admit, and when I did, it was a shock. It was the ghost of my dead brother Danviou!"

This was apparently just as great a shock for the emperor, whose eyes widened in astonishment. A murmur of surprise rose from the crowd. Danviou? The dead emperor?

"I had wished with all my heart that my brother was still alive, but without much hope," the empress continued sadly. "And then I learned something new, something equally significant. When my brother spoke to Tara, he called her 'My daughter'! That's when I realized that a miracle had taken place. I had lost my brother, but he'd had time to have a child! A young girl who is a worthy descendent of Demiderus. Like our illustrious ancestor, she has just saved our universe for the second time!"

All eyes now turned to Tara, whose brain practically shut down under the pressure. What could she possibly say to this?

The emperor saved her the trouble.

"Lisbeth, that's impossible!" he cried. "Danviou disappeared more than fourteen years ago. Are you saying he had a daughter? And that the daughter is the little Duncan girl? It's grotesque!"

"I don't see why," said the empress, thoughtfully looking Tara over. "She has the Demiderus white strand in her hair, I saw my brother's ghost—"

Sandor cut her off. "Trickery and deceit! It's too easy! Some stranger shows up, claims she's the heir to the empire, and without further ado we roll out the purple carpet for her. I won't be a party to such a masquerade!"

He was so angry, he'd turned bright red.

"I haven't claimed anything at all," Tara calmly pointed out. "And I never said I was the empire's heir. Anyway, I'm going back to Earth to be with my family—my mother and my grandmother. You can keep your empire. I wouldn't want it for all the gold in OtherWorld."

Now the emperor felt offended.

"What do you mean, you don't want it?" he spluttered. "You have no idea how lucky you are to be the heir of an empire as magnificent as ours. It's an honor, it's . . ."

Suddenly he realized what he was saying. He opened his mouth, closed it again, and scowled at Tara.

The empress repressed a little chuckle.

"I don't need any more proof," she decreed. "I know that this child is of my flesh. She's the spitting image of Danviou. Look at that blond hair and those deep blue eyes. Tomorrow I will announce that the imperial heir has been found. And here is your present, darling."

Ignoring Tara's reticence, she put something in her hand. Everyone was very curious and leaned closer. Tara opened the small purple and gold package she'd been given. Inside was a ring. More specifically, a signet ring, exquisitely engraved with Omois's emblem, the strutting hundred-eyed purple peacock. Without thinking, she slipped it onto her left pinky. The ring was too loose, and she was about to comment on this when it suddenly tightened itself to a perfect fit. Alarmed, Tara went to remove it, and the signet ring obediently slipped off.

"Turn it three times around your finger," suggested the empress, with a sly glint in her sapphire eyes.

Tara put the ring back on and did so, somewhat cautiously. The ring had barely completed its third turn when an enormous purple ifrit appeared, making the courtiers jump.

"Greetings, mistress," he said in a voice like thunder, bowing to Tara, "What is your desire?"

The girl gulped, feeling panicky.

"This is Meludenrifachiralivandir, one of our most valuable ifrits," explained the empress. "He's been in our family's service since Demiderus. Now that you're the crown princess, he's exclusively yours to command. No one will be able to take the ring without your permission, and if somebody tries to cut off your finger, hand, or arm, Meludenrifachiralivandir will instantly appear."

Tara nearly choked. *Oh really? Before or after part of me is chopped off?* She preferred not to ask the question. Just the thought that somebody might want to do such a thing made her feel sick.

"Er, what do I do to send him back into the ring?" Tara asked.

The huge ifrit looked at her as if she were talking Martian.

"I don't live in that object," he said in a pinched tone. "It's merely the intermediary by which you summon me. My palace is in Limbo Circle Six."

"Oh, I'm very sorry," said Tara. "On Earth, genies live in lamps, rings, baskets, you know, stuff like that, so . . ."

Meeting the ifrit's frankly scornful look, her voice trailed away.

"If these genies, as you call them, choose to live in weird places, that's up to them," he growled. "Personally, I much prefer a palace. So, my young mistress, what do you desire? Dresses, jewels, gold, exotic animals . . . ?"

As he spoke, each appeared before the stunned courtiers. The dresses were long, short, slit, straight, and flared, cut from muslin, velvet, silk, and brocade, and covered with silver or gold. The jewels were sumptuous: sapphires, emeralds, pink, white, blue, and red diamonds in bracelets, rings, tiaras, diadems, crowns, and sparkling brooches displaying animals, flowers, fruits, and insects. The animals included puppies just begging to be petted, a tiny pink and blue pegasus that was so adorable it set Gallant's teeth on edge, and an affectionate little pocket panther. It was all dazzling, unbelievable, fantastical.

"The advantage is that none of this will disappear, because it wasn't created by magic," Lisbeth explained. "Everything is real. The fabrics are woven by Circle Six demonesses, and the rest is built or sculpted by the circle's artisans. The only thing that Meludenrifachiralivandir can't provide you with is food. Well, not without getting it from a regular kitchen, that is. Demons don't cook."

"I know, I saw that," said Tara, her throat tightening at the memory. "But there's something I don't understand. I thought demons had to stay in Limbo."

"We ifrits have a special status," proudly explained Meludenri-fachiralivandir. "We disagreed with our fellow demons when they invaded your planets. We felt that everybody was entitled to a place in the universe. So we fought on Demiderus's side against our own kind. After the other demons were defeated, he thanked us by allowing us to come back to OtherWorld. At first, we didn't do much. Then, because we were bored, we offered to lend a hand to the planet's inhabitants and, in particular, those in Omois."

Watching Tara's confusion at being confronted with the growing pile of jewels and dresses, the empress felt an incipient case of the giggles. She firmly repressed it, not wanting to make fun of her newfound niece.

"You have worked with unusual speed, oh great Meludenrifachiralivandir," she said in a friendly way. "We probably won't want all of this for now. Tara must get accustomed to using the ring. Please say hello to your wife and children for me."

The ifrit bowed to her, then to Tara, and made all the marvels disappear, which caused the female courtiers to sigh with regret. He then vanished with a distinct little *plop!*

At this, Cal felt a little envious. Not for the jewels or the dresses, which he didn't care about, but for the incredible potential. "An ifrit! Ye gods! The things I could do with an accomplice like that!"

Sparrow nudged him in the ribs.

"Keep quiet," she whispered, her eyes on Tara. "I think our friend may have a little surprise for the empress, as well."

"Why?" asked Cal, taken aback. "Is it her birthday too?"

Sparrow gave him a dimpled smile, but didn't answer.

Tara faced the sovereign, and in a firm voice said: "I claim my imperial favor!"

The empress, expecting Tara to thank her for her extravagant and unique present, sat back in her chair, looking distrustful.

"For what reason?" she asked levelly.

"I don't want to be the empire's crown princess," said Tara in a tense silence. She took off the ring and held it out to the empress. "I want you to let me go back to Earth, to my mother and my family. I renounce this title."

It took the courtiers some time to fully understand what they had just heard. Then all at once a unanimous cry of protest arose, causing a terrible din.

The empress took a deep breath, then nodded. She wasn't surprised by Tara's reaction. The girl hadn't mentioned her imperial status, even though she'd clearly known about it for some time. The signet ring had only been a lure—the lure of absolute power represented by the ifrit. It hadn't worked. Too bad.

"A present is a present," she said. "I couldn't take that ring back even if I wanted to. Keep it."

Tara wanted to protest, but the empress stopped her. "Your adventures have often put you in danger. Meludenrifachiralivandir isn't there only to create baubles. He might save your life someday. Don't reject this gift."

Reluctantly, Tara had to admit that the empress was right. And she swore she would never use the ring except in the most hopeless situation.

The empress spoke again: "Now, I'd like to ask you a favor in turn."

"What?" asked Tara cautiously.

"I'd like to go to Earth with you and meet your mother. That's all."

Tara looked at her suspiciously, but the young woman's smooth face was unreadable.

She finally nodded. "If you really want to, I don't see any reason why not."

"Perfect!" said the empress, jumping to her feet. "Let's go!"

"What, now?" asked the disconcerted emperor. "But we have to alert the guard, secure the area, inspect the—"

"Now!" interrupted the empress firmly. "I'll just take Xandiar as my escort."

A loud, anguished groan rose from the back of the room.

"That's . . . that's impossible, Your Imperial Majesty," stammered the guard captain, who looked about to pass out. "I can't guarantee your safety all by myself! Let me assemble a battalion, and we—"

"I am the Imperial Spellbinder and the Empress of Omois!" she snapped angrily. "I know how to defend myself. And I say we're leaving immediately, with you as my only escort. Is that clear enough, Xandiar, or should I call the executioner to help unplug your ears?"

The guard captain gulped, then snapped to attention. Standing tall, he clicked his heels and put his four fists over his heart. "Perfectly clear, Your Imperial Majesty. At your orders!"

The emperor yawned, adjusted his breastplate, and tossed his long blond braid back.

"I don't have anything special to do right now," he said indifferently, "so if you don't mind, I'll accompany you as well, my dear. Two bodyguards don't strike me as too many."

The empress thanked him with an affectionate smile.

Manitou was feeling ill. His jaw dropped when the empress revealed Tara's secret, and how his stomach was playing tricks on him. *Do Labrador retrievers get ulcers?* he wondered. Because all this business with Tara was sure to give him one. Reluctantly, he followed the little group toward the Transfer Portal. Manitou felt frightened. He didn't know what he was afraid of, but he could feel fear crawling under his skin like some slimy animal.

Cal, who clearly shared his anxiety, waved his friends close and whispered: "I don't think this expedition is such a good idea. Why do you think she wants to go to Earth?"

"No idea," muttered Sparrow. "But if she goes, she'll be meeting Isabella."

"Yikes!" he grimaced, remembering Tara's formidable grandmother. "I hadn't thought of that."

"I don't know Isabella very well," she said, "but I have a hunch that the clash between their two personalities could be intense. We'll have to stick close to Tara, because Isabella and Empress Lisbeth might hurt her without meaning to."

Robin approached, looking fierce. "I'll make mincemeat of the first person who harms a hair on Tara's head!"

"That's not what I meant," said Sparrow, smiling at the half-elf's impetuousness. "They might not hurt her physically, but psychically. The empress will probably fight to have her come live in Omois, because Tara is a symbol of the country's future. And her grandmother isn't likely to give in, because she loves her and will be concerned for her safety, and also because she knows that having the Omoisian heir under her tutelage will give her an unbeatable political advantage."

"Oh, I see," said Robin. "Then it'll be up to us to show our love for Tara, not because she's a granddaughter or an heir, but simply because she's our friend."

This was too much for Cal, who couldn't resist.

"Oh, yes!" he exclaimed, hand on heart. "Love, always love. You have to show her your love!"

Fabrice shot Cal a sharp glance.

"What do you mean he has to show her his love?" he asked in a threatening tone.

"It means I really love Tara a lot," answered Robin, while looking daggers at the little thief. "As much as you do, even though I haven't known her as long."

"Hmm, well, don't forget that Tara is *my* best friend," grumbled Fabrice. "And has been for a long time, as you say . . . so . . ."

Sparrow rolled her eyes, and Cal cackled. Luckily for the little thief's continued good health, his parting wisecrack was drowned out by the commotion caused by the empress's arrival at the Transfer Portal.

Courtiers prostrated themselves as she passed, and the guards saluted with a resounding clicking of heels. On learning that the sovereign intended to leave, they unanimously announced that they were coming too.

After some confusion and a fair amount of ill temper, Empress Lisbeth refused to be dissuaded, to Xandiar's great distress. In the end, just nine humans and four familiars wound up in the Transfer Room: the empress and emperor, Xandiar, Tara and Gallant, Manitou, Sparrow and Sheeba, Cal and Blondin, Fabrice and Barune, and Robin.

Lady Kali nearly fainted when she realized that the two rulers were traveling with just a single escort, but when the party appeared in his castle, Count Besois-Giron practically had a heart attack.

"Your . . . Your Imperial Majesty?" he blurted, when he realized who was standing before him. "I mean Majesties . . . but . . ."

"We are accompanying our *friend* Tara back to her mother's," said the empress calmly. "I don't often get the chance to visit your pretty planet, so I came along for the ride."

The count wasn't stupid. The empress and emperor had just a single guard with them, who looked stressed-out and miserable, who jumped at the slightest sound, and whose hands clutched his four sword pommels. Secrecy was in the air, and Fabrice discreetly gestured for him to play it cool. *Fine,* thought the count. *I'll save my questions for later.*

The count bowed elegantly and offered to take them to the manor house by car. An unmarked sealed car with tinted windows. But the empress declined.

She felt like *walking*. The count tried to tell her that the nonspells would never have seen someone like her, but she ignored him.

"Very pretty flowers!" she told Igor the gardener, who gaped at her. Of course he didn't understand a word she said, because there was no Interpretus spell at Besois-Giron Castle.

"Nice rolling thing," she smilingly told the mayor of the village when she met him on his bicycle. He was so surprised that the bike wound up in the ditch, with the mayor still on it.

"Beautiful dresses!" she called to two pretty girls, who promptly decided to grow their hair long and, with knowing snickers, admired the handsome emperor puffing out his chest.

"Delicious looking fruits," said the empress at the stall of a green-grocer, who practically swallowed his mustache.

Tara was watching Empress Lisbeth'tylanhnem out of the corner of her eye. The empress seemed amazingly cheerful for someone who'd just suffered such a stinging defeat. *What the heck is she up to?* Tara wondered.

The empress liked everything. The blue sky, the yellow sun, the green trees (though she found the color a bit monotonous), the red roses, the white horses, and the black bulls (though she preferred them with wings; they looked more graceful that way). The more she praised things, the more worried Manitou became. If dogs were able to sweat, he'd have spent all his time mopping his brow. He panted instead, and his tongue lolled out so far he nearly tripped on it.

"Good grief," he muttered to himself. "We're going to have to cast a half-dozen forgetting spells to wipe out people's memories of the empress."

Fortunately, Xandiar wore a cape that mostly hid his four arms, and Tara and her friends had transformed their familiars so they looked like big dogs. So except for the empress's staggering beauty, and her crown, flowing pink hair, and jewel-strewn clothes, and the emperor in his golden breastplate, they could almost pass unnoticed.

Almost.

The villagers, who'd been alerted by some mysterious gossip line, were all out watching them with astonishment. Manitou sighed when a man from the local newspaper ran into his office and emerged with a camera.

"Tara," he called discreetly. "Can you please overexpose that guy's film and fast?"

"Sorry, Grandpa, I can't," she said, watching as the reporter squeezed off shot after shot of their little parade.

"Tara dear, I know you're hesitant to use your power, but this is an emergency!"

"It's not because I'm afraid of using my power," she retorted indignantly. "It's because he's using a digital camera. It doesn't have film!"

"Blasted newfangled gadgets!" growled the dog. "Well, do whatever you have to, but stop him taking pictures, now!"

Tara concentrated and wiped the camera's memory chip clean. It was a dirty trick to play on the poor man, but she didn't have a choice.

When they reached the gate of the manor house grounds, Isabella and Selena were waiting. They didn't look especially surprised, so the count must have made a discreet cell phone call to warn them.

Selena paid no attention to etiquette or protocol. Ignoring the empress and the emperor, she ran to hug Tara so tightly it practically squeezed the breath out of her.

Tara didn't try to free herself, but instead returning the hug with joy. She hadn't realized how much she'd missed her mother!

"Darling, darling!" Selena kept repeating. "I was so afraid. At first we were getting news from Chem, and then suddenly all communication with Travia was cut off. We didn't know what was happening. We thought we'd lost you!"

Tara was just as moved and was about to answer when she was interrupted by a discreet cough behind her.

"Hrrm," said the empress, clearing her throat. "Are you my late brother's wife?" she asked in perfect Lancovian.

Selena stiffened, and after giving Tara one last kiss, straightened up. She looked anxious. "Yes, that's right. Though I've only recently learned that we're related, I'm indeed your sister-in-law."

The empress gave her a big smile, while eyeing her up and down.

"I'm very glad to meet you," she said, while thinking that Selena shouldn't give her too many problems. "I wanted to get to know the mother of our remarkable Tara and talk over a few things in detail."

"I'm also glad to meet you, Your Imperial Majesty," coldly broke in Isabella, who hadn't stirred. "I am Isabella Duncan, Tara's grand-mother."

Lisbeth turned and met the old woman's green eyes. Evaluating her adversary, the empress thought, *Hmm. This one will be tougher.*

Selena broke the silence.

"But please, come into our home," she said with a smile that displayed her charming dimples. "Let's not stay out here. We've probably already given the gossipers enough to chew on for the next decade."

The empress raised an eyebrow but said nothing. She strode majestically across the grounds, this time without any commentary.

They entered the old pink stone manor house and Tara sighed with pleasure. She was home at last!

Selena led them to the little yellow parlor. Isabella's spellbinder servants Tachil and Mangus had prepared delicious refreshments, and the empress waited until everyone had a sandwich and a cool drink before attacking. Sipping her lemonade, she started with Selena.

"So, tell me a little about how you met my brother," she said with a smile.

Tara hadn't expected a question like that, and she listened up. She, too, was eager to learn more about her parents.

Selena smiled at the memory.

"He fell on top of me," she explained. "He'd just arrived in Lancovit, and his flying carpet had 'mechanical' problems—right over my head. Before I knew what was happening, I found myself buried under it. I had just spent a good hour fixing myself a very complicated hairdo, and was going to show it to some friends. When I saw that all my work had been wrecked because of Danviou, I got so mad I nearly turned him into a toad! He apologized, kneeled down to beg forgiveness—and fainted!"

"Fainted? Why?"

"He didn't realize he'd broken his leg in the fall. When he kneeled, the pain was so intense that he passed out. Naturally, I took him into our house."

"Oh, that's so romantic!" cried Sparrow, dabbing at her eyes with a tissue.

Cal looked at his friend as if her brains had melted and were running out her ears.

"I don't see what's so romantic about it," he remarked sarcastically. "It just shows how clumsy he was."

"By the time he came to," Selena continued, "I'd treated his leg with a Healus, but the injury was serious, and I urged him to stay off his feet for a while. That's when he started paying me extravagant compliments . . ."

"What kind of compliments?" asked the emperor, who found the young woman extremely attractive.

Selena blushed. "He said I was an angel who'd fallen from heaven. When I pointed out that he was the one who'd fallen from the sky and that he didn't look in the least like an angel, he laughed. He said that my hair was like black silk rustling through his fingers, that my skin was like a pink-tinged white rose, that my lips were like delicious red cherries. He was obviously feverish, because he was talking nonsense. So I suggested he stay with us for a few days. Mom was over at the castle for the biannual Lancovit-Hymlia-Selenda conference, so it was no problem. I put him in the guest bedroom."

"Wasn't that a little rash?" asked the surprised empress. "After all, you didn't know him! He could have been a thief or a murderer."

"I realize that," said Selena. "But I knew his injury was real, since I'd just treated it. He obviously came from far away, because he wasn't wearing Lancovian clothes. He was also obviously rich, because his spellbinder robe held a huge safe full of immuta-credits. In fact, he insisted on paying for all the expenses of his stay. He got me to talk about myself a lot, but didn't say much about himself."

"What did he tell you?" asked the empress.

"Only that he was destined for a future that didn't suit him. And that to escape that destiny, he'd chosen another path."

"He certainly did!" said Empress Lisbeth bitterly. "Leaving us to deal with the empire while he went off to fool around in Lancovit! Another path, indeed!"

"He wasn't fooling around!" snapped Selena, rigid with anger. "We were in love with each other right from the beginning! Danviou asked me to marry him several times, but I didn't want to. My mother didn't like him, and she did everything in her power to break us up. Finally, she even made me tell him that we weren't right for each other. I was weak and young, so I did as she said, and told Danviou that I didn't want to see him again. To make sure, Mom sent me off to live on a distant cousin's property, hundreds of miles from Travia. But my cousin there fell in love with me."

"Him too?" asked Empress Lisbeth. "You're a regular Miss Popularity, dear!" An acid undertone lurked beneath the empress' apparent sweetness.

Selena smiled weakly. "I could well have done without that, believe me. Then my mother decided to lock me up in a tower on the property and have it guarded by trolls, to make sure Danviou would never find me. She didn't trust me, and she knew he hadn't given up hope. He was still searching for me."

Selena shot a sideways glance at Isabella, who pursed her lips and didn't comment.

Tara was absolutely fascinated by the story.

"What happened then?" she asked.

"Your father found me. He fought with my cousin and the trolls and beat them. Then he countered the remaining spells that kept us apart and carried me off."

"Ooh, that's so romantic!" cried Sparrow, looking for her tissue again.

"Hmpf!" snorted Cal. "He climbed a wall and kidnapped her. Nothing to it! I can do that any day of the week."

"Cal?"

"Yes, Sparrow?"

"Shut up!"

"Hmph!"

"When I realized his love for me was so strong and sincere," Selena continued, "I confronted my mother. She wound up recognizing how deeply I loved Danviou. And we were married."

"What did you live on?" asked the empress a bit snippily. "On the money in the safe?"

437

"No," said Selena with a smile. "Danviou was a terrifically talented painter. His works are on display in many OtherWorld galleries, and the Lancovit Castle bought several for the king's private collection. Our only problem was the terrible antagonism between his familiar, an eagle, and my mother's tiger. They didn't get along at all, so we didn't see Isabella very often. Aside from that, we had some happy, peaceful years together. And the birth of our baby was our greatest joy."

"Well, well," remarked the emperor languidly, "I'm happy to see that our little brother managed to make out so well."

The empress turned to him in surprise.

"Does this mean you don't doubt Tara's legitimacy anymore?"

"No, I don't. Too many of the details fit. Danviou was forever painting canvases, creating holograms, and working on the palace frescos. He used to drive Dad half crazy with his colors when he was little. And he did take a safe full of immuta-credits when he went off, after leaving us that stupid letter in which he rejected his role as emperor. And his familiar was an eagle. Finally, there's the business with the flying carpet. One of the imperial guards' carpets disappeared that night. I'd guess that Danviou didn't want to risk being spotted by taking the Transfer Portal. The carpet must have flown him from Omois to Lancovit, which takes at least a month. Makes sense that the magic charge would be almost exhausted by then. So, I'm happy to recognize her legitimacy."

Sandor stood up and bowed very low to Tara. "Tara'tylanhnem T'al Barmi Ab Santa Ab Maru, welcome to our lovely family!"

The emperor had been so hostile to her from the very beginning, that Tara wasn't quite sure how to react to this changed situation.

"Thank you," she finally said. "What should I call you? Uncle Sandy?"

The emperor shuddered and sat back down.

"If you don't mind, dear niece, let's avoid overly familiar terms. I'd prefer just 'Uncle' or 'Sandor.'"

"Did Danviou ever talk about his family?" asked Empress Lisbeth, who had trouble accepting the fact that her brother had erased her from his life this way.

"Yes, he did," Selena answered softly. "He said he had a sister who was wonderful but very stubborn. And a half-brother who never listened to what he had to say, which was actually one of the reasons he left. He clearly had good memories of his childhood, even if he was very reluctant to talk about it. I sincerely believe he loved you and suffered from no longer being able to see you. But he often said that reuniting with you could put our child in danger. I asked him lots of questions at the time, because I didn't know what he was hiding from. Now I know."

"He was hiding?" asked the empress, clearly surprised. "What was he hiding from? Except shirking his duty by running away from Omois."

"Not what, but who. And when Tara was born, he became even more cautious. He was always telling me to trust him and not to try to understand his concern. I think he knew that Magister was already after him."

"Magister?" The emperor sat bolt upright in his chair, suddenly alert. "What does that animal have to do with this story?"

Tara answered for her mother.

"He needs me," she said. "After killing my father, he kidnapped Mom and held her prisoner for ten years. He set a spy to watch me and waited patiently for me to come into my spellbinder powers. Then he tried to kidnap me twice and finally succeeded. That's when he admitted that he needed me to get access to the demons' power objects, the ones that Demiderus and the four high wizards hid. Because

Those-Who-Guard and Those-Who-Judge, who guard those objects, will only allow the descendants of those five powerful spellbinders access to them."

At that, the empress turned very pale.

"Do you mean to say that you and I are a kind of key that would allow him to free the demons?" Empress Lisbeth stammered

"He isn't especially interested in freeing the demons," said Tara, "but if that was necessary for him to get absolute power, he'd do it in a heartbeat."

"He's insane," said Sandor. "Anyway, his quest is hopeless. I'm in no danger, since we don't have the same mother and I don't descend from Demiderus. My sister is well protected, and as Lisbeth's heir, Tara will be equally well protected in the palace."

Tara took a deep breath.

"Well, that's exactly where we disagree," she said. "Where do I get to choose in all this? What if I decide I want to be, I don't know . . . a ballet dancer, say."

Cal snickered, and she glared at him.

"Well, maybe not a ballerina, but how about a pilot? Or a doctor? I'm only thirteen, and I have no idea what I want to be when I grow up. You tried to make my father into a perfect emperor, and he ran away. You don't want to make the same mistake with me, do you?"

"But that's just it: You have no idea what being an imperial princess is like," countered Empress Lisbeth cleverly. "You might love it. How can you tell without trying it?"

"And it's not just that," said Tara with a sigh. "I haven't seen my mother for ten years, and I want to live with her—"

"We'll invite her too, of course!" the empress interrupted. "She's my brother's widow, so our protection also extends to—"

"That's out of the question!" snapped Isabella, angrily cutting the empress's offer short.

Manitou groaned. His implacable daughter had just entered the fray.

"We have no intention of exposing Tara to Magister's plots," Isabella continued. "Besides, she's a delicate adolescent"—Cal gasped. Tara, delicate?—"who needs a calm environment to grow up in. She is staying with us."

Tara looked up in surprise. Her grandmother hadn't suggested any conditions. Her rejection of the empress's proposal was total.

Empress Lisbeth spoke slowly, now worried that she might not be able to persuade her heir. "Lady Isabella, Tara demanded her imperial favor so she could return to Earth. What she doesn't know is that if the security of our state is threatened, an imperial favor doesn't apply."

"I don't see how the security of your empire depends on Tara," protested Selena, instinctively drawing closer to her daughter, as if to protect her.

"I can't have children," the empress said simply. "Our doctors have tried to figure out why, but we just don't know. Sandor is much loved and much appreciated, but he's my half-brother. We don't have the same mother. My mother was Empress of Omois, and my father was her prince consort. She married him after he divorced Sandor's mother. I ascended the throne when my mother died in the fire at her summer palace. Daril, my prince consort, ruled with me. Then they discovered that I was sterile. Daril was killed in a hunting accident."

"Sure seems to be a lot of accidents in the imperial family," Cal said to Robin, loudly enough for Empress Lisbeth to overhear. "I'm not sure it's a good idea for Tara to be part of it."

Thinking hard, the empress opened her mouth, then closed it. She nodded and, without reacting to what Cal said, continued with her explanation.

"So, I asked my brother Danviou to become my emperor. At first, he agreed, but the burden of the empire became too heavy for him, and you know what happened then. So I chose my half-brother Sandor as the new emperor, and we've been running the country together for the last fifteen years. But when I die, I won't have any descendants. Tara has Demiderus's blood in her veins, and she'll become the new Empress of Omois. Her children will rule after her, and our dynasty will live on!"

But Isabella wasn't about to back down. "My granddaughter will *not* go to Omois. She will stay here on Earth, with us. I am the Guardian of Earthly Surveillance and Identification of New Spellbinders, as well as a high wizard. May I remind you that our war against the demons cost us dearly? So dearly that Demiderus died soon afterward? And that just before he died, he made a mistake. He hid the demon kings' power objects here on Earth. Ever since then, I've feared the possibility that someone would acquire them and open the rift between our world and the demons'. Magister was able to seize Tara on OtherWorld twice. If he does it again, the security of our whole *universe* will be in danger. So by comparison, the security of just your empire isn't that important."

Well, with that, Isabella had managed to insult the Empress and the Emperor of Omois in one fell swoop.

Tara, who distinctly heard the empress's gasp of outrage, shot a look at Isabella, who stood wrapped in her dignity. *I would have preferred to defend myself*, she thought. *I'm not sure Grandma's being all that helpful.*

Emperor Sandor looked ready to grab Isabella by the throat, but Empress Lisbeth remained serene.

"Who is in charge of this place?" she suddenly asked. "Who is running the Earthly Surveillance?"

Isabella was momentarily thrown by the change of topic. "As you know perfectly well, a new OtherWorld country takes over the running and expenses of Earthly Surveillance every fifty years. We've been a Lancovian enclave for the last twenty years. In another thirty, it will be Meusian, since Meus is the next country in line. Why?"

The empress didn't answer right away. She was clearly thinking. "So, my heir will be raised in a Lancovian enclave, is that right?"

Isabella could tell that the young woman had something specific in mind, but couldn't figure what it was. Her answer was somewhat evasive. "She will be raised by her family. If Selena were Edrakin, she would be—"

"But she isn't!" the empress interrupted. "She's Lancovian. So I know what I have to do."

They all looked at her curiously.

Standing up, she carefully explained herself.

"I'm not sure I made myself quite clear before," she said icily. "If my heir doesn't come to Tingapore to receive the education suited to a future Empress of Omois, my people will have no choice."

Isabella's green eyes narrowed.

"What do you mean, no choice?" Her tone was now somewhat anxious.

"We'll determine that Lancovit is holding an imperial hostage."

"A hostage!" exclaimed Isabella. "That's really not—"

"And that being the case," the empress interrupted calmly, "we are declaring war on you!"

THE END

AN OTHERWORLD LEXICON

OTHERWORLD

OtherWorld is a planet where magic is widespread. It has a surface about one and a half times that of Earth. OtherWorld orbits its twin suns in fourteen months; its days last twenty-six hours, and the year has 454 days. Two satellite moons, Madix and Tadix, orbit OtherWorld and create extreme tides on the equinoxes.

OtherWorld's mountains are much higher than those on Earth, and the ore found in them can be dangerous to mine because of explosions of magic. There is less water covering the planet than on Earth. OtherWorld is 45 percent land and 55 percent water. Two of the seas are freshwater.

The magic that reigns on OtherWorld affects its fauna, flora, and climate. For this reason, seasons are very hard to predict. On

OtherWorld you can get three feet of snow in the middle of summer. A so-called normal year has no fewer than seven seasons.

Many different races live on OtherWorld. The main ones are: humans, giants, trolls, vampyrs, gnomes, imps, elves, unicorns, chimera, tatris, and dragons.

COUNTRIES AND PEOPLES OF OTHERWORLD

Dranvouglispenchir is the dragon planet. Dragons are huge, very intelligent reptiles. They know magic and are able to take any shape, but usually choose human. In opposing the demons that were fighting them to rule the universe, the dragons had conquered all the known worlds until they collided with earthly spellbinders. After the battle, the dragons decided that it made more sense to make allies of the humans rather than enemies, particularly since they still had to fight the demons. So they abandoned their plan to dominate Earth. However, they refused to allow human spellbinders to rule the planet. Instead, they invited them to OtherWorld to train and educate them. After several years of suspicion, the earthly spellbinders finally accepted and came to live on OtherWorld.

Gandis is the land of giants. Its capital is Geopole. Gandis is run by the powerful Groar family. The Island of Black Roses and the Swamps of Desolation are in Gandis. Its emblem is a wall of spellblock stones beneath OtherWorld's sun.

Hymlia is the land of dwarves. Its capital is Minat. Hymlia is ruled by the Fireforge clan. Its emblem is an anvil and war hammer on a mineshaft entrance. Dwarves are extremely strong, often as wide as they are tall. They are OtherWorld's miners and blacksmiths and are excellent metalworkers and jewelers. They are known for having cranky personalities, hating magic, and liking long and complicated songs.

Krankar is the land of trolls. Its capital is Kria. Its emblem is a tree beneath a club. Trolls are enormous, hairy, and green. They have huge flat teeth and are vegetarians. They have a bad reputation, because they feed on trees and decimate forests, which horrifies elves. They also tend to become impatient quickly and to crush everything in their path.

Krasalvia is the land of vampyrs. Its capital is Urla. Its emblem is an astrolabe under a star and the symbol for infinity (∞). Vampyrs are sages. They are patient and cultured, and spend most of their long existence in meditation, devoting themselves to mathematics and astronomy. They search for the meaning of life.

They feed entirely on blood from the cattle they raise: brrraaas, mooouuus, horses, goats imported from Earth, sheep, and so on. They can't drink the blood of some animals. In particular, unicorn or human blood causes them to go insane, cuts their life expectancy in half, and makes them deathly allergic to sunlight. Their bite then becomes poisonous and allows them to enslave any humans they bite. Moreover, if their victims are contaminated this way, they become corrupt and evil vampyrs. Those who fall prey to this curse are ruthlessly hunted down by their fellow vampyrs and all the OtherWorld races.

Lancovit is the largest human kingdom. Its capital is Travia. Lancovit is ruled by King Bear and Queen Titania. Its emblem is a white unicorn with a gold horn beneath a silver crescent moon.

Limbo is the Demonic World, the realm of demons. Limbo is divided into different worlds called circles. Demons are more or less powerful and more or less civilized, depending on the circle they occupy. The demons of Circles 1, 2, and 3 are wild and dangerous. The demons of Circles 4, 5, and 6 are often called on by spellbinders within service exchange agreements. Spellbinders can get things they need from the demons and vice versa. Circle 7 is the circle where the Demon King reigns.

The demons that live in Limbo absorb demonic energy provided by evil suns. If they leave Limbo to visit other worlds they must feed on the flesh and minds of sentient beings in order to survive. They were conquering the universe until the dragons appeared and defeated them in a memorable battle. Since then, the demons have been imprisoned in Limbo. They can only go to the other planets when specifically called by a spellbinder or by some other being with the gift of magic. Demons bitterly resent this restriction on their activities and are constantly searching for a way to free themselves.

Mentalir, the vast Eastern plain, is the land of unicorns and centaurs. Unicorns are small horses with a single spiral horn that can be unscrewed, cloven hooves, and white coats. Some unicorns aren't very smart, whereas others are true sages, whose intellect matches that of dragons. This peculiarity makes it hard to classify unicorns within the animal kingdom.

Centaurs are animals that are half horse and either half man or half woman. There are two kinds of centaurs: ones where the upper body is human and the lower is horse, and ones where the upper body is horse and the lower is human. No one knows what magical manipulation produced centaurs. They are a complex people and don't mix with others except to obtain essential necessities, such as salt or salves. Centaurs are fierce and wild. They won't hesitate to shoot arrows at any stranger crossing their land.

In the plains, it is said that the shamans of the centaur tribes catch Pllops, extremely poisonous blue and white frogs, and lick their backs to get visions of the future. The fact that the centaurs were practically exterminated by the elves during the great Starlings War suggests that the method isn't very effective.

Omois is the largest human empire. Its capital is Tingapore. It is ruled by Empress Lisbeth'tylanhnem Ab Barmi, Ab Santu T'al Maru and her half-brother Emperor Sandor T'al Barmi Ab March Ab Brevis. Its emblem is the hundred-eyed purple peacock.

Selenda is the country of elves. Its capital is Seborn. Like spell-binders, elves are gifted magicians. They look quite human, but with a few differences: their ears are pointed and their very light eyes have a vertical pupil, like cats. Elves live in OtherWorld's forests and plains, and are renowned hunters. They also enjoy fighting and games that involve defeating an adversary, like wrestling. For that reason they are often used in police or surveillance forces, so their energy can be used judiciously. When elves start growing magic corn or barley, the peoples of OtherWorld become worried, because it means they will soon go to war. Since they won't have time to hunt in wartime, the elves start growing crops and raising cattle. Once the war is over, they return to their ancestral way of life.

Another peculiarity of elves: males carry the babies in a little pouch on their stomach, like marsupials, until the children are able to walk. Also, a female elf can't have more than five husbands.

Smallcountry is the land of gnomes, imps, fairies, and goblins. Its emblem is a stylized globe surrounding a flower, a bird, and an arachne.

Gnomes are short, stocky, and usually blue. They feed on stones and are miners, like dwarves. They wear their orange hair in a quiff, which is an effective detector of dangerous gas. As long as it sticks straight up, all is well. But the moment it begins to slump, gnomes know there is dangerous gas in the mine, and they evacuate it. For some reason, gnomes are also the only people who can communicate with Truth Tellers.

P'abo are the small, playful imps of Smallcountry. They are the creators of the famous fortune-telling lollipops called Soothsuckers, which are also called prophesicles. P'abo can project illusions and briefly make themselves invisible. They also love gold, which they keep in a hidden purse. If you find the purse, you can make the imp grant you two wishes in order to get its precious gold back. But it's risky to ask an imp for a wish, because they are experts at misinterpretation, and the results can be unexpected.

Tatran is the land of the tatris. Its capital is Cityville. The tatris are unusual in that they have two heads. They are very good at organization. They often have executive jobs or work in the highest levels of government, both because they like to and because of their physical peculiarity. They have no imagination and feel that only work is important. They are the favorite targets of the P'abo, the playful imps, who are unable to conceive of a people without any sense of humor. The imps have desperately been trying to make the tatris laugh for centuries and even created a prize for the first of them to accomplish that feat.

OTHERWORLD FLORA AND FAUNA

Arachne: A spider-like animal from Smallcountry, like the spalendital. Gnomes ride arachnes, and their silk is famous for its strength. They have eight legs and eight eyes, and an unusual scorpion-like tail with a poison stinger. Arachnes are highly intelligent and enjoy challenging their future prey to solve riddles.

Baaa: Sheep with beautiful white wool, baaa are adapted to OtherWorld's extremely variable seasons and can shed their wool or grow it in a few hours. Baaa herders take advantage of this peculiarity at shearing time. They make their flock think the weather will turn very hot, and the animals immediately shed their fleeces. OtherWorld residents often say, "As credulous as a baaa."

Ball orchid: A beautiful flower that owes its name to its green-and-yellow root ball. Ball orchids are parasites that grow very fast and can kill a tree in a couple of seasons. Then, by moving their roots, they can attack another tree. OtherWorld trees secrete corrosive substances to deter ball orchid attacks.

Bizzz: A large red-and-yellow bee that has no stinger, unlike earthly bees. The bizzz's only defense is the secretion of a toxic substance that poisons any predator that eats it. Bizzz make an incomparable honey from OtherWorld's magical flowers. OtherWorlders say, "Sweet as bizzz honey."

Blood fly: A cattle fly whose sting is extremely painful.

Brill: A delicacy that grows in sheltered parts of the magic Hymlia Mountains. The dwarves who harvest brill don't eat it. Instead, they sell it at fancy prices to OtherWorld merchants. The dwarves find this amusing because in Hymlia brill is considered a weed.

Brrrraaa: Huge cattle with thick wool, which giants make into clothing. Brrraaas are very aggressive and will charge anything that moves. As a result you often encounter brrraaas exhausted from chasing their own shadows. OtherWorld residents say, "Stubborn as a brrraaa."

Camelin: A fairly rare plant with the unusual property of changing color to match its environment. In the Mentalir plains, its usual color is blue; in the Salterian deserts, it turns pale yellow or white, and so forth. This property is retained when the plant is harvested and woven into a fine cloth that changes color according to its setting.

Cantaloop: A voracious, carnivorous plant that feeds on insects and small rodents. Its garishly-colored petals have sharp spines that harpoon their prey. Cantaloops are considered a delicacy, but they are aggressive and grow to the size of a large dog, making them hard to harvest.

Chatrix: Chatrixes are big, black hyena-like animals with a poisonous bite. They hunt only at night. Though fierce, they can be tamed and trained. In the Empire of Omois they are sometimes used for guard duty.

Cruditor: A small, lemon-yellow rodent much like a rabbit. Because the OtherWorld environment is so colorful, cruditors can easily escape their predators. Their flesh is bland, but will feed a starving traveler or a patient hunter. Cruditors are also raised in captivity.

Crouicc: Large, blue, omnivorous mammals with red tusks, crouiccs are raised for their delicious meat. Famed for having difficult personalities, wild crouiccs can tear up a field in a couple of hours. OtherWorld farmers often protect their crops with anti-crouicc spells.

Drago-tyrannosaurus: A relative of dragons, but lacking their intelligence. Drago-tyrannosauruses have tiny wings and can't fly. They are fierce predators and will eat anything that moves and often whatever doesn't. They live in the warm, damp Omois forests, making those parts of the planet especially unsuitable for tourism.

Gambole: An animal often used in sorcery. A small rodent with blue teeth, the gambole burrows so deep into the OtherWorld soil that its flesh and blood become impregnated with magic. When dried and ground, gambole powder makes the most difficult magical operations possible. It also produces hallucinations, and some spellbinders use it for personal consumption. This practice is strictly forbidden on Other-World, and gambole addicts are severely punished.

Gandari: A rhubarb-like plant with a slight taste of honey.

Glurp: A green and brown saurian with a small head that lives in lakes and swamps. It is extremely voracious. It can spend hours under-water without breathing, waiting to catch an unsuspecting animal that has come to take a drink. It builds nests in hiding places along the shore, and stores its captures in underwater holes.

Kalorna: A beautiful forest flower with pink and white petals whose slightly sweet flavor is enjoyed by OtherWorld herbivores and omnivores. To avoid being eaten into extinction, kalornas have evolved three petals that work like eyes. These can detect the approach of a predator and allow the flowers to quickly hide underground. Unfortunately, kalornas are also very curious. They often stick up their petals too soon and are promptly eaten. OtherWorlders say, "As curious as a kalorna."

Kax: A plant used to make an herb tea so relaxing that it's best only to drink it when you're in bed. On OtherWorld, it's also called relax-kax, because of its action on muscles. The sentence "You're a real kax" refers to someone who's very soft.

Keltril: A luminous, silvery metal that the elves fashion into breast-plates and armor. Light and very strong, keltril is practically inde-structible.

Ko-ax: A two-toned frog that is the glurp's main food. Glurps locate them easily because of their particularly annoying croaking: "Brek-ek-ek-ek-ex, ko-ax, ko-ax."

Kraken: A gigantic octopus with black tentacles. It is found in OtherWorld's oceans, but can also live in fresh water. Krakens are a well-known danger to sailors.

Looky-look: A giant golden turkey that constantly struts around, gobbling. It is very easy to hunt. OtherWorld residents often say, "Dumb as a looky-look" or, "Vain as a looky-look."

Manuril: White, juicy manuril shoots are a very popular Other-World side dish.

Mooouuu: A two-headed stag without antlers. When one head is feeding, the other watches out for predators. Mooouuus walk side-ways, like crabs.

Mrmoum: A fruit that is very difficult to harvest, because mrmoum trees are huge animated plants that can cover as much area as a small forest. As soon as a predator approaches, mrmoum trees sink into the ground with the characteristic sound that gives them their name. It can be startling to be walking around and see an entire forest of mrmoum trees suddenly disappear, leaving only a empty plain.

Mud Eater: Inhabitants of the Swamps of Desolation on Gandis, Mud Eaters are large, hairy creatures that feed on insects, water lilies, and the nutrients in mud. The primitive Mud Eater clans have little contact with the planet's other inhabitants.

Newsrystals: OtherWorld's newspapers, which spellbinders and nonspells read on crystal balls, tablets, or smart phones.

Nonspell: Nonspells are humans who lack spellbinder powers.

Pegasus: A winged horse that is about as smart as a dog. Pegasi don't have hooves, but instead claws, in order to perch easily. They often build their nests at the top of steel giants.

Popping peanut: Popping peanuts get their name from the characteristic sound they make when you open them. They produce a scented oil widely used by OtherWorld's greatest chefs.

Puffer sardine: A fish that blows itself up when attacked. Its skin then becomes so taut, it's almost impossible to pierce. On OtherWorld, people say, "As tough as a puffer sardine."

Red banana: Just like an Earth banana except for its color.

Sacat: A large, flying, red-and-yellow insect that produces a honey that is much sought after on OtherWorld. Sacats are poisonous and very aggressive. Only dwarves can eat sacat larvae, which they consider a delicacy. Elves and humans would wind up with a swarm of them in their stomach, because their digestive juices can't dissolve the shell of the larvae.

Scoop: A small winged camera, the product of OtherWorld technology. Possessed of rudimentary intelligence, the scoop lives only to film and transmit images to its crystalist.

Snaptooth: An animal originally from Krankar, the land of trolls. Snapteeth look like fluffy, pink plush toys, and it's hard to tell their front from their back. They are extremely dangerous. Their extensible mouth can triple in size, allowing them to swallow practically anything.

Soothsucker: The fortune-telling lollipops, also called prophesicles, created by the playful P'abo imps. Licking away the candy's outer layers reveals the prediction in the center. Even if you don't understand it, the prediction always comes true. High wizards of many nations have studied these mysterious candies to understand how they work. But the P'abo guard the secret well. All the wizards got for their pains were cavities in their teeth and extra pounds on their hips.

Spalendital: A giant scorpion from Smallcountry. When domesticated, they are ridden by the gnomes, who also work their very tough hide. Gnomes practically wiped birds out from their country, which opened an ecological niche for insects. Since these no longer have any natural enemies, they keep growing larger and more numerous. As a result, Smallcountry is overrun with giant scorpions, spiders, and millipedes.

Spellbinder: Literally "someone who knows how to bind spells." Spellbinders have the gift of magic. They chant or recite spells to focus their thoughts and materializing their wishes. Some very rare spellbinders don't need spells. Their power is so great that it manifests itself without chanting. Earthlings corrupted the term after the spellbinders left for OtherWorld, and refer to them as sorcerers and sorceresses.

Steel giant: Enormous trees that can grow to 600 feet high, with trunks 150 feet around. Pegasi often build nests in steel giants to keep their progeny safe from predators.

Stridule: Similar to an earthly cricket. When they travel in swarms, stridules can be very dangerous, devastating all the crops in their path. They produce very fertile saliva that is commonly used in magic.

Tatchoo: A small yellow flower whose pollen, used on OtherWorld as pepper, is extremely irritating. Sniffing a tatchoo is guaranteed to unclog any nose.

Traduc: A large, smelly animal raised by centaurs for their meat and wool. "You stink like a sick traduc" is a widespread OtherWorld insult.

T'sil: A worm found in the deserts of Salterens, a t'sil hides in the sand and waits for an animal to pass. It jumps on it and burrows into the skin or carapace. Its eggs then enter the host's blood stream and spread throughout its body. About a hundred hours later the eggs hatch and the t'sil worms eat through their victim and emerge. Death by t'sil is one of the most horrible on OtherWorld. This explains why few tourists go trekking in the Salterian Desert. An antidote exists against the common t'sil, but none against the golden t'sil, whose infestation is inevitably fatal.

Tzinpaf: A delicious carbonated apple-orange cola beverage that is both refreshing and stimulating.

Vlir: A small golden prune much like a plum, but sweeter.

Vrrir: A six-legged, gold-and-white feline, a favorite of the Empress of Omois. She cast a spell on her vrrrirs so that they don't realize they are imprisoned in her palace. Instead of furniture and sofas, they see trees and comfortable stones. The courtiers are invisible, and when vrrirs are stroked, they think it is the wind blowing through their fur.

Whaloon: A huge red whale, two-and-a-half times the size of an Earth whale. Its extremely rich milk is traded by liquidians, like tritons and mermaids, to solidians, who live on dry land. Whaloon butter and cream are sought-after delicacies.

Yumm: A kind of large red cherry the size of a peach.

About the Author

Sophie Audouin-Mamikonian is not only the most widely read fantasy writer in France, she's also the crown princess of Armenia. Sophie was inspired to start writing the *Tara Duncan* series after reading Shakespeare's play *A Midsummer Night's Dream* in 1987. Seventeen years later, in 2003, she published *Tara Duncan* in France and eventually in eighteen countries.

Born in southern France in 1961, Sophie was mainly raised by her grandparents, who spoiled her with candy and carefully chosen French classics: Alexandre Dumas and Victor Hugo along with Corneille and Molière. Possibly as a result, Sophie started writing stories at a very young age. Stuck in bed by a bout of appendicitis at age twelve, she picked up a pen and hasn't put it down since. Before earning her living as a writer, she earned a master's degree in diplomacy and strategy, and worked in advertising with Jacques Séguéla at the Publicis agency in Paris.

Sophie is the niece of author and director Francis Veber, who wrote the screenplay for the movies *Dinner for Schmucks* and *Three Fugitives*. She is also the granddaughter of Pierre Gilles Veber, who wrote the script of the original 1952 film *Fanfan, la Tulipe*, which was remade in 2003 with Penelope Cruz.

Tara Duncan has been adapted for television by Moonscoop–Taffy Entertainment (*Casper, the Friendly Ghost*; *The Fantastic Four*) in co-production with the Walt Disney corporation and can be watched on Kabillion Channel. It is already broadcasted in twenty countries.

The Tara Duncan Show will begin on September 1, 2013, in the Gymnase Theater, and Sophie is scared to death because she will play a part in it! When not writing, Sophie divides her time between her husband, her two daughters, and the medical organization Pain Without Borders.

ABOUT
THE
TRANSLATOR

William **Rodarmor** is a journalist, editor, and French literary translator. In addition to the *Tara Duncan* books, his young adult translations include *The Book of Time* trilogy by Guillaume Prévost (Scholastic, 2007–09), *The Old Man Mad About Drawing* by François Place (Godine, 2003), *Catherine Certitude* by Patrick Modiano and Jean-Jacques Sempé (Godine, 2001), *Ultimate Game* by Christian Lehmann (Godine, 2000), and *The Last Giants* by François Place (Godine, 1993). His translation of *Tamata and the Alliance,* by famed sailor Bernard Moitessier, won the 1996 Lewis Galantière Award from the American Translators Association.

William has traveled all over the world but has a special fondness for France, about which he edited and translated two anthologies in Whereabouts Press's *Traveler's Literary Companion* series: *French Feast*

(2011) and *France* (2008). He is especially proud of two things: sailing solo from Tahiti to Hawaii in 1971 and winning the cartoon caption contest in the *New Yorker* in 2010. William lives in Berkeley, California, and often travels to New York City.

Thanks and Acknowledgments

To my tender and luminous family, my husband Philippe, and my daughters Diane and Marine, who continue to valiantly support their wife and mother with humor and lucidity. Thank you, darlings. Without you, this book would not exist.

It took seventeen years for my girl wizard Tara Duncan to see the light of day. I wrote *Tara Duncan and the Spellbinders* (*Tara Duncan et les Sortcelier*) in 1987, the year my daughter Diane was born. That is the first book in this series. But at the time, I couldn't get a single French publisher interested. I waited, kept writing, and sometimes cried my eyes out. But my very sweet husband Philippe kept saying, "You have so much talent. You'll see; one of these days Tara is going to take off."

That day came thanks to a boy wizard with glasses and a scar on his forehead. Harry Potter's success had such an impact in France that when I sent out my manuscript for the nth time, three publishers suddenly wanted options on it. Since then, the *Tara Duncan* books have been published in eighteen countries, adapted for television by Disney and Moonscoop, and sold some eight million copies.

Thanks go to my marvelous family, which has supported my stories about dragons for some twenty years now—you are heroes! To my publisher Tony Lyons, who gave me the chance to be published in the United States, the eighteeth country in which *Tara Duncan* has been translated. Let's hope we conquer the world together!

Thanks to Jennifer Lyons, my wonderful and dynamic agent; to my translator William Rodarmor, who ties his brain in knots rendering my improbable wordplay; to Karissa Hearn, who is publicizing my book in the United States; and especially to my marvelous American fans who write me (and whom I answer!) at tara@taraduncan.com.

To everyone, thanks for reading my books. You are true friends.

Sophie Audouin-Mamikonian
Paris, Winter 2013

Tara Duncan and the Spellbinders

by HRH Princess Sophie Audouin-Mamikonian

Translated by William Rodarmor

Though only twelve years old, orphaned Tara has developed strange telekinetic powers that allow her to bend space and levitate others high above the ground, as if they are lighter than air. Her two best friends, Betty and Fabrice—often the victims of Tara's uncontrollable abilities— are the only ones who know about Tara's secret. Even her grandmother and caretaker, Isabella, doesn't have a clue. That is until Tara learns that she is a spellbinder, descended from a long line of powerful magic- wielders born on the planet OtherWorld. Forced to flee her Earth home when Magister, the Master of the Bloodgraves, attacks, Tara escapes to planet OtherWorld, where she finds loyal friends and learns about her mysterious powers. But when Tara discovers that her mother is alive and being held captive by Magister, will she be able to save her?

Tara Duncan is an inspiring heroine, whose adventures and personal struggles will captivate readers already hooked by fantasy adventures and characters like Harry Potter. This is the first installment of the Tara Duncan series—an epic adventure full of magic and bravery that is sure to cast a spell on young readers!

$16.95 Hardcover